ART'S BLOOD

SIGNS IN THE BLOOD

Also by Vicki Lane

SIGNS IN THE BLOOD

ART'S BLOOD

And coming soon
from Dell

IN A DARK SEASON

OLD WOUNDS

VICKI LANE

A DELL BOOK

OLD WOUNDS
A Dell Book / July 2007

Published by
Bantam Dell
A Division of Random House, Inc.
New York, New York

Dell is a registered trademark of Random House, Inc., and the
colophon is a trademark of Random House, Inc.

ISBN 978-0-440-24359-5

Printed in the United States of America
Published simultaneously in Canada

www.bantamdell.com

OPM   10 9 8 7 6 5 4 3 2 1

For Justin, who helps me find the time;
for Eileen and Toby, fine examples of grace under pressure;
and for John, who abides

ACKNOWLEDGMENTS

As usual, I can't say enough about Ann Collette, my terrific agent (who doesn't need a white hat to be one of the good guys) and Kate Miciak, my amazingly astute editor (who won't ever let me take the easy way out). Thanks to the team at Bantam Dell: Caitlin Alexander, Loyale Coles, Nicole Hubert, Katie Rudkin, and special thanks to Jamie Warren Youll for the great covers.

And my grateful thanks to all the following: Chris Wattie, Jerry Wolfe, and Sharon Littlejohn, in Cherokee; Karol Kavaya for her *enthusiastic* help with research at the casino; and Buddy Harwood, instructor of the Concealed Carry Handgun class, for his patience.

Thanks to Kathy Hendricks (my own private Sallie Kate) for real estate information; to Tony Earley for friendship and telling me about the skunk ape; to Joan Medlicott for introducing me to many of her fans; to John Ramsey Miller for goofy emails. And thanks to Bob and Susan Adams and Jim and Libby Woodruff for providing an ivory tower on the coast where I could write and watch the waves at the same time.

I first learned about the booger dance in George Ellison's *Mountain Passages: Natural and Cultural History of Western North Carolina and the Great Smoky Mountains* (The History Press, Charleston, SC, 2005). As far as I know,

Maythorn's use of hair from the booger "to make the magic stronger" is my own invention—I have no authority for the booger dance being used in this fashion.

The story of how the Pleiades were created can be found in several places. Two of the best are James Mooney's *History, Myths, and Sacred Formulas of the Cherokees* (Bright Mountain Books, Historical Images, Asheville, NC, 1992) and, as retold by Kathy Littlejohn, in *Living Stories of the Cherokee* (University of North Carolina Press, Chapel Hill, NC, 1998).

An excellent website, www.pcf45.com (copyright © 2002 Robert B. Shirley), and a newspaper article by Guy Gugliatto gave me my information on swift boats in Vietnam. The incident I describe is, of course, fictional.

PROLOGUE

Saturday, October 1

The glowing computer screen, the only light in the dim gloom of the tiny, windowless office, cast a sickly green hue across the young woman's exhausted face. She slumped back in her chair and let out a profound sigh that spoke of surrender...and relief. At last it was done: the story that had, against all her careful defenses, clawed its way into existence. The story that had haunted her for too many long years, tapping with urgent, insistent fingers on the clouded panes of her memory, the story that she had pushed away like an unwanted and unloved child. Now, at last, she had allowed it into the light, had unbound it, had let it speak.

The words crawled down the screen and she scanned them critically. Enough details had been changed; it would pass as fiction. But the heart of the unresolved matter was there. She had put down all she knew...all she remembered, after so long.

She watched as the account of that terrible time passed before her blurring eyes. As the last page came into view she paused, pulled off her reading glasses, and wiped them on her sleeve. She drew in a long, shuddering breath, fighting back unwelcome tears. It had been worth it—painful but cathartic. It had been necessary, she told herself. And the story was powerful—her best work ever.

Rereading the last words, that desolate closing paragraph, she frowned. This was it, wasn't it? What more was there to say? For a moment she sat frozen, paralyzed by the flood of memory and emotion that threatened to overwhelm her. Then, with sudden decision, she clicked on the PRINT icon. The machine stirred into action and as the white pages pattered into the tray, the young woman's lean body began to tremble.

"Maythorn?" It was a tentative whisper. Shoving her chair back, she felt held in place, mesmerized by the growing stack of paper before her. The soft murmur of pages falling one upon another mocked her. *You think this is all but you're not done.*

So many questions remained unanswered. *You have to keep going. This won't be enough for her.*

The final sheet of paper inched its way out of the whirring printer.

"Mary Thorn."

Her voice was stronger now. The name was a declaration of the buried grief and doubt of the past nineteen years.

She pulled the sheaf of paper from the tray and stood, clutching the pages to her heart. Closing her eyes, she tilted her face to the ceiling and cried out, in a voice to wake the dead:

"Mary Thorn Blackfox, I *see* you!"

Still gripping the pages, Rosemary Goodweather reached for the telephone and punched in her mother's number.

1.

Dark of the Moon

Monday, October 3

"Bloody hell!"

The three dogs raised their heads, startled by the vehemence of Elizabeth's unexpected outburst. Their morning reverie disturbed, they looked at one another as if considering abandoning the sun-warmed porch for more peaceful surroundings. But when no further words, angry or otherwise, were forthcoming, heads sank back to outstretched paws and the three resumed their private contemplations.

Elizabeth Goodweather sat on her front porch, staring unseeing at the distant Blue Ridge Mountains that disappeared into ever-hazier rows along the eastern horizon. She was blind to the nearby wooded slopes with their first gildings of copper and gold, oblivious to the clear blue sky marked only by a pair of red-tailed hawks riding the cool autumn currents, and deaf to the birds' shrill, descending calls. The breakfast dishes in the kitchen behind her were still unwashed; the mug of coffee she held had grown cold without being tasted. She sat motionless but her mind whirled in tumult—a congregation of seething thoughts, feelings, and desires, all unresolved.

Two days ago she had been on the verge of… *on the verge of what, Elizabeth? Phillip asked if I was still grieving for Sam, if I would ever let someone else into my life. And I said something really profound about being willing to take a chance. And I was… I am… but then, just then… Oh, bloody hell!*

But at just that exquisitely crucial moment, Rosemary had called. Her brilliant, reliable, *sensible* older daughter. Assistant professor of English at UNC–Chapel Hill and not yet thirty, Rosemary had been writing a story based on the disappearance of a childhood friend almost twenty years ago. *And in the writing, something let loose. All those years that she wouldn't talk about Maythorn… and then Saturday… oh, god, it was awful to hear Rosie so… so* unhinged.

"Mum!" Her daughter had whispered, sounding more like the ten-year-old she had been than the self-assured academic she had become. "Mum! I have to find out what really happened to Maythorn."

Rosemary had been all but incoherent, babbling about her lost friend, about memories that had resurfaced… *and Maythorn's granny and something called the Looker Stone… and what was the really weird-sounding thing?… the Booger Dance? Whatever the hell that is.*

Maythorn Mullins, the child of a neighboring family, had been Rosemary's friend—*she's my best friend, Mum,* and *she's my blood twin! We were both born on January 11, 1976, and we both have brown eyes and we are exactly the same tall! We cut our fingers and swapped blood and now we're blood twins!* The pair had been almost inseparable for two idyllic years. Then had come the Halloween of 1986 and with it the disappearance of Maythorn from her family's home.

A massive search through the hollows and coves of Ridley Branch and adjoining areas had revealed nothing.

Some believed that the child had run away—there were whispers of an unhappy family situation. Others were sure that a kidnapping had been attempted and had somehow gone wrong. Still others shook their heads. They swore that the child was somewhere on the mountain—dead or alive.

But as a weary Sam had said to Elizabeth, on returning from the steep slopes and thickets of Pinnacle Mountain, "Liz, she could be hiding…or hidden…anywhere out there. There's just no way of searching every inch of these woods."

Wide-eyed, but remote, Rosemary had watched mutely as the futile search continued. Her responses to questions about Maythorn, from Sam and Elizabeth, as well as from the authorities, were little more than monosyllables. Tearless, she had shaken off attempts at comfort. Elizabeth could still remember the sudden stiffening resistance of her daughter's thin body when she'd tried to gather the child up in her arms for consolation.

"Don't, Mum," Rosemary had said briefly, gently removing herself from the embrace and retreating to her own room. And though she had eventually returned to her usual talkative self, any mention of Maythorn was met by a blank stare or an abrupt change of subject. Soon it seemed that she had simply chosen to forget the existence of the little girl she had called her blood twin. Elizabeth and Sam, caught up in the thousand details of their new life, had gratefully accepted Rosemary's return to normalcy. By unspoken mutual agreement, they no longer mentioned Maythorn around their older daughter.

A local man was questioned by the police and released for lack of evidence. The Mullins family drew in on itself and, after a year had gone by with no ransom demand and no sign of the child, they moved away, eager to leave behind the unhappy memories that haunted their home. Marshall County put the mysterious disappearance away in a seldom-visited drawer and life resumed its pleasant and accustomed shape.

Rosemary's unexpected and unsettling call on Saturday had alarmed Elizabeth deeply. All thoughts of romance and Phillip Hawkins vanished like dry leaves before an icy wind. She had listened in baffled incomprehension to her daughter's frantic chatter till Rosemary had run down, had calmed and begun to sound more like her usual self.

"I'm sorry, Mum. I didn't mean to spring it on you quite like this. Really, I'm fine. It's just that I've been so immersed in the story and when I printed it out now— well, I felt like I had to talk to you about Maythorn. Stupid, I should have waited. Listen, Mum, I've got to go. I'm meeting a friend in a few minutes. I'll call you tomorrow or the next day when I've made some arrangements and figured out exactly what I want to do."

Rosie finished talking and hung up and I . . . I just stood there holding the phone and staring. She had stared at Phillip Hawkins who, at the insistent ring of the telephone, had released her and tactfully moved to the cushioned nook at the end of the kitchen to busy himself with her three dogs while she answered the call. She had looked at him in bewilderment, as if she had never seen him before, as if he were a stranger who had unexpectedly materialized in her home. Granted, a stranger whose right hand was scratching behind the ears of James, the tubby little dachshund-Chihuahua mix, while his left was busy fondling Molly's sleek head. The elegant red hound's amber eyes gazed soulfully at Phillip as if *she* knew him very well indeed. And at his feet, shaggy Ursa lay on her broad back, offering her black furry belly to be scratched.

"What?" He'd looked up with a quizzical smile, which was rapidly replaced by a puzzled frown and a look of concern. As she continued to stare silently at him, he had disentangled himself from her dogs and come toward her. She'd stared at the burly man with the soft dark eyes and nut-brown balding pate, trying to reassemble his pleasant features into a familiar face.

"Elizabeth, sweetheart, what's wrong?" Suddenly the stranger was replaced by the familiar friend, the good man she'd come to rely on. She put down the phone and burst into tears.

He had put his arms around her again and she had relaxed against his comforting bulk. When her voice was under control, she asked, "Did you ever see that movie years ago—*Alice's Restaurant?* Well, like Alice said, I feel like a poor old mother hound dog with too many puppies snapping at her tits. I mean, I'm already worried about Ben and Laurel, after what they've just been through, and now *Rosie*...

"Sam and I thought it was all over—that she'd forgotten that awful Halloween and the days and weeks that followed. We were so grateful that she seemed . . . seemed *untouched* by it all that we just pretended it never happened, let *her* pretend there'd never been a little girl called Maythorn. But now it's all come back. I should have known. . . .

"Don't you see, Phillip? . . . I owe it to her . . . to both of them . . . to see it through to the end this time."

Somehow it had gotten sorted out. Phillip had listened as she explained and, before she could finish, had pulled her to him again. She hid her face on his broad shoulder and wrapped her arms around him, trying unsuccessfully to capture the joyous abandon she had felt before Rosemary's call.

His fingers traced a path along her cheek. "Hey, Elizabeth, it's okay. This is something you have to do. And if I can help, you know I will."

Gently, he cupped her chin in his hand and raised her head. "Elizabeth, what we were ... where we were heading just before that call ... where I hope we're still heading—that can wait a little longer."

The deep brown eyes were steady on her and he smiled tenderly as he said, "Miz Goodweather, I want your full attention for what I have in mind."

Elizabeth could still see his crooked smile as he had said good-bye. This man, an unwelcome stranger in her life not so long ago, had over the past year, in almost imperceptible increments, somehow become very dear to her. *Almost even ... necessary.*

The thought was disturbing and she brushed it aside. *But he's added something to my life ... and he's always been patient and kind, even in the beginning when I kept trying to ignore him.*

Phillip Hawkins and her late husband, Sam Goodweather, had been buddies during their years in the navy, and when Hawkins, a former police detective, had moved to the Asheville area, he had tried very hard to befriend Elizabeth. Her emotions still raw with the pain of her widowhood, she had rebuffed him until the suspicious death of a neighbor had forced her to seek his help.

The more time we spent together, the better I liked him. And then this nightmare we've just gone through in Asheville ... She shuddered at the vivid memory of a chase through dark corridors—a memory of blood and mirrors and madness.

Thank god for Phillip! A very solid bit of comfort and sanity to hang on to in a world gone askew. And if Rosie hadn't called just when she did, I'm pretty sure he'd have still been here the next morning. I was so ready. . . .

Impulsively, she jumped to her feet and hurried inside to the phone. She put in his number, her thumb flying over the tiny keys. *He might not have left for school yet— Didn't he say his first class isn't till ten?*

The line was busy. She hit REDIAL. Still busy. Again. Busy. *Maybe he's trying to call me. Okay, Elizabeth, put the phone down. Go do the dishes and—*

The shrill ring of the phone in her hand startled her and she fumbled eagerly for the ON button.

"Phillip! I've been trying to—"

"Mum? It's me, Rosemary. I've come up with a plan."

Shit! said Elizabeth to herself. She sat down heavily on the cushioned bench. "Hey, sweetie. Okay, tell me about it."

"All right, Mum, here's the thing. I've got a few Fridays free this semester and my only Monday class is in the afternoon. So that will give me some long weekends to be there at the farm and I'm going to work through this—I have to do it if it kills me. I've been making a list of places to visit and people to talk to—things that will help me remember. I do have a seminar this Friday, but I still want to come on and get started. If I leave right after class, I could be there in time for dinner. Then if I leave the farm Monday morning around eight, I'll make it back with time to spare. One thing I know I want to do eventually is go over to Cherokee. I need to find out more about the Booger Dance."

Elizabeth Goodweather frowned. The frantic whisper of Saturday's call was gone—Rosemary's tone was calm and perfectly controlled—maybe a little too controlled.

"Sweetie, you know I love for you to come home whenever. We've hardly seen you at all since you bought your house. Laurel was complaining just the other day that it's been months...and I'd love to go with you to Cherokee—someone was telling me recently how good the museum is—but, Rosie, did you say *Booger* Dance? Are you serious? What's a Booger Dance and what does it have to do with Maythorn?"

"I'm not sure, Mum...but I think it's important. It's something that came to me as I was writing the story. You know I went with Maythorn a few times to visit her grandmother over in Cherokee. Remember, she was called Granny Thorn and she was a full-blood Cherokee—living on the Qualla Boundary. Anyway, one of my last memories of Maythorn is her telling me how she was making a mask for the Booger Dance so she could stop being afraid of someone. I went online and found out what I could about the dance. It all seemed really familiar...like I'd seen it. I'm not sure; maybe Maythorn's granny took us to one that last weekend we stayed with her. Or, I don't know—it's vague; maybe she just told us about it.

"And then...it seemed like more and more memories of those two years started coming back to me, from the first time I saw Maythorn to right before...right before she disappeared...and I remembered a bunch of things she told me. Mum, I don't know what's important and what isn't but I do know I have to follow this to the end."

Phillip Hawkins looked at the clock. This was his first semester of teaching criminal justice at AB Tech, Asheville's two-year community college, and he had a class at ten. There was still time. He reached for the telephone.

No. He clicked off. *What was it she said? Like a hound dog with too many pups? I need to back off—Elizabeth's got enough on her mind right now.*

He stared at the phone, still undecided. Saturday night had been the first time he'd seen her cry—*Sam mentioned that about her, how she almost never cried, tried to hide it, like it was a weakness.*

Back in their navy days, during those last long months before they were discharged, back when the one thing that loomed in their minds couldn't be spoken of, he and Sam Goodweather had fought against the boredom, the danger, and the loneliness by talking about their girlfriends. Phillip had not met Elizabeth—would not meet her till years later at Sam's memorial service—but he had known from the picture Sam carried that though she was not really beautiful, her long dark brown hair and startling blue eyes compelled you to look again.

Sam had told the story over and over—how he'd gone into a used bookstore in Tampa, while home on compassionate leave, in search of something to take his mind off the past, something that might give him a new direction. He'd been browsing the cluttered back room when he spotted a battered copy of *Walden,* a book he'd been meaning to read for years.

"I reached for it just as this tall girl with dark hair down to there reached for it too. My hand touched hers, and I swear to god, it was like a goddam jolt of electricity. Then she looked at me with those blue eyes and that was it. It was like I couldn't get my breath."

The tall girl had insisted that they flip a coin for the book. She had won the toss but when Sam invited her for coffee that turned into lunch and she learned that he was on his way back for his final tour of duty, she gave the book to him, first writing her name and address in it. A correspondence had ensued, and a little over a year later, soon after Sam's discharge, they had married.

And me, I married Sandy. No electricity there. Just a pregnancy that wasn't. A pretty, empty-headed, little cheerleader with a cute giggle . . . at least, it was cute for the first month or so. Hawkins glanced toward the bookshelf where he kept framed photos of his son and daughter. *Still, there were some good times—and the kids, they were worth it. I don't know, maybe if I'd had a different job, we'd still be together. Maybe.*

He shrugged his shoulders and ran his hand over his shiny scalp. *Nah, Sandy's happier with her life now than she would ever have been with me. She's got a nice tame husband who goes antiquing with her and plays bridge and crap like that.*

Phillip looked again at the pictures of his children. *Good kids, both of them. But they've got their own things going now—Seth keeps talking about bringing Caitlin to Asheville so I can meet her. And Janie—*

Abruptly he picked up the telephone again and hit the familiar number. The harsh burr of the busy signal taunted him. He waited briefly and touched REDIAL. Once again the mocking busy signal rasped in his ear. Glancing at the clock, Phillip Hawkins muttered a brief imprecation, threw down the phone, and hurried out the door.

ROSEMARY AND MAYTHORN

June 1984

WHY ARE YOU *living in a barn? The solemn little girl stared down at Rosemary from the top of the granite outcropping. My mama says you're hippies.*

Eight-year-old Rosemary, climbing laboriously up the slopes of the mountain pasture, a stout hickory stick clutched in one hand, was deep in her pretend of an explorer in unknown lands. At the unexpected sound of a voice, she glanced up in surprise. Two dark eyes in a brown face, half-hidden by a thick shock of black bangs, regarded her steadily from the top of the big rock that she had marked as the goal of her exploration.

We are not either hippies. *My grandmother says that, too, but we're not! We're the Goodweathers. And this is Full Circle Farm. My mum named it. And we're just living in the barn till Pa and Uncle Wade can get our house built.*

Rosemary pointed down the mountainside to a flat, bull-dozed area where two shirtless, tanned men in work boots, straw hats, and cutoff jeans were busy installing a window in the unfinished shell of a modest house. A tall, slender woman in a blue work shirt and faded jeans toiled up the steep road that led to the building site from the barn below. A thick braid of dark hair hung nearly to her waist. In one hand she carried a thermos jug while with the other she held tightly to the unwilling fist of an energetic redheaded toddler. The child broke loose and tried to outpace her mother but soon took a tumble and sat down hard on her overalled bottom. Resisting any attempts to help her up, the child staggered to her feet, and ran. Once again her tiny boots slipped on the gravel and the scene was repeated.

That's my mum and my little sister. Rosemary jerked her head negligently in their direction. *Her name's Laurel. She's only three and a half and she can be a pest.*

I have a little sister named Krystalle and she's a pest too. The dark child patted the rock beneath her in a proprietary manner. *You want to come up on Froghead?*

Is that its name? Rosemary scrambled up the steep slope and climbed onto the tilted surface of the big rock protruding like a granite thumb from the mountain pasture. She moved cautiously up the incline and lowered herself to lie on her belly beside the other child. *Who named it?*

Me. The dark girl patted the rock again as if it were a living creature beneath her. *It's one of my special places. I know all about this mountain. My mama stays so busy with Krystalle that she doesn't care what I do. Long as I get home for supper. A lean brown arm indicated a knapsack that lay beside a pair of binoculars. I pack my lunch and sometimes I stay out all day.*

I'm Rosemary. What's your name? Rosemary cast an admiring glance at the other child's long straight black hair and bronze skin. *You look like an Indian.*

I am an Indian. Granny Thorn's a full-blood Cherokee and my real daddy was mostly Cherokee. My true name is Mary Thorn Blackfox but mostly everyone calls me Maythorn. My mama told them at the school that my last name is Mullins now, 'cause my real daddy's dead and she's married to Moon.

Moon? Is he an Indian too? Rosemary propped herself up to look at this interesting stranger more closely.

No, he's just ordinary. Maythorn pulled the binoculars to her and trained them on the big pear tree near the house site. The two men, the woman, and the redheaded child were sitting on a stack of lumber in the shade of the tree while the men drank from tall glasses.

Is one of those men your daddy? Slim brown fingers adjusted the binoculars for a closer view.

He's the one wiping his face with the red bandana. Now he's tickling Laurie. His name's Sam but I call him Pa. The other one's Uncle Wade. He's Pa's brother and he's staying here this summer to help build our house.

Hmmph. The binoculars stayed in place. *I figured they were brothers—both with red hair and all.* The lenses turned toward Rosemary. *Do you like your uncle?*

Rosemary wrinkled her brow at the glittering lenses. *What do you mean? He's my uncle! He's really funny and nice and he tells dumb jokes all the time.* The impassive lenses continued to hold her gaze. *And he's teaching me how to play the harmonica. Why wouldn't I like him?*

Dunno. The binoculars turned back to survey the scene below. The tall woman was rising and the toddler shook her head violently, stamped her foot, and attached herself, limpet-like, to her uncle's leg. The mother squatted down to look her daughter in the eye, spoke a few words, and slowly Laurel released her hold. The storm passed and the little girl grabbed the empty jug, waved a cheerful good-bye to the two men, and set off pell-mell down the road, the jug bumping the gravel with every step. Her mother hurried after her, pausing to look up the mountainside in Rosemary's direction.

Instantly Maythorn lowered the binoculars and flattened herself against the rock. Rosemary lifted up and waved *in her mother's direction. I'm up here! It's really cool! There's a—*

Below, Elizabeth, with one eye on Laurel, who was nearing the old tobacco barn—their home for the duration—waved abstractedly at her older daughter and called out, Okay, Rosie, just don't go any farther off. I'll ring the bell when it's lunchtime. Be careful up there.

She turned and hurried after the fast-moving little redhead, who was disappearing through the open doors of the barn loft.

Mum's got to watch Laurel all the time. There's holes in the barn floor she could fall right through. Pa and Uncle Wade fixed a safe corner for her—kind of like a corral. There's an old rug that covers the floor and we put her bed and all her play things on it. There's a kind of fence around the rug and she's not supposed to try to get out.

Where do you sleep? Maythorn's binoculars moved to the barn and studied the picnic table and rocking chairs under the raw new shed at the side of the barn.

We all have mattresses on the floor and sleeping bags on top of them. Except for Uncle Wade—he has his own tent in the other barn, that little one behind those trees. My special place is in the corner across from Laurel. I have a rug, too, and a bookshelf with my favorite books—the rest of them are in boxes down below till the house gets done. And I have a trunk for my clothes and a box for my very most important stuff. It's like camping out, except we don't have to worry about rain. And when it does rain, it sounds cool hitting the metal roof, like a million fairies tap dancing. Sometimes I wish we could live in the barn forever. We have kerosene lamps at night and we sit outside and watch the lightning bugs. And we bathe in the branch or in a big round tub if we want hot water. It's really fun.

Maythorn abandoned the binoculars and rolled onto her side, leaning on one elbow to study Rosemary. Do your mama and daddy yell at each other much? Mine do. I'm glad I have my own room to get away from them. I wouldn't want to live all together like you do. That's why my mama said you all are hippies.

No, they don't yell at each other! Rosemary was aghast at the idea but, after brief consideration, added, *Sometimes Pa yells when things mess up—like when the truck wouldn't start yesterday. He yelled and said bunches of bad words but he wasn't mad at any of* us.

What were the bad words he said? Maythorn gazed with interest toward the house site, where Sam Goodweather was hoisting another window into place.

I'm not allowed to say them. But I guess I could spell them for you. He said D-A-M and S-H-

A cowbell clanked and Rosemary jumped to her feet. *I have to go now.* She paused, reluctant to leave her newfound friend. *You could come down and eat lunch with us. There's plenty. I could show you my books and stuff.*

No, thanks, I've got my lunch right here. And I've got some other jobs before I go home, some other things I have to see about.

What do you mean? You're just a kid—and it's summer vacation! What do you have *to see about?*

Things. It's my job. Maybe I'll come down another day.

The bell sounded again, louder and longer. Laurel was standing at the edge of the shed, waving the cowbell wildly from side to side.

Okay, maybe another day. See ya. Rosemary slid off the rock and started down the slope. A thought struck her and she whirled to address the binoculars that were following her retreat.

Maythorn, what kind of job? What do you do?

The sun glinted on the lenses, throwing bright lances into Rosemary's blinking eyes.

I'm a spy, said Maythorn. I find out stuff.

* * *

Lunch was on the table in the welcome shade of the new shed. Bread and cheese, cold cuts, crisp green lettuce, and thick slices of tomato were heaped on two old ironstone platters. Elizabeth was fixing a plate for Laurel—five carrot sticks, half a cheese sandwich with tomato, no lettuce. No mustard, mayo on the slice of bread next to the cheese, not the one next to the tomato. Perched on a cushion atop the picnic table's bench, Laurel swung her legs and drummed her plastic cup on the table while singing the ABC song, loud and tuneless.

Hey, Rosie, did you have a good adventure? I saw you up on that big rock. Her father smiled his crinkly smile at her. Better wash your hands, Punkin.

Uh-oh, Sam, don't you remember? Uncle Wade's mouth turned down in a sad expression. We used up all the water in the branch. Rosie'll have to wash her hands with something else. Maybe leaves . . . or rocks . . . or—

Uncle Waa-ade, that's silly. You couldn't possibly use it all up! Rosemary made a face at her uncle and hurried off to the little stream, where a wooden trough set over a big rock provided a steady flow of icy, clear water. A bar of soap sat on a nearby rock and a faded green towel hung from a convenient spicebush.

When she returned, her mother had already made her a sandwich—just right—with lettuce, tomato, sliced turkey, and mayonnaise. She slid onto her place on the bench and the family held hands as Sam said, Let's be thankful.

The brief blessing done, they ate. Everyone was starving—it had been hours since breakfast—but Rosemary was full of her news. She swallowed her first huge bite of sandwich and announced, I have a new friend. She's a real Indian and her name is Maythorn.

2.

EVERLASTINGS

Wednesday, October 5

"Aunt E?" Ben's lanky frame filled the doorway. "I need to talk to you."

Elizabeth looked up from the wreath she was constructing. A giant hoop of twisted grapevine, nearly five feet across, lay on the worktable before her, surrounded by baskets of dried herbs and flowers. Branches of silvery-needled, aromatic lavender jostled pungent green-needled rosemary. Spikes of deep purple lavender blooms, olive-green bay, velvety convolutions of blood-red cockscomb celosia filled the baskets, as did the seed-pods of iris, poppy, nigella, and lotus, all gathered at summer's end. Willow hampers held masses of airy white baby's breath and clouds of hydrangea in moody blues and mauves that whispered of tea gowns and *fin de siècle* decadence. Along the workshop's back wall, sheaves of cattails and ornamental grasses drooped elegantly from tall wooden crates.

Half of the wreath's framework was already covered with swathes of the dried foliage, painstakingly wired in bunches onto the bare vines. Elizabeth reached for a handful of rosemary branches and, nodding at her nephew, began to trim them to a uniform length. "Sure, Ben, what's up?"

But he hesitated in the door, sunlight haloing his red-gold hair. "I've got the van all loaded for a delivery run and Julio's going with me—he's going to drive."

"Okay...?" Elizabeth twisted green wire around the clump of rosemary, forming a tight little bouquet. Ben lingered, seemingly unable to go on. Taking pity on him, she added, "It'll be good for Julio to learn the route too—in case you or I couldn't—"

"Yeah, that's what I was thinking." At last Ben came toward her. He stood by the table, aimlessly picking up and putting down her pruning shears. Elizabeth continued with her work, trying not to reveal her growing apprehension. *He's not here to chat... but he's having trouble saying what he came to tell me... I wonder...*

"Big wreath, huh? Must be a special order."

She gathered a handful of the hydrangea blossoms and made another bouquet. "Yep, it's for the show house in that fancy new development up on Turkey Run. Evidently it has a huge stone fireplace and they needed something this big to hang above it."

"Development!" The word was flung at her like a curse. "Why can't things stay the same? They're going to ruin this county—turn it into something like Gatlinburg—waterslides and cutesy gift shops and shit!" He jabbed the pruning shears into the scarred surface of the worktable. "I *hate* how Marshall County's changing. When I used to visit, back when you all first moved here, there wasn't all this... this *crap.*"

Thump. Thump. Thump. The sharp tip of the shears dug little triangular gouges into the unfinished pine. "And all these new people! Driving fancy foreign cars and they're walking around Ransom in *overalls,* for god's sake, like they think that'll make them fit in." *Thump, thump, thump.* Three more gouges were added to the tally. "And they're buying up the old buildings and turning the town into a different place. A gourmet *deli* where the old dime store used to be! And an Internet café next door!"

Elizabeth gently took the shears from her nephew as he waved them at her. "Ben, that dime store closed at least fifteen years ago. And it sat empty, just like the old grocery store and all the other little businesses that shut down. When the new road opened and made it easy to get into Asheville, folks just started doing their shopping where it was cheaper. And where their jobs were. And speaking of new people—what are we?" She clipped the ragged stems of a bunch of lavender. "Plus, you have to admit, the deli has great sandwiches. And it's a kind of gathering place—whenever I'm in town I always see people I know there."

He was shamefaced now, looking with startled recognition at the marks the pruning shears had left on the table. "Yeah, I've been eating there too, now and then. But I still wish—" He broke off. Then the words burst out. "Aunt E, I'm sorry but I've got to get away from here for a while. I don't know…I might go to Florida.… Mom's been after me to come down for a visit and… well, I just need some time to think about things."

Elizabeth's first instinct was to throw her arms around her nephew, but his face warned her off. Only a few days past, Ben's romantic involvement with a beautiful but troubled woman had ended abruptly. Much of the drama had played out right there on Full Circle Farm; indeed, a wreath the girl had made not long ago hung on the wall by the door, and Elizabeth tried not to let her eyes go to its somber circle of rosemary. The dark red roses that adorned it had dried to resemble nothing so much as clotted blood. *Rosemary for remembrance... why didn't I think to take that down?*

"...feel really shitty about leaving. I mean, here you made me a partner in the business and all, but if I don't get away..." Ben was pacing now. "I wouldn't leave if I didn't think Julio and Homero could take up the slack."

He was right, of course. Now that Julio's brother-in-law Homero was joining him in the little house across from the workshop and drying sheds, the work would still get done. And if Julio's wife and children were able to make the move from Mexico soon, there would be even more help. Elizabeth raised her hand to lay it on Ben's arm, to arrest his pacing, to achieve some sort of contact.

"Hey, Ben, it's okay. Things slow down along about now. It'll be fine. We'll manage...."

"I'll get everything caught up and I'll make sure that Homero understands the work before I take off." Quivering under her touch like a high-strung horse ready to bolt, he had hardly heard her. "I just have to be away from here before—"

"Ben, it'll be fine." She fought to keep any hint of chagrin from tainting her reassurances. "I understand. Really. When do you want to leave?"

He closed his eyes and exhaled a long sigh of relief. "I was afraid you'd be pissed." He looked around the workshop, then went to the big permanent calendar that mapped out the farm's yearly schedule. Tracing his finger along the days of October, he frowned. "I don't know... maybe next week? Once we get the greenhouses ready for winter, the load ought not to be too much for the guys."

Elizabeth returned to her wreath, struggling to conceal her feelings. "Rosie's coming home for the weekend.

I know she'd want to see you before you take off. What if I plan a family dinner for Friday night? Then you could leave Saturday or Sunday, if you wanted."

Ten uncomfortable minutes later, the van's door slammed and Elizabeth heard the roar of the engine and a spatter of gravel as Ben and Julie drove off. *It'll do him good to get away. He's hurt and confused and needs to figure things out.... And a little time with Gloria will probably remind him why he came here in the first place.*

Ben Hamilton, the only child of Elizabeth's much-married (and much-divorced) sister, Gloria, had been born in the same year as Elizabeth's daughter Laurel, and from an early age had spent his summers at Full Circle Farm. After graduating from college, he had come to Elizabeth and asked to learn the ins and outs of her work—growing and selling herbs and flowers. Ben had quickly become a valuable asset to the farm and Elizabeth had made him a partner in the business.

And now he's leaving. Just when I'd started depending on him. Just when... But he said it wouldn't be for long. I don't know... this thing... this romantic entanglement may have hit him harder than I know. Oh, Ben...

She tidied up the worktable, moving mechanically: putting the unused flowers back in their baskets, returning the wire, the pruning shears, and various implements to the proper places, bringing a semblance of order to the chaos of the crowded workshop. The familiar spicy-sweet smell of the dried herbs interwoven with the new-mown hay aroma of dried grasses and flowers filled her nose. The baskets of dried flowers were a muted rainbow, a soft symphony of color. Poignant melancholy swept over her as she surveyed the rich harvest of her summer's labor. *Everlastings. They call dried flowers everlastings. But, in point of fact, they're only good for about a year.*

Then they fade and get dusty and covered with cobwebs. And you toss them out.

Her spirits lifted as she ate her lunch—a quick bowl of ramen with dried shiitake slivers, cut-up green onions, a bright red blob of fiery *Sriracha* sauce, and an egg poached gently in the broth. Her silver spoon broke into the bright yolk nested in the soft white noodles, and she paused to enjoy the picture the vivid colors made in the cobalt blue bowl—*a picture of domestic comfort, like those old Dutch paintings.* She smiled to find herself so cheered—*and by a twenty-cent pack of noodles too. Am I a cheap date or what?*

As she washed the few dishes, the sight of yellow leaves whirling against the clear blue sky beyond the kitchen window called to her. *Maybe a walk before I go back to the shop—I could stand to get away myself.*

Lacing up her boots, Elizabeth looked around for the dogs. They were usually frantic with joy at the prospect of a walk into the woods, but at the moment they were nowhere to be seen. Off on their own adventures, no doubt.

"Alone, alone, all all alone!" She declaimed Coleridge's melodramatic lament in a mock-lugubrious tone and found that she was smiling again as she walked toward the grassy track at the top of the pasture. In the shade by her toolshed, she paused to check the stack of oak logs that Ben had inoculated with mushroom spawn. A lone shiitake the size of a silver dollar, its chestnut cap edged with tiny mocha dots, protruded from an upper log.

Nearby, a shaft of sunlight through the trees illuminated an unruly patch of hardy begonias, shining through the intricate tracery of the red-veined leaves and setting alight the delicately pinky-tan winged seedpods that dangled from slender red stems like inverted candelabra.

Beneath the trees a carpet of fallen leaves covered the still-green grass and made a satisfying crackle as she shuffled through them. Not much color yet—the occasional scarlet and some gold amid lots of brown. The earthy smell of leaf mold was pleasant and she inhaled deeply. *To every thing there is a season.* The words ran through her head as she pushed open the metal gate and stepped into the sunshine of the pasture.

The vista here always took her breath. At the house, the view from the porch had, year by year, become more limited as the trees below grew taller. Someday she would have them cut down, Elizabeth thought, and restore the view to what it had been when she and Sam first came to the farm. It was beautiful, even with the trees blocking the view, and the far peaks of the Blue Ridge were still visible in places, but sooner or later, steps would have to be taken.

She set out across the path that ran into the woods. The wild flowers of autumn, starry lavender asters, deep purple ironweed, and bright goldenrod dotted the mountainside above and below her. At the edge of the woods, where there was more moisture, a patch of deep blue-violet lobelia pooled at the foot of a tall persimmon tree.

Stopping to drink in the view, Elizabeth sat on a rustic bench, one of four Sam had set along this walk. The locust logs that supported the broad oak plank were showing signs of decay and the seat was slightly wobbly. *More change. But you can't make time stand still.* She pivoted to look up the hill, up to the southern ridge that separated Full Circle Farm from Mullmore—the one-time home of the Mullins family. The slope was thick with black pines, and the sound of the wind through them was a melancholy moan. *"Soughing"—that's what the wind is doing. What a great word—like "wuthering."*

She stood and looked at the ridge, considering. The ghost of a trail curled up the slope and disappeared into the pines. *That must be the route that Rosie and Maythorn used. Rosie took Sam and me and Laurel along it, that time we went to Krystalle's big birthday party—that awful party. That would have been '85, the year before Maythorn disappeared.*

The path was still recognizable—probably part of the dogs' vast network of appointed rounds—and Elizabeth studied it, appraising the possibilities. *It was so beautiful and manicured over there . . . all that professional landscaping . . . the rose garden . . . and it's been almost twenty years since anyone's lived there. I wonder what's left.*

She thought about her unfinished wreaths down in the workshop, but the faint trail was too enticing. She started up the slope. Behind her the wind riffled the poplar trees, twirling the leaves with a thousand brittle rustlings to sparkle gold and green in the sun. Higher up, the pines grew close and dark, their long shadows thrusting toward her, but beyond them there was sunlight.

She paused to look back at Full Circle Farm. A hawk was circling high over the fields below and she saw the flash of his pale belly and then the copper gleam of his broad tail. He circled once more, then set his wings and soared south in her direction, crowning the ridge and dropping down into the hidden cove that had been Mullmore.

Elizabeth climbed steadily toward the ridge, carefully pushing aside the pine branches when their prickly fingers brushed her face. Here the trees grew so close that most of the usual clutter of multiflora rose and blackberry bramble had not been able to gain a foothold. Her boots trod noiselessly on the soft duff of pine needles and she was soon at the top, at her line fence.

And here was the scuttle hole that Sam had built so many years ago, a narrow, zigzag parting in the fence that a person, but not a cow, could slip through. As she angled herself through the opening she could hear him saying, *Now maybe those girls won't keep snagging their clothes trying to crawl under the barbed wire.* And for two years the path and the scuttle hole had seen almost daily use as the two little girls ran in and out of each other's homes, families, lives. Elizabeth stood there on the other side of the fence, remembering. *And then it stopped. I don't think Rosie ever came up this way again. I know I didn't.*

Long rays of afternoon sun shafted through the old hardwoods—maples, poplars, hickories, and oaks—that guarded the upper slopes of Mullmore. Emerging from the deep, chill shade of the pines into the brilliance of this south-facing slope was like coming into another country, a dreamlike, mazy kingdom of slanting autumn light. A small wind trembled through the treetops and a shower of brilliant leaves swirled around her. *Like Danaë,* she thought, *when Zeus came to her disguised as a shower of gold.* Caught in the dream, she held out her arms and lifted her face to feel the leaves flutter against it. She stood there as the air grew still and the leaves fell to the ground. Then she set off down the trail that led to the clearing below...and to whatever remained of Mullmore.

3.

SLEEPING BEAUTY'S CASTLE

Wednesday, October 5

The trail wound through the trees, a narrow ribbon twisting down the wooded slope. Far below her and only partially visible through overgrown shrubbery and rampant wild vines, Elizabeth could see the dark red tile roofs of the abandoned house and outbuildings. Mullmore lay in the heart of the sheltered cove that previous generations had known as "the ol' Ridder place." Almost two hundred acres, it had once been a prosperous farm, comprised of steep woodland, gently rolling pastures, and an unusually large stretch of level bottom—so-called "tractor-land," much prized for ease of cultivation. But when the Mullins had bought the property at a staggering price—"Paid cash for it too" the local grapevine had insisted, "cash out of a suitcase"—it had swiftly become apparent that they did not intend to farm.

The log barns had been sold—dismantled and hauled off on trucks. And the weathered old farmhouse, with its gently sagging porches festooned with ancient rambling roses, had been demolished in favor of the massive, four-storied brick Tudor-style house that rose in less than a year. The fact that no local builders were employed had rankled the native inhabitants of Ridley Branch and they had watched, incredulous, as truck after truck of building supplies were followed by a small fleet of campers, bearing the crew of workers. Soon the dwelling under construction was spoken of as "a mansion house" and speculation ran wild as to what the "millionaire new folks" would do next.

All the construction and landscaping had been finished when we moved here, but people were still *talking about it. I think some of them were a little disappointed when we built such an ordinary, modest house.* Elizabeth's neighbor Dessie, gone now, but always vividly alive in memory, had declared, "Why you uns ain't a bit like them Mullinses! You and yore man is just as *common!*" It was a compliment, Elizabeth had come to realize.

She continued her descent, out of the forest into the rolling meadow that had circled the many-gabled house like a smooth jade collar. Smooth no longer. She picked her way through a maze of rampant growth: locust saplings in thorny and painful profusion; tall pokeweed that leaned over her, its strong magenta stems culminating in dangling clusters of hard emerald berries; and then a regiment of pale gray-green thistles, standing like prickly sentinels, their purple blooms mostly gone to down. A bevy of goldfinches, disturbed at their feeding, rose up from the thistles in a twittering cloud and scattered in their curious swooping, faltering flight.

I can understand why the Mullins would have wanted to leave after such a tragedy. But why didn't they try to sell the place? The great house loomed in the center of the cove bottom: a towering mass of deep purple-red brick relieved by multiple half-timbered gables. The lower windows were masked with plywood, but the upper ones were bare, their multiple panes winking blindly in the sun. It was an impressive piece of architecture and could have taken its place in a prosperous gated community without exciting comment. *Tudor revival—"stockbroker Tudor," I think the Brits call it. But here—I don't know—it's like a spaceship in a cornfield.*

It probably *had* been a cornfield, she mused, standing at the outer edge of the formal landscaping that had transformed this particular bit of Appalachia into the semblance of an English estate. Before her, the empty swimming pool gaped, its azure-tiled basin stained by the detritus of many seasons. She walked to the edge and saw that among the drifts of leaves and rotting black walnut hulls were the scattered and bleached bones of some large animal—a deer? *It must have blundered in and couldn't get out.* She turned away, with a sick pang, saddened as always, at the suffering of animals in a manmade world. *The suffering of the innocent.*

Broad limestone paving, now almost invisible beneath the fallen leaves, ringed the pool. Stately urns that she had last seen filled with late-blooming azaleas, their pink and coral blooms massed in tight perfection, now overflowed with a jumble of dead or dying weeds and a few tiny persistent seedling maples.

She remembered the scene as it had been twenty years ago: the pool shimmering turquoise, the assorted parents, drinks in hand, milling about, while at the far end of the pavement, in the open pavilion, a top-hatted magician entertained his audience of children. The pavilion was shuttered now, the children grown. *Except for Maythorn.* Elizabeth stood bemused, unwelcome memories flooding back, threatening to overcome her.

Well, here you are at last! Patricia Mullins had separated her-

self from a chattering crowd and hurried on clicking high heels toward Sam and Elizabeth. Tight blue jeans outlined her shapely legs and her blue chambray "work shirt," heavily embellished with rhinestone studs, was partially unbuttoned to display an impressive bosom. Y'all must be worn out, letting those girls drag you through the woods like that. You should have come around by the road. She grabbed Sam's elbow possessively and tugged him toward the bar. You come right over here and get a drink. I'm just dyin' to introduce my big handsome neighbor to some of my girlfriends. Elizabeth, you want to go on and take Miss Laurel in with the kidlets? They're having such fun. She had paused, looking Elizabeth up and down. You might want to freshen up a bit—you know where the little girls' room is.

"Bitch!" Elizabeth had hardly known that she'd spoken, and the harsh sound of her own voice startled her. With a last bitter glance around her, she moved across the terrace and down three wide shallow steps into the remains of the sunken rose garden that lay at the back of the house.

Twenty years ago, at that horrible party, it had been early June and the roses had been at their best. Fat and sprawling, the blowsy petals had shed an intoxicating fragrance, marred only slightly by the acrid smell of the fungicides and insecticides necessary to achieve such perfection. Each curving bed had been devoted to a single variety. Roses ranged from the deepest reds at the garden's center through corals, deep and then lighter pinks, yellows, and, at last, on the perimeter, a mass of white. The effect had been glorious, especially when seen from an upper window in the house.

I was a fool to go up there with him—all because I was angry with Sam. I should have known.... She thrust the bitter memories aside and surveyed the ruin of the garden. *All that work and all that money... all gone to waste now.* Today, only a few roses remained amid the weeds—unruly whip-like stems with mildewed leaves—the hardy roses that sprout from rootstock even after the fancy grafted culti-vars have succumbed to disease or weather. A statue—a classic nude clutching her stony draperies ineffectually to her chest—had been knocked from its plinth to lie half-buried beneath a tangle of brambles.

The blackberry bushes seemed to be ahead in the Darwinian struggle of survival. They were everywhere, coursing thickly up the dark red walls of the house, bar-ring entry almost as effectively as did the plywood shut-tering the windows. They snagged her clothes and skin with their thorns as she threaded her way out of the rose garden to the deserted tennis court beyond.

The net was long gone but the composite surface had, astonishingly, held firm against nature's rampant incur-sion. A mat of fall leaves covered the faded green surface and Elizabeth was surprised to see what looked like—no, what *were*—the fat tracks of an ATV, an all-terrain vehi-cle. *Hunters, probably, fooling around. The fence must be down somewhere, or they've cut it to get in. I'm obviously not the only one curious about Mullmore.*

A loud *crack,* like a gunshot, made her gasp and look wildly around. As she peered up into the woods, the dull glint of metal caught her eye—the copper roof of the gazebo—*Our landscape architect said we had to have a folly to anchor the central axis of the garden, the Bitch had prattled to a seemingly entranced Sam.* Almost instantly, there was a sec-ond sharp report—a black walnut dropping from a tree onto the metal roof, with explosive results.

Elizabeth picked her way through more brambles toward the octagonal structure, remembering that it en-closed a spring and hoping that she could get a drink of water. She noticed that there seemed to be something of a trail through the thorny shoots—*Probably animals using the spring,* she reassured herself, as she stepped into the cool interior of the Mullmore folly.

No, not animals, not wild *animals, anyway.* The sordid little heap of Vienna sausage cans, the empty plastic bottles, cigarette butts, and snack-food wrappers told another story. *Hunters again. Why are some people so trashy?*

In the distance she heard the throaty growl of a vehicle. Suddenly she was extremely aware of three things: she was trespassing; she was alone; and she hadn't brought Sam's gun. He had always insisted that she carry it when she went hiking. *You might meet a skunk ape or a booger man,* he had teased her. *Or if you fell and broke your leg, at least you could make a racket so I could find you.*

She was out of the folly and jogging, as quickly as the brambles and saplings permitted, toward the cover of the wooded slope. Behind her, the vehicle's roar seemed louder. *This is probably foolish,* she told herself as she tore free of yet another thorny multiflora rose. *It's just hunters...maybe even someone I know.* But she didn't slow, though her sides were aching and her breath was coming fast. The vehicle was on the other side of the deserted house, hidden from her view, but approaching steadily.

At last she reached the shelter of the woods. Ducking quickly behind the trunk of a giant tulip poplar, she sagged against its comforting mass, closed her eyes, and tried to catch her breath. The motor below roared and then fell silent. She listened hard, but there was no further sound of the intruder. *The* other *intruder, Elizabeth.* Peeking around the tree trunk, she studied the scene below, but nothing moved and there was no further sound of human activity.

She waited, listening intently. When five minutes passed with no renewed sounds, Elizabeth reluctantly abandoned her hiding place and began the climb back to the ridge and the scuttle hole. She went slowly and quietly, slanting up through the trees in search of the path that she had followed before. At last she came to the trail, climbing with confidence now, eager to be out of this haunted realm.

Too many memories. It was a mistake to come over here.

The scuttle hole lay just above her and she moved gratefully into its crooked opening then stopped, frozen in place by a single high thin cry. A cry like that of a terrified child, it was a sound that reverberated in her memory. She stood there, not breathing, braced to hear it again, to be certain that she'd heard rather than imagined that mournful wail.

Nothing. No sound but the low murmur of the wind in the pines. Elizabeth looked up through the dancing green boughs to the sky over Mullmore...listening... listening. As she stared into the blue depths, a sudden shadow fell across her, and with a plaintive cry the raptor caught the current to ride the wind over the breadth of Full Circle Farm and down into the cove to the north.

A hawk, you idiot. It was a hawk you heard. Still, she lingered to be sure. There were no more cries and so she set off, back down the trail to the welcome familiarity of her own home. *Just a hawk,* she reassured herself, trying unsuccessfully to ignore the voice that whispered, *What if... what if... what if it was Maythorn?... or another lonely child? What if you're supposed to do something? Something that's been left undone?*

The doubts were still with Elizabeth as she finished the wreaths that afternoon; the doubts rode on her shoulder as she climbed up the hill to her house; they continued their nagging refrain as she ate her supper. She willed them to silence and called Laurel to leave a message about coming to dinner on Friday. Then she stretched out on the sofa, a mug of tea in one hand and her phone in the other.

She and Phillip had talked the night before and he had been firm in his insistence on giving her time and space to deal with Rosemary's problem. "Which doesn't mean I won't be staying in touch," he had said. "It's just that after all the drama you just went through with Ben and now Rosemary . . . well, what I have in mind . . ."

He hadn't quite articulated what he had in mind. *And I'm not sure what I have in mind either. I just know that I like being with him, that he makes me smile . . . that I miss him when I don't see him for a while . . . and that a few days ago I was ready to go to bed with him.*

She keyed in the familiar number and was rewarded by the sound of Phillip's voice. "I just got done with my night class and was getting ready to call you. Are you okay?" His tone was soft, concerned. "What about Ben? He seemed pretty low when I was out there Saturday."

She told him about Ben's decision to go to Florida for some time off, adding that she and Julio and Homero were up to taking care of the farm. "Remember, for several years I did it all by myself. We'll be fine, really."

"Yeah, but if I remember right, you said your business has more than doubled since then."

"Trust me, Phillip. We'll manage. What I called about . . ."

He turned down her invitation to family dinner that weekend, holding to his decision not to complicate her dealings with her daughters and her nephew. "But after that first dinner . . . I'd really like to meet your Rosemary.

Sam always said that she took after you and Laurel took after him."

Elizabeth considered. "Well…I guess that's mostly true…especially in personality. But really, each of them is very much her own person. Rosemary does have dark hair like mine. Or like mine was, anyway." The ever-increasing number of white hairs that silvered her long braid was always something of a surprise on the rare occasions she glimpsed herself in a well-lit mirror. The ancient, streaked mirror above the bathroom sink where she brushed her teeth was dim—and kind, like candlelight. "But she has Sam's brown eyes."

"Yeah, and Laurel has Sam's red hair and your blue eyes. Man, genetics is a real crapshoot, isn't it?"

They talked on, the pleasant, inconsequential chat of good friends reluctant to end their conversation. Phillip told her about his night class and some of the unlikely characters who were seeking a career in law enforcement. Elizabeth asked about his daughter, Janie, provoking a spate of fatherly complaint. "Well, I wasn't going to mention this, but she's up to her old tricks. Here she is, a senior, almost a senior, anyway—hell, she's changed majors so many times, I can't keep track—and now she's taking classes at night to become a massage therapist. What is it about Asheville? Every other young person you meet wants to be a massage therapist. And none of them wants to leave the area. Like something I read the other day said, you can't swing a cat in Asheville without hitting a massage therapist—"

"Phillip," Elizabeth interrupted, compelled by some lingering doubt. "This afternoon I went to Mullmore."

THE SISTERS

June 1984

I CAN'T GO *too far off. I promised Mum I'd stay close enough to hear the big bell if she rang it.*

Rosemary struggled after the brown, bramble-scratched legs of her best friend, moving swiftly up the old logging road. The long-abandoned trace was little more than a footpath now, switching back and forth through the woods above the Goodweathers' unfinished house. Maythorn's thin brown legs kept going, up and down, up and down, and her glossy black braids bounced against her shoulders with every step.

It's not much farther. And it's my most secret hiding place. No one in the whole world knows about it but me. At last she paused to allow Rosemary to catch up. *I think Indians used to stay there,* Maythorn confided, lowering her voice and looking around as if fearful of being overheard. *There's some kind of writing on the rock. I'll show you. C'mon.*

As she trudged up the slope after her friend, Rosemary glanced back down the hill. The bright metal roof that Pa and Uncle Wade had put on the new house was still visible through the trees. It wasn't so very far; she would surely be able to hear if Mum rang the bell. But now Maythorn was disappearing behind some clumps of bushes. Just beyond the tangle of green

were two huge rocks that leaned together like friends whisper-
ing secrets. Rosemary stared up at the towering giants,
amazed to find such a magical place within eyesight and
earshot of her own home.

Come on! *Maythorn urged. We have to get down and*
crawl here. Behind the bushes, a ledge of rock stuck out at
the base of the two massive boulders. Maythorn had already
dropped to her hands and knees. We crawl under here for
just a little bit and then there's a cave big enough to stand
up in.

Rosemary hesitated. A cave? Is it dark? We don't have
flashlights. She had been reading Tom Sawyer *and now that*
she was actually faced with it, the idea of going into a cave was
not appealing. Maythorn, we might get lost!

Oh, Rosie! Maythorn twisted to look back at her. It's not a
real cave—it's just a little room under these big rocks. It's
partly open at the top and there's plenty of light. Come on!
Follow me! And with a sudden slithering movement, she was
gone. Only her hiking boots were visible for an instant before
they, too, disappeared under the big shelving rock. Scrabbling
sounds could be heard and then Maythorn's voice, nearby,
but oddly muffled, called out, Come on! *If you come right*
now, I'll show you the Looker Stone.

With one last desperate look at the friendly twinkle of the
sun through the trees, Rosemary dropped to her knees and fol-
lowed.

It was a short dusty crawl through powdery dirt and old
leaves, but though the light was dim, Rosemary had no trouble
seeing the sunlight on the white sand that lay a few yards be-
yond. With one last frantic push, her head was out from under
the rock ledge. She quickly pulled the rest of her body free and
scrambled to her feet.

It was a little room, just like Maythorn had said. Big
enough for three or four people to stand in and open to the sky

in the middle, but at the sides where the big rocks were leaning, there would be some shelter from rain or snow.

Under there's where the Indians slept, I reckon. And the writing's back there too. Maythorn motioned with her head and the two of them crept closer to the wall of rock.

It's like in Tom Sawyer! *Rosemary crouched down to examine the markings more closely. I'll bet someone made those marks with smoke from a candle, just like in Tom's cave.*

Maythorn crowded close, her fingers sketching the outlines of the dark shapes just visible on the smooth gray rock. That's a snake there, she said, indicating a curving shape. And I bet that's an arrowhead next to it.

Rosemary peered. I think it looks like an S. And a crooked L. See, that curvy thing across the top—that could be the top piece of a heart... like a valentine heart.

That's dumb, Maythorn scoffed. Indians *don't draw valentines. That top thing is a bird flying. I say it's a hunting picture—probably what the Indian who drew that shot for supper.*

Okay, said Rosie, moving back into the sunlit center of the little hidden room. I guess you're right. She tilted her head back to admire the two boulders looming above her till their utmost peaks delicately kissed. Do these rocks have a name? Like Froghead has a name?

Maythorn scooted away from the wall and sat cross-legged in the center of the room. They're the Two Sisters. They were twins and they lived together all their lives and when they got old they prayed to the Great Spirit not to let one die and leave the other one all alone. And the Great Spirit heard their prayer and turned them into stone so they'd be like this for always and always.

Rosemary stared openmouthed at her friend and then up at the great rocks. They're cool, she said softly. I always wished I had a twin. Laurel's such a baby.

Maythorn fixed her with a considering look. At last she said, Well, our birthdays are the same. That makes us kind of twins.

Yeah, but I wish we were real *twins. I wish I was Cherokee like you.*

Maythorn smiled and reached for her knapsack. We can be blood twins, if you aren't chicken. Then you'll have Cherokee blood in you.

There was a pocketknife beneath the sandwiches in the knapsack and after a tiny hesitation, Rosemary agreed to the ceremony. The knife was so sharp that she hardly felt the tiny cut on the tip of her little finger. Then Maythorn nicked her own finger and they pressed the open wounds together.

Are there words we should say? Rosie gazed into Maythorn's dark eyes. Indian words?

I know what we can do, Maythorn said. We'll use the Looker Stone.

They unhooked their fingers from each other. Rosemary pushed hers against the rough cloth of her jeans to make it stop bleeding but Maythorn ignored the spot of blood on her own finger and rooted in her knapsack again. At last she pulled out a flat, roundish something in a soft leather pouch.

This is the Looker Stone, she announced, taking from the pouch a dark flat rock, only a little larger than her hand. Roughly and irregularly circular, it had a dime-sized hole in its very center.

Granny Thorn gave it to me. It was hers when she was little but she says it doesn't work for grown-ups. She told me the Little People made it. And if I look through it at someone, I'll see them without the mask they wear and know what they really are. Granny Thorn says most everybody wears a mask—

No, not a real mask. Maythorn made an impatient gesture as Rosemary started to speak. A mask like when you feel sad but you don't let it show or you smile when you really want to hit someone—that kind of mask.

Maythorn raised the Looker Stone to her eye and turned to face Rosemary. Now that we're blood twins, we don't have to wear that kind of mask around each other. But we'll do this like a reminder—a very solemn ritual.

Standing straight and still, Maythorn gazed at Rosemary through the hole in the dark stone. Slowly she brought up her free hand and stretched it toward her friend, palm to the earth. Adopting the solemn tones of a shaman, she intoned the words: Rosemary Goodweather, I see you.

4.

WATCHDOGS

Wednesday, October 5 and Thursday, October 6

Phillip frowned and leaned back on his sofa. Elizabeth's words had been urgent, even ominous, but they were immediately followed by a rich chuckle. "Good grief, I sound like the second Mrs. DeWinter: 'Last night I dreamed I went to Manderly,' or however it went." He could imagine her tanned face crinkling into a grin, her eyes sparkling. "But it *was* like a dream—"

"Elizabeth, hold on a minute. You lost me there. The second Mrs. who? And where's Manderly?"

He had finally grown accustomed to her way of speaking, the obscure quotes and allusions that seemed to bubble up sudden and unbidden from some inexhaustible spring. Her sources were many and eclectic—from Gilbert and Sullivan to Bob Dylan, Monty Python to Jane Austen, Shakespeare or the Bible to the Firesign Theatre and beyond. Phillip smiled to himself and waited.

"No, not Mrs. Who. That's *A Wrinkle in Time;* I'm thinking about *Rebecca.* I sounded like a character in *Rebecca* just now…a book by Daphne du Maurier." The throaty chuckle filled his ear again. "I'm sorry,

Phillip. I can't help it, the old English major thing, I mean. No, I was just trying to tell you that I hiked over the south ridge to Mullmore—the place in the next hollow where the little girl who disappeared used to live."

Her voice grew serious as she described her exploration of the abandoned estate. It was obvious that the sight of the empty house and overgrown garden had affected her deeply. And there was an edge to her voice that hinted at things not said. "It was so unreal...so... suspended in time...at least till I found all the trash someone had left in the gazebo...and till I heard a four-wheeler coming."

She tried to make a joke of her hasty retreat back to the ridge but he could sense an undercurrent of real terror "...I kept going like the booger man was after me. I don't know why I was so spooked—it was probably only some hunters, trespassing just like I was. But I was freaked to the point that when I heard a sound like a cry, I immediately thought it might be Maythorn. Even when I saw the hawk, I kept thinking..."

Her voice wobbled unsteadily again, and he was reminded of a child recounting a bad dream, unable to shake the spell of the nightmare. He broke in. "Tell me something, Elizabeth. You said they never found any trace of that little girl?"

"No, none. At first they kept thinking that she'd run away, that she'd turn up. She had some family over in Cherokee, a grandmother and some aunts and uncles. But they didn't know anything about it."

"Cherokee? You mean the Indian reservation? But I thought..."

"Maythorn wasn't Moon's child. She was the result of a brief affair Patricia had before she married Moon. She married him not knowing—at least she *said* she didn't know—she was already pregnant by someone else. The little girl was always called Maythorn Mullins. But she told us that her real last name was Blackfox or something like that. Her father was a Cherokee and extremely proud of it too. He was a physician and I think he became something of an activist in Native American causes...at least that's the impression Patricia gave me, the one and only time she mentioned him. Evidently Blackfox, if that's the name, insisted that Maythorn spend time with him and his mother over in Cherokee so that Maythorn would be aware of her heritage. But—"

"Maybe the father snatched her...that happens—"

"No, when we knew Maythorn, her father was already dead—some kind of accident, if I remember right. Most people, including the sheriff, decided she'd been kidnapped—since the Mullins were so wealthy, that seemed a likely motive. But there was never any contact...no demand for money. And as the months went on with no clue...it just got harder and harder to believe that she might still be alive. The assumption was that the kidnapping had gone wrong and the child had died."

She paused, then went on. "You know, eventually, I think, horrible as it sounds, the family would have been relieved if her body had been found...just so they wouldn't be trapped in that horrible limbo of not knowing."

"Did you see much of the family during that time... after the disappearance? I wonder—"

"No." Her reply was curt. "The two girls had been big friends but Sam and I really didn't have much in common with the parents...with Moon and Patricia. They never socialized with us back-to-the-land types much. I think our big free-for-all potlucks were not exactly Patricia's cup of tea—or Moon's martini, for that matter."

The harsh tones gave way at once. "Oh, Phillip, I sound like such a bitch. As you can tell, I didn't like the parents much. But truly, when it happened the Mullins didn't seem to want a lot of people clustering round and offering condolences—particularly at first, when we all kept thinking that Maythorn was going to come back."

They had talked on and on, neither wanting to end the call. Elizabeth had told him more about the Mullins but always with a curious hesitancy. *There's something else going on here, something she's not ready to talk about,* he had thought as they had finally, reluctantly, said good night. His years as a police detective made him fairly astute in reading people. *And I've sure as hell made a close study of Elizabeth . . . as close as she'd let me, anyway. I know there's something.*

Hawkins stood, stretched, then picked up his briefcase, full of papers to be graded. He turned off the lights in the living room and headed down the narrow hall to the small room that he now called his study, by virtue of having replaced the sagging double bed and rickety night table there with a foldout sleeper sofa and a small desk. Clicking on the lamp, he set his briefcase on the desk. *Might as well get through these . . .*

Three hours later he was finished. He padded down the hall, pulling off his shirt and T-shirt as he went and dropping them on top of the washer that lurked in the shuttered alcove just outside his bedroom door. The slacks and boxer shorts were next and finally the socks. *Now, that's handy. Hell, if we'd had a setup like this, Sandy wouldn't have had to bitch so much about the laundry.*

In the bathroom, he shuddered as he always did at the flamingo pink of the tiles and fixtures, wondering as he had before if the color might have had something to do with the house's comparatively low rent. He hadn't *needed* three bedrooms and two baths, but the thought that there would be room for both kids, should they, through some miracle, decide to visit him at the same time, had been reassuring and had allowed him to feel like a good dad for once.

Nice little house but you got to wonder about the woman—it had to be a woman—who picked out this crap.

The house was furnished and the price was right. And he hadn't expected to be here more than a year. So he had hidden away some of the more offensive items of décor: the teddy bears, the fussy pink and blue ruffled pillows, the framed prints depicting improbable cottages, lighthouses, and villages with light pouring from every window and flowers blooming profusely regardless of season. There was nothing he could do about the bed—a monstrosity of brass curlicues that seemed to have escaped from a Victorian bordello. He had replaced the deep rose velvet and satin coverlet with a no-nonsense navy blue bedspread—but the price of king-sized sheets had shocked him deeply and he continued to use the pink linens that had come with the house.

"It's a wonder my balls don't fall off," he muttered as he slid into bed. Hastily he clicked off the bedside light, to avoid the sight of the lace-edged top sheet across his hairy chest.

I bet she'd laugh her head off. I got a real feeling the sheets on her bed aren't all frilly. The ones in her guest room were just white—kind of a creamy white.

The thought crossed his mind—not for the first time—that maybe it was time to spring for some plainer sheets. *Old Sam's wife ... he always said she was a special lady. And here I come just to check up on her and then it hits me ... kinda like it did Sam, I guess.*

He rolled over, punching his pillow into a more comfortable shape. It was hard to articulate what it was about this woman that attracted him so—there were no words that really fit. Instead images flowed through his mind: homemade bread, warm and honest; a tall poplar tree, straight and green against the clear sky; the scent of rain falling on parched earth.

His thoughts wandered. *She was so . . . wounded there at first. Defensive and determined to be independent. I think she'd made her mind up not to trust anyone. But now . . .* He drifted into sleep, seeing a pair of deep blue eyes staring up at him, looking into his very soul.

The cell phone at his bedside beeped and, without turning on the light, Phillip reached for it.

"What? . . . Yeah, I have. . . . No, nothing on that front . . . What the hell time is it, anyway? . . . Oh, yeah, I know you boys work 24/7. . . . This is the country, man, we go to bed with the chickens. . . . Well, your sense of humor hasn't improved. . . . The voice murmured on: instructions, queries, hypotheses. Phillip was wide-awake now and he broke in. "There *was* one thing, though. It's probably nothing, but maybe I'd better get Blaine to check it out."

He explained his concern to the voice on the other end and, after a few more minutes, ended the call. Immediately, he keyed in another number.

"Hawkins here. Sorry to call so late, but I was talking to my friend and there could be a problem."

The cell phone beeped again as he was shaving the next morning. Hastily wiping away lather, he hurried to the bedside table. It was Blaine, who announced without preamble that he was on his way over with a bag of sausage biscuits, some good news…and some bad. He'd be there in ten minutes and he took his coffee black.

It was eight minutes and Blaine was at the door with a white paper bag in one hand. He wore jeans and a light windbreaker and it was his personal car rather than a cruiser parked in the driveway.

"Didn't want to give your neighbors too much to talk about," he drawled as he followed Phillip to the kitchen, where the coffeemaker was signaling, with a series of asthmatic gurgles, that the brew was ready.

They sat at the round table. Phillip chose two mugs from the house's collection: one with big-eyed kittens on it for Blaine; and another, adorned with sunflowers, for himself. Blaine eyed his mug balefully, but accepted it and tossed two paper-wrapped biscuits in front of Phillip.

"These aren't any fast-food sausage biscuits; these are from Sadie's Place—best in three counties."

The biscuits were tender and flaky, the sausage patty thick and spicy. Phillip smiled happily as he finished the first one and began to unwrap the second.

"You're a real pal, Mac. This makes a nice change from cold cereal." He bit into the second biscuit. "So, what's the story? You send some boys out to take a look?"

Mackenzie Blaine, sheriff of Marshall County, swallowed his coffee before replying. His shrewd brown eyes surveyed the kitchen. "Nice place you got here, Hawk. I wouldn't of figured you for a pink and baby blue type but—"

"Yeah, yeah, beneath this rough exterior…Come on, Mac, do we have a problem? You said good news and bad news."

Blaine took a paper napkin from the stack in the center of the table and fastidiously wiped the greasy crumbs from his fingers. His folksy, down-home accent disappeared. "I'm reasonably sure it's not what you were worried about. My deputies and I searched the premises and found evidence that two people have been camping out in the basement. We set a watch but no one has showed as of yet. And I talked to the Roberts—the neighbors just below the Mullins place. They confirm seeing a man on an ATV up that way a couple of times in the last week. And they came pretty close to giving us a positive ID."

Phillip refilled their mugs from the glass carafe. "So, you don't think it's..."

The sheriff leaned back in his chair, "No, I'm pretty sure this is a local bad boy—no connection to the folks your 'friend' is so worried about."

A frown creased Phillip's brow as he brushed the crumbs on the table in front of him into a tidy line then bisected the line with one finger. "How worried should I be about this local fella? I told you her older daughter's coming back, wants to—"

"Yeah, and undoubtedly your Miz Goodweather was over there playing Nancy Drew. Hawk, that little girl's disappearance was thoroughly investigated by my predecessors. I spent a little time this morning going through the files to make sure. I don't think there's going to be anything new turning up at this point in time...or at any other point in time either." Blaine scrutinized Phillip with knowing eyes. "How are you getting along with this so-called assignment, anyway? From what I hear, you're not finding it too unpleasant."

Phillip stared into the murky depths of his coffee mug. "Oh, hell, Mac, it's getting complicated. She's...I don't know...she's not what I expected."

The sheriff let out a weary sigh. "No doubt. But what

about your friend in DC and his concerns? How much do you think she knows?"

Phillip was silent as he tried to consider the questions thoroughly. Had his growing feelings for Elizabeth distracted him from the job at hand? Had he overlooked some vital—

No. He met Blaine's gaze and held it. "I'd swear she has no idea.... Sam said he'd never tell her any of it. She has no clue about what went down in Nam."

"Then that's good. As long as she's clueless—and as long as the other side doesn't come looking for her—she can go on with her flowers and herbs and you can go on playing teacher at AB Tech."

5.

THE SKUNK APE

Thursday, October 6 and
Friday, October 7

"**I sure as** hell hope so." Hawkins gathered up the mugs. "I wouldn't mind making it a permanent thing—the teaching, I mean—once this thing gets resolved. You know what, Mac: I really like this part of the world." He pulled open the dishwasher and added the mugs to an already crowded rack. "Living in a quiet little mountain town, teaching at a community college...it has its appeal."

Blaine chuckled. "And, no doubt, the widow Goodweather has her appeal. She's not bad, Hawk, for a woman her age. Maybe a little too much of an inquiring mind to suit me, but—"

Hawkins interrupted. "You want to tell me about this local bad old boy you think is hanging out at Mullmore?"

Blaine smiled at the abrupt change of subject. "Well, I'm pretty sure it's a fellow called Bib Maitland. And there's a kind of a tie-in with the whole Mullins case your Miz Goodweather is so interested in."

"It's her daughter who's got the bug up her—" Phillip broke in.

"Yeah, whatever." The sheriff waved aside the

objection. "Bib's been away for the past seventeen years—doing hard time for attempted murder. He got out a few months back and it looks like he might be up to his old tricks. See, nineteen, twenty years ago, he had a real war going on against all the transplants, all the new people moving into the area. Especially the Mullins. Of course, that was before I came here, but I talked to one of the boys who was around at the time and got the straight skinny. Seems Bib had married into the Ridder family that used to own the holler where the Mullins lived.

"Turns out, there's this old family cemetery up there and the law says the Mullins have to allow reasonable access. They fought it—didn't want the Ridders traipsing through their place. But they had to put up with it, at least now and then. So Bib takes his wife up there just before Decoration Day, and while she's cleaning off the graves, he's sitting there with a six-pack or so, looking around at all this fine property and getting drunker and madder every minute. He ends up by working himself into some kind of twisted fantasy that the Mullins have stolen the place from the Ridders.

"Then here comes Mr. Mullins, out with one of those long nets to skim leaves and stuff off the swimming pool down below the little knoll where the Ridder burying place is. Evidently the sight of this fella in his little short pants just sets Bib off and he starts pitching his beer cans down into the pool. He and Mullins get into a yelling match, but when Bib starts down the hill, Mullins runs for the house, threatening to call the law. Bib and the little lady take themselves off, no harm done, and Mullins thinks that's the end of it. Probably even feels pretty good about how he handled it.

"Then, a week later, the Mullins find their fancy pedigreed cat floating in the swimming pool. They pull it out and see someone's put a bullet in it. So the wife calls the sheriff's office, blubbering like her mama's died, and says someone's shot Miss Fancy. Well, Sheriff Holcombe—he was before Frisby, who was the one just before me—Holcombe doesn't wait to hear any more and he and two deputies take off for Ridley Branch, sirens howling and lights flashing. They've called EMS too, because all the information they have is that Miss Fancy's been shot." Blaine was grinning widely now. "See, they don't know Miss Fancy's a cat."

Hawkins made a show of looking at his watch. "Is this going anywhere, Mac? If Bib, or whatever his name is, isn't one of the people my friend is worried about—"

Blaine stood and stretched. "What I'm trying to tell you, Hawk, is maybe you do need to worry about this bad boy. He's just out of jail and, from what I hear, he's pissed at the world. His wife ran off and took their daughter with her, right about the time he got sent away, and he hasn't been able to find out anything about them. I don't know what Bib's up to at Mullmore, but if I catch him there, I'll notify his parole officer, for a start."

The sheriff moved toward the living room and the front door, then paused. "Hawk, I know this isn't what you and your boss—excuse me, your *friend*—are worried about, but if I were you, I wouldn't just ignore Bib Maitland. That whole Ridder clan he's married into is a shady bunch. They don't give a damn for the law; they've always lived outside it. It's a family tradition: the first Ridders to come into these mountains made liquor from the corn they grew in that big cove next to your lady friend. And what's left of the family today, living over there in a bunch of ratty trailers on Hog Run, *that* crew has been into everything from marijuana to methamphetamines, and we suspect they're behind a string of burglaries at some of the summer homes in the county. The decent folks won't have anything to do with them, but the Ridders stick together, marry cousins, and don't talk to strangers."

Blaine's eyes narrowed and he pointed an admonitory finger at Phillip. "I know that the folks you're watching for make one tough redneck seem like chicken shit. But if it was *my* lady friend and Bib was hanging around just over the hill, I believe I'd worry."

Elizabeth held the pillow to her face and breathed in deeply. It was still there—that smell of Old Spice and something else, something indefinable, that she associated with Phillip Hawkins. Only a week ago he had spent the night in this guest room. And she had lain in her bed just across the hall, sleepless for much of the time. *What if I'd just come in here and said, "Move over"? What if he'd come to my room?* She closed her eyes, imagining a quiet tap on her door, a gentle—*But he didn't, did he?*

"You fool," she muttered, and shook the pillows out of their cases. She stripped the bed and left it to air while she wiped the wood of the bed frame with fragrant lemon oil. Friday had come at last and the room was ready for Rosemary, except for clean sheets. A thought struck her and she sniffed at the bare pillow. Yes, that enticing smell was still there, even without the case. She carried the pillows into her own room, hugging them to her, and tossed them onto her bed. Next, marveling at her own silliness—*Like a bloody teenager, Elizabeth*—she removed the cases from her pillows and fitted them over the pillows Phillip had slept on, noting that maybe it was time to get some nicer sheets for her bed.

A frenzied barking from the direction of Ben's cabin caught her attention and she went to the window. Ursa was standing at the foot of the cabin steps, staring fixedly at the door. The burly black dog continued to bark, occasionally breaking into a high-pitched howl.

"Ursa!" Elizabeth shouted from the window. "Ursa! Ben's gone to Asheville. All gone!"

Ursa looked briefly in Elizabeth's direction, then resolutely resumed her barking. A squirrel skittered across the rusted metal roof and leapt for the Cherokee peach tree that grew nearby. Landing safely, it clung to a slender branch, flirting its tail and raising a mocking chatter that could be heard in the intervals of Ursa's persistent alarm. *Idiot dog,* Elizabeth thought, taking her pillows into the guest room to replace the ones she had appropriated.

Almost home at last! But as she neared the Marshall County Consolidated High School, Rosemary Goodweather was seized by a sudden impulse. She pulled into the right-hand lane and turned up the familiar road leading to the high school.

The parking lot was all but deserted and she quickly made a U-turn and came to a stop at the top of the drive. Yes, just as she had seen it for her four years here: first from the windows of a lurching, rowdy, yellow school bus, later from her very own car—an aging, déclassé little Honda—Full Circle Farm lay in the hazy distance. Rosemary breathed deeply as she gazed at the beloved pattern of dark woods and lighter pastures on the slopes of Pinnacle Mountain, and at the silver speck that was the metal roof of her childhood home, shining in the center. *Like a lodestone.*

She smiled, feeling the tug of home and family. Words from one of Shakespeare's sonnets ran in her mind.... *it is an ever fixed mark / That looks on tempests and is never shaken; / It is the star to every wand'ring barque, / Whose worth's unknown, although his height be taken.* Behind Pinnacle Mountain rose still higher peaks, toward which the late afternoon sun was rapidly sliding, its pinks and golds and reds gilding the mountain peaks and the banked, curdled clouds above them.

Home for supper... and Mum and Laur and Ben... and all the memories. Good ones and bad. Her eyes were wet with tears as she turned the car back toward the road.

Memories. Elizabeth looked around the table at her two daughters and her nephew, all eagerly assaulting the chicken cacciatore and all talking loudly. These three had grown up together for the most part, and although Ben had only spent summers with them, he was as much a part of the fabric of their life as any brother or son.

He had appeared in her kitchen shortly before the girls had arrived and asked Elizabeth not to tell Rosemary about the events of the previous week. "Not tonight, anyway. Let's just enjoy ourselves and not get into all the heavy crap."

That seemed to be Rosemary's wish as well. No mention had been made of Maythorn as yet. Rosemary had parked her sensible hybrid car at the workshop and climbed the hill to the house, leaving her suitcase for Ben to bring up in the little utility vehicle they used for hauling firewood and mulch. She had burst into the kitchen where Elizabeth was browning the cut-up chicken in olive oil and garlic, embraced her mother fiercely, and plopped down on the floor to visit with each dog in turn.

"It's so good to be home." Her voice had been slightly wistful. "Chapel Hill's terrific and I love my little house, but there's something about coming home."

Now the three cousins were indulging in noisy reminiscences of growing up on the farm, each seemingly untouched by past tragedies—though tragedies there had been. Laurel, whose recently cropped red hair formed an aureole of ringlets above her lime green turtleneck sweater, was the most vocal. As befitted the artist that she was, Laurel was dramatic and flamboyant at all times. Her sister, however, though always known as "the quiet one" of the two, was holding her own tonight. Rosemary's shoulder-length dark brown hair had been pulled back into a careless ponytail and she had changed her preppy slacks and neatly tucked-in shirt for a pair of faded jeans and a dark red sweatshirt. Her eyes glowed with affection as she vied with her sister in trying to remember exactly which of them had been the first to try to scare their young cousin from the city with tales of a creature lurking somewhere in the woods.

"It was Cletus who told us about the Skunk Ape. You remember, Mum." Rosemary turned to her mother for confirmation. "He swore he'd seen one in his roaming around—'Big ol' thing, taller 'n your daddy, and all covered up with black fur, walking on his hind legs like a man.' Remember, Mum? You told us it was a folk legend, like the Abominable Snowman—"

"Or Bigfoot." Laurel broke in. "But with a silver stripe down its back."

"Like a skunk." Ben looked from one young woman to the other and laughed. "And you sweet little girls had me convinced that there was one hanging around the old cabin. You said if it saw me it would spray me with its super-skunk smell and I'd have to live outside for ten years till the smell went away."

"It may still be around, Ben." Elizabeth raised an eyebrow and looked at her nephew with mock solemnity. "Ursa was over at your place earlier, barking her head off. I thought it was just a squirrel, but...well, it's been a while since there's been a sighting...."

Ben frowned. "You know, I think something *was* in my cabin today. When I came back from Asheville and started packing, there was stuff missing. Some food, granola bars and apples, things like that."

"Probably a raccoon." Laurel helped herself to more chicken. She flashed a wicked grin at her cousin. "Or maybe it *was* the Skunk Ape. Did you notice a strong smell?"

Ben didn't smile. "I noticed that my sleeping bag was gone. I don't think a raccoon took that. Or any other animal."

"Ben! Are you serious?" Laurel stared across the table, oblivious of the sauce dripping from the drumstick paused in midair.

Expressionless, Ben waited a beat. Then his face relaxed into a smile. "Well, I couldn't find my sleeping bag. But I did tell Julio a few days ago that he could borrow it for Homero to use. That's probably where it is. And there *was* some food gone. But the coons or possums are welcome to it."

It was just what a family meal ought to be, Elizabeth decided, when, after much talk and laughter—and several bottles of wine—they settled in the living room with coffee and hot apple crisp. She felt like a contented mother hen with her brood all tucked safely and happily under her wings—for the moment at least. James established himself in a tight little ball on the sofa next to

Rosemary while Ursa lay at Elizabeth's feet. Molly, after regally presenting herself for attention to Rosemary, Laurel, and Ben in turn, lay beside Ursa, her muzzle resting on the larger dog's shaggy shoulder.

But too soon, Ben was standing. "I hate to do it, but I need to get to bed. I'll say good-bye now: I'm gonna leave out at dark-thirty, while you all are still asleep." He hugged the two girls, then turned to Elizabeth. "Aunt E, I'll keep in touch. Everything should run smoothly; if there's any problem—"

She reached up to him. "Ben, we'll be fine. Tell your mom hi for me. And come back whenever you're ready."

His arms tightened around her and his voice was husky in her ear. "Thanks, Aunt E; I will."

Laurel had returned to Asheville soon after Ben's departure, saying that she had to help a friend hang a show the next day. She hugged her mother and sister affectionately, bemoaning the fact that she wouldn't be able to come back out to the farm till she finished an important commission. "Carter Dixon recommended me to some friends of his who're opening a restaurant. They've got two long walls they want murals on, and the work has to be finished in time for the restaurant's grand opening in November. So that's going to *totally* consume all my so-called free time this month."

Rosemary, yawning hugely, had retired to the loft room that she and Laurel had shared for many years. "I'd rather stay there than the guest room, Mum. Nostalgia, I guess. It's been so good—coming back and just all of us being happy and silly together. I'm going to curl up in bed and read some of my old books for a while. Tomorrow we can talk about what I need to do. But for tonight ... I just want to be happy." And she had climbed the steep stairs to the loft, worn copies of *A Swiftly Tilting Planet* and *Ozma of Oz* tucked under her arm.

Elizabeth switched off her reading light and rolled on her side. The faint Old Spice aroma at once filled her nostrils. *I didn't think about Phillip all evening, not once. The kids and I were so busy being family and remembering funny things that happened....I guess he was right not to come, it wouldn't have been the same. The kids all needed this time together...but things are changing....Rosie...*

Her head nestled into the soft pillow and she drifted away into a Never Never Land of past, present, and future. A smile crossed her dreaming face.

A low growl awakened her. She sat up, realizing that the massive object taking up the lower third of the bed and forcing her sleeping self into a cramped fetal position was a dog. "Hush, Ursa!" She reached for the dog's snout and held it shut. "It's just that coon at the birdfeeder again. No barking! You'll wake Rosie."

With a dissatisfied grumble, the big dog put her head down. Elizabeth switched on her light and looked at the clock on the chest of drawers beside the bed—3:32 a.m. She grimaced and then realized that she was very thirsty, undoubtedly the result of drinking more wine than usual. With a low command to Ursa to stay, she swung out of bed, shoved her feet in her slippers, and went noiselessly toward the kitchen. No lights were necessary; twenty years' familiarity guided her steps.

A dim light shone from the kitchen doorway and Elizabeth's brow wrinkled. *I thought I turned that off. Maybe Rosie—* Then small clinking and rustling sounds came to her ears.

"You'd better not be getting into that garbage,

James!" she hissed as she rounded the door and headed for the pantry. A light glowed faintly behind the curtain covering the doorway of the little room just off the kitchen. Here were stored canned goods, cleaning supplies, and dog food. The refrigerator was hidden away in this nook, as well as receptacles for garbage and recycling, and James had more than once whiled away an agreeable hour in here, examining the garbage and trying to get into the dog food container.

"*What* are you doing, you bad dog!" She whipped the curtain aside, sure of what she was about to see. "You're going to—"

What she did see stopped her mid-sentence. The refrigerator door was open—the source of the light—and a dark figure leaned into the interior. On the floor beside the creature's filthy feet were containers of leftovers, their tops awry. The smell in the little room was very strong.

Miss Birdie
and Cletus

June 1984

SUNDAY AFTERNOON: *lunch and the heat had made every-one drowsy. The grown-ups were rocking lazily in their chairs under the shed. Laurel lay sprawled on the mattress in her corner, fast asleep. Her red curls, damp with perspiration from the exertion of insisting that she didn't want to take a nap, were plastered against her plump cheeks. One arm encircled Rex, the stuffed dinosaur her mother had sewn of soft blue brushed denim; the other lay extended, hand splayed open like a fat pink starfish.*

Rosemary sat at the rough table under the window her pa had cut in the side of the barn. From this perch, she commanded a view of the winding gravel drive that snaked down the hill to the hard road, almost half a mile away. Just at the moment, she was two people. One was Rosemary Goodweather, writing in her diary, reading an Oz book, and enjoying an after-lunch glass of milk with a handful of cookies. The other was Shining Deer, the Indian princess keeping watch against enemies.

Rosemary took a careful sip of milk and dispatched a cookie in two bites. She put down her pencil and raised a hand to shade her eyes.

Shining Deer peered out of the window, scanning the hori-zon with her keen, hawklike vision. All was well in the Valley of the First People, from the nearer meadows where the deer and buffalo and spotted horses grazed in peaceful harmony to the tall Sacred Mountains that lay purple in the distance, many moons' ride from this place. No marauding settlers ap-peared to disturb—

Shining Deer stiffened. Around the nearest bend in the road came an old woman and a younger man. They both wielded sticks to help them in their ascent. The man was carry-ing something that dangled from his shoulder. Friends or foes? No matter. The tribe must be alerted! She would sound the alarm.

Pa! Mum! There's people coming! Rosemary ran to the door of the barn, eager to deliver her news.

There was a gratifying, bustling reaction. Her mother quickly looked around, picked up the empty beer bottles left over from the grown-ups' Sunday lunch, and hid them away in the recycling box just inside the barn door. Pa began to but-ton up his shirt and Uncle Wade retrieved his T-shirt and pulled it hastily over his head.

Who is it, Rosie? he whispered, with the sly look that meant he was getting ready to tease her. Is it the sheriff coming to get me for jaywalking in Ransom? No! He'll never take me! Promise you won't let him—

Hello the house! The old woman's voice rang out just as she and the young man came into sight. Elizabeth moved to meet them, smiling broadly.

Hello to you. The house isn't finished yet and we're camp-ing out in the barn. Were you—?

The woman, a plump little person in a printed cotton dress and worn tennis shoes, beamed at them all. So you uns is the Florida people Dessie was telling me about! Now, you must be Lizzie Beth, and I reckon this young un to be Rosie. Bright eyes *darted from Sam to Wade and back again. Law, look at that red hair! But which one of you fellers is Sam and which one is his brother? I don't believe I can make it out.*

The young man who had accompanied her hung back, looking at the ground and tracing circles in the dirt with his stick. Rosie studied him carefully. He was a grown-up—a dark shadow along his jawline told her that. But something about him was different. At last, seeming to feel her gaze, he looked up and his limpid blue eyes met hers with the sweet innocence of a baby. He smiled shyly and ducked his head again.

Ay law, where's my manners? I know who you uns is but I ain't yet named who it is come disturbin your Sunday rest. I'm Birdie Gentry and this here's my boy, Cletus. We live down the branch in that little log house nigh the church. Me and Cletus took us a notion to go a-visitin after dinner and Dessie said you was a friendly set of somebodies and you'd not care for us coming up here.

The little woman turned to her son. *Cletus, give Miz Goodweather that berry basket.*

Slowly, carefully, Cletus lifted the odd bark cylinder with its long vine carrying-strap from around his neck and held it out to Elizabeth. *Raspberries,* he said. *Me and Mommy picked em for you uns. And I made the berry basket.*

Please, said Elizabeth, you all come get a seat in the shade. She waved them toward the shed. Oh, Sam, Wade—just look at the beautiful black raspberries! Thank you so much, Cletus. Thank you, Miz Gentry. These look wonderful!

Now, honey, you just call me Miss Birdie like ever one does. Even my man, Luther, calls me Miss Birdie, and we've been wed these forty-four years. Luther would of come too but his arthuritis is painin him bad today. He made it to the church house this mornin for preachin but he 'lowed he'd just stay home this evening and leave the loaferin to me and Cletus.

Rosemary watched as her mother led the two visitors into

the shade and insisted that they rest themselves in the rocking chairs. Rosie! *her father called.* Take the pitcher, please, and go get us some cold water at the spring.

She set the blue-striped crockery pitcher on the flat rock below the pipe where the icy pure water poured out in a thin but steady stream. As the pitcher filled, she considered. *This Miss Birdie sounded a lot like Dessie but talked faster. They both used strange words that she didn't know but could guess at. Miss Birdie said that she and Cletus were loaferin around. Was that something to do with bread? Or shoes? No, probably it was like when Pa said he had to quit loafing and get to work on the house if they wanted to be in before winter. Nothing whatsoever to do with bread or shoes.*

The pitcher overflowed and she picked it up, using both hands, and walked carefully back to the barn. Mum had glasses ready and had put the raspberries into a bowl and set out a plate of cookies. The talk had wakened Laurel, who now sat in Miss Birdie's lap, blinking up at her.

Well, if hit ain't the purtiest thing! *The little woman twisted a red lock of hair around her finger.* Hit'll make a beauty, if hit lives.

Rosemary noted her parents' startled expressions but the old woman went on. *Now, I lost five: three never drew a breath, the innocent angels, and the other two was puny; couldn't do no good atall—went home to Jesus afore they could walk. Cletus is my onliest living one—and a comfort to my soul, I tell you what's the truth.*

Laurel was looking curiously at Cletus now. Suddenly she crawled down from Miss Birdie's knees and stumped over to the young man. She gazed up at him and was rewarded with the fleeting, shy smile. Charmed, she clambered up onto his lap and leaned back against his chest, gripping the strap of his dark blue overalls in a proprietary little hand.

Miss Birdie continued on, scarcely pausing to take breath.

Now, Dessie done told me all about you uns. Said you was naming to farm, soon as you got your house built. I see you already put you in a little bit of a garden. Course, hit's late, but you keep it hoed good and hit'll make you many a mess of beans.

Rosemary sat at the picnic table, eating raspberries one at a time, crushing each with her tongue against the roof of her mouth to savor the sharp sweetness. She liked listening to the grown-ups talk. Uncle Wade tried to ask Cletus how he'd made the berry basket, but Cletus just ducked his head again and said nothing. Miss Birdie did most of the talking; Mum barely had time to answer a question before the plump little woman was off again.

Now, I wonder, do you uns know the folks over the ridge? Bought the old Ridder place a few years back of this? They're from away too. They come to this country and laid out the money like one thing. I heared as how they tore down the old home place and built them a mansion-house. We was namin' to go visit them back of this and me and Luther and the boy set out one Sunday evening with a fresh turn of cornmeal in a poke for them. But when we got there, come to find they had put up a big old brick wall at the foot of their road and great high iron gates acrost it. And those old ugly yeller POSTED signs all along the line fence. Luther said he didn't reckon they was wantin no company and we ain't never seen them, ceptin when they go down the road. And they go back and forth like one thing! Hardly a day don't pass but first the woman and the little one goes out, then there's two men, brothers, I don't doubt, they're bad to go all the time. And I believe they must have six vehicles up there for the family—I never heard of such! Me and Luther ain't never needed but the one truck and hit's done us these thirty-four years.

Miss Birdie paused to sip at her water and Elizabeth pounced on the opportunity to say, No, we haven't met the

Mullins. Except for Maythorn. She comes over here to play with Rosie a lot. They—

Now, Maythorn's the dark-complected child, ain't that so? Looks like an Indian and roams the woods like a wild Indian too. But my Cletus is just the same. Miss Birdie looked fondly at her son.

I seen her in the woods lots of times. Cletus's soft voice was hesitant. She done found all my trails and hidey-holes. She's right smart for a little girl. And she's pretty—kindly like a baby deer.

That Miss Birdie's quite a character—nice little lady. And what about the way Laurie took to Cletus?

Rosemary could hear her father's voice, kept low in the darkness of the barn. They had all gone to bed when it got dark, Uncle Wade to his tent in the other barn, the rest of them to their mattresses and sleeping bags on the upper floor of the main barn. As usual her parents were talking over the events of the day. She liked hearing what they said when they thought she was asleep. Not that it was ever very interesting. Except sometimes Pa had bad dreams and he said a lot of funny words. But then Mum would wake him and they would whisper. Once it had sounded almost like Pa was crying. That had been scary, but Mum had talked to him very quietly and in the morning Rosemary hadn't been sure if she had dreamed it or not.

Laurie really has a thing for men. Her mother's voice was smiling. I'm afraid I see trouble down the road. How are you going to feel when she goes out on her first date?

Oh, I don't believe she'll date. Pa's chuckle made Rosemary feel warm inside, like always. Maybe when she's twenty-one— and if I go along. Thank god, Rosie has more sense right now than any three teenage boys. We won't have to worry about her.

There was a rustle in the darkness as one of her parents turned over. *Sam, did you hear Miss Birdie when they left, inviting us to come to church sometimes? That little church down the branch?*

Liz, you take the girls there and you know what it'll be. They preach hellfire and damnation and it'll scare the pants off the kids.

Her mother sighed. *I know.... It's just ... Well, it would be a nice way to join in the community. But you're right. There're other ways.*

Hellfire and damnation. Rosemary whispered the words, tasting their sounds. They felt dangerous—strong and hot in her mouth. Hell ... fire ... dam ... nation.

Her father's voice was a sleepy murmur now. *Miss Birdie asked if Wade and I could patch the roof on their cabin and I told her we would. Don't worry, Liz—we'll get to know these folks on our own terms.*

There was silence and Rosemary began to make a story. Shining Deer stretched out on her bed of sweet-smelling pine boughs, watching the moon climb the blue-black sky. The Indian princess was waiting for Ranger, her pet wolf, to return from the hunt. Far in the distance she could hear owls calling and—

Sam. Mum's low voice broke into the story. *I had a letter from my mother.*

Pa didn't answer but Mum went on. *She and Gloria want to come visit ... to see this place we've bought ... and the house we're building.*

There was a loud sigh and her father said a bad word.

6.

CALVEN

Saturday, October 8

The dark figure pulled back, out of the depths of the refrigerator. Luminous eyes stared up at Elizabeth out of a dirt-smeared face. For a frozen moment the two stood silent. Then, with an unearthly screech, the intruder lowered its shaggy head and tried to butt its way past Elizabeth. A bulging plastic bag was clutched in one filthy hand and a carton of milk in the other.

"Hey, now wait just a minute. I think we need to talk." Recovered from her momentary alarm, Elizabeth caught one bony arm in a firm grasp. "Who are you and what are you doing in my refrigerator?"

"Lemme go! I ain't—"

"Mum?" Bright light flooded the room. Rosemary stood in the doorway, blinking owlishly. "Mum, what— Who's that kid? And why is he ... she ... so dirty?"

The child, for a child it was, gave one fierce, hopeless tug, but Elizabeth held firm. The little arm was so thin that her fingers met around it, making her feel unpleasantly like a bully. The wide eyes gazed at her in appeal, then narrowed. "I ain't no girl. My name's Calven. Please, ma'am, I just needed me somethin' to eat. I done run off from Bib."

"Mum?" Rosemary looked very young, standing there in her faded plaid flannel night shirt, shining dark hair tumbled about her face. But she spoke sternly. "Mum, do you want me to call the sheriff?" Behind her, Ursa and Molly poked inquiring heads into the kitchen.

The boy's arm jerked again, but Elizabeth again held firm. "No, Rosie. At least not now. Let's find out what Calven has to say for himself." Gently she propelled the boy to the cushioned bench in the corner of the room, taking care that she and Rosemary were between the boy and the door.

"Rosemary, why don't you fix Calven a sandwich and a glass of milk? He can have something to eat before he tells us what he's doing here." She eased the carton of milk from the boy's grimy clutch and handed it to her daughter. Rosemary raised her eyebrows in a brief question, but began to assemble the ingredients for an impromptu meal.

The two dogs bounded into the kitchen, jostling each other in their eagerness to investigate. "No! Down!" Elizabeth scolded, envisaging a disastrous confrontation as the faithful dogs, bent on protecting her, attacked the intruder. She grabbed their collars and hauled them away from the boy. To her surprise, he leaned out and began to pat Ursa's broad back. The big dog's plumy tail was waving happily as, Elizabeth realized, was Molly's.

Feeling vaguely ridiculous, she released the dogs. They instantly crowded up to Calven, obviously recognizing an old friend.

"Hey there, ol' Molly; hey there, Yoursa." He looked up at Elizabeth. "I know them two, seen 'em in the woods back of this. Read their names offen their collars. They're right friendly, ain't they? I wisht I could have me a dog but—"

He broke off as Rosemary set a glass of milk and a plate with a thick ham and cheese sandwich on the little table under the window. His eyes widened at the sight and he darted forward.

Again Elizabeth interposed. "Maybe it would be a good idea for you to wash your hands first, Calven." She spoke gently but firmly. "There's a bar of soap over there at the sink."

The child frowned but mutely complied, leaving dirty smears on the dishtowel Rosemary gave him to dry his hands. Then he slid onto the bench, hunched over his plate, and began to devour the sandwich. *Wolf his sandwich,* thought Elizabeth, watching him snap off huge bites and swallow them, virtually unchewed, helping them down with noisy gulps of milk. Rosemary refilled his glass two times before the plate was empty. Then she gave him a bowl of the leftover apple crisp, topped with a scoop of ice cream.

Calven's spoon chased the last crumb of the dessert around the bowl, scraping furiously. Reluctantly he abandoned the implement and picked the bowl up to lick off the remaining film of ice cream. "Son, I tell you that's good stuff. I kin *hide* me some ice cream." He looked hopefully toward the container Rosemary was returning to the freezer.

"Calven, I don't think you better eat any more right now. Let that settle a while. I don't want you to get sick." Elizabeth looked at the thin dirty child, wondering what had brought him to her kitchen in the middle of the night. *He said he ran off from Bib—who or what is Bib? . . . Is this some neighbor's child? Barefoot, for god's sake, and it's chilly out there. And filthy . . . he can't have bathed in weeks. How old is he? Ten? Eleven? Maybe not that old; he's not very big.*

The boy was singularly unattractive: scrawny and pallid beneath the dirt. He wore a too large pair of camouflage pants, belted around his bony hips with a green bungee cord. A rip high on the side revealed no underwear, only pale, dirty flesh. The worn, faded T-shirt beneath the camouflage jacket—again, several sizes too large—advertised a waterslide in Gatlinburg in colors that had once been lurid but were now overlain with embedded grime. His hair, dark with grease and dirt, hung in limp hanks to his shoulders. And he stunk.

Elizabeth's nose wrinkled but then as she watched, she saw that Calven had saved back two bits of crust and was offering them to the attendant Ursa and Molly.

She smiled. "They like you, Calven."

He looked at her with an answering grin and his gray-green eyes suddenly came alive. "I like them too. They's my friends."

With a wrench, Elizabeth forced herself to the job at hand. "Okay, Calven, I need for you to tell me who your folks are. They're probably worried sick about you and—"

"Huuh!" It was a derisive snort. "Ain't no one worried about me but Bib. And I already told you—I done run off from Bib."

"Is Bib your father?" Rosemary stacked the dishes in the sink and came to sit beside Elizabeth.

"Him? Naw! He's just my mama's boyfriend. Mama, she's in the hospital and her mama—that's my mamaw—has to stay with her most all the time, so she done tole Bib to look after me. Weren't no need—I kin do fer myself, long as there's some food in the trailer. I kin fix macaroni and cheese out of a box and I kin cook frozen pizza. But Bib said we was goin' campin'."

Calven squirmed on the bench. "Funny kind of campin', you ask me. We been stayin' at that great huge house just over the ridge. I never seen so many rooms as that place has but Bib fixed us a place in the basement. There's some says that house is haunted; my mamaw done told me folks has seen the ghost of a little girl over there. Bib says there ain't no ghostes. And we ain't seen none neither. But when Bib goes off like he does now and again, I tell you, I git out of that house fast as I can."

The boy cut his eyes at Elizabeth with an air of sly amusement. "Bib had done told me to keep a lookout while he was gone t'other day. I seen you come over the ridge, down that same little trail ol' Molly and Yoursa follows. Seen you walkin' around like you was in a dream, talkin' to yourself and lookin' at stuff. I thought maybe you was a crazy woman."

He sniggered. "Not too crazy, though. You took off like one thing when you heard ol' Bib a-comin'. I like to bust out laughin' when I seen you haulin' ass up through them briars."

Elizabeth studied the boy. Phillip had called her on Thursday with a carefully worded suggestion that she abandon any further exploration of Mullmore for the time being. He had taken pains not to appear to be telling her what to do, saying only that the sheriff thought that some questionable characters could be using the abandoned house for some undefined but probably nefarious activities. And now here was one of them, eating ice cream in her kitchen. "Calven, why are you and...Bib camping out over there, anyway?"

The child shrugged. "You got me. I asked Bib and he tole me weren't none of my business." He leaned toward them and confided, "I reckon he might be lookin' fer something. He's goin' through all them empty rooms, a-tappin' at the walls and floors. And he got him one of them detectors; been walkin' up and down, inside and out with it."

"Mum, didn't Dessie tell us that there was a place there before the Mullins built that…that mansion? A real old farmhouse? I know sometimes people used to bury their money for safekeeping. Maybe that's—"

"That there whole cove used to belong to my mama's people." Calven spoke with a certain pride, a deposed prince, reduced to rags but not without dignity. "They was some of the first that come into this country and they held that place fer nigh on two hundred years afore them Mullins bought 'em out. Mama tole me that my papaw's daddy was one of the richest men in the whole county."

"Calven, I still want to know why you were in my house—in my *refrigerator*—in the middle of the night. And I need to know where you *should* be."

"I done *tole* you. I run off. Bib come back right after you hightailed it outta there t'other day. I didn't say nothing to him about you bein' there 'cause…'cause you weren't doin' no harm but I didn't know Bib'd see it that way. And, son, I tell you what's the truth: you don't want Bib takin' against you. So when he asked had I seen anything, I tole him no.

"But then that night, me and him was asleep in the basement and we heard someone comin'. We got out just in time and was hidin' up in this place Bib fixed. We seen it was the sheriff and some deputies and we heard them talkin' about some woman had been over there that very day. Bib lay there a-listen' and I knowed he was goin' to whale the tar out of me fer not keepin' watch. So, when the sheriff and them left, Bib tole me to head back over the mountain to the trailer and he'd see me there and I'd git what I had comin'.

"Well, ol' Bib, he slipped back down to the house to git his stuff and I took off fer the ridge over to Bear Tree like he done tole me. But I got to thinkin' and figgered that without my mama nor my mamaw there to hold him back, he'd be like to kill me. So I just went along the ridge top a ways and come down here in you unses holler. I slept in your barn last night and I got me some food from that cabin over yon. But I was still hungry and—"

"Your mama and mamaw live on Bear Tree Creek? What are their names?" Elizabeth interrupted, hoping at last for something concrete.

"All us Ridders live there on Hog Run Branch—just off Bear Tree. My mama's Prin Ridder and my mamaw's name is Mag. Bib used to be married to my mama's sister but she done run off and took their little girl too. Mama says that's one reason Bib's so mean—losin' his little girl like that."

Hog Run Branch. Elizabeth remembered traveling up that way with her friend Sallie Kate over a year ago. *We passed a kind of clearing with four or five really awful trailers and a bunch of kids playing in the branch. There was a rotting deer head in the water. And a fire with a sofa smoldering on it.* "Squalor Holler," Sallie Kate had called the little community.

And this Calven, he was probably one of those kids. So now what? Do I take him back and deliver him to this Bib, who's going to "whale the tar out of him"? No, of course not.

"Tell you what, Calven. How about if we find out what hospital your mama's in and we take you to her and your grandmother? Would that work?"

The pale eyes regarded her suspiciously. "Right now?"

"No, tomorrow...that is, later today, after we've all had some sleep. There's a comfy bed in the room across the hall from mine. But first, I think you'd better get cleaned up, okay?"

"I'm amazed you talked him into a bath." Rosemary and Elizabeth were sitting in the living room, waiting for Calven to emerge. Elizabeth had turned down the bed in the guest room and readied it for her unexpected visitor. From the bathroom beyond the study, the shower could still be heard.

"Well, it was bribery. I'm afraid I told him if he bathed really good and washed his hair that he could have another bowl of ice cream." Elizabeth furrowed her brow. "I got out a new toothbrush for him to use after the ice cream—I'm not sure how I'll bribe him for that."

The sound of running water ceased. They waited, almost holding their breath. At last came the creak of the bathroom door opening and the pad of bare feet.

"*Son,* that felt *good!* We ain't had no hot water at the trailer ever since the tank busted. And campin' out like we been doin', ain't nothing but ice-cold branch water."

Calven—clad in an old pair of Laurel's sweatpants, hastily shortened by cutting off the lower third of the legs, and an equally old sweatshirt—stood in the doorway, enthusiastically rubbing his wet hair with a towel. He looked much better, though still pale and woefully undernourished. And his hair, now that it was clean, was revealed as silver- blond.

"I'm glad it felt good, Calven." Elizabeth reached out to scratch Ursa behind the ears. "You know, even these dogs like baths—once they're in. Do you want that other bowl of ice cream now?"

*   *   *

The second bowl of ice cream had been devoured; the teeth had been brushed—no bribe needed this time; the filthy clothes had been dumped into the washing machine. Calven had crawled eagerly into bed, docilely accepting Elizabeth's assurances that they would take him to his mother and grandmother the next day.

As Ursa and Molly positioned themselves on the guest room rug, Elizabeth and Rosemary said good night to the child. Elizabeth left the hall light on and started for her bedroom, but Rosemary clutched at her arm, whispering urgently, "Mum, do you think it's okay ... I mean, just to leave him? Should we lock the doors or—"

Elizabeth laughed. "Sweetie, I couldn't lock him in if I wanted to. The front door key has been lost for I don't know how many years and I don't think there ever was a key to the outside door in the guest room. And I'm not about to stand guard over him. The idea of taking him to see his mother and grandmother seemed to suit him. If they can't take care of him ... Well, we'll talk about that in the morning."

But in the morning the boy had vanished, leaving Ursa and Molly happily snoring on the bed where he had slept. His wet clothes were still in the washer, but a loaf of bread and a jar of peanut butter were missing from the kitchen. On the counter lay a paper towel with a note scrawled on it. *Thanks and plees don't say nothing or I could get kiled.*

7.

Bib Maitland

Saturday, October 8

"Phillip, I feel like an idiot."

Elizabeth's first move, on realizing that Calven was really gone, had been to call Phillip. Rosemary was still asleep; there was no point in awakening her just to tell her that she had been right, that someone *should* have kept watch. So it was Phillip who heard the first unchecked outpourings of Elizabeth's guilty conscience. She quickly outlined the events of the previous evening, trying to present a coherent account. Soon, however, she felt a growing tide of anxiety washing over her and heard herself beginning to babble.

"I'm afraid he'll be in danger...he's just a little boy... and he's barefoot and he's afraid of this Bib. I should have made sure....And you *warned* me not to go back over there and I should have realized—"

She broke off, hating the way she sounded. *Like a bloody fool—appropriately enough.* Forcing herself to breathe deeply, she struggled to reorder her thoughts.

"Elizabeth," his voice was like a calming hand on her shoulder, "it'll be okay. This isn't your fault. Tell you what: I'll get hold of Blaine. He'll find the boy and get him to his folks."

At last she put down the phone, feeling somewhat re-assured, though still unhappy with her own negligence. *Now I have to tell Rosie.*

Rosemary, just out of bed and in search of coffee, listened to her mother's rueful tale. Elizabeth was folding Calven's clothes, still warm from the dryer, and Rosemary watched as she smoothed out the camouflage pants, carefully aligning the inseams as if readying the ragged garment for careful pressing. She studied her mother's worried face and seemed to see her clearly for the first time in many years. *This has really upset her—she looks tired and ... and older. And she's almost dithering. This isn't like Mum.*

"He left a note. It's there in the kitchen. And he took some bread and peanut butter, not that it matters. The sheriff's going to be looking for him. I called Phillip right away and he—"

Rosemary was amazed to see a blush creep over her mother's tanned face.

"Well, I know I've mentioned him—Phillip Hawkins—he's ... he *was* a—"

"A friend of Pa's—I know. From the navy." Rosemary took pity on her parent, seemingly so incapable of explaining what had been a topic of great interest to both her daughters and her nephew. "Mum, I know all about him. He used to be a police detective somewhere over on the coast—was it Beaufort? He's divorced and has a daughter at UNCA and you've been seeing a lot of him recently.... The miracle of e-mail," she elucidated, in response to Elizabeth's startled look. "Ben and Laurel are a lot better at keeping in touch than you are. They tell me it's starting to look serious. So, am I going to get to meet this guy at last?"

It must be serious, decided Rosemary as she hiked up the familiar slope toward the big rock Maythorn had called Froghead. *Mum's eyes just lit up when she talked about him. The tiredness vanished and she looked like herself again. . . . I hope he's nice. Laur and Ben seem to like him a lot, judging from their e-mails in the past year. . . . I wonder if . . .* But she abandoned that train of thought. Though she recognized that her mother was still reasonably attractive at the advanced age of—*what is it, fifty-one or fifty-two?*—and though she was well aware that, theoretically at least, sexual activity could continue unabated well past even her mother's age, still, some things were just too weird to think about. She set her eyes on the granite outcropping above her and plodded on.

I have to go back to the beginning . . . and this is where I first saw Maythorn. Rosemary stopped and looked up at the great rock. Her eyes were misty as she remembered. *It was like magic, like an imaginary playmate suddenly materializing in front of me. And she was an Indian. I remember how that seemed so incredibly cool. I had always wanted to be an Indian myself.*

She stared at the rock's rim, willing a dark face, black eyes shining below thick bangs, to appear, just as it had twenty-one years ago. Holding her breath and wishing, she waited, silently invoking all of childhood's mystical powers. With the same deep faith, she had once fervently stared at the antique armoire in her grandmother's house, convincing herself that if she believed hard enough, it *would* be the doorway into Narnia. Hardly breathing, she kept her gaze riveted on the unchanged loom of granite that hung dark above her.

Maythorn, come back. The words were a plea, an invocation. Rosemary waited, feeling inexplicably *near* to something, as if she teetered on the brink of an unseen time and place, some parallel universe where two little girls who had once played and plotted together had never been separated. In an instant, a vision of an adult Maythorn flashed into her mind: the Maythorn that might have been. A sense of irretrievable loss swept over her and the vision blurred and vanished.

The spell was broken. Shaking off irrational hope, Rosemary climbed to the back of the rock outcropping and crawled out onto its surface. The smooth granite was warm from the sun and, as she had done countless times before, she flattened her palms against it, feeling its bulk as a thing alive beneath her. Above and behind her, there was a clatter and cawing in the woods as raucous crows roused a sleeping owl and harried it from its perch. She watched as the big bird, imperturbable amid the scolding crowd, flew on soft, silent wings over her head to the deep woods on the farther side of the hollow.

Rosemary crept to the end of the rock and stretched out so that she could look down at the house and garden. *We would stay up here for hours, watching Mum and Pa and Uncle Wade and Laurel. She said we were spies, gathering information.* Rosemary watched as her mother moved through the garden below, cutting back dead asparagus stalks and pulling off the lower leaves of some tall collard plants.

Her mother had been relieved that Rosemary had not demanded to begin her research at Mullmore. "Phillip says"—there had been that extraordinary light in her mother's face—"Phillip says the sheriff is keeping an eye on the place but that I—that *we* should stay away till he . . . till Phillip can go back with us. And the little boy *did* say that this Bib character is mean."

Rosemary lay on the rock, feeling the sun beat down

on her back. The air was chilly, though windless, and the warmth stored in the granite felt soothing. She watched her mother moving to and fro as she had watched so many times. In faded blue jeans, an old blue corduroy shirt, a quilted cherry red vest, and a disreputable straw hat, Elizabeth looked much as she always had. Not remarkable, just Mum, a fixed point in the universe. From this distance, the gray was not apparent in the long braid that hung down the back of the red vest.

As her eyes drifted shut, Rosemary let her thoughts wander at random. *Maythorn . . . short for Mary Thorn . . . her grandmother's name . . . and her real father was named . . . what? . . . Blackwolf . . . no, Fox, Blackfox . . . and Maythorn kept a notebook that she wrote stuff in . . . she wouldn't ever let me see all of it, but I got one of my own and she showed me how she wrote up "reports" . . . we were so serious . . . stuff like "10:22 a.m.—WG takes truck to mailbox——12 noon——LG rings bell" . . . I wonder if that notebook of mine is still in our secret hidey-hole . . . if I could find it. . . .*

Rosemary rolled over and tugged her baseball cap low to shade her eyes. She stared out from under the brim up at the sky. *It's really working . . . just being here . . . letting myself remember . . . but there's so much . . . and I'm not sure—*

The roar of a big truck laboring up the hill shattered her reverie and she turned back over to see who it was. The vehicle had not yet come in sight, but her mother was emerging from the chicken yard, where the hens—red, white, brown, and speckled—were greedily pecking at the culled collard leaves. Rosemary watched her mother walk to the edge of the road, head cocked curiously. At last, around the bend came a large white pickup truck, its sides heavily spattered with mud. An even more mud-spattered four-wheeler rode in the pickup's bed.

* * *

Elizabeth waited apprehensively as the big truck came to a stop beside her. She noted the four-wheeler in the back and the big, rough-looking man in the driver's seat. *Oh, shit. I've got a real feeling this must be Calven's mama's boyfriend—the guy Phillip warned me about.*

Trying to project an assurance she did not feel, as well as an ignorance of who the man was and what he wanted, she smiled as she walked around to the driver's side.

"Can I help you?" She raised her voice and spoke at the closed window, keeping her expression and tone neutral. It was not unknown for strangers to come up the road. It happened several times a year. They came in search of lost hunting dogs; they came to take a look at the old Baker place where their Aunt Lulie had grown up; they came to offer a *Watchtower* and invite Elizabeth to do Bible study with them; they came by mistake, having turned too soon or too late; they came, openly curious about who lived up here. There had never been a bad experience with a stranger in all her years on the farm and she fervently hoped that her luck was not about to change.

The man at the wheel cut the engine and rolled his window down. "Well, now, maybe you can do that very thing. What it is, I'm lookin' fer my boy. We was out huntin' over yon." His head jerked in the direction of the ridge that separated Full Circle Farm from Mullmore. "We was headin' back to Bear Tree and he took off on his own. Reckon he could of got turned around and come down in yore holler." His thin lips sketched a smile that revealed a mouth of snaggled, brown-stained teeth. One was missing and its mate seemed to have been half broken off. Dark stubble covered his gaunt cheeks and greasy black hair straggled from under a dirty orange hunting cap. The man's gray eyes were close-set and seemed to miss nothing. Even as he spoke, they ranged over the chicken house, the barns, the house itself.

"I'm sorry, I can't help you." Elizabeth smiled, hoping she looked both innocent and unintimidated. "No lost boys here. If he turns up, I could give you a call. *The operative word being* 'could.' *Not that I would.* Do you want to leave your phone number, Mr.... ?"

"Name's Maitland. And I ain't got no phone just now." The smile was replaced by a glare of distrust. "You sure you ain't seen him? I done tracked him along the top, and looked to me like he come down this way." The penetrating gray eyes bored into her and she had to struggle to maintain her composure. *God, I hate lying. But I can't say that I saw the boy. The best defense...*

She assumed a look of interested concern. "So, do you think he's lost, or was he running away for some reason? Maybe just playing around? I can see how you'd worry, though. What age is this boy? He's your son?" *Over to you, Mr. Maitland. Let's see how you do at telling the truth.*

Bib Maitland's scowl relaxed briefly and he made another frightening attempt at a smile. "Aah, you know how kids is—tell 'em they cain't do this or that and they git their noses out of joint. Little Cal, he's as butt-headed as his mama and he's bad to sull up and run off everwhen he cain't git his way. He's probably headed back home right now. I just thought, bein' as I was up this way, I might try and find him, give him a ride back to Bear Tree. But long of you sayin' as you ain't seen him, I reckon—"

Delighted with the success of turning the questions back on her questioner, Elizabeth pressed on. "Maybe we should call the sheriff and let him know Calven's missing. Since you don't have a phone, I'll be glad to—"

"How come you to know his name's Calven?" Maitland snapped, voice and eyes cold and suspicious. "And what fer are you so quick about callin' the law? This ain't none of your business, you hear me?"

His angry eyes looked past her and she turned to follow his gaze. It swept the slope, following the trace of the trail that led through the pasture and up into the woods toward Mullmore. He studied the path intently for a few seconds then fixed Elizabeth with a withering stare. "I know who you are. You and your man are more of them goddamned Florida people. I remember back when you uns bought the place from ol' lady Baker. And I'll lay money you're the nosy bitch what called the law on me t'other day."

The vehemence of Maitland's words was like a hurled weapon and Elizabeth pulled back from the truck. She opened her mouth to say something—just what, she had no idea—but Maitland continued, leaving no room for interruption and spitting venom with every syllable. He leaned out the window, his narrow, pale eyes holding her.

"You new people come to these mountains, buyin' up our land and sendin' the price of an acre up to where a pore man cain't afford to farm no more. You let your dogs run loose in folkses fields and amongst their livestock and you put up yore yeller signs to keep folks from huntin' the same woods they hunted with their daddies and them *their* daddies afore that. You think you know everything they is to know and you think you can tell us how we ought to do, but I'm here to tell you, lady, you don't know shit."

A fleck of spittle hit her cheek and Elizabeth fought back all the words that were tumbling over one another in an eager desire to justify her right to be here on this land— this land she had loved and tended for twenty-some years. But her inner good sense prevailed. *Walk away, Elizabeth. The guy is not rational. There will be nothing you can say that won't just piss him off even more.*

Wiping her cheek, she backed away from the truck,

then deliberately crossed the road behind it in order to approach her house through the garden. *If I walk up the road, he might follow me, ranting all the way. I'll cut through the garden and the front yard and go in the basement door.* Once in the house she could call the sheriff, if this man didn't leave. And Sam's gun was there.

8.

LONG SHOTS AND FORLORN HOPES

Saturday, October 8

Elizabeth climbed the slope on the far side of the garden, keeping her pace deliberate and unhurried. *Like dealing with a mean dog—run and it'll chase you; walk away slowly and, with any luck, it'll leave you alone.* From the corner of her eye she could see that the truck had not moved and that Bib's head was turned toward her. As she reached the front yard and started for the basement door, the truck's motor growled to life. She stopped and waited, relieved to see the big vehicle back off the gravel, turn, and head down the road.

When it was out of sight she looked up the mountainside, to see Rosemary hurrying down the narrow cow trail toward the house. A smile spread itself across Elizabeth's face. *Back then she'd come barreling down the mountain just like that, pigtails flapping and arms waving when we rang the bell for lunch. A skinny little monkey of a girl. Our sweet Rosie. So happy with her life here. And so pleased to have found a friend next door. If only...*

The memories stung. *She grew up overnight, it seemed. All the lovely, carefree silliness and make-believe stopped as if it had never existed. I hope ... I hope that digging back into all of it is the right thing. ...*

"Who was that in the truck, Mum?" Rosemary's cheeks were flushed and her glossy hair had escaped its ponytail to tumble about her face. "I thought I heard him yelling, so I came down."

"Let's go in and get some lunch, Rosie. I'll tell you all about it." Elizabeth reached out to pull a clump of cockleburs from the tail of her daughter's old flannel shirt, suddenly feeling the need to touch this lovely creature that she had birthed, raised, loved, and protected till at last it was time to let her go out on her own. Surely, by most standards, Rosemary had a good life: a rewarding career, the respect of her peers.

But one thing had always nagged at Elizabeth, and that was Rosemary's apparent avoidance of any emotional involvement. *Unlike her sister, who gets involved at the drop of a hat,* thought Elizabeth as they climbed the stone steps that led from the front yard to the house. *And that worries me too. Are mothers ever completely happy with the way their offspring turn out? God knows, I'm luckier than most with my girls. But I just want them to be happy.*

The phrase echoed in her mind. How many times had her own mother used that same excuse as she urged Elizabeth to do something entirely alien to her nature: dancing classes, joining a sorority, studying to be a secretary? *At least I try to stay out of their lives and keep my worries to myself. And the girls and I get along far better than my mother and I ever did.*

As she heated up some Spanish bean soup from the freezer, Elizabeth told Rosemary about Bib Maitland and his evident animosity toward newcomers.

"As long as he's hanging around next door, I don't think it's a good idea to go over there. I know you came home hoping to do just that, but maybe there are some other things you could do."

Rosemary's brow wrinkled and she looked down at her bowl of soup. For a moment she was silent, her spoon prodding at the thick spicy mass of garbanzo beans and sausage. She seemed to be working out some complicated problem in her head, but then her face brightened and she smiled at her mother.

"No worries. I think that the best thing I can do this weekend is find out where the Mullins went and try to get in touch with them. Didn't you say they still own Mullmore? Maybe we can find out from the tax office or something where they are now."

Elizabeth considered. "It's Saturday—the tax place will be closed. But I could give Sallie Kate a call. She's probably at her office and she may know something about Mullmore. I'm pretty sure I remember hearing her say that she had some buyer it would be perfect for but the owners refused to sell."

They finished their soup and left the bowls on the table while Elizabeth called her longtime friend. Sallie Kate was a successful realtor who delighted in matching the right people to the right places. She took pride in walking the lines of the properties she listed, no matter how steep or wooded, and probably knew as much, if not more, about Marshall County property as any native. Elizabeth punched in the number and was delighted when the phone was answered on the second ring.

"Country Manors. Sallie Kate speaking."

"Hey, Sallie Kate. This is Elizabeth. I'm looking for some information. It's a long story I won't get into 'cause

I know you're busy, but it's about Mullmore—you know, the big place next to us? Do you have any idea who owns it now?"

"Mullmore? Omigod—the realtor's wet dream. Lord knows *I'd* love to list it. I approached your ex-neighbor—What's-his-name Mullins—way back when they moved off, but they weren't interested in selling. And at that time, the way the housing market was, I doubt they could have gotten what they put into the place. So I didn't pursue it. But now, with all the deep pockets moving into the county, I've had several buyers that wouldn't think twice about spending that kind of money."

Sallie Kate chuckled and Elizabeth could hear her tapping at the keys of her computer. "Let me just take a look in my Long Shots and Forlorn Hopes file ... I know I've got something about Mullmore in there. Honey, sometimes I stay awake at night just *fantasizing* about what I could do with the kind of commission I'd get from a sale like that. ... Oh, yeah, here it is."

Again, the throaty laugh gurgled in Elizabeth's ear. "Lord, honey, how could I have forgotten? There was this couple came to me back in '99, right when lots of folks were hedging their bets in case the Millennium ended Life As We Know It." The capital letters were clear in Sallie Kate's tone. "You remember all those poor souls who suddenly decided they had to find a place in the country to ride out whatever might happen. *Anyway,* there were these rich folks from Delaware and the wife had heard of Mullmore—you know it was written up in one of those fancy house magazines back when it was first built—and these people had found out somehow that it was sitting vacant. Well, you couldn't get in to see the place, not legally, with those big old gates across the road, so these Delaware people hired someone to fly them over the property in a helicopter and, grown up as it was, they were hot to buy it. I told them it wasn't listed, but the wife did everything but throw herself down right here on the rug in my office and have a hissy fit, she wanted that place so bad.

"So, I decided to try to get up with the Mullins and see if they might be tempted to sell—quite a few years had passed since they'd moved and that big house just sitting there empty and losing value every day. I went to the deeds office and come to find out Mullmore had been handed over to some kind of foundation called Redemption Walk."

Sallie Kate paused as a voice in the background seemed to be asking her something and Elizabeth could hear her saying, "Lord, honey, I don't know. Tell them it's a good price and the owners are in no hurry to sell. Don't let those people waste your time with a piddling little offer like that."

Then she was back. "Now, where was I? Oh, yes. Well, I couldn't find out a thing about this so-called foundation, but I did learn the taxes on the property were paid through an attorney in Asheville. I got up with him and told him what kind of offer the Delaware people were prepared to make and, honey, he broke my heart. I had already mentally spent that commission and he more or less told me to get lost: Mullmore was not for sale. Lord, I was the one about to pitch a hissy fit when he hung up. I swear, if I—"

"Sallie Kate," Elizabeth, clinging desperately to her purpose, overrode her friend's lamentations, "Sallie Kate, what was the attorney's name?"

"Oh, he was one of the Mullins. Hang on while I scroll

down here.... Yeah, his name was Jared Mullins, Jared R. Mullins."

It was almost too easy, Rosemary thought, running her finger down the page of tiny print. No Jared Mullins, but two listings for a J. R. Mullins in the Asheville directory. One was followed by the designation "atty" and a downtown address; the second, evidently a home address, was a street that her mother recognized as being in the upscale Beaver Lake area.

"Okay, Rosie." Elizabeth pushed the phone across the table. "You've got your first lead. Maybe you'll be lucky enough to catch Jared at home. He'll remember you, don't you think?"

Rosemary stared at the telephone as if it were some unfamiliar piece of technology, then slowly picked it up and studied the keypad. *Jared. She remembered him—a handsome, oddly mysterious presence in the Mullins household—more like an uncle than a brother to his sisters—his stepsister and half-sister. Maythorn and Krystalle had both danced attendance on him in their different ways, eager for his approval. But there had been an uncle there, too, at least some of the time...*

She realized with a start that her mother was waiting for an answer. "I don't know.... Jared didn't pay much attention to me. He was...at least, he *seemed*...a lot older, almost a grown-up. He could drive and his parents let him drink beer and—"

"And you were his sister's best friend and in and out of their place all the time." Elizabeth stood and stacked their bowls to carry to the kitchen. "Of course he'll remember you. You see what you can find out; I'm going to go do these dishes."

Rosemary hesitated, bit her lip, then tapped in the

number. Three, four, five rings, and she was about to click off—*No way I could explain this to a machine*—when suddenly there was a voice in her ear.

"Hello?"

"H-hello," she stammered. "Is this Jared Mullins?"

"Yes..." An instantly guarded response, as from one wary of telemarketers. "This is Jared Mullins. And you are—?"

"Rosemary Goodweather. I'm Maythorn's friend." She heard a sharp intake of breath followed by a stifled sound, and hastened to clarify her words. "I mean, I *was* her friend, back before... My family lived... *still* lives just over the ridge from Mullmore. Maybe you don't remember me—"

"Rosie? Rosie from the next hollow? I almost hung up on you. I thought it was another one of those sick prank calls."

The voice at the other end that had been so coolly suspicious was suddenly warm, even welcoming. "Little Rosie... I can hardly believe it! You know, I haven't thought about you or any of the good things about back then—well, in a long time. I guess it was easier just to forget it all."

"I *know*, I've been the same way." Rosemary found herself nodding in agreement. "But recently... That's why I wanted to talk to you. Maybe you can help me....you see, I feel like I might be able to find out what really happened to her."

There was a silence and then Jared spoke. "Oh, Rosie... Rosie, Rosie, Rosie." There was no mistaking the leaden ring of finality in his response.

"No, I'm serious...really. Jared, I know it sounds absurd—after all this time, and I'm sure your family has done its grieving and moved on. Please, believe me—the last thing I want to do is reopen old wounds needlessly, but...but if it would finally bring a resolution to the whole mystery—"

"Rosie, what makes you think that you can—"

"I know, what can *I* do that wasn't done nineteen years ago by the sheriff's people and the tracking dogs and the private investigators. It's just a feeling, but it's so strong that I can't ignore it—this nagging sense that there's something I *know* about all this but have forgotten. That's why I was hoping to get in touch with all your family—somewhere, somehow, I'm hoping for the word or the...*whatever* that will jog my memory."

When Jared didn't comment, she hastened on. "I guess I sound like a lunatic. Believe it or not, I'm a fairly respectable academic—I teach English at Chapel Hill—and I am not now, nor have I ever been a psychic."

There was a short, humorless bark of a laugh at the other end of the line. "Oh yeah, we had a few of those call back then—they'd get everyone all worked up, just when we'd begun to accept the reality, the *fact* that she was gone and we'd never see her again. Even now, there's one odiously persistent woman who keeps insisting that she has news of Maythorn from the Other Side. She calls me every year just around Halloween. When you said you were Maythorn's friend...well, I thought it was just another sicko."

There was a deep sigh. "Rosie, I have to be honest. I don't think you're going to get anywhere with this, but I have to admit I'm curious. Tell me what you want and when we can meet."

Jared's voice took on a curiously wistful tone. "You know, I never forgot you."

Ten minutes later, when the call ended, Rosemary went into the kitchen, where her mother had somehow been managing to keep herself occupied and out of the way by washing one saucepan, two bowls, and two spoons. Now she was wiping down the countertops and cabinet fronts with the purple contents of a spray bottle.

Rosemary smiled affectionately at her parent. *Good old Mum, she knows not to hover.* Elizabeth tossed her sponge into the sink, poured two cups of coffee, and lifted her eyebrows. "So? I take it he didn't hang up on you."

"No, he did remember me and he was quite nice. I told him what I was trying to do and he said he'd be glad to help. I asked about the rest of the family and he said his father and Patricia separated shortly after the family moved away and he wasn't sure where Patricia and Krystalle were now but that his father would know." Rosemary cradled her cup in both hands. "I'm supposed to meet him at the Grove Park Inn for a drink around five."

"Well, that should be interesting." Her mother sat down beside her on the cushioned bench. "I don't really remember Jared. I guess I must have seen him a few times back then, but I don't have a picture in my mind of him. What did he look like?"

Rosemary shut her eyes, remembering. "He was really handsome. He had that white-blond hair, kind of short except for the really long rattail. I remember thinking that was the coolest thing in the world. Didn't I try at one point to get you to cut my hair that way? And those blue-gray eyes...sometimes they looked almost silver. I could probably recognize him by the eyes, even if he's gone bald and gotten fat."

She sipped her coffee, remembering. She and Maythorn had been up in a giant beech tree by the old family graveyard on that little knoll just above the Mullmore swimming pool. They had been munching on sandwiches and reading comic books when the sound of someone bouncing on the diving board caught their attention. It was Jared, in the skimpy black Speedo that Maythorn's little sister had dubbed a "wienie-boy suit," and even now Rosemary could remember the vague stirrings that the sight of his tanned, long-muscled, nearly nude body had aroused in her ten-year-old heart.

"I hope he *hasn't* gotten fat." The words escaped before she could stop them and she felt her face redden as her mother turned a questioning gaze on her. "I mean, it would be embarrassing if I couldn't recognize him because he had gained so much weight."

"No doubt." Elizabeth's wry smile said that she, too, remembered the crush young Rosie'd had on Jared. "We'll hope he still has the rattail too. But, sweetie, did you ask him about the foundation that owns Mullmore now?"

"Yes, I did. It's his dad—Jared said that his dad has put all his money into this foundation. Evidently he went through some kind of spiritual crisis after Maythorn disappeared and now he's gone all saintly. He runs a homeless shelter in Asheville called Redemption House."

PATRICIA MULLINS

October 1984

YOO- HOO! A *sudden rapping on the kitchen window accompanied the trilling call. Yoo-hoo! Anybody home?*

Rosemary, stretched out in a patch of sun on the blue-and-white vinyl floor, was playing with the new puppy Pa had brought home from the animal shelter last week. Dinah, a wobbly little black-and-tan hound, stiffened in alarm at the sight of an unfamiliar face pressed against the window, promptly left a puddle on the newly installed vinyl and scuttled under the woodstove, her toenails clicking.

The woman at the window smiled broadly as Rosemary met her gaze. She waggled her fingers in a friendly way, then held up a basket with a huge orange bow on it and called out, Is your mama at home?

Rosemary started for the door, pausing to call to her mother, who was up in the loft helping Pa paint the walls of their bedroom.

Mum, there's a lady—

I know; we saw the car from the window. I wish I didn't have quite so much paint on me. Her mother appeared at the top of the steep stairs, wiping her hands on an old T-shirt. Go on, sweetie, open the door.

Elizabeth started down the stairs and Rosemary reached for the doorknob. The lady with the basket was very fancy. She looked like the Barbie doll Grammer had given Laurel for her birthday. Mum had made a face when she saw it. This lady had on tottery high heels and tight pants, just like Barbie. And fluffy yellow hair and big blue eyes. There was blue stuff on her eyelids and her mouth was very red. And, just like Barbie, her bosom stuck out a lot.

I'll bet you're Rosie! Maythorn told us about you. I'm Maythorn and Krystalle's mama. Just ran by to bring you all a little housewarming gift. She thrust the basket with its orange bow and decoration of paper autumn leaves at Rosemary. Beneath the transparent yellow plastic that covered its contents, Rosemary could see an interesting array of little boxes and cans and jars.

How nice of you! Mum was downstairs now and smiling at the lady. I'm Elizabeth Goodweather, Rosie's mother. Please come in. I'm afraid we're a bit of a mess—we had to move in before the house was finished. It was getting too cold to stay in the barn any longer.

Well, hi, Elizabeth! A belated welcome to the neighborhood! I'm Patricia Mullins. Our girls have gotten to be such friends and I'm ashamed not to have come over sooner. It's just been hectic—all summer long Krystalle was doing pageants and I hardly had time to turn around. And this fall she's started piano and tap and charm lessons—it seems like I'm back and forth to Asheville every day. I was just bringing Krysty and Maythorn back from their hair appointments and I said, Well, I'll pick up a nice housewarming basket for our new neighbors and run it by.

I'm going out and talk to Maythorn. Rosemary tried to slip past the lady, but her mother said, Do you have time to stay for a cup of tea, Patricia? I can find some cookies and milk or juice for the girls.

Well, maybe just a quick visit. Rosie, tell Maythorn to hold Krysty's hand coming up the steps.

Rosie pulled on her shoes without bothering to lace them and hurried out to the car. It was big and shiny green. On the front it said "Range Rover" and there was a bumper sticker that said "Pageant Mom: Princess on Board." She could see a car seat with a little girl about Laurel's age in it. The little girl had fluffy hair just like her mother's. There was no sign of Maythorn.

Rosie stood on tiptoe and peered through the window. A muffled voice said, *Go away.* A small figure was slouched down in the seat, a red jacket pulled up to conceal her head.

Maythorn! It's me. You all are s'posed to come on in; Mum made brownies last night and we can have some.

No! Go away!

May-tho-orn's ma-ad! chanted the child in the car seat. *May-tho-orn's ma-ad!*

Rosemary opened the door to the back seat and tugged at her friend's jacket. *Come on!*

The jacket slipped down and Maythorn stared defiantly up at Rosemary. Her glossy black hair had been cut and styled into a tangle of curls, and smeared traces of lipstick and blue eyeshadow gave her brown skin a bruised and wounded look.

Now do you see why I didn't want to come in? She told the lady at the hair place to do this. *I wiped off the stupid makeup, and when I get home I'll wash all this gunk out of my hair. I just hope it's still long enough to braid.*

Maythorn! Help me down! I want to go inside and have bwownies! The child in the car seat was tugging frantically at the restraining straps. She too had been made up: pearly pink lipstick, a hint of blue eye shadow. Her blond curls were caught up with a shiny lavender bow that exactly matched the velvety little dress she wore. White tights covered her stubby legs and on her tiny feet were shining patent leather shoes with bows and low heels.

Rosemary stared curiously at Maythorn's sister and put her mouth to her friend's ear to whisper, Is she a midget? She looks grown up but she's so little.

No, stupid. She's only four years old. Maythorn undid the seat belt and held out her hands to help the child down.

You weren't very sociable, Sam, staying up there in the loft.

From her room, Rosemary could hear them. Mum and Pa were in the unfinished living room, sitting in the rocking chairs by the woodstove.

I had to finish the painting, Liz. Besides, I came to the top of the stairs and said hi before she left.

You did that. And let me tell you, Sam Goodweather, you made quite an impression. When I walked her out to her car she kept going on about how handsome and manly you were. And how she's always had a thing for redheaded men. I have a real feeling that's why we're invited over for dinner next Saturday.

Oh? So the mighty Mullins have decided to take notice of the lowly hippies next door, have they? What do you think, Liz—will we have anything to talk about with these people?

We can always talk about the kids—did you know that Rosie and Maythorn share a birthday? And Krystalle and Laurel are close in age.... But I doubt we're going to have much in common beyond that....

Mum made a disgusted sound and went on in a lower voice. Sam, did you see that child, how she was gotten up? She's just six months older than Laurie and she had makeup on! Evidently Patricia drags her to all these kiddie beauty pageants. It's kind of creepy; I suggested to Krystalle that she and Laurie go in the kitchen to play with the puppy, and the child just sat there with her ankles crossed and said she didn't want to get dirty. Four years old! She reminded me of my aunt Dodie. And as different from Maythorn as night and day.

Didn't Rosie say that Maythorn's real father is dead? Pa got up and shoved another log into the woodstove.

Oh, Patricia gave me the whole story. She ran off with Will Blackfox when she was quite young, "almost a child" was what she said. She said she was "just swept off mah feet," he was so handsome. He was a med student and she "just lost mah head like a silly girl."

Rosie smiled. Mum was making her voice all soft and breathless, just the way Maythorn's mom talked. Maythorn's mom had blinked fast while she talked. Her long, thick black eyelashes had looked like spiders hanging on to her blue eyelids.

So she married the handsome doctor? Pa's voice was grinning.

Well, no. I think she moved in with him and was planning a wedding. But when she found out that he wanted to live in Cherokee and run some sort of free clinic there, she backed right out of the relationship. And shortly after—and it must have been very shortly—she met Mr. Mullins. Who is known as Moon and who, according to local rumor, has more money than God. "Why, we just looked at each other and knew it was The Real Thing."

Pa was making a kind of groaning noise, but Mum kept on. "Why, it was a real whirlwind courtship. Moon just wouldn't take no for an answer, and we eloped two weeks later."

And where does Maythorn fit into all of this? Was she already—

Yep, already on the way. But Patricia said she had no idea. Right there in front of the kids, she described how surprised she was when the nurse brought her "this little brown baby."

Saturday came and the Goodweathers piled into their old Toyota Land Cruiser and started out for Mullmore. Pa had grumbled some but Mum had said that she really wanted to see this mansion that Dessie and Odus had talked so much about. Rosie did too; Maythorn had never said much about her home and Rosie was dying of curiosity. And Laurie was happy because she was wearing her new bright orange corduroy overalls and yellow turtleneck tee. She was strapped in her car seat and loudly singing: *Here we go to Mullamoe, to Mullamoe, to Mullamoe! Here we go to Mullamoe...POP goes the weasel!*

The big iron gates were open as they turned up the driveway. *It's like a real road,* said Rosemary, *not all bumpy like ours.*

Sam—Mum's eyes were wide as she looked at the pavement that stretched ahead of them—*what would it cost to make a road like this?*

Liz, it's one of those "If you have to ask, you can't afford it" things.

And look at the landscaping! Japanese maples and azaleas and rhododendrons—it's a miniature Biltmore Estate.

Rosemary remembered going to Biltmore. Mum had declared she needed a day off and had taken the two girls to wander the huge house and gardens. It had been okay but a little boring. Her favorite part had been sitting on the terrace to eat ice cream. She had pretended that it was her house and that all the tourists were people she had invited to visit. The whole time they were at the Biltmore House, Laurie kept asking again and again when they would see the king and queen.

The road curled through the trees. Then there was a sharp turn and they were in a big wide meadow that was surrounded by wooded slopes. Right there in the very middle of the meadow rose a big house. Rosemary felt a little pang of disappointment when she saw it was nowhere near as big as the Biltmore House. Still—

Oh, my god, it's a Tudor mansion. Look at that, Sam!

The big house was part redbrick and part cream-colored stuff with wide strips of wood making patterns on it. Rosemary stuck her head out of the window to see it more clearly—one, two, three, there were four stories! And five chimneys, and instead of one big roof there were lots of different ones. The windows were made of tiny little diamond-shaped panes that shimmered in the fall sunshine like a thousand winking eyes.

It's like a house in a fairy tale, Rosemary decided, eager to be out of the car and exploring.

MULLAMOE! crowed Laurel, as they pulled round the circle drive and came to a stop at the broad marble steps. Heeere's Mullamoe!

9.

ROAD TO REDEMPTION

Sunday, October 9

The note was propped against the coffeepot. *Mum,* it read...

Sorry to do this but my mind is so full of tags and rags of half memories right now that I think I'll be better off alone, where I can sort things out a bit. Driving always calms me, so I'm heading back to Chapel Hill now. It'll be a good chance to let all this information simmer. I've realized that I have to go slower—one thing at a time—so I'm not going to try to follow up on Jared's father this weekend.

I know you had invited Phillip out today and I'm really sorry not to be here. But I'll be back next weekend.

Mum, it's as if the past is a huge lake and I'm diving deep, trying to find something. But I have to keep coming up for air in the present. If I could just stay under long enough, maybe I could find what I'm after. I know this must sound crazy to you—but don't worry, I'm fine. Just a little overwhelmed with the task I've set myself, I think.

I'll give you a call when I get back to my house.

Love you. R

"Rosemary decided to go back to Chapel Hill today instead of tomorrow. She said she felt overwhelmed by all the old memories." Elizabeth gripped the telephone a little too tightly and went on. "I have to tell you, Phillip, I'm not happy about her and this...this wallowing in the past. I'm afraid she's going to be hurt—either by what she *does* find, or maybe by what she doesn't. But since I can't stop her, I'm going to help her. I want to talk to Maythorn's stepfather and find out how to get in touch with Patricia. The sooner Rosie's satisfied, the better. And anything I can do to speed the whole thing up—"

Phillip broke in, his voice calm. "Why don't you come by my place and I'll go with you to see this guy? It'll be something different to meet a born-again saint. And then let me take you to dinner here—there's a new Thai place I think you'd like."

"Well...Sure, that would be great." Elizabeth looked again at the note in her hand. She felt like crying. "Thank you. This is so unfair to you, Phillip, and you're being a really good sport. I don't know what's up with Rosie—she was looking forward to meeting you, but then something changed.

"Nothing to do with you," she added hastily, "more that Rosie's...preoccupied. When she went in to Asheville to have drinks at the Grove Park with Jared, she was just going to get some basic information about where the rest of the family is living. Then drinks stretched into dinner. And when she finally got back, she was really quiet; said something about how seeing Jared had made her realize how much she had forgotten.

"But Phillip, the other thing I called about—have you talked to Sheriff Blaine today? Has he found out anything about the little boy—about Calven?"

"No, I'm afraid he hasn't. He told me he sent someone out to look around Bib's trailer over on Hog Run

Branch, but there was no sign that anyone had been there recently. He did talk to Calven's grandmother, but she didn't know anything either—evidently Calven's mama isn't likely to live and the old lady's all to pieces."

"Phillip, I'm really worried about that little boy. It's like Maythorn all over; he's simply vanished. And *his* family's not wealthy—no chance of kidnapping here."

She had picked him up at his house in Weaverville and they were on their way into Asheville to find Moon Mullins at the mission he called Redemption House. Her anxiety about Calven jostled with concern for Rosemary and a nagging feeling that something had been left undone.

"I think this is different," Phillip replied. "I told you what his grandmother said. 'That young un's got kin all over the county *and* he's got sense enough to find him a place to stay.' She was worried about her daughter, not Calven. He's probably just fine. But Blaine's still on it."

She said nothing, her thoughts still with the little boy on the run. Phillip watched her for a moment, then said, "Let it go, Elizabeth; you've got enough to worry about. What was the deal with the note she left?"

Elizabeth sighed, knowing he referred to Rosemary. "It was a weird, rambling sort of note; it made me wish to god she'd just forget about the whole thing."

"But that's what she did before, isn't it? And it didn't work." Phillip reached over and rubbed his knuckles against her arm. "Elizabeth, this is the right thing for her to do. And it's right that you're helping." His hand rose to brush her cheek. "Why don't you tell me about the Mullins family and when you first got together with them? Give me some background."

"The first time we went to Mullmore…I'll certainly

never forget *that*. Phillip, I can't begin to describe how weird it was that first time we went to their house. There we were, so-called 'back-to-the-land hippies,' just moved from the barn, where we'd lived all summer, into our unfinished house—I mean, we hadn't even put in a septic tank yet, so we had an *outhouse*, for god's sake! And here, just over the ridge from our humble abode, we're being met at the door of this veritable *castle* by what seems to be a *butler*."

Phillip's lips curled in amusement. "Tell me about the family. I looked at the newspaper stories and talked to one of Blaine's deputies who was around back then, but I'd like to hear what *you* thought of the Mullins."

"Well, we'd seen a good bit of Maythorn during the summer but it wasn't till fall that we actually met the rest of them. What did I think?"

Elizabeth fell silent, trying to remember her first impressions of the Mullins—first impressions untainted by later experience. She smiled at a sudden memory. "Patricia came over to invite us to dinner—we didn't have a phone yet. When she left, Rosie said that she looked like a Barbie doll. And she did! I'm afraid that Sam and I referred to her as Mrs. Barbie for a while. My first thought was that she had married up—out of her class." A rueful laugh escaped her. "Lord, is that un-PC or what? I sound like a Victorian novel—or my mother. What I really mean is that Patricia wasn't as educated as her husband. I'm sorry to say I pegged her as a dumb blonde; though, in time, I came to see that she was really quite sharp."

She hoped that Phillip hadn't noticed the bitterness creeping into her voice. But his expression was neutral as he asked, "And what about her husband—Moon?"

"Moon was smart enough to make it through some Ivy League college—though the kind of money his family had may have helped some. He used proper grammar and seemed well read, but the main thing about Moon is that he was a drunk. Not a falling-down or yelling sort of drunk, he just worked on a bottomless glass of iced tea and vodka all day long, and by the afternoon he wasn't particularly coherent."

"Yeah, Blaine's guy mentioned that about him. 'Drunk as an owl' was what he said. But the deputy put it down to the shock that the whole family was going through at the disappearance of the little girl."

Phillip's face grew still as if he were trying to unravel some knotty conundrum. Elizabeth waited for further comment but none came. Finally she said, "Moon was drinking heavily when we first met them.... Patricia told me all about 'his little problem' that first time we went over there."

She glanced over at him. "Phillip, you aren't thinking that...?"

His head jerked. "Wha–? No, I'm not thinking about Mullins. I was wondering about 'drunk as an owl.' I always think of owls as pretty solemn, *sober* types. Sorry. Go on. Who else was there in the household?"

"Maythorn, of course, and her half-sister, Krystalle—a baby Barbie—very like her mom. Krystalle was four or five years younger—around Laurel's age. And Jared, the step-brother. He was from *Moon's* first marriage. I guess Jared was at least sixteen back in '84; I seem to remember he had his own car."

"What was he like?"

"Rosie seemed impressed with him last night; she said he was very helpful—"

"No, not now. *Then.* What was Jared like then?"

"I don't really remember him that well. He was very handsome...they all were. I started looking through some old photo albums last night after Rosie went to bed—I was pretty sure that the Mullins had sent us one of those Christmas cards that first year, with a family picture. And that I'd stuck it in an album."

She reached for the envelope propped on the dashboard in front of her. "Just seeing the pictures brought a lot back." *Maybe more than I wanted,* she added silently as she passed the envelope over to Phillip.

"There're *three* guys." Phillip was frowning at the photo card. "The one with his arm around Mrs. Barbie—appropriate name, by the way—I assume is Moon. But then there're two more—and they've all got that white-blond, blue-eyed Aryan look. Kind of creepy, actually. And Mrs. Barbie and Barbie junior are blondes too—Maythorn's definitely odd man out in that family. Wonder if she felt that way. But who's the third guy? It just says 'Season's Greetings from all the Mullins.'"

"That third one would be Mike—Moon's younger brother." Elizabeth's eyes were fixed on the highway. "He was there as a kind of mentor-slash-tutor for Jared. I think, if I'm remembering this right, Jared stayed with his mother when Moon left her for Patricia. Then, not too long before we moved here, Jared's mother sent him to live with Moon. I don't remember if I ever heard why exactly; I think Patricia mentioned his mother couldn't handle him." *Whereas Patricia let him do anything he wanted. Most of the time she treated him as though he were her age, flirted with him outrageously . . . and god knows what else.*

Elizabeth realized that her jaw was set in an unbecoming clench and that her teeth were beginning to grind. "But anyway, Moon's brother, Mike, had some experience working with quote 'troubled youth' and he was brought in to kind of pal around with Jared. As I told you, Moon was hopeless—he just wandered around with that drink in his hand and occasionally told the lawn crew that came in twice a week from Asheville what to do. And Patricia had about as much idea of how to deal with a teenage boy as . . . as a Barbie doll would."

The large brown-shingled house sat on the corner of a busy street, just across the expressway, where the stores and businesses of Asheville faded into a run-down residential area. The size and location of the building, together with the long utilitarian-looking clapboard addition at the rear, hinted at its probable past as a boardinghouse from an earlier time, when invalids flocked to Asheville for the health-giving mountain air. A sign by the front walkway read, REDEMPTION HOUSE. Patches of well-trodden grass and weeds on either side of the walkway were adorned by semicircles of white plastic lawn chairs, all occupied by bedraggled-looking men and women enjoying the mild weather and warm sun. They ranged in age from teens to completely indeterminate.

A heavy, pasty-faced woman in green sweatpants and an ample Hawaiian shirt stubbed out her cigarette on the arm of her chair, tossed the butt into the scrawny evergreens that did service as foundation planting, and hailed Phillip and Elizabeth as they approached the steps.

"You folks in the market for good help?" she rasped. "I work cheap. Cook, clean, take care of kids? Hell, I'm a goddam Mary Poppins."

"Thanks, but we're looking for Mr. Mullins. Is he here today?" Elizabeth attempted a nonchalant demeanor as she and Phillip made their way through the lounging residents, who watched their progress with varying degrees of interest.

"Moon? Shee-it, *Moon's* here every day." A gaunt black man seated next to Mary Poppins looked at the cheap watch on his wrist. "Meetin' ought to be windin' up right about now. Go on in; closed meeting but you can wait in the hall."

As they entered the wide hallway, its yellow-painted walls covered with motivational posters, rosters, and sign-up sheets for various activities, the door to the right swung open and a swarm of chattering people surrounded by a fog of cigarette smoke poured out into the hall.

Most kept moving toward the front door; a few started for the broad wooden stairs that swept majestically toward a landing graced by a full-length stained-glass panel depicting Jesus as a gentle shepherd; and a small group made for the door at the back of the hall, from which issued the industrial clatter and steamy odors of an institutional kitchen.

Elizabeth and Phillip stood transfixed as the swarm of humanity surged around them. When the hallway cleared, they saw a tall thin figure coming slowly out of the room. His arm was around a well-dressed man who seemed to be in the throes of some deep emotion.

"Thank you, Moon. I . . . I can't tell you what it means." The well-dressed man had his hand over his face. Phillip took Elizabeth's arm and swung her around to put their backs to the two men. They stood there, pretending to study the poster of a kitten dangling by its front paws from a branch. "Hang in There," the poster urged.

"It's an AA meeting," Phillip whispered. "Most of the participants take the anonymous part very seriously."

Behind them, good-byes were being exchanged. There was the sound of the front door opening and closing. Then a quiet voice inquired, "How can I help you?"

She would have recognized him anyway, she decided. The silver-blond hair was mostly silver now and the pale blue-gray eyes were clear instead of reddened. Moon's face, once puffy and soft, was now thin and ascetic. But the gentleness of his manner was the same, as was his careful selection of each word. Yes, she would have recognized him anywhere.

"Mr. Mullins—Moon—I don't know if you remember me...Elizabeth Goodweather? We lived in the holler next to you...out on Ridley Branch—"

The tall thin man took a step toward her and held out both hands. "Elizabeth! I'm...I'm amazed! How long has it been? You've hardly changed, but..." He eyed Hawkins curiously. "Sam?..."

Moon Mullins, it turned out, did not know of Sam Goodweather's untimely death six years earlier.

"I stay so busy with the work of the foundation...and I rarely read the newspaper or hear the news. I got out of that habit during my lost years."

A rueful smile played across his still-handsome face. "Almost ten years gone from my life forever. After Maythorn...went away, everything fell apart. I know now that I was a drunk back then—had been a drunk for years. But it took the...the tragedy to bring things to a head. I fell so deep into the bottle that I lost my wife and daughter; my son went back to his mother. My drinking drove them away and I became the lowest of the low."

A slow smile played across his features as he went on. The familiar words, polished to smoothness by frequent repetition, slipped easily from his lips. "And the Lord saw me in my wretchedness and took pity on my misery. He led me to an AA meeting and step by step I came back to the world, to the pleasures of a cool glass of water, the low voice of a friend, the glory of the morning sun. I had been a stranger to these simple gifts for too long, wandering in low dives and dark streets."

A quiet radiance shone from his face. "I've been sober for nine years, eight months, and four days. When I turned my life over to a higher power, I also turned over my assets. Now that I have nothing, I find that I have everything. The foundation and the people we help are my life."

Moon led them to his small, starkly furnished office, where he offered them coffee in plastic foam cups. He listened gravely as Elizabeth explained her mission, saying when she'd finished that he was willing to help in spite of being dubious of any positive outcome. "And little Rosie's a professor of English now? It hardly seems possible. So many years gone, so much lost to me now."

He sat, head bowed, looking at his folded hands. Elizabeth followed his gaze and noticed that the wrist of his left hand was heavily scarred.

"Mr. Mullins, there've been some problems with trespassers on your property out in Marshall County—" Phillip began.

"Not *my* property, Mullmore belongs to the foundation," Moon corrected him. "I own nothing now— the land and buildings on Ridley Branch belong to Redemption Way—and very soon we hope to begin work to turn Mullmore into a retreat for recovering alcoholics. It's my hope that Mullmore's tragic past will become a future of hope for many."

He glanced at his cheap wristwatch. "I have an interview scheduled in a few moments. Was there—"

"I was hoping that you could tell me how to get in touch with Patricia. I thought I heard she'd moved away."

"She did, for a time." Moon's face was tragic. "It was my fault; the booze had such a hold on me that she didn't want me around Krystalle. I don't blame her anymore. When we divorced she managed to forbid me any contact with my daughter—I haven't seen Krysty since then. But they moved back to Asheville five or six years ago. You've heard her, I'm sure. She went back to her maiden name—Patricia is now Trish Trantham...she dispenses advice daily and nationwide. You know—'Tell Trish.'"

10.

MEMORIES AND MESSAGES

Sunday, October 9

" 'Tell Trish'—*that's* Patricia?"

Even Elizabeth, who rarely listened to the radio or read newspapers, had heard of Trish Trantham. Highly in demand as a motivational speaker, Trish Trantham also wrote a weekly column, and her syndicated radio show was a part of the national consciousness—or conscience, some claimed. Blazoned in dashing emerald-green script across the façade of one of the largest spaces in a shopping center in West Asheville, the increasingly familiar logo "Trish Trantham Lifeworks" marked the headquarters of a swiftly expanding empire.

"That's Patricia." Moon stood, looking toward the door. "After the loss, we both made radical changes in our lives. Please let Rosemary know that I'll be happy to talk with her if it will help. I'm sorry there isn't more time just now, but I have an appointment." The door opened and a dark-skinned young girl wearing a short tight skirt, platform heels, and a black bustier stood looking blankly at them. Her face was heavily made up and her garish yellow-dyed hair was braided into neat cornrows.

"Hey, Moon, I'm here like you said. You want me to…" She jerked her head toward the door.

"That's all right, Soledad, these friends are leaving now." Moon put out his hand. "Elizabeth, it's been good to see you. Mr. Hawkins, a pleasure to meet you."

As the door closed behind them, Elizabeth caught a glimpse of the girl walking into Moon's outstretched arms.

The lawn chairs were all still occupied, and as Elizabeth and Phillip made their way back to the jeep, two men left their seats on the lawn and trailed after them. The self-proclaimed Mary Poppins called out, "You been talking to a goddam *saint;* you remember that!"

The larger of the two men, a hulking heavyweight, came up beside Phillip and jabbed a sausagelike finger into his arm. "You hear what she said? All of us at Redemption House feel that way. Moon looks after us and we look after him. Don't want no one comin' around giving him any trouble, know what I'm sayin'?" Again the finger prodded, deeper and harder.

Phillip looked up placidly at the dark figure looming above him. "Hey, man, we got no problem here. This lady is an old friend of Moon's. Relax."

"Well, I *was* a little disappointed," Elizabeth told Phillip as they drove off. "I thought maybe you'd do some fancy police detective move and flip that big guy over your shoulder when he poked at you."

"Sweet Jesus, woman, did you notice that hulk had about five inches and a hundred pounds on me? Who do you think I am—Jackie Chan?" Phillip shot an incredulous glance at her, then grinned. *He looks like a man completely at home with himself,* she thought. *I like that.*

"Nope," he continued cheerfully. "I'm just not that touchy. I learned a long time ago that touchy people don't live as long as us mellow types." He looked back at the throng on the lawn and the bulky figure that still stood on the sidewalk. "Mullins has quite an admiration society there. I believe I'll ask around—find out what kind of rep this Redemption House has. And who the hell is Trish Trantham?"

"Phillip, you really don't know? And I thought *I* was out of touch with things. Trish Trantham is like...she's like an advice columnist on steroids. She has a syndicated column and a call-in radio show and—"

He was staring at her in amused amazement. "You listen to stuff like that? Somehow I wouldn't have figured you for—"

"Just now and then—when I'm in the car and I've forgotten to bring along a book on tape." Elizabeth found herself scrambling to explain. "I'd heard of her—there was a lot of controversy because of some very un–politically-correct stands she's taken. So one day I turned on the radio, looking for classical music, and it was set to AM instead of FM, and there she was. I had no idea she was my ex-neighbor. She takes these very absolute positions, and the thing I find intriguing is that sometimes I completely agree with her and other times I have to turn off the radio, she makes me so mad with her Bible-based authority and her moralizing attitude. It's a kind of fatal fascination—like trying to understand how someone who seems so sensible in some ways can come across as a total right-wing reactionary in others.

"But now that I know who she is..." Elizabeth's jaw tightened and she was silent for a few moments. Phillip waited expectantly, but she didn't speak, busy with an angry inward rant. *That bitch! Ms. Family Values. There she sits calling women sluts and she—*

"Now that you know who she is..." he prompted.

At last the words came, in a furious eruption. "The woman is a total hypocrite!"

Phillip looked at her in surprise. "How's that?"

She regretted the outburst immediately. And, unwilling to explain the reason for it, she resorted to a vague, "Oh, I guess it's just the holier-than-thou attitude that comes across. And the narrow-minded certainty thing. You know, 'God said it; I believe it; that settles it.' And the fact that when I knew her she wasn't...particularly..." Her words trailed off lamely.

"People do change," Phillip observed, adding, to her annoyance, "Case in point—Moon. From a drunk to a saint." He plucked the envelope with the Mullins family Christmas card off the dashboard, slid out the photo card, and examined it closely. "He's healthier-looking now too." He frowned at the picture. "What about the brother? Is he still around?"

Elizabeth's attention was focused on the road. "I doubt it; I think he moved to California. He used to talk about wanting to go to...Big Sur, I think it was." She concentrated on keeping her face expressionless.

"I guess Rosemary can find out when she talks to Moon later on." With a last glance at the family picture, Phillip returned the card to the envelope. "Funny to think...I mean, there they are, all happy together, good-looking bunch of folks. And a couple of years later...it all falls apart. Looking at this picture, you'd say they had everything."

He tossed the envelope back on to the dash. "So, what can you tell me about Mike?"

I could have told him that Mike Mullins was one of the most handsome men I've ever seen, that he was well read, witty, caring. I could have said that there was a time that my blood sang whenever Mike Mullins looked at me.

But, in fact, she had told him none of this. She had muttered a few inanities about Mike's acting as a role model for Jared, as Moon was a rather detached father. Phillip had not seemed to notice her reluctance to talk about Mike.

And then I did to Phillip exactly what Rosemary did to me this morning. Just left.

Realizing that she could not—*could not!*—discuss Mike Mullins and Patricia—*Trish Trantham, for god's sake!*—any further with Phillip, Elizabeth had rapidly concocted an excuse: No, she couldn't stay in town for dinner as they'd planned earlier; she really needed to . . . to get back home and close up the chickens. She'd forgotten, there had been a marauding bobcat and she needed to close the chicken house door before dark.

He gave me such a strange look. As if . . . as if he was disappointed in me.

A wave of nausea swept through her body and her eyes blurred. *This can't wait. I owe him honesty. If we . . .*

Briefly she considered turning back, but then remembering the newly acquired cell phone in her shoulder bag, she pulled to the side of the road and stopped. She was nearly home, only a few miles from the bridge that crossed the French Broad at Gudger's Stand, but it was suddenly an urgent necessity that she speak to Phillip and unsay the lie.

She stared at the still unfamiliar buttons on the tiny instrument, trying to remember. Recent events had convinced her of the usefulness of a cell phone, and earlier in the week she had made a special trip to Weaverville to buy one. The saleswoman in the cell phone store had made it look laughably easy as she programmed in Elizabeth's most-often-called numbers. Rapidly demonstrating the various features and modes of use, the woman's lacquered fingernails had clicked busily on the little keypad as Elizabeth looked on, nodding as if she understood. Now, however, Elizabeth found that she had only the vaguest recollection of how the thing worked.

Okay, this is the power button. Turn it on. A twiddle of sound, and the little screen lit up. MENU and CONTACTS seemed to be her choice. Dubiously she prodded the tiny button under MENU with her thumbnail. No, that took her to MESSAGES. Over to EXIT. This time she chose CONTACTS. A blue bar highlighted SEARCH.

Right, that's what I want to do. Now we're getting somewhere. She hit the same button and she was back to the choice of MENU or CONTACTS. *Shit!*

Angrily, she hit a button at random and found that the screen showed a list of numbers. *Okay. And this center square button scrolls the list up or down.* Yes, here was Phillip's home phone. And maybe this little button... To her great amazement and relief, the screen informed her that it was calling the familiar number.

She put the apparatus to her unaccustomed ear, thrilled to hear Phillip's phone ringing. There was a click and the voice mail told her to leave a message.

"Phillip...it's Elizabeth....I need to apologize....I... oh, hell...I need to talk to you. I'll try your cell."

Now to end the call. An experimental prod at a likely button informed her that she was now on a loudspeaker. Baffled, she chose the simple expedient of mashing the power button to turn the phone off.

The second call went better as she quickly found the combination that led her to the number for Phillip's cell phone. She waited eagerly, listening for the familiar gravelly voice, anxious to explain herself, but, once again, was forced to leave a message on the voice mail.

Cursing her own stupidity, she pulled the car back on to the road and continued on her way.

And then she remembered a question Phillip had asked, a question that she had been unable to answer. "What did your local neighbors think about the girl's disappearance? What did Miss Birdie think? You've told me how sharp she is—how nothing happens without her knowing about it. I'll bet she had an opinion about what happened."

Elizabeth glanced at the car clock—4:53. *I can run in for a quick visit and ask what she remembers about that Halloween. Then when I talk to Phillip later, at least I can answer that question.*

Miss Birdie's little log cabin was halfway between the bridge at Gudger's Stand and the entrance to Full Circle Farm. It sat on a low knoll surrounded by what, till recently, had been tobacco fields. The end of government price supports for tobacco, as well as the death of her son two years previous, had meant that now, at eighty-three, Miss Birdie was content merely to tend a large garden. A small herd of a neighbor's cows grazed happily in the former tobacco fields now.

The plank bridge over Ridley Branch rattled as alarmingly as it always did, but Elizabeth drove across undaunted, noting that the creek was still in full spate after the heavy rains of the week before.

The little woman was in her kitchen, seated at the formica-topped table, a bowl of cornbread and buttermilk in front of her "Git you a chair, Lizzie Beth." Her

bright blue eyes twinkled. "And git you some of this cornbread and buttermilk."

"Just a little, Miss Birdie." Elizabeth poured herself a
small glass of the thick, creamy liquid. Tiny flecks of yellow clung to the sides of the gallon jar. She cut a narrow
wedge from the partial cake of cornbread and dipped it
into the buttermilk. The gritty, slightly salty bread was
perfectly complemented by the smooth, tart buttermilk.
Elizabeth smiled.

"It's delicious, Miss Birdie. Almost makes me wish I
still kept a cow."

"Now, hit *is* good, and that's the truth. When Louvanda
brung it by this mornin', I told her I was going to make my
supper of it. Git you some more, honey."

After a few moments of quiet communion as they enjoyed the simple meal, Elizabeth broached the subject of
Maythorn Mullins. Miss Birdie laid down her spoon and
fixed Elizabeth with a steady gaze.

"And you say your Rosemary's a-wantin' to find out the
truth of it?" Birdie's wrinkled face held some unreadable
expression—was it sorrow or anger? "Well, I believe hit's
about time *someone* does, don't you? That was a terrible
thing—terrible fer them folks what lost their little girl and
might near as bad for them folks what got fingers pointed
at 'em, saying they might of knowed something about it."

The old woman's voice quavered. "Lizzie Beth, honey,
don't you remember? Back then, they was folks thought
my boy Cletus might have done away with that little girl.
I believe they's still some that think it."

How could I have forgotten? I guess I was as bad as Rosemary—
just wanting to blank out that whole year. But now that Miss
Birdie reminded me—now I remember.

Maythorn's disappearance had ignited the latent distrust that existed between some portions of the newcomer and local communities—what had been a gently smoldering perception of deep differences had burst into flame, threatening to divide the two groups forever.

In the weeks and months following the girl's disappearance, families and groups had taken sides. Native-born residents tended to believe that some outsider had come in and kidnapped the child, hopeful of squeezing a big ransom from the wealthy family. "Just seems to me like that's what it had to be," Miss Birdie had said. "And then somethin' bad happened—like with that pore little Lindbergh baby."

Among the newcomers, however, a different mind-set emerged. A local man who had previously been warned against trespassing on the Mullins' property had been taken into custody, questioned, and exonerated. Then, Patricia Mullins, desperate and distraught, had told anyone who would listen that "It had to be that half-wit who roams the woods all the time." Evidently, Maythorn had mentioned encountering Cletus and, with visions cobbled together from *Deliverance* and some B horror movie, Patricia had accused Miss Birdie's simpleminded son of murder.

Nothing had come of it—beyond a great deal of bad feeling. There had been no evidence whatsoever to link Cletus to Maythorn's disappearance, but still there were those in the newcomer community who muttered to one another in undertones at the sight of Cletus roaming the woods with his shotgun. Indeed, several families who moved away gave the unsolved case as their reason for doing so. "That, and a sheriff who would let a half-wit wander around with a shotgun in the first place."

Sam and Elizabeth had ignored these whispers,

believing in Cletus's innocence. And, after a few years, the entire event had been forgotten. Cletus continued to range the woods. And no more young girls vanished.

Remembering that unpleasant episode had done nothing to lift Elizabeth's spirits. She trudged wearily up her steps. *First, I'll try to call Phillip.* She ignored the three dogs, eager for their dinner and whining anxiously as she entered the house. Instead, she made straight for the telephone in the little office.

She felt a surge of delighted expectation as she saw the blinking light on the answering machine. Eagerly she touched the PLAY button to retrieve the message.

"This here is Bib Maitland, that pore ignorant redneck what you called the law on when I weren't doin' nothing but huntin' on land what had belonged to my woman's family, time out of mind. I just wanted you to know I done a little askin' round about you and yore family."

There was an ugly chuckle. The menacing voice continued. *"Well, what do you know? Come to find out your man done got hisself killed in a airplane wreck. Now, ain't that too bad. There you are, 'thout no man to look after you. S'posin' I was to pay you a little visit one of these nights—"*

Without waiting to hear the rest, Elizabeth's finger stabbed the ERASE button. Then she went to her bedroom and took Sam's gun from its hiding place.

11.

WAITING GAME

Sunday, October 9

Phillip yawned, checked his watch again, and shifted restlessly behind the steering wheel. The flight must have been delayed. That, or there was trouble. He scanned the short-term parking lot but there was no sign of the man he had been so urgently summoned to meet.

Seems like he would have called—Dammit, did I leave my cell off? Phillip yanked the phone from his belt, powered it on, and tapped the keys impatiently. The screen lit up and at once he saw that there were two messages from Elizabeth. *Well, Ms. Goodweather... got those biddies safely off to bed?* He stared at the screen, fighting the annoyance he felt at the memory of Elizabeth's inexplicable retreat. *This game is beginning to get damn tedious... and goddam frustrating.*

The sudden vibration of the instrument in his hand startled him and he barked a peremptory "Hawkins" as he keyed the CALL button.

"I'm here." The voice from the past was low, but eerily familiar. "Are you in the vehicle and location he told me?"

"Yeah, I'm—"

"Thirty seconds."

The call ended and Phillip peered into the halogen-lighted gloom to see a tall figure in dark trousers and a black windbreaker striding briskly toward his car. There was a quick triple tap at the window, an ID was pressed briefly against the glass, and Phillip unlocked the door.

The man was in his late fifties or early sixties, his weather-beaten face marked with broken veins and the deep wrinkles of an outdoorsman. Thinning hair was pulled back in a short graying ponytail and he wore steel-rimmed glasses. As he slid into the seat beside Phillip, his face split into a wide grin.

"So Del told you he got in touch with me? I guess you guys had figured I was out of things for good."

"Gabby!" Phillip clapped his old shipmate on the shoulder. "Good to see you, buddy." He studied the man beside him, looking for traces of the brash young gunner's mate he had last seen being loaded onto a medevac chopper. *God, do I look that old? Of course, he was hit pretty bad and in and out of rehab centers for years. A user, too, Del said. But he's clean now supposedly. And running a security business of some kind.*

"Yeah, I was surprised when Del told me you were flying in and I had to drag my ass out here in the dead of night to talk to you. What's up?"

"Things are starting to move and Del thought I should be here too." Gabby grinned wickedly. "I've picked up some special skills since the old days and Del knows he can trust me to get the job done. First off, though, I need to bring you up to speed."

Gabby glanced at his watch. "I'll be renting a car and staying in Asheville. And this..." He pulled a very small cell phone from his pocket, "...this will be how we communicate from now on. There's a real possibility that both your cell and your landline are no longer secure."

"Whoa!" Hawkins held up a hand. "What happened? I talked to Del just a few days back and everything was routine."

"Maybe so. But you must not have been watching the news. Landrum's set to make his move. They're shuffling the Cabinet around and he's a shoo-in for Defense. With his Medal of Honor and that little show he can put on with his missing arm and legs, there won't be many hard questions. And he has political ambitions that reach way past a cabinet position. This war we're in isn't likely to go away very soon, and come the next election, Landrum's going to sound more and more like the man for the top job. He has all the money he needs and solid backing from the right wing. With all this at stake, Del figures that Landrum's people will be desperate to find and destroy the deposition and photos that Red threatened him with. So we have to find those photos first…no matter what the consequences."

As he drove back to Weaverville along near-deserted roads, Phillip Hawkins was mired deep in memories. Memories he struggled never to revisit in the waking hours—and had prayed to be free of in his dreams.

Early 1970 and the whole SEALORDS operation was winding down. There were just a few days to go before it was all handed over to the Vietnamese and emotions ran high. *We'd been in-country so long and most of us had known from the beginning that it was hopeless. But the situation was eating at Landrum. He'd always been moody, driven—but that last day... We should have done something after the thing with the girl on the bicycle.*

Images assailed him. Patrol: The PCF—Patrol Craft, Fast, in the military's inverted language, more commonly known as Swift Boat—chugging down the canal; the crew of six almost stupefied with the hypnotic thrum of the dual diesels and the blazing sun of the Mekong Delta. Sam had been playing with his new camera, a recent acquisition in the marathon poker game that went on back at base. He had been snapping shots, first of water buffalo near the river's edge and then of his crewmates.

The Lieutenant had the tub, *Catch a few rays,* he had said, as he pulled off his shirt and leaned back beside the dual .50 caliber machine guns there high atop the little vessel's pilothouse.

A bird-boned girl in black pajamas pedaling madly down a dirt path beside the canal, a baby in a sling on her back—*Her little brother or sister? She had to be too young to have a child of her own*—the baby's dark head bobbing rhythmically with the motion.

And the sudden bark of the .50 caliber machine gun from the tub, the girl's arms outflung as she and her burden parted company: she, cartwheeling in slow motion into the shallow water at the canal's edge, while the swaddled infant fell to the path and the ancient bicycle wobbled crazily on for a few feet before teetering and crashing.

The PCF had continued on, the men who were topside looking up at the gun tub in paralyzed silence, watching as the dual guns swung round, coming to bear on the target that was rapidly falling behind them. Hawkins had been aware of the groan that had come from... Was it Sam? Or had he made that sound himself? And then, before anything could be said, before anyone could move, the stuttering thud of multiple rounds hit the swaddled bundle, which jumped and skittered off the path into the murky, blood-dyed water where the girl lay, facedown and still.

"Sometimes they have grenades." Lieutenant Landrum had been matter-of-fact. "That's two less gooks in the world. And before we're out of here, I plan to take out some more."

It was war, Phillip and Sam had reminded each other later. Girls that young and younger had lobbed grenades, aimed rifles....

Hawkins winced. The girl and the baby had been bad enough—but on that same night, as their Swift Boat made its way back to base...

It didn't bear thinking of. *We should have disarmed him. He'd lost it, big-time. Me and Sam and Del... Would the others have gone along with us? I don't know....*

This time it was a tattered group of farmers, mostly old men and women with children at their sides. They were pulling a dilapidated handcart of some sort—*That was his excuse; he said it might have been weapons*—and Landrum had ordered the rating at the helm to slow the boat to an idle. There had been no Vietnamese liaison available when they set out on patrol so it was left to Sam, whose command of Vietnamese was generally adequate, to call to the group to stop and turn the cart over so that its contents could be viewed.

The boat rocked gently in the muddy water as Sam tried to make himself heard over the low rumble of the idling diesels and the sudden alarmed chatter of the villagers. The big, lanky redhead had repeated himself over and over, forcing the unfamiliar words across the little strip of water that lay between them and the frightened group of people.

They called back in high, incomprehensible syllables and the handcart remained upright, its contents hidden. Slowly the little crowd began to move away from the canal edge, toward a distant village.

A familiar metallic cranking caught Phillip's ear as Sam continued to call out to the Vietnamese to stop. He had turned to see the Lieutenant at the mortar on the fantail, his face calm, as he calculated his shot. The sudden *puumph* of a round had been followed by the explosion of the handcart. At least half of the civilians were down. A second and a third round in swift succession accounted for the rest.

"Hit it!" Landrum had called out to the helmsman. "Let's get back to base." He had remained by the mortar, head turning from side to side, scanning both banks of the canal. Phillip remembered feeling that if he had looked into the Lieutenant's eyes at that moment it would have been like staring into a void.

Sam had started toward Landrum, sputtering and incoherent with rage, but Landrum's only reaction had been to raise his .45 automatic and level it on his raging subordinate.

"Back off, Red," Phillip had whispered, hastily pulling his buddy away. "He's over the edge...look at his eyes. Nothing we can do about those folks. Keep quiet and I'll back you in reporting this later—hell, we all will."

At their side Delfino Reyes, the quartermaster, who had just emerged from belowdeck, gave a mutter of assent. "Court-martial time, man," he told Sam.

But before they reached the floating base in the bay, Nemesis, or something like it, had reached out with a savagely avenging hand. Their boat had come under heavy fire. Two of the six-man crew had been hit. Landrum, while trying to drag the wounded men to safety, was ripped apart by the hail of bullets.

He was still alive when they limped into Sea Float, the base at the mouth of the Delta. But the medics who took him off the Swift Boat shook their heads knowingly.

"He's lost an arm; both his legs are toast; and he's gut-shot too. You might as well say good-bye now. Your buddy's bought the farm."

And that was the last we saw of Lt. J. G. Laurence Landrum. We figured he'd be dead in a few hours, and besides, we were licking our own wounds. The hell of it was, he'd saved Gabby and Vermin at the risk of his own life—how do you explain someone like that?

Hawkins, Sam, and Delfino had talked it over. *What's the point,* Del had argued. *What's the point of reporting this shit when the one guy responsible for it is as good as dead? We gotta go back to the World, not him. And who's gonna believe he did it all alone?*

But it makes me sick. Phillip could still hear the raw agony in Sam's protest. *I thought we were here to help these people. That little girl, that baby . . . she was trying to get away from us, for Christ's sake. I even got some photos . . . if I didn't screw up and they show what I think they show, there'd be an air-tight case. . . .*

I hear they're calling returning vets "baby killers," Del insisted. *Girls spittin' on 'em and shit like that. Not me, man. I say we forget about it. They can give him all the posthumous medals they want to. I'm not saying a word.*

A conspiracy of silence was born. The three—Phillip, Sam, and Delfino—were the only ones left to tell the tale.

Of the two men Landrum had saved, the boatswain's mate, Vernon "Vermin" Monroe, had died the next day and John Hayes, the gunner's mate known as "Gabby," had been flown stateside, where he would undergo numerous surgeries and several years of rehab. It was said he remembered nothing of his last day in Nam.

Landrum too had been airlifted out, leaving both legs and most of one arm behind. He had not been expected to survive, and the three who remained simply agreed to forget . . . if they could.

The horrible grace of the dead girl, cartwheeling in a lazy arc, long black braid streaming behind her—that was the image that Phillip had found impossible to erase. Sam couldn't either. On the few times the two had met since Nam, they had talked of their shared experiences, at first tentatively, neither wanting to summon up bad memories if the other had somehow managed to outrun them. But then, as they admitted to each other the truth—the reality of the nightmares, the flashbacks—meeting every few years to talk about the past had become a therapy. A burden that could not be acknowledged to any who did not carry it was somehow lightened by their occasional meetings.

And then, that last time, six, seven years ago. Sam . . .

They had met in DC: Sam, Phillip, and Delfino. Del, to everyone's surprise, not least his own, had stayed in the navy and had soon been selected for officer's training. He had excelled; promotion had followed promotion and he was now attached to the Pentagon in some highly classified capacity. When Del's wife had planned a trip to

Florida with their five children to visit her mother and nearby Disney World, Del had seized the opportunity to invite Sam and Phillip for the weekend—to visit once more the great half-sunken Wall that memorialized the dead of the Vietnam War, and "to catch up on things."

They were settled in his spacious kitchen, well provided with cold beer and Thai takeout, when Del had said quietly, "There's something we need to talk about. Do you guys know that Landrum is still alive? He's got more money than God, he's got the Medal of Honor, and he's got the President's ear. Word is, if the administration wins the next election, Landrum will be calling in his markers."

Del took a long pull at his beer, then clapped the empty bottle down. "I don't know about you guys, but I think it's time for us to go public with what happened— *before* Landrum became a hero. It'll mean the end of my career, but I can't see that sick bastard getting away with it any longer."

He had fixed Sam with a steady gaze. "Red, I hope you still have those pictures."

IN THE WINTER WOODS

February 1985

ROSIE I'M GOING *for a walk. I need for you to stay here with Laurel.*

Mum was putting on her heavy blue jacket. Rosemary's Christmas gift, the knitted hat, the kind the kids at school called a "boggin" was pulled down over her ears, and her boots were already laced up. Dinah frisked clumsily at her feet, alerted by the magic words—going for a walk.

Rosemary laid down her battered copy of The Dark Is Rising. *Can we go too? Where are you going? I'll go get my—*

No, sweetie, Laurie's taking a nap. Plus, she has the sniffles—she shouldn't be out in the snow. And you played outside with Maythorn all morning. Now it's my turn.

Where's Pa? He could watch Laurie.

Her mother's face took on the look that had become too familiar recently. I'm being patient but don't push me, the face said.

Your pa is down in his shop working on the kitchen cabinets, Rosie. And all you have to do is stay here and read, just like you've been doing. I'm going to take Dinah and walk along the path into the woods. I won't be gone more than an hour. And when I get back we'll make popcorn and hot choco-late. If there's a problem—a real problem—you can go out to the porch and ring the big bell.

You didn't argue with Mum when her face and voice were so stern. Rosie nodded a brief okay and returned to her book, quickly losing herself in the wonderful adventures of the boy who, all unaware, was born to a special task. She was deep in the story when the scrape of boots at the front door made her look up.

Hey, Rosebud, her pa called. The shoulders of his jacket were dusted with melting flakes, and little white waffles of snow sprouted on the doormat when he stamped his feet.

Pa, I want to go outside. Mum went for a walk and said I had to watch Laurie, and Laurie's still asleep—

Sure, run along. I'm done in the shop for the day. Pa sat down on the chair near the door and started pulling off his boots. I'll take over here. You wrap up warm.

It would be fun, Rosie decided, to track her mother, just like a real Indian would. Maythorn had bragged so often about all the Indian lore she had learned from her uncle and grand-mother that Rosemary felt the disadvantage of her own up-bringing weigh heavy. She'd show Maythorn that she had skills and powers too.

Snow was falling lightly. As she crossed the icy little branch that flowed beside their road, she could see the indentations her mother's boots had made, slowly filling up. Nodding wisely to herself, Rosemary pursued the footprints along the road at the top of the pasture. Dinah's pawprints circled and looped and ran off and came back, while Mum's headed straight for the woods.

Maythorn sat quietly in the old deer stand. It was little more than a rough platform wedged into the branches of an ancient maple, but it had makeshift sides and the remains of a roof. Spikes had been hammered into the smooth bark to make a ladder, and once inside, she knew she could not be seen from the ground. She had discovered this hiding place, near the path where the wild things walked, and had found that if she sat very still and waited, something would come along. Only yesterday two does, followed by a male yearling, had tiptoed so close beneath her, she could hear the huff of their breathing.

Though she had dressed warmly, she knew she would not be able to remain still for much longer. Her feet already felt like they were asleep; perhaps—A crunching sound alerted her and she leaned forward to peer through the crack between the boards. Dinah, Rosie's dog, was circling the base of the maple, snuffling loudly. Her quivering nose covered every inch of the whitened ground, and then she began to sniff at the trunk. Suddenly she reared up, put her front paws against the tree trunk, and released a mournful howl.

Maythorn sighed and stretched. Might as well go home and get warm; no wild thing would approach now that Dinah had made all that noise. She started to lower herself through the hole by the trunk, then stopped. Someone was coming—and they were crying.

On the path below her, she saw Rosie's mom. She had pulled off the bright knit hat from her head and was using it to wipe her eyes. She stood there sobbing for a few minutes, her head bent, then she straightened. Dinah, she said, in a wobbly voice, is there a possum or something up that tree?

Maythorn stayed just as still as she could, not even breathing. This was interesting. Rosie's mom crying? Rosie always talked about how happy the Goodweather family was—everyone loving everyone. And that's how they all acted, at least whenever she'd been around. This was very interesting. She began to wish that she had brought her notebook.

More crunching, more footsteps, but from the other way

this time. Dinah stopped scratching at the maple's trunk and darted toward the approaching figure.

Well, you caught me trespassing, neighbor. Mike smiled that white toothpaste smile at Rosie's mom, who hastily wiped her nose with the back of her hand and smiled back.

Hey, Mike, this is a pretty place to walk, isn't it? How'd you happen to be over this way? Rosie's mom's eyes were all red and her voice was wobbly, but Mike didn't seem to notice. He came up closer, still smiling that toothpaste smile.

Like the bear that went over the mountain, I guess—to see what I could see. I was following the trail the girls use and just kept going.

Maythorn wondered if it was worth freezing her butt off to hear any more of this. But then Mike said, Do you mind if I walk with you? and Rosie's mom said, That would be nice, and they started down the path that led deeper into the woods. Briefly, Maythorn thought about shadowing them for practice, but decided it would be impossible, even for an Indian, to stay hidden from Dinah's busy nose.

She waited to make sure they were out of sight, and was starting down again when she heard Rosie coming. It had to be Rosie, because she was humming that dumb song she always liked to sing about a frog going courting.

. . . sword and pistol by his side, uh-huh, uh-huh, warbled Rosie in an off-key undertone, as she came slowly along the path. Her head was bowed and Maythorn saw at once that she was carefully following her mother's footprints in the snow.

Hummph, let's she what she thinks when she gets a little farther. Maythorn watched, grinning as her friend neared the spot where Elizabeth and Mike had stood talking.

There was someone else on the trail! Mum had stood and talked to them—a man, Rosemary decided, putting her foot inside one of the big footprints. Maybe that creepy Cletus—he's always out in the woods. And they went this way.

She trotted down the path, smiling to think how surprised her mother would be when she appeared. A little way on and the path veered sharply as it wrapped around the mountainside. Just beyond that turn was one of the benches Pa had made for Mum so she could sit and look at the view. Maybe she would be there. Humming, Rosemary hurried on.

The brightly striped boggin was the first thing she saw. But the other person—it wasn't Cletus. She recognized the fancy coat, all tan leather and creamy sheepskin. The arms were wrapped around her mother, almost hiding her blue jacket. It was Maythorn's Uncle Mike. Kissing Mum. And Mum was kissing back.

All at once Rosemary felt bitter cold. Her mouth filled with salt saliva like she might be going to throw up. She stood there, feeling sick and sad, then spun around and ran clumsily back up the path. Her eyes were full of tears.

High in the deer stand, Maythorn waited. Soon Rosie came staggering along the path, out of breath with running and crying.

Rosie's mother was a few minutes behind her, calling out, Rosie, wait, I need to talk to you. She was crying too.

12.

REMEMBRANCE OF
THINGS PAST

Friday, October 14

Chilly mist was rising from the gray river as Rosemary and Elizabeth crossed the bridge at Gudger's Stand. It was only 7:20 but the early start was necessary if they were to have a full day in Cherokee and its environs—the Qualla Boundary, homeland to the Eastern Band of Cherokee...and Maythorn's father's people.

Elizabeth clutched her travel mug of hot, black coffee, wishing that the car would warm up faster. Rosemary was driving, her creased brow indicating that she was deep in thought...or memory. Elizabeth concentrated on the scenery. *I wish I could paint this,* she thought, her eyes devouring the rapidly passing scene—autumn reds and yellows, bright against the haze...a plume of white smoke, billowing from the chimney of a house otherwise swallowed by fog.

Then they were winding up the narrow road, climbing from the river and out of the mist and she was ravished by the sight of the early sun shining through a yellow-leafed poplar, illuminating its interior to reveal, like a dark skeleton, the framework of trunk and branches. On, up toward Dewell Hill, where the land opened out.

Rich honey-gold sunlight lying on the brown and umber fields brought to mind the California *plein air* paintings she had admired recently on a trip to the art museum. The car whirled past a weathered tobacco barn, doors open, revealing bright tobacco hanging to cure, the rows looking like tattered ball gowns.

They always make me think of Blanche DuBois, for some reason. Or Miss Havisham. Elizabeth started to speak and then stopped herself. Rosemary was still preoccupied with her own thoughts. *And that's what this trip is for—to help her remember the time she and Maythorn went to stay for a weekend with Maythorn's granny. She doesn't need my idle chatter.*

Now the roadside was a tapestry of evergreens interspersed with bare gray trunks and an occasional maple, a cloud of greeny-yellow leaves shading to coral where frost had nipped. Ahead, an old silver-gray log barn topped by a rusted metal roof perched on a hilltop—a scene from years and years ago ... and today.

And then they were on the Ridley bypass, where the sun glared off the white lines at the edge of the pavement. A steady flow of cars, an amazing number of cars, in both lanes were coming to the high school and middle school or traveling to Asheville. *Where do they all come from?* Elizabeth mused. *When we moved here there was so little traffic that it wasn't unusual to see two pickups stopped in the middle of the road, the drivers talking to each other. And there was only one traffic light in Ridley, and that was more for show than anything else.*

The highway to Weaverville and the dark loom of the Blue Ridge appeared in the distance. But soon the rolling pastures gave way to subdivisions and the scenery grew generic—strip malls, fast-food places—and Elizabeth's thoughts turned inward.

She had finally spoken with Phillip, after so precipitously abandoning their dinner plans for Sunday and fleeing home to avoid talking about Mike Mullins. Repeated, unanswered calls on Sunday night had left her wondering if he was angry with her—"*Fed up*" *is probably the right phrase*—and just not answering. But he had returned her calls on Monday morning and had seemed much as usual. *I did* apologize; *I just didn't actually explain. That can wait till tomorrow night.*

The week had been hectic. She had spent long hours working double time to fill orders for dried flower and herb wreaths so that she would be free when Rosemary returned. Ben's absence meant that she also had to make sure that Julio and Homero tended to the thousand and one details of collecting seeds, watering the greenhouses, and harvesting the last of the tender edibles. There had been no killing freeze yet, but she expected one soon.

She and Phillip had talked briefly and, she thought, affectionately, each night. But she had delayed explaining to him the feelings she'd once had for Mike Mullins. *Tomorrow, when he comes out tomorrow, then I'll explain.*

She tried to make a picture in her mind of just how she would do this. Privacy and keeping her inmost feelings to herself had been a way of life for so very long that it was second nature to put a cheerful face on an unhappy situation.

And there's another thing I didn't tell him. He would have wanted me to call the sheriff about that message from Bib Maitland. And you should have, you know, nagged the irritating voice of her common sense.

I did replace the lock, she reminded the voice, in hope of silencing it. Bib's threatening message had led her to the unusual step of replacing her front door lock set so she could lock the doors at night. *And I hate that—after all these years of not worrying.*

"That's where there used to be all those big white cows— what are they called? Charolais?"

Rosemary had finally broken her silence and was nodding toward a development of multistoried houses, packed tight in what had been a pasture only ten or fifteen years ago.

"How can people choose to live like that, Mum? Instead of building a MacMansion, why don't they opt for a smaller house with more land around it?" Rosemary scowled at a particularly offensive example in which most of the façade was given over to a three-car garage. "I feel sorry for kids growing up without fields and woods to roam in like we had."

Elizabeth was silent, remembering her own childhood. She had grown up in a similar suburb—the houses not so large, the lots only slightly more spacious. But to her the yard had been a kingdom; the block, a familiar continent; and the immediate neighborhood, a world that was hers to explore, on foot or bike. *We had the same freedom to roam that she's talking about—within bounds, yes, but bounds that felt boundless. What was it Thoreau said about traveling much in Concord?*

She began to attempt to explain this to Rosemary, but now they were entering the steady rush of traffic on the interstate that led to Asheville. "I can't believe all these cars!" Rosemary groaned, carefully merging into the flow of commuters. "When did it get this bad? I had no idea...."

Farther on were more unhappy changes. The creepy

old Victorian farmhouse that they'd always loved for its dark green Gothic trim had been wrenched from its foundations. It sat forlorn on trestles, awaiting relocation, while heavy earthmoving equipment scoured the red soil it had once rested on. The mournful evergreens that had lined the property were gone and a sign proclaimed that THE HEMLOCKS——LUXURY CONDOS! would soon rise on this site.

Rosemary's expression darkened. "Why do things have to change all the time? I *hate* what's happening here! You know, I've always looked forward to someday coming home to the farm and building a house in the woods. If I ever have children I want them to grow up like Laur and I did."

"Laurel said something similar the other day. You don't know how glad I am that you all feel that way. So many people thought we were crazy, taking you two away from the so-called civilization of Florida. And during the early years, things weren't always as smooth as I would have liked them to be for you and Laurel—I mean, beside the horrible fact of Maythorn's kidnapping…murder…or whatever it was. I know I wasn't always as good a mother as I wanted to be. But if you both feel that your childhood was happy, then that makes *me* feel really good."

Rosemary's eyes were fixed on the road. "I think that Laurie was always happy. And I was too, mostly. When things didn't seem right, I could always lose myself in my books or my 'pretends.'" She glanced at her mother. "You may not have realized it, but for several years when we first moved to the farm, I wasn't me—I was an Indian princess named Shining Deer."

"Were you unhappy a lot of that time?" A sudden pang of guilt gripped Elizabeth. "I was afraid that changing schools—"

"No, it wasn't that." Rosemary seemed to be selecting her words with great care. "Once I could understand what the teachers and the other kids were saying, I liked school a lot. It was more…" She hesitated. "I guess I was picking up on the fact that you and Pa weren't always very happy yourselves."

Well! And here I thought… "What made you think that, sweetie?"

"Just…just a lot of little things. I hadn't thought about it in years because I know how strong your marriage was. But all this remembering has made me think about that time when we had first moved in the house, and before Maythorn…went away. I remember funny noises at night—when you and Pa had your bedroom over ours."

Elizabeth felt herself blushing. "Rosie, do you mean you heard us—"

Rosemary smiled, a little sadly. "No, Mum, I think I figured *those* noises out fairly soon. I'm talking about hearing Pa shouting out in his sleep, yelling in some strange language. And then I think I heard him crying… and sometime you cried too."

I feel like crying right now. You poor child. Too much like me—keeping it all private. Well, that's enough.

"Rosie, your pa was suffering from what they eventually diagnosed as Post-Traumatic Stress Disorder. You know he was in the navy during the Vietnam War."

"I thought that the stress thing happened to guys who'd been in combat. Pa just said he was on a ship all the time and it was bloody boring."

Elizabeth hesitated. It had taken years before Sam had told her about his time in Vietnam—and he had told her very little. *He insisted that it was just routine, but when the nightmares started I knew he had to be lying. And he was so adamant about not letting the girls know.* She laid a hand on her daughter's arm.

"Rosie, sweetie, your pa was part of a six-man crew on a Swift Boat, patrolling rivers and canals in Vietnam. He said it was all pretty tame right up till their last patrol. Then their boat got hit and two men were killed and one wounded really badly. I guess that was what the dreams were about. And the strange language was Vietnamese—he said he'd learned enough that if they didn't have a liaison guy along—a native speaker—he could usually communicate. Oh, Rosie, I'm so sorry that you never asked us about it—I didn't know you'd heard him."

Elizabeth turned her face to look out the window. She continued. "We were both going through a bad time—leaving Florida and jumping into this different life, building a house, getting used to all the new things about living on the farm; it was hard on both of us. And, for your father, I guess the stress triggered those old bad memories. We never had any idea that you girls—"

"Was stress why you were kissing Maythorn's uncle that time I saw you in the woods?"

13.

TO THE BOUNDARY

Friday, October 14

Rosemary's words, precise and merciless, were like a sudden slap. Elizabeth turned to her daughter, but Rosemary's face was expressionless and her eyes were fixed at some point far down the road.

Well, hell. "*How all occasions do conspire against me*"... *or however that goes.* "Rosie, did you just now remember that... along with the Maythorn memories? Or have you been wondering about it all this time?"

"I never forgot *that.*" Four clipped words and a waiting silence.

They turned onto 40W to Canton. The sun was at their back now and from the passenger seat Elizabeth could see the black shadow of the car running ahead and to the right of them. A single tree—an oak?—glowed deep purple-red against the soft-green pines. There were tangles of bittersweet in the trees—that vine, so beloved of decorators in the fall, with its beautiful orange-red berries in papery yellow husks, was gathered to be sold at farmers' markets. An invasive introduced plant, bittersweet had come to rival that other alien, kudzu, in draping and strangling the native trees.

"Rosie, I tried to explain it to you then. I saw you standing there and—"

"I always wondered if you'd gone out on purpose to meet him. You wouldn't let me come with you."

Ahead of them the green mountain slopes were warmed with a haze of autumn color. *Deal with it, Elizabeth; you owe her an explanation now.*

"It was like this, Rosie—and I'm not trying to make excuses, I'm just trying to explain the way I was feeling at the time—your father's nightmares had gotten worse, but instead of talking to me about them, he kept turning me away. And yes, there was the whole stress of the move and the difficulties of ordinary daily living—do you remember when our pipes froze and for weeks we were hauling buckets of water from the branch? And school was closed and you and Laurie were in and out of the snow and having to change your clothes six times a day."

She bit her lip, knowing that she could go on and on and on without ever truly explaining what had led to that moment in those snowy woods—the moment Rosemary had witnessed.

"I don't know…call it cabin fever, sweetie. But I was feeling trapped and so alone. Your pa was doing everything he could to help—everything except taking me into his confidence and letting me help *him*. And then…"

Sam had been working in the house and, seizing the opportunity to leave the girls in his care, she had taken the jeep, piled high with several weeks of dirty laundry, into the Washeteria on the Ridley bypass. Leaving eight machines churning over the Goodweather wash, she had sought the comfort of a sandwich and a cup of coffee in the Burger Palace next door.

She was reading her library book and munching on her Chik-N-Burger when Mike Mullins slid into the seat across from her. "Howdy, neighbor," he had said with a smile that was almost blinding. "Where's Sam?"

The Goodweathers had seen little of their neighbors since that visit in October. In November Elizabeth had called Patricia with a dinner invitation and had been indecently happy to learn that the Mullins would be unable...the Harvest Home Pageant was coming up and Patricia and Krystalle...busy, busy, busy. Elizabeth had breathed a sigh of relief and decided to wait till spring, when the house would be nearly complete and the comparison with Mullmore not so stark.

They had gone back to Mullmore for a huge Christmas party, complete with Moon rigged out in a Santa suit, boozily passing out expensive gifts to each partygoer. The girls had disappeared into a swirl of excited children; Sam had been cornered by two new friends who wanted to talk about the possibilities of purchasing farm equipment together; and Elizabeth stood by a window, holding a glass of punch that was far too sweet, wondering how soon they could return home.

Mike had a way of showing up when I was unhappy. And when I was unhappy, I probably said more than I should have. I was so pitifully glad to have someone who seemed interested....

"So was it planned or what?" Rosemary made no attempt to hide her impatience with her mother's long silence. "I'm just curious."

"No, not planned...at least not by me. A few days before, before the day you remember, I was in town doing laundry and grocery shopping. You girls were home with Pa and I was in the Burger Palace getting lunch. Mike came in and sat in the booth with me. We were talking about how the wintertime could make you a little crazy if you didn't get out now and then, and I told him that I tried to take a walk every afternoon. But it wasn't...it wasn't an assignation."

Elizabeth glanced over at Rosemary. Her daughter's face expressed something between suspended disbelief and outright doubt.

"Rosie," Elizabeth forced herself to speak the words, "what you saw was totally unpremeditated. Your father and I had an argument earlier in the day—I'd suggested he should get help for the nightmares, and he told me, in rather harsh terms, to mind my own business. And the water was frozen and Laurie had been so grouchy all day—I was feeling really sorry for myself and went for a walk, and there was Mike. He saw I'd been crying and asked me to tell him what was wrong and he was so...so warm and...so *understanding.*"

God, this sounds like a bloody soap opera, she lamented inwardly. *But I have to explain.* "It was just a stupid thing, Rosie. I cried on his shoulder; he kissed me; and for a minute I felt like...I don't know what exactly. But then I saw you standing there on the trail and I realized what I was doing. I tried to explain it to you back then, but you wouldn't let me."

All the long-put-away guilt flooded over her and she stared at her daughter's impassive face and the eyes that seemed only to see the road ahead.

"Rosie, please, I'm so sorry if—"

Miraculously, Rosemary turned toward her, her smile

filling up the car. "Mum, it's okay. I think I understand—not that it's my business, anyway. That was one moment, over twenty years ago. I know that what you and Pa had was a lot better than any other marriage I've seen. What I saw...well, it definitely shook me at the time. I was already a little worried about you and Pa because you both seemed unhappy. But at some point I realized that it was possible for people to have arguments and still love each other."

Her daughter's lovely, long-fingered hand reached out and squeezed Elizabeth's. "Oh, Mum, I don't know why I even brought it up. It didn't blight my childhood, or anything like that. But I *had* wondered. And thank you for answering my question."

Elizabeth stared out the window, her eyes brimming with tears, unable to trust herself to speak. They drove on in silence until, passing the turn to Newfound Gap, Rosemary pointed at the sign. "Look at that!" she exclaimed. "Newfound by who...whom?"

"Excuse me?" Elizabeth came back to the present at the sound of her daughter's voice. "What do you mean? I've always thought that was a kind of romantic name."

"No, I was remembering one time Maythorn's uncle told us that name was a reminder of the arrogance of the white settlers—how they gave names to tracks and traces that already had names, names the Cherokee had given them. He told us that Newfound Gap had been used by Indians for thousands of years and to call it newfound was stupid—and disrespectful."

"You really loved going to Cherokee. I remember that first time, you came back with some kind of Indian bread you'd made and you couldn't stop talking about all the things you'd learned. You never seemed to envy Maythorn the fancy house and all the money, but I remember your pa saying that we were a bitter disappointment to you in our lack of Native American blood."

"We went back a few more times, I think, but it's the first visit I really remember. The last time was in the fall of '86, just a few weeks before..." Rosemary's hand sketched a small gesture, and she went on. "Anyway, it was always an amazing experience. Granny Thorn spoke mostly Cherokee and she lived in a little log house and she showed us how to cook Cherokee food and how to do Cherokee dances. I'm remembering more every minute."

"What about the uncle? Do you remember his name? Maybe we can find him if he's still in Cherokee. Was he a doctor like Maythorn's father?"

Rosemary frowned. "No...I think he was an artist of some kind. He talked about making real Cherokee art and what he called phony Noble Savage stuff. He said tourists liked the phony stuff better."

"Do you remember his name?"

"I didn't, but Jared did. It was Driver Blackfox. I'm hoping we can find him and he can tell me about the Booger Dance—I keep remembering that phrase and somehow I think it's important. And I'm almost sure it comes from that last weekend."

On they drove. As they neared Canton, the car plunged into mist again—man-made and foul-smelling this time, an ugly low-lying, murky haze.

"What in god's name...?"

"I'm pretty sure it's a paper mill." Elizabeth rolled up her window. "I've heard that Canton residents say it just smells like money to them."

A stand of poplar trees, green leaves tarnished to brown, their edges crisped by frost. From their midst, cell towers bristled. A modest billboard set back in a pasture advertised Cherokee Tribal Bingo in blazing letters. Rosemary nodded toward it and made a face. "Yuck."

Elizabeth laughed. "Sweetie, there's worse to come. Did you know the tribe has a casino now? At long last, the Indians are scalping the white folks."

A pair of crosses and some faded artificial flowers, side by side on the shoulder, marked the site of a double traffic fatality...farther on, a simple white-painted wooden cross...and farther still, a cross of bleached-out plastic flowers, leaning drunkenly. Waynesville...Lake Junaluska...and then development run amok—tattoo parlors, pawn shops; "junque" barns; riding stables; Mom-and-Pop strip motels; home sites for sale; mountainsides covered with phony-looking log houses instead of trees; motel after motel; campgrounds; a rock shop, with a display of big chunks of brightly colored glittering pieces of glass, red, blue, green, purple, orange; Halloween harvest displays...

Rosemary's face was growing grimmer by the moment, and as they drew to a stop at a red light, she burst out, "This is...this is *terrible!* I don't remember it being like this at all." She looked from the sign urging her HAVE YOUR PICTURE MADE WITH A REAL MOONSHINE STILL! to a garish billboard for SANTALAND—THEME PARK AND ZOO.

"Mum, what if Marshall County gets like this? Laurel and Ben mentioned that there're lots of new people buying up buildings in Ransom and land all over the county. What if...?" She gestured wordlessly to the unlovely conglomeration of tourist traps.

A nightmare vision of quaint, quiet Ransom, suddenly transformed into a tourist mecca filled Elizabeth's mind. The prospect was unnerving. "Rosie, I don't know." Visions of herself with a shotgun, holding a developer's bulldozer at bay, flitted through her thoughts.

But as they left the gaudy jumble of the commercial strip and began to climb toward Cherokee on a winding road through undisturbed forests, both women relaxed. And by the time they saw the sign for the Cherokee Indian Reservation and the beautiful long views across wooded mountains, there was a powerful sense of coming to a hidden-away place...a Shangri-La. They began to see homes: modest houses and trailers. The side roads were marked with standard green street signs but—and Elizabeth felt a thrill as she noticed—the signs were in English *and* in the beautiful curling symbols of the Cherokee syllabary, the alphabet invented in the early 1800s by Sequoyah to give his people a written version of their language.

Elizabeth motioned to one of the signs and Rosemary nodded happily. "I see, Mum. That's so cool."

Deeper in, there were more and more homes, mostly modest brick ranches; a billboard: "TALK TO YOUR ELDERS ABOUT DIABETES"; Cherokee Church of God (Pentacostal); trailers, campgrounds; three kettle-style barbecues and a cluster of lawn chairs outside one house, evoking an image of a cheerful family gathering; signs for the Wolfetown Community, Macedonia Baptist Church, Bigwitch Baptist Church, Hornbuckle Tree Farm....

And then the tourist heart of Cherokee—Santaland, almost deserted at this hour, and a sudden shock as the Casino Hotel loomed ahead, at least three times taller than any other building in sight. Behind it, the casino itself, an odd building that managed to look like ancient Egypt rather than Cherokee, its huge parking lot stretching empty before it.

"Only nine-thirty—it'll be interesting to see what it looks like later in the day. You want to gamble, Rosie?" Elizabeth grinned at her daughter, trying to project an air of knowledgeable raffishness.

"Have you ever been in one of those places?" Obviously Rosemary was not deceived. "I have, once when I was at a conference. Really awful—full of cigarette smoke and zombies. Somehow I don't see you there. No, I thought we could start at the museum. That's the first place Driver took us."

14.

STONEWALLED

Friday, October 14

"Driver wanted to make sure we understood about the Trail of Tears and how many died on the Long Walk—that was the main thing." Rosemary watched as her mother minutely examined the museum's display re-creating a cozy Cherokee home of 1838. Its inhabitants could be glimpsed through a window at the rear, being led away by armed and menacing U.S. soldiers. The few bits of blue-and-white china on the table where a meal had been in progress seemed unbearably poignant.

"Driver told us Granny Thorn's people were some of those who hid from the army—hid for years and years till the government agreed to a reservation right here. And there were other Cherokee who were forced to walk all the way to Oklahoma, and then, when they could, they turned around and walked right back."

The recording that accompanied the exhibit had just finished the bleak tale—Cherokees torn from their homes and farms and forced onto the Long Walk to the inhospitable West, but still Elizabeth stared into the little room, saying nothing.

"Mum?" Rosemary ventured. She was alarmed to see her mother's blue eyes swimming with tears.

"This just really gets to me—there they were, there they'd *been* for time out of mind, and all of a sudden white settlers want their land. The white soldiers cut down the Cherokee's peach trees and burn their corn...."

Rosemary waited as Elizabeth scrabbled in her shoulder bag for a bandana, blew her nose vigorously, and went on. "But the thing of it is—the *real* thing—is that it's always happening. Like the Cherokees probably displaced some earlier, weaker tribes who had beat up on someone before that. And back when we moved to Marshall County, the descendants of those same first settlers who had helped get rid of the Cherokee felt threatened by how many new people were moving to the county, new people with different ideas about how things should be run. And now *I'm* feeling threatened by the folks moving in with mega-bucks to spend and their own vision of what the county should be. Fancy summer homes, bigger and bigger ... gated communities that say 'us, not you.'"

Mum's really on a rant, Rosemary thought, eyeing her mother with incredulity. *She hardly ever—*

"Not that I think these really rich people would want to turn Ridley and Marshall County into a tacky tourist trap like we just drove through. But I'm afraid it'll be a *tasteful* one—you know, art galleries and spas and high-end crafts and places to eat with goat cheese and arugula."

She broke off and blew her nose again. "What a hypocrite I am. I *love* goat cheese and arugula. And I was thrilled when the deli opened up and there was a choice in Ransom other than burgers or meat and three. Ben and I had this conversation not long ago, and I was giving him all sorts of stuffy wisdom about change being part of life. I guess I'm just feeling endangered. Sorry, Rosie, I'll get off it."

They passed through the remaining exhibits in silence. At this early hour, they had the museum almost entirely to themselves. As she moved from display to display, Rosemary felt the remembered presence of Maythorn and her uncle Driver. *He was so passionate about their heritage. See and remember, Mary Thorn Blackfox, he'd said it over and over. See and remember.* In her mind's eye she saw him, a dark-skinned young man with long braids and glittering eyes, his strong hand gripping Maythorn's thin shoulder as he directed her attention to one of the glass cases. *See and remember.*

When they returned to the lobby, Elizabeth crossed to look at the artifacts and Indian crafts filling the showcases on the walls. Rosemary's attention was drawn to a display of carved masks representing various animals— a long-beaked bird, a wolf, a bear. She studied them, frowning. *These aren't the kind I remember. I wonder…*

Leaving her mother rapt in contemplation of a display of basketry, Rosemary returned to the desk where they had purchased their tickets. Business was still slow and the two Cherokee men—one young, one white-haired— seated behind the desk were chatting leisurely.

"Excuse me," Rosemary said, as the younger man stood and came to the front, "I had a few questions. What can you tell me about the Booger Dance? Is it still performed?"

The two men exchanged startled glances. The younger— "Wattie Calhoun" his name tag read—shook his head slowly. "No, not for a long time. It's, you know, kind of…"

"But I think I saw it when I was here nearly twenty years ago." Rosemary persisted despite Wattie Calhoun's clear discomfort with the subject. "Was it performed for tourists back then?"

The older man said something in the strange, somehow halting tongue that she recognized from the recordings she had just heard in the museum as Cherokee. He was evidently teasing the younger man, for the latter's olive complexion deepened several shades as he continued to shake his head. "No way they ever did the Man Dance for tourists. You remember wrong."

Now Rosemary was blushing. She remembered from her online research that the Booger Dance involved a certain amount of rowdy horseplay with water-filled gourds brandished like phalluses. *And some of the masks were semi-obscene too. This poor guy, having to deal with Crazy White Woman Asks Indelicate Questions.*

Impulsively, she changed the subject. "My best friend's uncle used to live here and I think he had something to do with the museum. I was hoping to get in touch with him again. His name is Driver Blackfox. Do you know him, by any chance?"

Wattie Calhoun's face went blank and the older man said something in rapid Cherokee. The younger man relaxed.

"No, I can't say as I know of any Driver Blackfox. Sorry." He picked up a jumble of papers that lay on the desk before him and turned away from her. "Sorry, I can't help you." He muttered something to the old man, who rose and followed him through the door at the rear of the ticket office.

"Rosie, look here!" Her mother's voice was full of barely contained triumph. "Over here—these carvings!"

The case was full of recent examples of Cherokee craft—intricately woven baskets of dyed river cane, and carvings in wood and soapstone. A graceful owl carved in some pale wood hovered, wings half-extended, over a sleeping fox executed in black walnut. Beside the pair a neatly lettered card read D. BLACKFOX——2002.

"You said he was a woodcarver, didn't you?" Her mother's face glowed with excitement. "Let's ask in the gift shop if this is Driver."

The women in the deserted gift shop brightened at the sight of potential customers. Elizabeth and Rosemary made a circuit of the store and Elizabeth became absorbed in the book section. With a surreptitious look at her oblivious parent, Rosemary picked up a very small, very expensive Cherokee basket, beautifully woven in intricate patterns with river cane, both natural and subtly dyed. *I'll give it to her as a thank you for helping me with this— what is it, a quest?*

Feeling that perhaps her purchases might buy her a little information as well, she handed the cashier her credit card. "I really love that carving out in the hall, the owl and the fox. Do you have any smaller things by Driver Blackfox for sale? The large pieces are way out of my price range."

The dark-eyed young woman laughed. "Sorry. We used to have a few, but he's only doing big things now. You might find—"

"Tla!" The older man from the ticket desk was standing behind her and staring fixedly at the three women behind the counter. He barked out a short sentence, then wheeled and stalked out of the shop. The three women looked at one another, and silent messages were exchanged without the flicker of an eyelid.

"And sign this. Thank you so much." The cashier thrust the credit card receipt at her. Before she handed it back, however, Rosemary tried once more. "Where did you say I could find more of Driver Blackfox's work?"

The young woman plucked the slip from Rosemary's fingers. "Driver? Oh, I thought you said something else. I don't know any Driver." She pushed the bag with the little basket in it across the counter. "Thank you. Have a nice day."

"Okay, the people in the other gift shop were equally uncooperative. The woman at the cash register was putting down the telephone as I walked in and she stared at me with just a hint of a smirk, like she knew exactly what I was going to ask her. *And* what she was going to say. Talk about stonewalling."

Rosemary gave the steering wheel an annoyed jerk. "I wonder if it would be worthwhile going someplace official or if that wouldn't do any good either."

Elizabeth looked up from the book on the history of the Eastern Band that had been her single purchase. "We could drive out to Big Cove and look for his house."

"Excuse me?" Rosemary stared at her mother, who was grinning madly now.

"While you were getting stonewalled, I went and found a payphone. With a phone book." Elizabeth pulled out a crumpled sheet of paper. "There are a bunch of Blackfoxes, including a Dan, a Davy, a Doris and L.D., a D.G., and two plain *D*s. But there is also, as big as life, a Driver on 538 Robert Junaluska Road in Big Cove. I have a phone number, but somehow I think we might do better to go unannounced."

Does it seem familiar? It took a long time to get to Maythorn's granny's house from the museum, I think I remember that much.

The road was curling through woods and fields, at times along a broad, shallow creek, water racing over smooth rocks. They passed several campgrounds and homes set in clearings. Large gardens abounded. Rows of drying cornstalks stood sentinel, pale crisp leaves fluttering like stiff flags in the autumn breeze.

"This book I got about Cherokee says that Big Cove is the most remote and the most traditional of the various communities in the Qualla Boundary." Her mother peered at her over the top of reading glasses. "What's this up here?"

They had come to a large open area. Tiny orange flags fluttered everywhere, marking off rectangles of various sizes, some of which were covered with canopies of bright blue plastic. Several utilitarian trailers sat at one end of the site and an assortment of cars and trucks lined the entry road. A large sign proclaimed that this was the future site of an educational complex.

"I don't see any construction going on. What do you suppose . . . ?" Elizabeth craned her neck to see the activity as they passed.

"I'll bet it's an archaeological dig—maybe one of the towns that was destroyed by the army when they forced the Cherokees out. Probably this whole place is full of history and they have to do a dig and study it before they can build over it."

Rosemary smiled to herself. *There's undoubtedly a metaphor to be made here, but with two English majors in the car, it's also undoubtedly not necessary.* She looked over at her mother, who returned her glance with a nod.

"Exactly," said her mother.

They were deep into the Big Cove area when Elizabeth spotted the road they sought. A narrow, unpaved ribbon, it ran between tall trees and thick undergrowth. As they followed it, they passed a mailbox marked with the number 316. A modest brick house sat at the end of a long driveway. There were no cars and no sign of activity.

Rosemary looked eagerly up the road. "'Further up and further in!'" She glanced across at her mother, who was smiling.

"That's from the Narnia books, right?"

Rosemary nodded. "I taught Maythorn to say that when we went exploring. We were all over the mountain that last year—it was so wonderful to have all that space to roam." She fell silent, hearing an echo of her father's voice. *She could be hiding... or hidden... anywhere out there.*

Elizabeth's face was troubled. "That was one of the reasons your father and I wanted to live here, away from all the crime and random violence of the cities. And I *still* believe we were right." Rosemary heard her breathe deeply before the next words tumbled out. "My mother had a fit when she heard about Maythorn. She was convinced that you and Laurie would be next. She threatened to sue for custody of you two, said we had put you all in a dangerous environment."

"What? Did she really?"

"Oh, nothing came of it. She never could have won—but she *was* genuinely worried about you two. She loved you all a lot, you know. In the end, that's what matters. At least, that's what I've always told myself."

The road had degenerated to a one-lane track when they found themselves at a dead end. A garden lay to one side and on the other was a small log cabin, surrounded by a chain-link fence. A sign beside the closed gate warned:

BITING DOGS. There was a mailbox, but it bore neither name nor number.

"What do you think, Rosie? Does this look like where you came before?"

Rosemary stared at the house. A porch ran across its front, and beneath the roof's overhang were several straight-backed chairs, and a tree stump serving as a table. The doors and windows were shut, mute and unrevealing.

"I . . . don't know." *But there's something . . .* "No, I don't think so. There's no water. At Granny Thorn's there was the sound of water, I'm sure of it."

"But this must be Driver's place." Her mother pointed to a lean-to shed attached to the cabin. A half-finished carving of what appeared to be a bear stood on another stump under the shed. "There's a pickup parked out back. Let's see if anyone's here."

At once, Elizabeth was out of the car and approaching the gate. Just as she put her hand to it, two massive brindle hounds tore around the small house. They hurled their bodies against the gate, which sagged and rattled alarmingly under their attack. Elizabeth backed up and began to speak in a low, calming voice to the animals, but the dogs ignored her friendly overtures and continued to test the holding ability of the gate latch.

"Mum! Get back in the car! What if they—" But her mother was already retreating.

"So much for my way with dogs." Elizabeth took her seat again and put up her window. "Maybe we'd better leave; if they come over the fence, they'll probably chew up your tires, and then where would we be?"

She stared back at the little cabin and its canine guardians as Rosemary turned the car and started back down the road. "Really gorgeous hounds. I wonder what breed they are? They're bigger than Plotts . . . maybe some mastiff there or—Wait a minute! I think I saw someone at the window."

Rosemary stopped the car. Behind them, the barking dogs raced up and down along the fence nearest the road. After several minutes and no further sign from the house, Rosemary sighed and drove on.

"I don't know, sweetie," Elizabeth said. "Maybe I didn't see anything. But what do you want to do? I wrote down the number—we could try calling." She reached for her cell phone. "If anyone's there—" She tapped in the number and handed the phone to her daughter.

A woman's voice was on the answering machine. She spoke the number and a few words in what must have been Cherokee. In the background, the hollow tones of a wooden flute played.

"If this is the home of Driver Blackfox, I really need to get in touch with him. I was a friend of his niece Maythorn—I mean, Mary Thorn Blackfox." Rosemary gave her name and phone number, as well as a further entreaty, and waited. *Maybe if someone is really there, they'll pick up. Maybe . . .*

"No good," she told her mother. "I guess I can try writing."

"Let's go on up the road a little more." Elizabeth was searching the book she had bought. "There's a waterfall we could go see."

A waterfall. Rosemary closed her eyes. *At Granny Thorn's there was always the sound of water.*

GROUNDHOG FALLS

October 1985

THE TRAIL FOLLOWED *the rushing branch beside the laurels. It was steep and slick with fallen leaves and the damp of the recent rain. Driver was just above them, striding quickly up the steep, narrow path.*

Further up and further in. Rosie whispered the words to herself, her breath coming in short bursts. *We are going deep into the land of the Cherokee, led by Driver, the son of the chief. We will meet the Wise Woman, who will teach us the forgotten ways of our people. My sister and I are of the Chosen Ones.*

There were logs, velvety with moss, across the trail at the steepest places, like steps, but you had to be careful not to skid on the slippery parts. Tall ferns grew in lush patches, their emerald plumes bowing as the three woods-wise Indians passed stealthily by.

Driver, wait up. Maythorn stopped at a turn where the path led to a footlog over the racing water. *Rosie needs to rest. Her face is turning all red.*

I'm okay. She tried not to sound out of breath. *I can keep up.* She would not ask how far it was, not for anything.

But Driver stopped and looked at her. He smiled and his teeth were white and strong against his dark skin. Rosie's rosy, he said. You sit and rest a minute on that log over there and I'll tell you a Cherokee story.

As Rosemary and Maythorn settled themselves on the log, Driver squatted effortlessly beside it and began to roll a cigarette. He lit it and inhaled deeply. *I'll tell you about the boys who didn't want to stop playing, just like my grandfather told it to me when I was little.* Driver settled himself on his haunches and blew out three rings of smoke, one after another.

Well, it was a long, long time ago, back before the white man was here. In this one Cherokee village there were seven boys who played together every day. All seven were best friends, just like you two girls are best friends. And every day they would get together and play games and run around and wade in the creeks and roam in the woods, just like you two.

Driver smiled his white smile at them and went on. *But most of all, those boys, they loved to dance. They would make a circle and dance and dance till the sun went down and the moon came up, never paying attention when their mothers called them to come to supper. And after a while, their mothers got mad. The seven mothers got together and said, Let's teach these bad boys a lesson. When they come in to dinner late, let's give them stones to eat.*

So the next day the seven boys were playing together as usual and, as usual, when their mothers called, they just kept on playing, pretending that they hadn't heard. Their mothers called them again, but still they didn't come. Again and again the seven mothers called, but the seven bad boys just didn't pay any mind.

Finally, when it was black dark, the boys got so hungry, they decided to go home. They went home and they were bad hungry—ready for some chestnut bread or maybe some squirrel stew. They could smell the good smells of what their parents had been eating and their mouths were just watering.

Rosie's mouth began to water too. She'd never had chestnut bread, but it sounded nice. She wasn't so sure about squirrel stew.

What happened then, Driver? Maythorn's voice was impatient. *Did their mothers really give them rocks to eat?*

That's exactly what they did. The seven mothers filled the bowls with smooth river rocks and set them down in front of the seven bad boys. This is all there is for boys who won't come when we call them. We've already eaten up all the good chestnut bread and all the rich-tasting squirrel stew, the seven mothers and seven fathers said.

Well, that made those boys so angry that they jumped up and yelled at their parents. I told you that they were bad boys. They jumped up and yelled, If this is all the food you've got for us, we're gonna go back outside and dance all night! And they ran back out to the middle of the village and joined hands and started dancing around in a circle.

Then the seven mothers and seven fathers felt bad and ran after them, but the seven boys just kept dancing faster and faster and faster. They danced so fast that their feet began to leave the ground. Pretty soon they were just a big spinning circle a few feet off the ground.

Stop! yelled the seven mothers. Stop! the seven fathers hollered. But the seven boys went faster and faster and their dancing circle kept rising higher and higher and higher.

Now Driver was standing and with his hand he was showing how the circle kept rising up. Rosie and Maythorn sat quite still, their eyes wide as if they were watching the ring of furiously dancing boys.

Driver's hand rose up above his head as he continued the story. *Finally, when the dancing boys were as high as the head of the tallest man there and all the mothers were wailing and crying and all the fathers were getting pretty worried too, at that very moment, the tallest man reached up and tried to grab one of the boys by the ankle.*

Standing on his tiptoes, Driver stretched up his arm as far as it would go. He wiggled his fingers and caught at the empty

*air. Finally the tallest man caught one of the boys. He pulled as
hard as he could, and suddenly that boy came falling down.
He fell so hard and he fell so fast that when he hit the ground,
he just kept going till the earth covered him right up. But the
other six boys didn't stop their dancing. Now they were a fast-
moving, spinning blur, rising higher and higher all the way up
into the night sky, right into the middle of all the stars.*

The girls looked up at the sky where Driver was pointing.

*Tonight I'll show you a little circle of six stars way up there.
The white men call it the Pleiades but our old people say it's
those six boys, still dancing.*

There was a silence. Then Rosie whispered, *What about the
boy who went into the ground, Driver? What happened to
him?*

See that tall tree over there? Driver nodded his head. *That's
a pine tree. That seventh boy turned into a pine tree. You see
how the top points up? That's because the boy's pointing up at
his friends. And the pine stays green, even in the winter, so you
can see it pointing at the six dancing boys in the sky.*

The two girls, mouths open, were staring up, squinting their
eyes, looking for the lost boys. Driver clapped his hands to get
their attention.

Okay, let's go. Granny'll be looking for us. He held out
both hands and pulled them to their feet as if they were weight-
less.

Crossing the foot log was scary. Driver and Maythorn walked
on it as if it was just part of the path, but when Rosie stepped on
the slender tree trunk, damp and slippery above the water, she
had a funny swimmie feeling in her head. She edged out cautiously, taking tiny steps and trying to be brave.

Do you want me to come get you, Rosie? Driver had
stopped again and was looking at her with a funny expression.

She took a trembly breath. No, she answered and, looking straight at him, she walked right across without stopping.

Good girl. We'll make a Cherokee of you yet, he said, and patted her shoulder. She felt that swimmie feeling again, but this time it was nice.

They continued on, always up, always along the creek, and she began to hear a dull roaring sound, like a heavy rain. It got louder and louder with every step they took, till finally she tugged at Driver's shirt. What's that noise? she wanted to know.

He grinned. Didn't Mary Thorn tell you? That's the old groundhog, old o-ga-na, grumbling in his cave.

She must have looked uncertain, because Driver squatted down beside her and said, You don't worry. Won't nothing harm you at Granny's. Come on now, good girl, o-s-du a-ge-yu-tsa, we're almost there.

One more turn, and the sound was very loud now. They pushed through the twisty-branched, shiny laurels that grew taller than Driver, and there before them was a little bridge—with handrails, she was happy to see. Beyond the bridge a snug log house nestled beneath more big laurels. Ferns grew on its wood-shingled roof and a wisp of smoke curled from the chimney. On the sagging porch stood a tiny, wrinkled woman in a dark green skirt and faded red blouse. A gray wool shawl covered her thin shoulders and her scanty white hair was parted in the middle and pulled back into a single thin braid. She held her arms open wide and said something Rosemary couldn't understand.

She says to make your manners to Groundhog Falls first. Driver jerked his head and Rosemary turned, and gasped.

A vast wall of rock, towering nearly vertical—up and up toward a sky blue as a gemstone—stood before her. It's taller than a house, she thought. Maybe three houses. And wide—with many, many separate rivulets cascading from the top of the sheer cliff. Water poured over the edge in steady streams that hit projecting rocks, divided and redivided till the whole wall of living stone was a maze of streamlets, an ever-changing lacy pattern of white foam against black rock.

Rosemary stood and gaped. You never told me, *she accused her friend.* You never said anything.

Granny says it's better that way. Maythorn glanced at her uncle for confirmation. Better not to think you know what you're going to see. Granny says people see things better when they don't know what to look for, isn't that so, Uncle?

Late that night, lying in the little loft on thick pallets made from soft faded quilts, Rosemary and Maythorn whispered quietly. Granny was snoring gently in the bed that took up one corner of the main room and Driver had gone outside. His pallet awaited him before the guttering fire.

Why's he gone so long? Rosemary felt a little anxious. Granny mostly spoke Cherokee, though she seemed to understand English perfectly well. Driver had said that Granny wanted to keep the old language alive and that was why she wouldn't talk English. Maythorn, in spite of all her bragging, didn't understand Cherokee as much as she had pretended to. Plus, Driver was a strong man, and here in the middle of the woods, with wild animals all around, and the constant roar of the falling waters that could hide the sound of stealthy footfalls—He's not going far away, is he? Rosemary whispered.

Maythorn sat up cross-legged on her pallet. The fire's glow illuminated her dusky face and danced on her glossy braids. The longer we stay here, the more Indian she looks, realized Rosemary, wondering if her own braids gave her some of the same coveted appearance.

Driver has trouble sleeping nights. Maythorn's face was somber. He has bad dreams because he's the one that shot my daddy. I was there when it happened.

15.

INTRUSION

Friday, October 14 and Saturday, October 15

"So, Jared's taking you to see Trish Trantham tomorrow—is that still the plan?"

Before Rosemary could answer, Elizabeth slowed the jeep. "That's weird—I thought for sure I left the outdoor lights on. I figured it'd be dark when we got back and ... I don't know, maybe the power's out. It still happens now and then—but usually only when we've had a lot of rain."

She pulled the car to a stop in the driveway and opened her door. No dogs. It was well past their feeding time and she had expected to be greeted by James's eager barking as well as the accusing glare that Molly had down to perfection. But all was quiet. Nothing.

"Molly! James! Urrr-sa!" As they climbed the steps to the porch, Elizabeth whistled and then called again for the missing trio. No response. "They must have given up on us and gone off on a toot. But I've never known *James* to go off—"

"Mum, I thought you locked the door. Look, it's wide open. Do you think that kid is back?" Rosemary pushed past Elizabeth, hitting the switch by the door and flooding the living room with light.

It was like a blow to the stomach, Elizabeth thought. First she felt sick. And then angry. Very, very angry.

Every drawer in the living room had been pulled out— contents dumped on the floor. The shelves that lined the back walls gaped empty; the books lay in tangled heaps on the floor. Sofas, tables, chairs were all overturned and pictures had been pulled from the wall and tossed to the floor to rest atop the other carnage.

Room by room, it was the same. Closets and cabinets had been disemboweled, drawers and shelves ransacked. Mattresses lay askew on beds, and in each room an untidy pile of Elizabeth's possessions lay on the floor.

"Mum, we have to call the police." Rosemary was reaching for the telephone. "It must have been that kid. Or the creepy guy who came looking for him. And we shouldn't touch anything."

"Where are my dogs?" was Elizabeth's only reply.

Phillip looked up from the papers he was correcting. He'd been puzzling over a student's definition of "recidivist" as "a person who receives stolen goods but gives them back," when he realized that the muffled beep of his cell phone was sounding from somewhere. He pulled himself to his feet and went in search of the jacket he had worn earlier.

It was Sheriff Blaine. "Hawk, we got a situation here. I'm on my way to your lady friend's place right now. Her daughter called—"

"What is it? Is Elizabeth okay? What's—"

"She's fine. She's outside looking for her dogs, the daughter said. But it sounds like someone's tossed the house pretty good. I thought you'd want to know."

Now the phone on his desk, his landline, was ringing. "Hold on, Mac."

Elizabeth's voice was small and frightened. "Phillip, could you come out here? Tonight?"

He made the call to Gabby as he sped toward Marshall County. His old shipmate seemed unsurprised by the news, saying only that Del had been afraid of something like this.

"Maybe it's time you come clean with her. Red may have told her more than he let on to us. Hell, she may know exactly where the stuff is hidden. Or she could know something without exactly *knowing* she knows it, if you follow me. But once we have that deposition and the pictures—especially the pictures—the other side won't have any reason to go after her."

Mackenzie Blaine was waiting for him in one of the sheriff department's four-wheel-drive vehicles. "Thought I'd give you a ride up, Hawk. My boys are done and Miz Goodweather and her daughter are trying to put things back together."

The sheriff's eyebrows lifted slightly as Phillip tossed a little overnight bag into the back seat of the SUV. "Good idea. Those two women are pretty shook up. And Miz Goodweather said that the Mexican fellas who live down here are off for the night at some fiesta over in Henderson County. I doubt whoever it was would come back, but just as well for you to be here. Something like this can really—"

Phillip broke in. "What's your take on this, Mac? Does it look like robbery, or what?"

The sheriff started the car and flipped on his headlights. "I don't like it. Miz Goodweather thinks it was Bib

Maitland—says she had a threatening message from him on her machine back on Sunday night—"

"What? She never—"

"No, and she erased the message. So we got nothing there. But—"

"What about prints? Was anything taken? If you find Maitland in possession of stolen goods..."

Blaine slowed the SUV as the headlights caught the forms of Ursa and Molly in the field just ahead of them. "Those her dogs? She's been worried sick about two dogs that are missing. We found that little one hiding under the porch—doesn't seem hurt, just pretty scared. Those two look okay. They hers?"

Phillip leaned forward to peer out the window. "Yeah, those are hers. Looks like they're headed home now."

He watched Molly loping gracefully up the road, followed by Ursa, whose broad-beamed body plodded laboriously just ahead of their car. Phillip smiled as the big dog sat down to scratch, eliciting a muttered curse from the sheriff as he stopped the vehicle.

"That one moves at her own pace, Mac. Tap the horn; she'll get up eventually."

As they waited for Ursa to move out of the road, Phillip said, "Listen, Mac, have you sent someone to pick up Maitland? Because if you're shorthanded, it would be my pleasure. I'm still sworn in as a deputy from that thing with the militia last year—"

"Slow down, Hawk, I'm not so sure it was Maitland. This doesn't look like ordinary vandalism or burglary."

Blaine enumerated his points. Nothing seemed to be missing. A locked door had been opened as if by a locksmith. "If it was Bib trying to scare her, I'd expect to find stuff broken or torn up. This was more like someone looking for something. And unless they found what they wanted when they pulled out that last drawer, I'm thinking they're still going to be looking." The sheriff continued, looking troubled. "And the daughter—what's her name, Rosemary? She's saying stuff like this is all her fault, but that she has to find the little Mullins girl. Hawk, it's a helluva mess."

A helluva mess doesn't come close. Phillip looked in dismay at the heaps of books and objects covering the rose red Oriental carpet. A deputy, who was picking up and stacking some of the books in random piles, looked up in relief at the sight of Sheriff Blaine.

"Miz Goodweather and her girl are out back lookin' fer them other dogs." He set an outsized copy of *Moby Dick* on top of a stack of fat paperbacks by James Michener. "Reckon she's read all these books?"

Leaving Blaine and the deputy in the chaos of the living room, Phillip went quickly to the guest room where a French door opened onto the wooded area behind the house. There, more confusion greeted him: ransacked drawers; a wooden chest turned on its side, spilling out a collection of sepia-toned pictures; blankets twisted over the mess on the floor. The outer door opened and a dark-haired young woman stepped into the room. Seeing Phillip, she froze, but before he could explain himself, Elizabeth burst through the door and hurled herself into his arms.

Hours later, Phillip and Rosemary had been introduced, the sheriff and his deputies had gone, a modicum of order was restored to the house, and all three dogs had been fed and were happily asleep in Elizabeth's bedroom. *I wonder who else is in there now,* Rosemary mused.

Rosemary had taken herself off to bed upstairs, firmly closing the door behind her, while her mother and the burly ex-detective still sat talking quietly in the living room. *She went into his arms like she belonged there.*

Rosemary smiled. *It's good to see her able to lean on someone again. She's insisted on absorbing all the shocks and troubles by herself for too long. And he seems to really care about her—the way he insisted on staying till we find out who's behind the break-in. And for once Mum didn't argue.*

Rosemary yawned and snuggled into her bed. The thought that her mother might have found someone after five—*no, almost six*—years of widowhood was comforting. *Who knows, maybe there's hope for me.*

As she drifted into sleep, images from the day in Cherokee followed one after another. A mask in the museum, a gourd rattle in a gift shop, the waterfall that had been their last stop. Surely she had seen it before. But it was bigger than she remembered, much bigger. Wasn't it usually just the opposite? Didn't things remembered from childhood always turn out to be smaller, less impressive?

It was good of Jared to offer to go with me to see Mrs. Mullins—or rather, Trish Trantham. The thought emerged unbidden. *He said it was unfinished business for him too . . . and that it was fate that had brought me back. Maybe tomorrow . . .*

Phillip Hawkins stepped noiselessly out to the little porch that lay beyond the guest room's French door. He took his cell phone from his belt, punched in a number, and began to speak quietly. After a moment he shook his head in disgust and ended the call. He stood in silence, absorbing the sounds of the night, weighing and assessing each rustle and creak that came to his ears. At last satisfied, he went inside and set his phone on the bedside table, then put his pistol beside it. *Back in the guest room again.* With a sigh, he sank into the bed. The luminescent dial on his watch told him that it was after two a.m.

I need to come clean with Elizabeth about this situation with the deposition . . . but not while her daughter's here. It's going to be tricky—she's not going to like it that I didn't explain to her why I came here in the first place. How much did Sam tell her? I know he didn't want her to know about that last day—he was afraid it would change the way she felt about him.

He rolled over and shoved the extra pillow off the bed. *And now I'm afraid it's gonna change the way she feels about me. And that can't happen.*

Elizabeth stared out her window at the moon-glazed slopes. The swelling golden disk had moved out of sight now and was sinking toward the west, but its light still bathed field and woodland. *It must be nearly full. Probably why Molly and Ursa were gone. Moonlight brings out their wild side.*

She glanced at the closed bedroom door. *I wish . . . Oh, please, Elizabeth! With Rosemary here? And what if I . . . what if he . . . ?*

The faint lingering aroma of Old Spice on the pillow-case mocked her. *Maybe you can dream about him.*

It was no gentle rosy-hued idyll, nor was it one of the disturbingly erotic dreams that occasionally jolted her awake, to lie there breathless and troubled at the hunger in her body. No, it was the old familiar nightmare—the bad dream that had haunted her since childhood.

The bad lady at the top of the stairs was waiting for her, and now she had to climb the stairs, though her feet seemed to stick on each step, and the bad lady was glaring down at her, and the bad lady was raising her hand, and the little girl was crying, Help, Help, but no one was—

"Elizabeth!"

And now the bad lady was grabbing her shoulder and shaking her. The bad lady was saying, "Elizabeth! What's wrong? Was someone in here?"

She jerked awake and lay there, shivering. Slowly, reality returned. She sat up and turned, to see Phillip standing at her bedside, his left hand on her shoulder. The moonlight glinted off the barrel of the gun he held in his right hand.

She blinked, and at that moment they both became aware of the fact that he was naked.

"Sweet Jesus!" He snatched one of her pillows off the bed and lowered it modestly in front of himself. "I thought I heard you calling for help. I thought... What the hell did I hear?"

Without thinking, Elizabeth reached for him. "Put the gun down, Phillip, and come to bed."

16.

THE MORNING AFTER
THE NIGHT BEFORE

Saturday, October 15

All the doubts, the hesitation, the unspoken fear that her body, no longer young, would reject or be rejected by a lover, all these vanished like the fleeting bad dream. And when she woke in the morning to hear his soft, regular breathing on the pillow beside hers and then to feel his warm hand settling gently on her belly, it was good. It was very good.

"You said you were having a nightmare—I guess coming home and finding your house torn apart like that could do it. Were you dreaming ol' Bib was coming after you?"

Phillip had propped himself up on the pillows and was watching the ever-changing scene beyond the three big east-facing windows. Mountaintops, like islands, emerged from the sea of mist below them, as the red ball of the sun slowly inched its majestic way from behind a central peak. The question hung in the air between them but he continued to study the view, giving her time, time and space to answer.

She studied him—this man in her bed. The creamy

white sheets were pulled decorously high on his hairy chest and he kept his eyes on the windows, though one hand rested lovingly on her thigh. Molly and Ursa had been let out before dawn; James was deeply asleep, curled tightly on his little bed, and the house was hushed. The question hung there.

In the early morning light Elizabeth felt suddenly shy. She pulled her nightshirt back on—the long-sleeved tee that had fallen to the floor beside the bed—then resettled herself beside Phillip. His arm lifted and drew her closer as he continued to watch the sun rise. She relaxed against his comforting warmth.

"No, it wasn't Bib I was dreaming about. It's just a nightmare I have now and then—have had for as long as I can remember. It comes when I'm feeling stressed. Sam got used to it—he said he'd hear me calling out and he knew to wake me and save me from the bad lady."

Briefly, she described the recurring pattern of the dream, trying to make light of it and wondering at the same time if Rosemary was awake. Phillip was watching her attentively.

"You've always had this dream?" He was lightly running his fingers along her arm. "Is it based on something in your past? When I was a kid I had a recurring dream about drowning, and my mother told me it was probably because our family house got flooded during a hurricane when I was four or five. But I didn't remember the hurricane at all."

"I think it's from seeing *Snow White* at a young and extremely impressionable age. Evidently the wicked stepmother scared the bejesus out of me and I had to be removed from the theater—shrieking." She laughed and captured his roving hand in hers.

* * *

Phillip had made a discreet exit from her bedroom to collect his clothes. Elizabeth dressed quickly and went to the kitchen, thankful that Rosemary was not yet up. *I'll tell her... but not quite yet. Although I feel like it's written in neon all over me. What a night! What a very surprising night!*

She busied herself with the coffeemaker and a pan of frying sausage. She and Rosemary had tidied the kitchen the night before, while Phillip replaced drawers, rehung pictures, and righted heavy objects in the other rooms. The sight of accustomed order was reassuring. *Accustomed order... And just where does Phillip belong in the scheme of my life? I thought I'd learned to rely on myself, and then a silly nightmare has me yowling for help.*

In spite of herself, she smiled. Somewhere, far in the back of her head, the Hallelujah Chorus was shouting out in triumph. She took a large blue crockery bowl and began to break eggs into it, nodding in time to the crashing chords that reverberated in her imagination.

"Mum, how in the world can you look so cheerful?" Rosemary was standing in the kitchen doorway, dressed, but yawning and rubbing her eyes. "It's going to take most of the day to get those books back on the shelves. I'll help, of course, but I'm meeting Jared at noon and—"

"Don't worry, sweetie, Phillip's going to help me." Elizabeth ducked her head into the refrigerator in search of some cheese to add to the eggs. She wondered if her daughter had noticed how *beautiful* the name "Phillip" was. She hoped that she could maintain a straight face till Rosemary left for her date.

Phillip ambled into the room just as she was taking the sausage out of the pan. "Good morning!" His cheerful smile included them both. "Do I smell coffee?" Without waiting for an answer, he took a mug from the counter and filled it, pouring a mug for each of them as he did so.

Elizabeth could feel him watching her as she stirred the beaten eggs in the sizzling sausage drippings. "Rosie, would you put forks and napkins on the table? And juice?"

While Rosemary was out of the room, Elizabeth turned to look at Phillip, a thing she'd dared not do under her daughter's acute eye. They were standing only a few feet apart: he with his coffee mug in one hand, she with a spatula. All the words that had not yet been said seemed to travel unspoken between them, binding them together. *Is this the communion of souls I've read about?* His soft brown eyes were locked with hers and a look of deep tenderness mixed with *Could it be sadness?* was on his face.

Her daughter seemed oblivious to the seething, middle-aged emotions that roiled the very air around the table. Rosemary ate her breakfast and chatted amiably with Phillip, asking about the time he had served with Sam Goodweather in the navy.

"Pa never talked much about it; of course, he was really ambivalent about the whole Vietnam era. It seemed to me that he felt…tainted by having been in the military at that time. Once he told me that he sometimes wished he'd gone to Canada and avoided serving in a war he had grown to be ashamed of."

Phillip looked unhappy but said only that Sam had nothing to be ashamed of. "None of us knew when we signed up how things would go. My dad was in the big one, WW Two, and I grew up feeling proud of the fact that he had fought the bad guys. Things were more black and white back then—a clearer line between good and evil. Now..."

He's going to run his hand over his head, thought Elizabeth, anticipating the familiar gesture that meant Hawkins was perturbed in some way.

He ran his hand over his head, as if polishing his shiny balding pate. "Now it's really screwed up—young men and women dying in Iraq for what turns out to be 'faulty intelligence.' The country we were going to turn into a democracy slipping closer and closer toward anarchy... innocent civilians dying right and left... the United States, *my* country, sponsoring and justifying torture. And it's all run by guys who've always managed to avoid putting their own asses in harm's way, who have no idea—"

He caught himself and shrugged. "Sorry, Rosemary. You punched the wrong button. Let's just say I love my country but I'm not so happy with the way it's being run just now. Why don't you tell me about the courses you're teaching?"

"Miss Birdie, did you notice any strange cars coming and going yesterday? I wondered because—"

"Nary a one, Lizzie Beth. 'Course, I was gone from home what you might call the better part of the day. Me and Dor'thy went up to her brother's place to git us some apples to can. I aim to fix me some dried apples too. Git you'ns a chair in here by the stove, Lizzie Beth. Hit's turned off right cool this mornin'. Reckon they'll be givin' frost afore long."

Elizabeth, Rosemary, and Phillip had spent the morning dealing with the chaos left behind by the unknown intruder. The books that had been flung to the floor were now stacked in neat, mostly alphabetical piles to await a thorough vacuuming. "They needed it, anyway," Elizabeth had declared. "But not now—it'll take most of a day. I'll do it later in the week." Once the rest of the house had been restored to livability, Rosemary had left to meet Jared and have lunch with him before visiting his one-time stepmother.

After a quick sandwich, Elizabeth and Phillip had gone to see Miss Birdie. Elizabeth's little neighbor was a one-woman traffic monitor for Ridley Branch, almost always aware of any strange vehicles that passed on the seldom-traveled country road. And it was just possible that she had seen Maitland's vehicle.

"I heared as someone had broke into yore place. I was talkin' this mornin' to Bernice and she said her boy had heard it on the scanner. Said the high sheriff was up yore way last night." Birdie's bright eyes darted to Phillip. "Hit's a good thing Lizzie Beth's got her a man to stay there, what with Ben off in Florida. I know you'll take good care of my Lizzie Beth, now, won't you?"

"Yes, ma'am." Phillip seemed to be blushing but he returned Miss Birdie's gaze without wavering. "I mean to do that very thing."

Elizabeth wondered if the other surprising event of the previous night was obvious to Miss Birdie. Her neighbor's sharp eyes and keen intuition were uncanny at times. *Or maybe Bernice's boy heard it on the scanner. God knows, very little escapes my neighbors.*

Miss Birdie was nodding in approval. "Now, that's what I told Dor'thy. When she heared that Ben had gone to Florida to see his mama, Dor'thy took to worryin' 'bout Lizzie Beth way up there and all alone.

"'They's so many new folks comin' into the county and all and you don't know nothin' about them,' she says. 'Shoot, Dor'thy,' I tole her, 'Lizzie Beth's got her a gun and I know she ain't afraid to use it. What's more, she's got her a feller. I reckon he'll see she ain't too lonely.'"

Miss Birdie's eyes twinkled at Phillip. "Why, I believe—"

"How *is* Dorothy, Miss Birdie?" Elizabeth broke in, desperate to change the subject. "I haven't seen her car here in a while. Is she looking after someone again?"

Miss Birdie's cousin Dorothy had spent much of her life as an aide in nursing homes and, though she was now well into her seventies and retired, she continued to "see about" any of her ailing, elderly friends and relations who were in need of an energetic and bustling helper.

"Ay law, Dor'thy's got her hands full now and that's the truth. She's taken on her sister's grandboy. He's right much of a handful, but I reckon Dor'thy can tame him."

Delighted to be off the subject of Phillip, Elizabeth prompted Miss Birdie to continue. "I'm sure Dorothy can handle anything. Where're the little boy's folks?"

Birdie shook her head. "Oh, hit's a sad tale. Why hit's so awful, it could make a story for the daytime tee-vee, and that's the truth. His mama's at death's door and I don't believe she ever said who the boy's daddy is—if she knew. Prin's been a wild thing all her life, layin' up with first one good-fer-nothin' and then another. And when Prin got bad sick and had to be took to the hospital, the pore little feller was left with that rough ol' rascal she's livin' with now—same one as once was married to her own sister. Now, I don't think that's right, do you?"

Elizabeth could only nod mutely as Birdie continued her story. "So Mag Ridder, what's Dor'thy's little sister, asked Dor'thy to take the boy and raise him up right. Her and Dor'thy both grew up there in that house where Morris Roberts and his family live now. But then Mag took up with them Ridders—they still lived way up there in the holler back then—and next thing you know, she's married Royal Ridder—a no-count feller—and her and Dor'thy fell out."

Bewildered at the twists and turns of this tale, which seemed likely to rival a biblical account in the telling of generations, Elizabeth grasped at the name snagged in the stream of remembrances. "Did you say *Ridder,* Miss Birdie? Is that the name of the little boy Dorothy's taking care of?"

"Why, yes it is. Now, Dor'thy's sister Magdalene married Royal Ridder, who was the last of the family to live up there where them Mullinses bought."

Elizabeth and Phillip sat transfixed as Birdie traced the Ridder family's gradual descent from prosperous farmers into poverty and crime. Royal and Magdalene Ridder had produced numerous children, among them Princess and her older sister, Precious.

"Now, just like her mama, Precious married a wild feller who was bad to drink and quarrel, but then they had the prettiest little yaller-haired girl, called Tamra. Law, she looked just like an angel. They all fairly worshipped that child—even her daddy, big ol' feller, and rough as a cob. He got him a job on a road crew and was doing good. Why, he even come to church a time or two. Then what happens but Precious ups and runs off with some feller from away."

Miss Birdie's face grew troubled. "I never would of thought it of Precious. She was the smartest one of them Ridder children. Why, she'd finished high school and was takin' courses to be a nurse. But one day she just packed up her bags and left a note on the kitchen table sayin' she's going off with someone as can give her the kind of life she wants.

"It was a heavy blow to Bib, that was the feller's name, but he carried on just the same as usual. Told little Tamra her mama'd be back soon. And he was right—not a week later, Precious must of come for Tamra, for Bib come home to find another note. This un's from Tamra, saying as how she's goin' to be with her mama.

"Well, sir, Bib read that note and did he ever cut a shine! He got knee-walkin' drunk and set out in his truck to look for Precious and his little girl. He didn't get far before the law stopped him, and then he set to on that trooper and the trooper like to died. Bib got sent to prison, and not a word has Mag heard from Precious in all that time. Presh hadn't never even sent her mama a picture of the little girl—and I tell you what's the truth, it like to broke poor Mag's heart. And now, that sorry Bib is out of prison and he's taken up with Presh's little sister, Princess. I wouldn't be a bit surprised iffen he didn't have something to do with why Prin's in the hospital now. Ain't no wonder Mag wants Dor'thy to take on little Cal—git him away from that ol' Bib."

17.

OLD FRIENDS

Saturday, October 15 and Sunday, October 16

"She's so *firm* … really straight-talking. … She put her finger right on what I need to do. Of course, some of what she says is painful: she doesn't have time to beat around the bush. And you have to be strictly open and honest with her … she comes down hard on you if you try to evade her questions, but, believe me, it was an *amazing* experience. … What? … Well, of *course* it was expensive; she mainly does big workshops. … Oh, there must have been several hundred people at the one I went to last year. … No, she and her daughter also do intensives limited to twenty or twenty-five. Those are great—I did one in April and another in July. … I *know* I told you about that one. … Perilous Patterns? … You know, Lydia, I think *you'd* benefit from the PP intensive; it's all about how we make the same stupid mistakes over and over. … *No,* I'm not calling you stupid … you told me yourself you keep marrying the same needy, passive-aggressive types. …"

The emerald green door with the forbidding notice NO ENTRANCE / ONE-ON-ONE IN PROGRESS had opened and shut firmly behind a large woman in a long dark red skirt and jacket. The woman, intent on sharing her experience with a friend, took no notice of Rosemary and Jared sitting on the bench next to the door, but floated away from them, cell phone still to her ear. Wild gray ringlets, springing Medusa-like from her head, quivered as she talked to her unseen friend and waved an enthusiastic arm.

"No, I'm sure that Rudolph—excuse me, *Randolph*—is different.... Anyway, the intensives were so helpful to *me* that I decided to sign up for a one-on-one with Trish.... Yes, she *told* me to call her Trish.... *Trish* said she saves a few days a month for these one-on-one sessions... they drain her energy far more than the group sessions, so she has to limit them. But she knows that there are some who will benefit so much *more* from the intrapersonal time that she feels it's part of her *calling*....

"Well, we focused on my addictive behaviors... Trish says I won't make any more progress till I can detach myself from my need for constant approval and reinforcement.... Don't you think I sound more self-assured already?"

Rosemary and Jared watched with keen interest as the woman retreated down the mini-mall's corridor, still talking and still waving her free arm.

Jared glanced at his watch. "Five more minutes till our appointment. I'm sorry I hurried us through lunch, but when I spoke to the secretary she made a big deal of saying that Patricia—excuse me, *Trish*—is a very busy woman who *requires* punctuality." He looked around at the drab surroundings and sniffed. "You'd think that at least they'd have a waiting room where we could sit."

"*Jared!*" The vibrant green door swung open again and a petite blonde in immaculate white wool trousers and a creamy cashmere pullover stood framed in the doorway, both hands extended. "And little Rosie! Please, come in."

"Well, she wasn't at all the way I remembered her. And there was this weird kind of tension going on between her and Jared. We didn't stay long because she had to catch a plane, but she said that she'd be back Wednesday."

Sunday morning had come and, except for the stacks of books still arrayed at the end of the living room, it was almost as if the break-in had never happened. Almost.

Rosemary looked across the table at her mother. And Phillip. *Speaking of a weird kind of tension. But this is a different kind... more like a private joke between the two of them.*

Her mother looked up from her bowl of fruit and yoghurt. "So where did you and Jared end up going for dinner? I got your message that you wouldn't be home till late, so we—so I didn't wait up."

Phillip was sipping his coffee and staring out at the birdfeeder where blue jays and cardinals, towhees and mourning doves jockeyed busily for position. A faint smile played at the corners of his mouth but he said nothing.

"Jared had tickets to a Keb' Mo' concert, so we ate at that new place just across from the theater. But I wanted to tell you about Patricia—Trish. She's so *different* now. She used to be such a... such a..."

"Ditz? Is that the word you're looking for?" Her mother's tone was innocent.

Rosemary considered. Phillip had abandoned his birdwatching and was studying *her* now. It seemed strange to see him there, sitting at the end of the table where Pa had always sat. Strange, but okay too. She smiled at him.

"I guess 'ditz' is the word. Or 'airhead.' Back then, Phillip, she was like a life-sized Barbie doll. You know, all make up and wearing tight clothes and flashy colors. And she didn't seem particularly intelligent or educated. But now she's a vision of understated elegance in shades of white—spouting polysyllabic psychological jargon."

She turned to her mother, who was basking in the morning sun like a contented cat, her eyes half-closed. "Mum, I really would like for you to go back with me to talk to her. To Trish, I'm still just little Rosie. It felt like she was humoring me but not actually answering my questions. Anyway, next week is Fall Break. I have classes on Monday and Tuesday, but I'll be able to come back Wednesday. Trish said she would have time on Thursday to talk. It's apparently the only so-called 'free' day she has for the next month."

Her mother did not respond but continued her inward reverie, an annoying little smile flickering on her lips.

"Mum," Rosemary raised her voice. "Will you plan on doing that with me next Thursday?"

"Sure, sweetie," Elizabeth replied in an absent tone. "Next Thursday." Her blue eyes were open wide now but they were distant and she was smiling broadly.

Feeling vaguely annoyed at her mother's lack of interest, Rosemary rose. The scrape of the chair on the tile floor seemed to awaken the daydreaming Elizabeth from her private musing.

"Wait a minute, Rosie. You haven't told us what Patricia—excuse me, *Trish*—said. How does she feel about your digging into all these old memories? It sounds as if she's come to terms with the past and moved on." Her mother's eyes twinkled. "God, now I'm talking like a soap opera. But really, how did she seem?" Mum's eyes were fixed on her now and she was at last paying attention. Rosemary sat back down.

"It was a little odd. She acted like she was really glad to see me…and Jared too. You know, Jared told me he hadn't seen her since they left Mullmore. That was when Moon's drinking really got out of hand. Trish filed for separation and Jared went back to his mother. He didn't even see his father for years. It wasn't till Jared was through law school and on his own that Moon got in touch. He was sober and doing the twelve-step bit. Moon asked Jared's forgiveness for all the things he'd done or not done when he was drinking…and he offered Jared a job in Asheville as administrator of the Redemption Walk Foundation."

"And what happened to change Patricia into Trish Trantham?" Elizabeth leaned on her elbows, waiting eagerly for the rest of the story.

Rosemary smiled. *That's better. Now she's back with me.* "Evidently she had some sort of epiphany when Krystalle refused to do any more beauty pageants. All that energy she'd used as a pageant mom had to go somewhere. So she enrolled in college and ended up with a master's in Psychology. She said something about helping troubled people as a memorial to Maythorn."

"But how did she end up with the bloody *empire* she's got? Daily radio show, conference centers all over the place—the woman's a household *word*, for god's sake. She's just a step or so beneath Billy Graham or the Pope for a lot of people. 'Trish Trantham says…' You hear it all the time. And it's *Patricia!*" Elizabeth made a face. "I can't quite get my head around that."

"Trish said that the tragedy had taught her a lot and

that she had chosen to grow from the experience rather than be buried by it. Of course, Jared told me later that Trish received a huge settlement when she and Moon parted ways; maybe that money made things easier as she expanded her business. But you know, Mum, it really is her personality—the self-assuredness, the quick, decisive, seemingly common-sense answers. All that's what makes her so popular as an advice guru. *You* know; you've heard her on the radio. Everyone has."

"Not me." Phillip stood, picking up his plate and coffee cup. "She sounds like quite a go-getter, though." His eyes lingered on Elizabeth, who smiled up at him—a long, sweet, lazy smile that Rosemary didn't remember ever seeing on her mother's face.

Rosemary studied Phillip as he picked up the rest of the breakfast dishes. *Not nearly as tall or handsome as Pa, but he looks . . . trustworthy. I would have thought he was Italian or something ethnic like that, he's so dark. But "Hawkins" is an English name. Not that it matters: Mum likes him, and that's what counts. And thank god he's going to be around, at least till they get that horrible guy who tore up the house.*

A thought struck her. "Phillip, do you think they'll arrest him, that Bib What's-his-name? I mean, you can't stay here forever—" She broke off, seeing an amused look pass between her mother and the burly ex-detective.

"I mean, I know you have classes to teach. Is Mum going to be safe here during the day?" Her mother and Phillip both looked as if they were suppressing a good deal of inner mirth. *I feel like a kid trying to figure out what the grown-ups are doing,* Rosemary thought with exasperation.

"It's going to be all right, Rosemary." The steadiness and certainty in Phillip's voice were a welcome balm. *A very nice guy to have around,* she decided.

He went on. "Sheriff Blaine will have a deputy checking by when I can't be here. And with Julio and Homero down at the lower place—I've talked to them about keeping their eyes open—I don't think you need to worry." He carried the stack of dirty dishes to the kitchen and she could hear the water running.

Her mother yawned, looking uncharacteristically relaxed. Usually Mum had so many chores to attend to that she didn't linger long at the breakfast table. It was nice to see her be a little lazy for once.

"What do you need to do today, Rosie? Do you feel like you're getting any closer to ... to whatever it is?"

Mum was looking at her with that grown-up face again. Rosemary felt a twinge of annoyance. *Is she humoring me? Probably. Maybe this is all a wild-goose chase. But I had a thought a minute ago ... what was it? I felt like a kid trying to figure out what the grown-ups are doing. Like those notebooks Maythorn and I used to keep.*

Realizing that her mother was still waiting for an answer, Rosemary jumped up from her chair and gave Elizabeth a quick hug. "Am I getting closer? Mum, I really think I am. I just remembered something that might be huge! I need to find my secret spy notebooks."

They left Rosemary digging deep into the cubbyholes of her childhood room. Several old trunks and ancient family suitcases had been appropriated by the girls as storage receptacles for outgrown toys, costumes, dolls, books, and stuffed animals—outgrown but too dear to discard or give away. Elizabeth had watched, amused, as Rosemary turned out the contents of the first suitcase: a pink-and-purple stuffed dragon; a canvas bag of smooth river rocks; a flat box that housed a number of small seashells, each one carefully glued down and labeled; a dirty and much-mended pair of tan faux-suede breeches with fringe down the seams, and a matching shirt—an outfit Elizabeth had sewn for Rosie's ninth birthday.

Along with an identical set for Maythorn. That weird fabric was a bitch to work with too. Elizabeth ran her hand over the smooth fabric, noting the wear to the seat of the pants and the incipient holes in both knees.

Something nudged her memory. *And didn't I have to put Maythorn's pants back together after her little sister cut them up with scissors? But it was worth it—they loved these outfits.*

"Look at this! I'd forgotten all about my horse collection." Rosemary had a cardboard shoe box open on the floor beside her. One by one she was pulling out little bundles of what looked suspiciously like toilet tissue. She began to unwind the yellowing wrappings.

"It's Fireboy!" A small, improbably bright red plastic horse was revealed and set upright on the floor. Eagerly, Rosemary began to unwrap the next bundle. It turned out to be an identical horse, but this one pure white.

"Snow Stepper!" Rosemary proclaimed, and reached into the shoe box.

Elizabeth smiled fondly. "Listen, sweetie, Phillip has to go back to his house to pick up some stuff if he's going to be staying here for a while . . . till they arrest that guy. I'm going to take him down to his car, okay?"

If Rosie's colleagues in the English Department could see her now, surrounded by plastic horses. But maybe this is all part of what she needs to do to bring back the other memories she's so sure are there. I know that most of these things got put away after Maythorn disappeared. It was all stuff they'd both played with, and it was just too painful for Rosie to deal with.

Rosemary looked up and a smile of pure happiness illuminated her face. "Okay, Mum. I'm just going to dig through all this stuff. But I'm going to have to take my time. It's like ... like finding old friends I'd forgotten."

Elizabeth went carefully down the steep stairs. Behind her she heard Rosemary's delighted crow: "Silver Star! Midnight!"

CLETUS

Spring 1986

HEY, ROSEBUD, GET *your shoes on. We're going to make a quick trip into Ransom. Mum and Laurie aren't back yet and I've got to take that flat tire in to Jim Hinkley.*

Rosie lay on her stomach, arranging the colorful array of plastic horses she had spread out on the living room rug. Some of Laurel's Legos had been pressed into service as a makeshift corral and throw pillows from the sofa formed a mountain range. Behind the corral's impenetrable barriers, three mares—Blue Moon, Misty, and Seafoam—moved restlessly back and forth, looking for a way out. The cruel rustlers who had captured them were all asleep, dead to the world after drinking a bottle of whisky apiece, and the fearless stallion Fireboy was leading the rest of the wild horse herd over the mountains in a bold attempt to crash through the walls and rescue—

Did you hear me, Rosemary? Pa's big boots were right beside her and he sounded impatient. *Get your shoes on right now. Just leave all that stuff,* he said, as Fireboy came galloping down the mountain.

Without waiting for her answer, Pa walked toward the door. Quickly Rosemary breached the corral walls and scooped up the three captive mares. Scrambling to her feet, she put them and their rescuer, Fireboy, on the far side of the throw pillows, safe from the sleeping rustlers. *There,* she whispered. *Now if they wake up before I get back, you'll be safe.*

Her sneakers were on the front porch and she hastily shoved her feet into them and hurried down the steps to where Pa was waiting by his truck. A thought struck her.

Pa, have you seen Dinah? She was out all night and I haven't seen her once this morning.

Pa heaved the flat tire into the back of the truck. *Don't worry, baby; she'll be back. Hounds just like to run in the woods. Remember, we heard her barking so much last night, like she had something treed? She's probably basking in the sun somewhere, catching up on all the sleep she missed.* He pulled open the door. *Hop in. This won't take long. And your pup'll probably be here waiting for you when we get back.*

As they drove down Ridley Branch, Rosemary kept a close watch for Dinah. She didn't think that the young hound ever went far from home, but you never knew. Only last week something terrible and unexplained had happened to Maythorn's pet cockatiel. Most likely a silly accident, Mrs. Barbie had said, but Rosie wasn't sure.

There's Miss Birdie and Luther out hoeing their potatoes. Pa tapped the horn and waved at the plump little woman and lean old man, working in their garden patch just the other side of the branch. *Wonder where Cletus is? He must be off on one of his hunting trips, roaming the woods like Dinah.*

Miss Birdie says "taters," not "potatoes." Rosemary stuck her arm out the window and waved too. *And she says "maters" and "baccer" and—*

It's kind of a shortcut, Rosie. Just like people say "fridge" for "refrigerator" or "TV" instead of "television" or—

Are we ever going to get a TV? She knew what the answer was, but had to ask, anyway.

I don't think so, Rosebud. Pa reached across and tickled her knee. *There's not that much on that's worth watching, and besides, it might take away from your reading time.*

He always said this. And it wasn't worth arguing—from the little TV she'd ever watched, either at Maythorn's house or when they'd lived in Florida and went to dinner at her Grammer Grey's condo, she knew that it was mostly stupid and sometimes gross. And the pictures were never as good as the ones in her head.

Look up there, Rosie! I hope your mum sees this when she comes back this way. She'll love it!

What is it? Is it a carnival or something? Can we stop? In the side yard of a small green house overlooking the road, bright colors of every description flapped and danced in the wind. Pa slowed the truck, and Rosemary realized, with some disappointment, that it was just a bunch of quilts, hanging from clotheslines stretched between big trees. A slender woman in a blue housedress was adding yet another dazzling rectangle to the last empty space. Pink stars spun on a green background as the breeze lifted the quilt. The woman stepped back as if to admire the sight, then, catching sight of their truck, she raised her hand in a friendly wave.

They left the tire at Jim Hinkley's filling station, and while Jim fixed the tire, Pa took her to the Burger Doodle for lunch. That wasn't its real name, just what Mum and Pa called it. It was right next to the laundromat and Mum always made a face when Rosie and Laurie wanted to eat lunch there.

Can I have a chili dog? Mum was really picky about what food she would let them get when they ate out and Pa some-

times was the same. But today he just said, Sure, whatever you want. He paid for their order and handed her the slip of paper with their number on it.

When they call twenty-six, can you go get the tray? I'll be right outside at the payphone. He glanced at his watch. I've got to go make a call.

She felt very grown up, sitting alone in the orange booth, and when the lady behind the counter, the one with the net squshing her hair down, called out, Twenty-six! Rosemary went and got the tray and carried it very carefully back to their table. Through the window she could see Pa at the payphone, dialing a number.

The chili dog was delicious—just as she'd imagined it would be. Foot-long, the menu had said, and it was—so long that both ends hung off the paper plate. And so much chili that it spilled out of the big soft bun and left an orange stain on the plate. It was messy to eat and Rosemary pulled napkins one after another from the little black dispenser on the table to wipe her face and fingers.

She had eaten almost all of the chili dog but still Pa hadn't come to get the BLT sitting forlornly across from her. Rosemary drank the last of her Dr Pepper (another rare treat), wiped her fingers once again, and slid out of the booth.

Pa had his back to her as she came out of the door of the Burger Doodle. The phone was to his ear and he was talking real low. No, she doesn't know anything about it, he was saying. But I need to see you . . . soon.

It was almost two o'clock when they got back home. Mum and Laurie were still gone—doctor appointments took a long time, Pa said, even when it was just a checkup. Dinah wasn't there either. Rosemary looked at the bowl of dry dog food they'd put on the porch last night, but it was still full and the chunks of canned dog food sitting on the top were dry and dark.

You go on back to your horses, Rosebud, Pa said. I've got to get started on the mowing. Mum and Laurie'll be back soon.

Three o'clock and still no Mum and Laurie. No Dinah either. Pa was down near the barn now, following the big noisy mower in a neat pattern. The rich smell of freshly cut grass filled the air.

Rosemary went out to the porch. She tried to imitate Pa's shrill whistle, but gave up after a few sputtering attempts. Diii-nah, she called. Diii-nah! The lawn mower, though at a distance, was still loud and drowned out her voice. I have to look for her, she decided. I'll start up in the woods where Dinah was barking last night.

Up the old logging road above the house, climbing steadily higher, stopping now and then to call Dinah's name, Rosemary went. The mower was still growling in the distance and Mum's jeep had not yet returned. Finally Rosemary stopped to rest, feeling tired, and a little sick at her stomach. A series of burps reminded her unpleasantly of the chili dog.

She had stopped in a little clearing where the sun shone warmly down, just the kind of place where Pa had said Dinah might be sleeping. Rosemary found a flattish spot and sat down with her back to a big rock. She remembered to look for snakes first, just like Pa and Mum always told her, then she leaned back and closed her eyes.

She awoke feeling cold. The sun had moved and she was in the shade now. And squatting beside her was Cletus. And Dinah!

A piece of baling twine was threaded through her collar and the other end was in Cletus's hand. Dinah's head was drooping as if she was very tired.

Cletus stared at Rosemary with a strange look. I wondered when you was goin to wake up, he said. I'm fixin' to cook me some dinner. You kin have some too. He motioned to a little fire burning in a circle of rocks just a few feet away. A shotgun, its wooden stock polished with long use, leaned against a tree.

Cletus's eyes never left her face. They were red, as if he hadn't slept, and there was black stubble all over his chin. I catch all kinds of things and cook 'em fer my dinner.

Rosemary felt a little uneasy, as she often did, around this man who talked like a little boy. Slowly, she began to stand. Cletus, let me have Dinah. I need to take her home for dinner.

Cletus made a funny hiccuping kind of sound and she realized that he was laughing.

Dinah's dinner, Dinah's dinner, Dinah's dinner, he chanted, rocking his head from side to side. Then, still staring at Rosemary, he reached into the knapsack that lay on the ground beside him and pulled out a limp gray body. With his other hand he took a jackknife from the bib pocket of his overalls, snapped it open, and made few deft cuts on the little carcass. Wiping the blade on his leg, he closed the knife and returned it to his pocket.

Looky here! Cletus held the dead squirrel up by its bushy tail and inserted a finger into one of the cuts he had just made. I'm undressing him. He gave a tug and with a crackling sound the skin began to separate from the body. Rosemary watched in shocked disbelief as Cletus peeled the skin away, as easily as she pulled off her socks.

In a few seconds, Cletus was holding a raw red horror by its bushy tail. He grinned at her and said, I'll fix you some dinner.

With a sudden heave, Rosemary rid herself of the partially digested chili dog. Wiping her mouth on her sleeve, she snatched the baling-twine leash and ran down the logging road for home, hauling the startled Dinah behind her.

She left the weary Dinah on the porch, gobbling down a long overdue bowl of dog chow, and crept quietly into the house to rinse out her mouth. The jeep was back and Mum was probably wondering where she was. And probably she was going to get in trouble for going off and not telling Pa.

I'm going to get it now, she whispered. Maythorn always said that when she was late going home. Rosemary wondered what it was.

Laurie was asleep on the sofa in the living room with one of Rosemary's horses clutched in her hand. From Pa and Mum's room came the sound of low voices. And then the sound of Mum crying.

18.

REVELATION INTERRUPTUS

Sunday, October 16

Hand in hand, Elizabeth and Phillip strolled down the leaf-strewn driveway, toward the little pond just beyond the herb field. The three dogs trotted behind them and the sweet-sad lilt of mariachi music floated across the field from the little rent house shared by Julio and Homero. Above, the sky was very blue.

She looked at Phillip, who, as usual, seemed perfectly happy and at home. He smiled at her and squeezed her hand. They walked without speaking, as if neither wanted to break the spell. *If nothing is said, nothing will change,* she thought. *It will always be a beautiful fall day, clear and mild, with music in the air and this amazing, unlooked for, deep joy welling in my heart.*

Down the rock steps and across the wooden foot-bridge that spanned the shallow branch. The pond lay bounded on one side by the herb field and on the other by a pasture. A rustic pavilion, almost hidden by the coils of a rampant wisteria, jutted out over the still water, and two dark-stained Adirondack chairs awaited them there.

Elizabeth took down the metal can of fish food that

hung from the rafters of the little structure, away from the clever paws of marauding raccoons. She tossed a handful of the pellets onto the still surface of the pond and waited. Phillip stood at her side, peering into the green depths.

They came slowly at first: one whiskered patriarch rose to engulf a little clump of the floating pellets, then a second and a third. Sleek, sharklike bodies, dark shadows in the water, made a shocking contrast to the pale gape of their wide mouths as they swept the water's surface, passing to and fro and skimming up the tiny morsels. Elizabeth tossed more of the food as three and then four more of the giant catfish appeared, swirling gracefully about in a harmless feeding frenzy.

When the last crumbs had disappeared, Phillip turned to her, taking both of her hands in his. She faced him squarely, returning his questioning gaze with a smile that, she felt, grew from the very center of her being.

"Well, Ms. Goodweather."

"Well, Mr. Hawkins."

Phillip pulled her to him and kissed her. Then, reluctantly pulling away, he said, "I think we need to talk."

"If you say so." Elizabeth nodded to the chairs, set companionably side by side. She sank into the nearer one and propped her feet on the bench that ran around the open sides of the little pavilion. Phillip took the other chair, but instead of settling himself comfortably, he sat on the edge of the seat and ran his hand over his head.

A sudden chill of misgiving swept through Elizabeth. *Here I've been floating along in a dream of never-ending bliss, like a bloody character in a feminine hygiene commercial running through a meadow of wildflowers, and he's about to tell me . . . what? . . . I don't know . . . that he's not really divorced . . .*

that he was too polite to say no when I pulled him into my bed . . . that he's really looking for someone much younger and cuter . . . that the past two nights really didn't mean anything.

He seemed to read the apprehension in her eyes and reached again for her hand. "Elizabeth . . ." His grip was strong and he squeezed her fingers as if hoping to communicate his feelings without words. "I want you to know . . ."

Up came the free hand to his head, but he caught himself and lowered it. He cleared his throat. "Elizabeth, I'm not good at the talking part of all this . . . but I want to say a couple of things. I should have before this but . . . first of all, I'm glad you had that nightmare. The past two nights have been like . . . like coming home to the place I'd been trying to find all my life."

A surge of joy and relief swept over her. She started to speak but he shook his head. "Only, I feel like maybe there were some things I should have told you before we . . . before I . . ."

He was still clasping her hand tightly and his eyes were fixed on her in some unspoken question. She leaned toward him.

"Phillip, you don't need to tell me anything. *I'm* the forward huzzy who dragged you into her bed. And I enjoyed every bit of it and I'm not sorry and you don't owe me any explanations or anything. We already established that we were both disease-free, and I'm obviously not going to get pregnant, and I'm not looking for any kind of—" *You're babbling, Elizabeth,* her inner censor warned her.

Phillip put a gentle finger to her lips. "Elizabeth, sweetheart, please be quiet and let me talk. I'm trying to be serious here—I *am* serious, dammit. This is important. I want there to be more between us than just—"

"Do you?" She felt a sudden cautious drawing-back forming in her mind, a reluctance to formalize this new step with words. *Are you sure about this man? Can you ever be sure about anyone?* "Do you really?"

The brown eyes never wavered. "You bet I do. Elizabeth, we've known each other for over a year now and we've been through some rough experiences together. I think I knew almost from the first that I'd like to spend the rest of my life with you. But first, there're some things about the past—about *my* past—that I need to tell you. I—"

"Please . . . Really, Phillip, I don't care about your past! I know you've been divorced for years. I assume there've been other women and all that, but what can it have to do with us, with now?"

Suddenly the dogs, who had been sprawled out on the grass absorbing the welcome rays of the autumn sun, sprang up and pattered across the footbridge to the road that ran alongside the stream. A thin boy, in immaculate, new blue jeans and a crisp white shirt, was rounding the bend. At the sight of the three dogs racing toward him, he dropped to one knee. He almost disappeared in a wagging swirl of black and brown as shaggy Ursa rubbed herself against his chest, James leapt to lick his face, and even the usually aloof Molly wedged her elegant head under his arm to get his attention.

A little way behind the boy came two elderly women, one with a tall walking stick, the other holding her frailer companion's elbow.

With a last squeeze of Phillip's hand, Elizabeth smiled ruefully and stood. *So much for romantic solitude!*

"Phillip, it's Miss Birdie and Dorothy. And that boy...
that's Calven."

He watched as Elizabeth hurried to meet the two women
and the boy. When Miss Birdie had told them yesterday
that her cousin Dorothy was taking care of Calven
Ridder, he had passed on the information to the sheriff,
who had been conducting a fruitless search for the missing boy. Mackenzie Blaine had then confirmed that the
boy's mother, still in critical condition at the hospital,
had expressed her wish that the boy be kept away from
Bib.

*And here they all are. And I still haven't come clean with
Elizabeth. The longer I wait, the harder it's going to be for her to
understand—if she will understand. Oh, goddammit all to hell! I
wish that there didn't have to be all this back story. I wish that it
had been me, not Sam, reaching for the copy of* Walden *in that
used bookstore way back then.*

He hauled himself to his feet, feeling obscurely guilty
at that last thought, and sauntered out toward Calven
and the dogs, who were thundering across the foot-
bridge. Elizabeth and the other woman were helping
Miss Birdie negotiate the rock steps. Elizabeth flashed
him a quick smile, then returned her attention to her little neighbor.

Calven stopped short at the sight of Phillip and
looked hesitantly back at his aunt. Phillip smiled and
put out his hand. "Howdy, son. You must be Calven. My
name's Phillip. I'm a friend of Miz Goodweather's."

The boy stood there, looking indecisively at the outstretched hand. Dorothy called out, "Calven Ridder, you
mind your manners and shake Mr. Hawkins's hand. He's
a policeman and he won't put up with unmannerly little

boys. And would you look at the grass stains on your nice Sunday shirt! Now, Birdie, you got to watch this last step here; I don't want you to take a tumble."

The little group of women moved slowly across the bridge and even more slowly the boy raised his hand. He did not meet Phillip's gaze and the dirty little hand made no response to Phillip's gentle clasp.

"Your aunt got that wrong, Calven—I'm not a policeman anymore. I'm a teacher now. You want to throw some horseshoes?"

The boy looked over at the horseshoe pits near the fence. Brightly painted horseshoes hung over one of the fence planks: blue, yellow, red, and white. He considered a moment, then a smile of great sweetness lit up his face. "I git the red ones!"

While Calven took some practice tosses, Phillip went docilely to pay his respects to Miss Birdie and be introduced to Dorothy. The two older women were ensconced in the Adirondack chairs and Elizabeth was perched on the bench, listening as Dorothy held forth.

"...and when we got to the church house, there's a piece of paper tacked up saying as how Preacher's car's broke down and mornin' meetin's gone to be delayed one hour and a half. And I says to Birdie, 'Birdie, we cain't just set here a-suckin' our thumbs; let's take us a walk down the road.' And when we got so far as you unses mailbox, Calven there, he takes a notion he wants to go look at your fishpond. That boy's got more energy than a feist pup and that's the truth."

Phillip stepped into the little pavilion and three faces swiveled to look at him. Dorothy's sharp eyes looked him up and down in critical assessment, like a horse trader surveying an unpromising nag.

"Mornin', Miss Birdie. Good to see you again." He bobbed his head at Dorothy, whose mouth was set in an uncompromising line. "Mornin', ma'am. You must be Miss Birdie's cousin Dorothy. Elizabeth's told me about you. I'm Phillip Lee Hawkins." He smiled in what he hoped was an ingratiating manner. "I'm sure glad you're able to take that boy in—he needs a good home."

"Birdie told me you was Omie Caldwell's nephew. Now, I knowed your mama, back this many a year. We was in nurse's aid training together, but then she went on to nursing school. Met that feller from away and they moved off to the coast." The sparkling eyes studied him. "You do favor her right much, now I come to study you— dark complected and that big nose. Her and Omie always did claim a Cherokee grandmother. How's Waneeta doin' these days?"

"Well, ma'am, I'm sorry to have to tell you, but my mama passed away back in '82." Phillip moved to sit beside Elizabeth.

Dorothy pursed her lips. "Now, I hate that. But it don't surprise me none. Some folks just don't do no good a-tall when they leave these mountains. You look right healthy, though. Reckon you could take on that mean old Bib, was he to come around again, aggravating Lizzie Beth."

Miss Birdie leaned forward and put a gnarled hand on his arm. "I'm proud you're here. I worry about Lizzie Beth something awful. Why, Dor'thy tells me they say that Bib—"

"Law me, yes!" Dorothy broke in. "They say he got drunk as an owl and was goin' on to anyone who'd listen about how new people had took what was his and how he was goin' to make 'em pay. It was down there at the river, where a bunch of them rough old fellers get together and drink beer. And the trash they leave behind them...They say as he was talkin' plumb wild and wavin' round a pistol. Then he climbed in his pickup and off he went. Back on Friday night, it was. And ain't nobody seen him since."

19.

Home Defense

Sunday, October 16

"Elizabeth, I'm serious. You need to do this. Like Rosemary said, I can't be here all the time. And I'd feel a lot better if you had some training." Phillip studied Elizabeth's face, hoping for some hint of acquiescence.

There had been time for four rounds of horseshoes before Dorothy and Miss Birdie summoned Calven for the walk back to the little church. Dorothy was still fussing and brushing at Calven's clothes as the trio disappeared around the bend in the road. Phillip could hear her scolding voice—"have to double-bleach that shirt, for sure"—as he and Elizabeth walked back to his car, holding hands. The mariachi music from the rental house had given way to the thump of some sort of Hispanic hip-hop.

"What do you think, Elizabeth? Can I sign you up?"

"I've got Sam's gun. And I do know how to use it." At her smile, little rays gathered at the corners of her eyes. "Why do I need to take a class?"

"When's the last time you actually fired that gun? And where do you keep it?"

She frowned. "It's in a closet in my bedroom...but I can't remember the last time I fired it. A while ago, I guess."

"Not good enough. If you're in danger, you need to be really comfortable using the weapon. And you need to be able to carry it with you." *Now's when I should tell her about the thing with Landrum. If his people tossed her house, the danger's serious. But I'm not sure...and it's going to take some explaining. Maybe tomorrow, once Rosemary's out of the way.*

Impulsively, he pulled her to him. Wrapping his arms around her, he inhaled her smell—shampoo, the lavender-scented lotion she used, and something else he couldn't identify.

"Please, Elizabeth. There's a class next Saturday. Let me sign you up."

She nuzzled at his ear. "Okay, Phillip. If you really think it's important, I'll sign up for the class and get my—what's it called?—concealed carry permit?" She pulled back and grinned at him. "How about I get one of those really cool ankle holsters?"

Elizabeth watched Phillip Hawkins drive away, reluctant to part with him even for a few hours. *I feel like a teenager, for god's sake. If I had a notebook, I'd be writing his name on it, over and over. This is...this is totally amazing. I never thought I'd feel this way again. How...how totally amazing.*

Shaking off the romantic lethargy that suggested it might be nice just to lie in the sun and wait till Phillip returned, she decided to make a quick tour of the greenhouses that lay at the upper end of the big growing field.

Everything was in order; Julio and Homero were taking diligent care of the trays of cuttings and the tender herbs and lettuces that would provide a harvest through much of the winter. Ben had left the farm in good hands, she decided, pinching off a sprig of basil and inhaling its spicy, clovelike fragrance.

Phillip's making such a big deal of this break-in. I don't know, I guess it couldn't hurt to take those classes. As Miss Birdie says, "They's a lot of meanness out there." But I hate feeling like I have to go around with a gun, for god's sake.

A chill ran over her and she felt the tiny hairs on her arms rise. It took a moment to pinpoint the source of her uneasiness, but then she realized what it was. The unexpected sound of quiet footsteps had sounded her internal alarm. Quickly, she swung around to face the door. Through the greenhouse's curving plastic wall she could just make out a shadowy form carrying . . . what *was* that in its hand? It was moving toward the door at the end of the greenhouse.

Looking around in desperation, her eyes lighted on a metal watering wand. It was laughably light, but as she gripped it she felt a bit more prepared. With noiseless steps she moved to one side of the door and raised the makeshift weapon above her head.

The intruder seemed to have trouble with the doorknob, but after a few abortive attempts, the door slowly began to move. Elizabeth gripped the slender metal tube resolutely and drew a deep breath.

As the door creaked open, there was the sound of muttered, unintelligible words, and the scrape of something metallic on the doorframe. Elizabeth braced herself.

And then, with a gusty exhalation, she relaxed. Julio's brother-in-law Homero, a long-spouted watering can in one hand, stood frozen in the entryway, his dark eyes wide at the sight of his employer, evidently intent on whacking him over the head.

"*Dios mio!*" He dropped the watering can and retreated several paces. "*Señora! No me—*"

"It's okay, Homero!" Appalled at her foolish alarm, Elizabeth dropped the wand and held out empty hands. "*Lo siento.* I'm sorry! I didn't know it was you."

Homero regarded her warily. In the distance she heard Julio calling out in rapid-fire Spanish. Without taking his eyes from her, Homero called back an answer. He had quite a bit to say.

"*Qué pasa aquí?* Whass happening, *Señora Elizabeta?*" Julio's familiar form appeared just behind his brother-in-law, who gave him a speedy and, to Elizabeth, largely unintelligible account of the past few minutes. Julio listened briefly, then waved his hands to stem the flow of words. "*Hombre, no importa.* The *señora* is a little scary, *no más.* Those *malditos* who get in her house make her that way."

Homero spat out another stream of words, motioning to the discarded watering wand. Julio nodded and laughed, then explained to Elizabeth, "Homero *dice qué* you want to scare those *pendejos* who get in your house, that thing there won't do no good. That thing—" He picked up the wand and, gripping either end, bent it till the ends met. "—it is a piece of crap. You want to protect yourself, you get a gun."

Phillip packed a few changes of clothes, as well as his lecture notes, textbooks, and the pile of ungraded quizzes that would have to be dealt with before tomorrow's class. He glanced around. It was easy to leave this place. It was a temporary shelter, nothing more. His fee-

OLD WOUNDS 215

ble attempts at remaking it to his own tastes had not amounted to much in the face of so much pastel paint and pink porcelain. *Suit me fine not to spend another night here.* He smiled reminiscently. *Sam, old buddy, she's everything you said.*

In the kitchen he filled a mug—pink with teddy bears all over it—with tap water and drank. *Even the water out there is better—no chlorine.*

As he set the mug on the countertop, a thought occurred to him. He pulled from his waistband the tiny cell phone Gabby had told him to use. A touch of his finger and it was ringing; three rings and Gabby answered. "Yeah?"

"What's up? Anything new on the break-in?"

"Well, I should be asking you. How's Red's little wifey doing? She okay?"

"A little nervous, but basically all right. She's a gutsy woman." Phillip hesitated. "The sheriff's got someone keeping an eye on the place." *No need to say who. This is information Gabby doesn't need, not yet.* "Listen, she thinks—and I guess it's a possibility—that the break-in was the work of a local fella with a grudge against her. I need to know: do you have any real reason to believe it was Landrum's people?"

There was a mirthless bark at the other end. "C'mon, man, get serious here! Of course it was them. They're in town and they have a limited amount of time. They want the appointment in place by the end of the month: the administration's set to move quickly. And Landrum's worst nightmare is that those photos of Red's will show up. Del's not willing to risk his entire career without the hard proof of those pictures. And even if you and me backed Del up, who are we? An ex-junkie and a small-town cop. Our word against Landrum's."

Gabby's voice grew sarcastic. "I'm assuming you haven't done what I suggested: just asked the widow Goodweather if she knows where Sam might have left some important papers. Hell, tell her about Landrum—I happen to know the woman's a bleeding-heart liberal; she'll bend over backward to help once she understands what's at stake here. Do what it takes, but find that stuff and get it to me ASAP. I can be in DC in a matter of hours, and once he has the deposition and the photos in his hand, Del can go right to the top. Landrum's political future will disappear and—"

"Okay, you're probably right." Phillip paced from kitchen to living room and back, as if trying to escape the demands of his old shipmate. "I'll see what I can do. But I'm going to have to take it slow—she has no idea about all this. And I want to wait till her daughter's gone back to Chapel Hill. Give me a few days."

This time it was a real laugh, a knowing cackle. "Need to be alone with the lady, huh? Spend some time getting close, *real* close to Red's old lady? You do that, pal, and you can find out what she knows."

Damn the cynical bastard. But how the hell am I going to explain this to Elizabeth? Phillip clicked off the cell phone and clipped it back on his belt. *It's taken her this long to trust me, and now . . . What happens if I tell her it was no accident that I showed up in Asheville? And all the Nam shit—how's she going to take that?*

"Goddammit to hell!" Phillip Hawkins looked down at his packed bag waiting by the door. With a sudden savage impulse, he snatched up the teddy bear mug and hurled it to the tiled floor. The sound of shattering ceramic made him smile. Stepping carelessly over the pieces, he picked up his bag and left.

Her jeep was parked by the barn, but Phillip could see no sign of Elizabeth. She was nowhere to be found—neither in the workshop nor the greenhouses. The sound of a slamming door caught his attention.

"*Señor!*" Homero was hurrying down the steps of the tenant house. "*Señor! Elisabeta* she say you drive car. She go—" His thick fingers pantomimed walking and he gestured up the road. "—*su casa.*"

"*Señor Felipe!*" Now Julio had emerged from the little house. He was carrying a primitive-looking machete and brandished it before him as he approached Phillip. "*Mira! Homero y yo,* we take care of those *pendejos* if they come back."

As he neared the comfortable-looking house nestled on the mountainside, its peaceful aspect called to him. It seemed to offer a promise of quiet content—of shared joys and deep companionship. The three dogs trotted to greet him, just as he had seen them greet Elizabeth—not sounding an alarm, but wagging and bowing, as if welcoming a returning family member.

Phillip pulled his belongings from the back of the jeep while the dogs milled about him, demanding his attention. He squatted down and patted each in turn, rubbing Molly's sleek chest, scratching behind Ursa's ears, fending off James's frantic leaping attempts to lick his face. All the while, his thoughts kept churning—a continuous, inescapable loop of uneasy foreboding. *She's let me into her bed. But will she let me into her life? Will I lose it all if I tell her the truth?*

20.

REFLECTIONS

Sunday, October 16 and
Monday, October 17

"They were in the very back of my closet, underneath an old science fair project—fourteen in all."

The cache of "spy notebooks" unearthed, Rosemary had spent most of the afternoon curled up on the sofa opposite the fireplace, head bent over the little hardcover composition books, occasionally sharing a delicious tidbit: "Listen, Mum, this is what Grammer Grey said when she came to visit and found out we didn't have a real bathroom yet, only an outhouse." But there had also been long stretches when she was silent, her face grave and her mouth tight as she read.

After supper, Phillip set up shop at the dining table, grading test papers. His face, too, had been solemn, as he groaned at some hapless student's particularly unfortunate response to an essay question.

Stretched out on the other sofa, a well-worn copy of Dorothy L. Sayers's *Gaudy Night* unopened on her lap, Elizabeth basked in the warmth of the cheerful fire and the comfortable, companionable presence of the others. *I hadn't realized it, but I've been lonely. This—this family life—is what I've missed.*

She looked from her daughter to Phillip, both so engrossed in their reading. *He's not what I might have imagined for myself… if I'd felt like looking. He's intelligent, but not much of a reader, and he's spent his life as a cop—really, what do we have in common beyond Sam? But here he is, and I like it.*

She glanced down at the book in her lap. *I've read this probably ten or fifteen times—and it's still romantic when Harriet finally gives in to Peter. At one time I might have said that Peter Wimsey was my idea of an ideal man—that literary turn of phrase and clever banter, not to mention the title, money, and perfect manservant.*

She studied Phillip, mentally comparing his stocky frame and shiny balding head to Lord Peter's slim, athletic form and buttercup yellow hair. *I like the way he looks—and, after all, Lord Peter's monocle would have been a bit much.*

As if aware of her gaze, Phillip looked up. He seemed on the point of speaking, then, with a quick smile, looked away and resumed his labors.

Elizabeth's face flushed. *But the thing that really mattered about Lord Peter, mattered to Harriet Vane, was that he respected her independence, that he prized her for it—all the other stuff just got in the way of her caring for him. It wasn't until she realized he saw her as an equal that she gave in to him. Is that what I find so appealing about Phillip?*

She turned her attention to her daughter. Rosemary's face—high cheekbones, dark eyebrows, and thick lashes—had taken on an added beauty in the fireglow. Elizabeth watched her as she read, luxuriating in the pleasure of having her older daughter near again. Just as Phillip had done, Rosemary seemed to become aware of Elizabeth's scrutiny. She looked up. "I'm not much company tonight, Mum." Her smile was rueful. "But you can't believe how amazing these are—how much stuff I wrote down back then." She nodded at the stack of note-books. "I'm about halfway through. There's a lot that may be useful, but I want to go through all of them before I come to any conclusions. If... if you want, you can read them too." A look of embarrassment flitted across her face. "Some of the stuff I wrote... well, I know better now. Remember, I was just a kid."

Sensing her daughter's reluctance to offer her private diaries, Elizabeth feigned a disinterest she did not feel. She tapped her own book. "Thanks, sweetie, but I'm involved with Lord Peter Wimsey right now. Besides, I think I'm about ready to turn in. I'll look at the note-books another time, if you like."

A look of relief flooded Rosemary's face. "Sure, another time would be fine. And once I've gone through all of them, I'll have a better idea of what's important and what isn't."

A short while later, Rosemary gathered up her note-books and said good night, carrying all fourteen slim books upstairs to her old room.

It feels ridiculous to be sneaking around like this, but... What do I say? "By the way, Rosie, Phillip and I are sleeping together now." I don't know—maybe I'll tell her when she comes back. Though, it's more likely that she already knows, and is too polite to embarrass her silly old mother.

As Elizabeth made ready for bed, she could hear Phillip showering in the guest room's bath. She brushed out her hair, rebraided it loosely, and climbed into bed, taking the side farther from the door, just as she had done when Sam was alive. She propped herself against the pillows, put on her reading glasses, and opened her book. The dogs, settled in their accustomed places, were

already deeply asleep. *That won't last, not with the full moon.*
They'll be whining to go out around two.

A light tap, and Phillip, modestly clad in a white terry-
cloth bathrobe, opened the door. A wonderful aroma of
soap and shampoo and man flowed into the room. He
came in and shut the door, careful to make no sound,
then, without speaking, he stood by the bed, seemingly
unsure what he was doing there. He cleared his throat, as
in preparation for a solemn declaration. Elizabeth put
down her book and waited.

"The thing is…" he began, then faltered. "The thing
is, I…Elizabeth, are you sure—"

Elizabeth leaned across the vacant side of the bed to
tug at the damp terry cloth.

"Phillip, I'm as sure as I'm going to be. We can talk
about it another time."

"And your mother allowed the abuse to continue, even after you
had told her about it?"

"Well, kind of… You see, Trish, the thing about it was—"

"No, I don't see, and I don't want you to tell me 'the thing
about it'; I want you to answer my question. I'll repeat it, just in
case you didn't quite understand. And this time, I want a yes or a
no. No 'kind ofs,' okay?"

There was a sniffle, a pause, and a choked sound that
was probably a yes. Elizabeth paused in her cleaning of
the empty bookshelves and turned up the radio volume.
She had decided to listen to the morning broadcast of
"Tell Trish" in preparation for the Thursday meeting
with her erstwhile neighbor.

Trish Trantham's hectoring tones continued. *"Beth-*
any, you have to take responsibility for your memories—you have
to remember things as they were, not as you wish *they had been.*

You've spent your life excusing your mother's behavior, trying to be the good little girl whose mommy loved her. Now, I'll ask you again, and I want a direct answer—no qualifying, no explaining—did your mother continue to permit your stepfather's sexual abuse of you?"

A stifled gulp was followed by a whispered *"Yes."*

"Now, that wasn't so hard, was it, Bethany?" Trish's harsh, demanding voice suddenly became warm and nurturing, her honeyed syllables rewarding the caller who had at last responded correctly.

A sob of relief and then Bethany quavered, *"No, I guess not. Th-thank you, Trish."*

"And do you see now that you don't owe this evil woman anything? You don't have to invite her to live with you; you don't have to spend time with her; you certainly don't have to allow her any contact at all with your children. Bethany, you have my permission to put this horrible woman out of your life forever."

"But, Trish, . . . she's . . . she's my mother."

"We're going to commercial break right now. Meanwhile, remember, if you have a problem, 'Tell Trish!' My number is—"

"That's enough of *you*, Mrs. Barbie." Elizabeth dropped her cleaning cloth as the radio began to burble the praises of vinyl siding. She jabbed the button to switch to CD and shoved in a reggae disk.

She had driven Phillip and Rosemary down to their cars a little before nine that morning so that they could be on their respective ways: he to his ten o'clock class at AB Tech, and she to Chapel Hill.

"I'll be back Thursday," Rosemary had promised. "Mum, how about if I meet you at the Trish Trantham Lifeworks place at one? That's when she said she could see us." With an enthusiasm she did not feel, Elizabeth had agreed. She had kissed her daughter good-bye, and watched her drive away. Phillip had taken his time, first opening his trunk as if in search of something, then going into the greenhouse to speak to Julio. Finally he returned and stood by the jeep's open window.

"Julio says that he and Homero will be right here all day and they'll keep an eye on the road. I'll feel a lot better once you've done some target practice." He started to say more, then stopped himself. His hand started up in the familiar gesture.

Elizabeth reached out the window and grabbed the hand, halting its upward sweep. "I know; you want me to be careful. And I will. It'll take me most of the day to vacuum all those books and put them back in order. And I'll keep Sam's gun nearby."

Phillip leaned to kiss the hand that held his. "Take care of yourself, my love."

She worked her way steadily through the stacks of books, vacuuming and returning each volume to its alphabetical destination. Slowly the newly cleaned shelves across the living room's back wall began to fill again. Douglas Adams... *Watership Down*... all of Jane Austen... Robertson Davies... Hermann Hesse... *Lost Horizons*... Kazantzakis (and the plangent sound of bouzouki music filled her head)... *The Just So Stories*... Michener's *Hawaii* and *The Source*... Ayn Rand (but she has no *compassion*! a philosophy professor had warned her); each volume that she touched recalled a time and place in her life.

And so many demanded the quick rereading of a favorite passage or a glance at a remembered illustration. Mary Renault's wonderful retellings of Greek history and myth... Salinger... *Treasure Island* (with the N. C. Wyeth

illustrations: cobalt skies and billowing rosy clouds)...
Vanity Fair and the lively Becky Sharp ... Thoreau.

A copy of *Walden,* one of the icons of the back-to-the-
land movement. She slid it from its faded green sleeve.
The front cover was a woodcut, green on cream, showing
Henry David Thoreau's famous little "tight-shingled
and plastered house, ten feet wide by fifteen long."
Elizabeth held the book in her hand and remembered. *I
owe you a copy,* Sam had said, handing it to her on his return from a trip, the same year of the deadly plane crash.
*The one you gave me when we first met didn't make it back from
Nam. But the ideas stayed with me. Besides, it was only a paper-
back—I hope this will be around a lot longer.*

He had handed it to her and put his hands over hers as
she clasped the book. *There's important stuff in here, Liz. The
things that brought us here; lessons we shouldn't ever forget. Keep
it safe.*

She opened the little book and flipped through the
pages. As far as she could remember, she'd never read this
copy—too caught up in life itself to spare time for the
somewhat precious observations of a young man who
had, when all was said and done, lived quietly and simply
for a few years before rejoining the common throng.

But there's some fine writing here, all the same, she thought,
leafing through the pages. *It taught an appreciation of simplic-
ity ... and a love of nature that has stayed with me, even if I don't
live as simply as Thoreau did. Of course,* he *didn't have children.*

She started to shelve the book, then, changing her
mind, set it on her bedside table. *I owe old Henry David another look,* she decided.

Elizabeth dusted off the last two books, *Virginia Woolf* and
Émile Zola—now, there's an odd couple, and returned them

·

to the shelves, then tried to decide what to do next. Not enough time to begin a major project, and too early to start supper. She looked speculatively up at the loft bedroom. *Those spy notebooks. She said I could read them. And I'd dearly love to get a glimpse into her mind back then. Children are so strange and wonderful. And Rosie was such an enigma—when she was Rosie, not pretending to be Running Deer or whatever the name of her Indian princess alter ego was.*

Minutes later, Elizabeth was sitting on one of the low twin beds in the loft bedroom. She plucked a speckled-covered notebook from the pile beside her, opened it at random, and read. *I know that it was a bad thing to do but <u>I don't care.</u> Mum and Pa have done bad things too.*

AT THE SCUTTLE HOLE

August 1986

WITH CATLIKE TREAD, *upon her foe she steals...dum, dum, dum, dee dum, dee dum, dee dum.*

The *Pirates of Penzance song was running through her head as Rosemary crept up the path to the scuttle hole. A little way off she could hear the bang of Pa's fence tool as he drove in more staples to hold up the barbed wire and fix the fence where the cows had knocked it down.*

Good thing Dinah stayed with Laurie, thought Rosemary, carefully inspecting the ground ahead of her so that she would not betray her presence by a snapped twig or a rolling pebble. I could never sneak up on Pa if she was with me.

Rosemary would have preferred soft moccasins for her spy work, but Mum always made her wear hiking boots when she went climbing on the mountain, and the clumpy boots made it extra hard to be quiet. Still, she could see Pa now, leaning down to drive in another staple, and he hadn't heard her yet.

Taking advantage of the banging, Rosemary advanced another few yards, then ducked behind a huge poplar just as Pa stood up and pulled off his T-shirt. He wiped the sweat off his face and flapped the shirt in front of him like a fan. The shirt was dark with perspiration and Pa stretched it out over the top strand of wire.

She had to stifle a giggle. It was fun being a spy. Maybe if Pa left his shirt there while he kept on working . . . maybe she could creep up and grab it without his seeing her. It would be like counting coup. That would show Maythorn what a good Cherokee Rosemary was becoming.

Pa moved a little farther along the fence, stretching wire and hammering it to the posts. Rosemary stayed behind the big tree, waiting for her opportunity. When he gets to the scuttle hole . . . then I'll make my move.

Well, hello there, neighbor. I heard all that racket and thought maybe it was some big woodpecker.

Rosemary peeked cautiously around the massive trunk. Rats! Mrs. Barbie. Just like her to come along and ruin things.

Howdy, Patricia. No, it's just me trying to keep the damn cows where they belong. Were you looking for Maythorn? She hasn't been over today—our Rosie's down at the house reading.

Oh, that Maythorn, she's here and there. I don't even try to keep up with her. You know, she has another little friend she visits—a local child called Tammy or something like that. Somewhere over there.

Mrs. Barbie's hand waved vaguely toward the top of the mountain. The big shirt she wore over a pair of purple shorts fell open, revealing a brightly flowered bikini top.

Her boobs are about to fall out, thought Rosemary in prim disgust. I'm glad Mum doesn't wear stuff like that.

Mrs. Barbie laughed. She had a silly, tee-hee-hee laugh. Well, as you can see, I was down by the pool. Then I heard the banging and got curious, so I decided to investigate.

From her hiding place Rosemary could see Mrs. Barbie take a step closer to her father and place one hand on his bare chest. She tilted her head to look up at him, batted her false eyelashes, and purred. But I'm glad to find you up here, Sam. I've been wanting to talk to you about something. Moon doesn't notice things and it's hopeless trying to discuss anything with him. Sam, I'm a little concerned about that retarded local who wanders all around. Do you think he's safe?

Pa looked at Mrs. Barbie's hand as he answered. Cletus knows these woods better than anyone, according to his mother. Yes, I'd say he's perfectly safe.

Pa took a step back but Mrs. Barbie followed him. She twiddled her fingers on his arm.

Oh, Sam, that's not what I meant. I mean, is he safe to have around the children? I think he may have kind of a thing about little girls, especially Krystalle. He's never done anything, but somehow—

I don't think there's anything to worry about there, Patricia. Cletus is at our place a lot and Liz—

That reminds me, how is Elizabeth? I hadn't seen her in ages, and then I ran into her at the grocery store last week and I almost didn't recognize her. She looked . . . oh, just so tired and unhappy. Is she all right?

Liz tries to do too much. And adjusting to this new life has been hard. Pa said this patiently, like he was repeating himself.

And it did sound familiar. Rosemary had heard her parents quietly arguing about this . . . and other things too.

Mrs. Barbie's voice dropped to a low murmur. Rosemary could just hear some of what she said. . . . Understand all too well . . . frustration . . . Moon . . . drinking problem . . . attracted to you.

There was a silence. With all the caution of her Cherokee training, Rosemary inched her head to where she could see what was happening. Patricia Mullins had her arms around Pa's neck. She was pulling his face down to meet hers.

Rosemary hadn't waited to see what would happen next. She was older than she had been when she saw Mum kissing

Maythorn's uncle ... a lot older ... and she knew what might come next. They hadn't heard her hurrying away down the trail.

She hadn't cried this time. Maythorn had taught her that Indians don't show pain or sorrow. That other time, a year and a half ago, she had boo-hooed like a big baby, but not now.

Instead of going back to the house, where Mum might ask questions, she had made straight for the Cave of the Two Sisters. There was comfort beneath the solid shapes of the leaning giants, always together, always faithful. She pulled out her spy notebook and began to write.

What was that? She froze and listened. The sound of something rustling through the bushes outside sent a chill over her body. Now it was scrabbling at the entrance to the hideout. A terrible thought came to her and she felt her mouth go dry.

What if it was Cletus? Miss Birdie said that he knew this mountain like the back of his hand. That meant he probably knew about this cave. Was it him scraping his way through the low entrance? Rosemary shivered as she remembered the last time she was alone with Cletus—when he had skinned the squirrel. Is he safe to have around the children? ... a thing about little girls—Mrs. Barbie's words echoed in her ears like the warning cries of circling crows.

The scratching and scrabbling grew louder, and Rosemary grabbed one of the fist-sized rocks that Maythorn had insisted they carry into the hideout. Ammo in case the enemy attack, Maythorn had said. Rosemary's fingers curled tightly around the rock.

A faded blue ball cap came into view in the low entrance and Rosemary dropped the rock. She sank to a cross-legged sitting position, hastily opened her spy notebook, and began to write, summoning all the nonchalance at her command.

Maythorn slid into view, breathing hard. One braid

had come undone and black hair spilled from under her cap. Her jeans were filthy and scratches covered her thin brown arms. She put her finger to her lips and listened intently for a few moments. No sound came from outside the hideout.

At last she relaxed and stretched full-length on the sandy floor. *They almost caught me,* she told Rosemary. *But I gave 'em the slip.*

Who was chasing you, Maythorn? Rosemary looked wide-eyed at her friend, her blood twin.

Those folks over the mountain. Tamra's dad and some others. They have a bunch of mean dogs. I'm pretty sure they're growing marijuana and they didn't want me to see it.

Rosemary knew all about marijuana. Officer Jim and Officer Deb had talked to the school assembly about the bad things that could happen to kids who smoked it. *How do you know it's marijuana,* she asked, wondering how long Maythorn had been going over the mountain to see this Tamra, wondering why Maythorn had never talked about another friend.

Jared told me. He buys it from them. I followed him over there one time. Maythorn rolled over, reached into the pocket of her knapsack, and pulled out a small tin cough-drop box. She sat up, and with a knowing half smile opened the box and waved it under Rosemary's horrified eyes.

A small box of matches and a lumpy-looking cigarette lay within the little container. Maythorn narrowed her eyes and looked at her friend. *Jared gave me this so I wouldn't tell Moon that he had some weed—that's what Jared calls it. And this is a joint.*

What are you going to do with it? Rosemary couldn't take her eyes off the forbidden object. *You could get in big trouble....*

What do you think I'm going to do with it? A rattle of

matches, a spurt of flame, and after several false starts, the joint was alight. You're supposed to breathe the smoke right into your lungs, Maythorn said. Breathe it in and hold it there as long as you can. Jared showed me how. He said it's like an Indian vision quest.

21.

THE SPY NOTEBOOKS

Monday, October 17

The defiant words, so incongruous in the young Rosemary's looping, sprawled handwriting, had been written with pencil, pressed so hard that the indentations were still visible. Two heavy, angry lines underscored the words "I don't care." With a sick feeling, Elizabeth turned back to the beginning of the entry.

August 9, 1986—Today I saw Pa kissing Maythorn's mom. And today me and Maythorn smoked ~~marywana~~ weed. I know that it was a bad thing to do but <u>I don't care.</u> *Mum and Pa have done bad things too.*

"Oh, god! The poor baby. It wasn't bad enough that she saw me that time with Mike, but then to see *Sam* acting the same way! And that *bitch* Patricia. Oh, my poor baby Rosie!"

Heartsick, Elizabeth closed the little book and thrust it away. She buried her face in her hands and rocked back and forth in misery. *I never wanted the girls to know anything about that... that stupid, stupid, passing craziness that hit first me, then Sam. I wanted them to have a perfect childhood, not worrying that their parents might get divorced, that one would leave. I never wanted them to carry around the kind of anxiety I felt when I was growing up—the emptiness, the guilt.*

She raised her head and looked around the little room that for so many years had been Rosemary's private lair. The unicorn posters had been taken down; the menagerie of stuffed animals had been dispersed; the lavender-blue walls had been repainted apple green. It was now "the loft guest room" not "Rosie's room." But the bookshelves still held many of Rosemary's childhood books and treasures. And, in some indefinable sense, the room retained the imprint of the Rosie that had been.

Elizabeth closed her eyes in a half-formed prayer. She wanted to believe that the angry words penciled in the notebook had been a momentary reaction, that the essential Rosemary herself had remained untouched. *But just a few months after this, Maythorn vanished. And Rosie stopped talking. Of course we thought it was the terrible loss of her friend. But was it also a reaction to what she saw as her parents betraying each other?*

"Get a grip, Elizabeth!" She sat up and drew a deep breath. *Rosemary is a happy successful woman. She did* not have a blighted childhood—*she told you so herself.*

"God, I hope that's true." She whispered the words and reached for the notebook as if grasping a nettle. It had become necessary that she follow this wherever it led.

The next entry was a week later. There was no mention of Sam and Patricia Mullins; instead, there was a terse *I don't like Tamra. All she wants to do is swim in the swimming pool and play dress-up with Maythorn's fancy clothes—the ones Maythorn won't wear unless her mom makes a big fuss. It's boring. We can't go to the hideout when she's around. I made Maythorn promise not to tell Tamra about the Cave of the Two Sisters. I don't think she will.*

Tamra…the name was vaguely familiar, but she couldn't put a face to it. As far as she knew, the Mullins girls had been the only children living nearby back then. Rosie and Maythorn had been close friends out of necessity, as well as inclination. Maybe Tamra was one of the pageant children that Patricia Mullins occasionally had out to Mullmore for play dates with Krystalle.

Elizabeth turned the pages, skimming through days and weeks. Some entries were businesslike notations of what Rosemary called her "work"—the spy game.

> *August 12*—*3:15 p.m. Bus driver stops at foot of the Buckman's road and waits for a long time. Buckman kids have already gotten off and gone up the road.*
>
> *3:23 p.m. Young guy in old blue Ford truck with one red door stops by bus. Herley tells us kids to stay put. He gets out. He has a Timberland shoe box under his arm. He talks to the guy (skinny, long hair, yellow tractor cap).*
>
> *3:27 p.m. Young guy gives Herley money and Herley gives him shoe box. Maythorn tries to get license number of the truck but it's all splashed with mud and all we could see was a J & a three.*
>
> *Billy Gentry and Shawn Clemmons got in a fight while Herley was off the bus. When Herley got back on, he said he was just giving his brother-in-law some boots he'd picked up for him in Asheville. Maythorn says he could be selling crack, like Officer Deb and Officer Jim told us about. She says not to say anything till we have more evidense.*
>
> *August 16*—*2:23 p.m. Maythorn and me are in our special tree in their woods. We can see the swimming pool*

and the gazeebo real good. Mr. Mullins is in the pool, floating around on a rubber raft. He has a plastic glass on his stomach.

2:34 p.m. Mrs. Barbie comes out & calls him. He doesn't answer.

September 13—Top of Pinnacle. 1:20 p.m. We brought our lunch up to eat in our Top of the World spy outpost. Maythorn says that if we are very quiet we could see some thing important. She won't tell me what.

1:35 p.m. Mike Mullins has come up the trail from Mullmore and is sitting on a log. He is whistling.

1:40 p.m. A lady in tight jeans with fancy yellow hair comes up the trail from the other side of mountain. She is looking around like she's scared. Mike whistles & she runs to him. He is hugging her very tight and now she is laughing. They go back down the trail to Mullmore. Maythorn says that is Tamra's mom.

Tamra again. Elizabeth's brow wrinkled. And just on the other side of the mountain. *Where did I hear that name recently?* She turned over a few more pages, looking for another mention of the name. There it was again, part of an undated entry—not a "spy report," but a sad little statement: *I don't like the Reaper Game. It's too scary. But Tamra & Maythorn think it's fun, so I have to play.*

She was lost in her daughter's past, trying to make sense of the childish scrawl and the accounts of things observed almost twenty years ago. *Where was I back then?*

And who is this Tamra? *And her mother? I had no idea that Rosie and Maythorn were spending all this time spying on everyone. That kind of thing could get them in trouble.*

A chill coursed through her body. *Maybe it did. Maybe that's what happened to Maythorn—what if the child saw something she shouldn't have? She wandered all over the place—not like Rosie, who stayed close to home . . . I think. Where the hell was I?*

The answer was obvious—she had been dealing with the house, the farm, the garden. They had been growing tobacco back then—long, exhausting days of hoeing, topping, spraying, cutting, hanging. Time had passed in something of a blur and she had been grateful that her quiet older daughter had seemed so content and happy with her friend. She and Sam had congratulated themselves that Rosemary didn't beg for a television set but seemed happy with her books and her explorations.

Does a mother ever really know her child's heart and mind? Elizabeth turned the pages before her at random, no longer trying to read, but simply acknowledging the enormity of her ignorance.

Cletus. The name of Miss Birdie's son, dead a little over a year now, jumped out at her from the page. *Cletus was in the woods near our hideout again.*

He had been a frequent visitor to Full Circle Farm back then. Cletus was known to be "simple," in the gentle parlance of the mountains. He could not read but he was, as his mother had often said, "a good hand to work," and when the Gentrys' tobacco and crops were hoed and fertilized, Cletus would often appear at Full Circle Farm, ready to lend a hand at any job. Sam had always paid him what they could, over Cletus's protestations that he just liked to help.

Laurel had had a deep affection for the shy young man, as had Sam and Elizabeth. Rosemary, on the other hand, had never been quite at ease around him. The idea of a grown-up who couldn't read, who was often more childish than her little sister, seemed to disturb her at some deep, involuntary level, and Elizabeth had soon realized that Rosemary, while dutifully polite to Cletus, made a point of avoiding him.

Elizabeth turned the page. *He tried to show me something he had in his pocket but I ran away. I don't like Cletus.*

The barking of the dogs alerted Elizabeth to Phillip's return. She went to the window and looked out across her garden. There he was, hiking up the road, a knapsack on his back, and on his face the happy look of a man coming home at the end of the day to a warm house, a good meal, and his heart's desire.

Instantly she abandoned the notebooks and hurried down the steep stairs.

As Elizabeth flung open the front door and her eyes met his, a tide of thankfulness swept over him. Phillip dropped his knapsack in one of the porch rockers, opened his arms wide, and engulfed her in a glad embrace.

"Everything okay today? No unwelcome visitors?"

"None, Phillip." She leaned against him, a sweet and comfortable armful. "Only, maybe, some unwelcome memories."

She had not explained, beyond saying that she'd been reading through Rosemary's notebooks. As they sat side by side on the sofa before the fire, enjoying their after-dinner coffee, Phillip rummaged through his thoughts for something to lift the solemn mood that seemed to have overtaken her at the mention of the note-books. That had persisted through dinner.

"Elizabeth, are you still up for the gun class on Saturday?"

"I'm not trying to back out or anything, Phillip, but... I don't know, I guess it seems a little excessive."

Okay, now or never. "Elizabeth, there's something else here you need to know about. I don't think it was Bib who broke into your house. And neither does Blaine."

She started to speak, but he plowed ahead. "Did Sam ever mention Lawrence Landrum? From Nam?"

22.

LAST GIFTS

Monday, October 17

She stared at him in complete bewilderment. "What does someone from Vietnam have to do with what happened to my house?"

"I'll get to that." He reached out, took her hand, and studied it for a moment. Fine-boned and long-fingered, it bore the calluses of hard work. He noted that the heavy wedding ring she had worn till very recently was gone, though a band of pale skin on her fourth finger was a ghostly reminder of the ring's long tenure. "Do you recollect Sam ever mentioning a guy named Lawrence Landrum—Lieutenant Landrum in Nam?"

"Sam made it something of a rule never to talk about Vietnam—at least when he was awake. For a long time though, he couldn't stop talking about it when he was asleep. He said a lot of names—I know I heard 'Phil' over and over. But no Landrum, as far as I can remember."

She looked down at her ringless hand where it rested in his. "You know, those dreams were a real problem between us for several years. I wanted him to get help—or to let *me* help him. I had the naïve belief that if he'd just once open up—but that wasn't going to happen."

"And the dreams?..."

"As time passed, the dreams went from being almost every night to once every few months, and then to just a couple of times a year. I think the nightmares had been triggered by the stress of moving from the suburbs to the farm—abandoning the security of the life we'd grown up with to come here. And as we got accustomed to life on the farm, the nightmares decreased."

She smiled sadly. "Eventually they stopped altogether. There were years that he never had a Vietnam dream and I was sure it was all behind him. But then for some reason, they started again. A couple of years before he died, the dreams came back. Really bad again, but this time he told me he knew what to do for them. And it must have worked, because after a month or so they stopped again. But, as I said, I never heard Sam mention the name Landrum. Who was he?"

It had been tricky, Phillip thought, but he'd done it. He'd told her the truth—most of it—as much as she needed to alert her to the potential danger. He'd carefully omitted the circumstances that had brought him to the Carolina mountains—*Let her believe that was coincidence.*

Elizabeth had listened quietly as he related, with a careful lack of detail, the events of that last day on the Mekong. She had even—*thank god*—nodded in understanding as he had explained the surviving crew's decision to remain silent about Landrum's psychotic slaughter of unarmed civilians.

"We thought he was done for—hell, even the *medics* said he'd bought the farm. And he'd been shot all to pieces while he was saving two of our crew...one of the bravest things I ever saw. He was a hero *then*, all right. We figured it wouldn't bring anyone back to report the incidents—we just wanted to get away and forget about it all as best we could. It wasn't till six or seven years ago that we even knew Landrum was still alive."

He studied her face anxiously. She was frowning in an effort of memory. Then she leapt up and disappeared into the kitchen. He could hear the muffled sound of paper rustling and the words "I know it's in here" followed by a triumphant "Aha!"

She returned, triumphantly waving a crumpled copy of *Time*. "It was in the recycling, near the bottom. I'm pretty sure that your guy Landrum was mentioned in the article about the far right and their influence on this administration. I wouldn't have remembered the name, but they made a big deal of how, unlike most of the folks at the top, this guy was actually a veteran and a hero, wounded while saving his men. There was a picture of him and his prosthetic legs and empty sleeve." She riffled the pages eagerly. "It's gotta be the same guy—they called him a power behind the scene. Lots of family money, which he's parlayed into a mega-fortune...Here it is!" She thrust the open magazine toward him. "Lawrence Landrum—is this your lieutenant? Even without the atrocity story, this guy's a total disaster. Just a little to the right of the Taliban."

He took the magazine, glanced at the picture, and nodded. "That's him. And Del, the one at the Pentagon, says this sick bastard is about to be named Secretary of Defense."

She plopped down beside him. "That *is* sick. But I still don't see what this has to do with my house being torn apart."

* * *

Elizabeth listened in shocked disbelief. *Pictures of an atrocity, thirty-five-year-old pictures...and a video-taped deposition...hidden in her house?* She shook her head. "It doesn't make any sense, Phillip. Why wouldn't Sam have just put them in a safe-deposit box or—"

"You know, Sam could be pretty paranoid sometimes. He told me and Del that safe-deposit boxes just advertised that you had something worth protecting. He was convinced that Landrum could have bought his way into a Swiss bank, much less the Farmers and Mercantile in Ransom. No, Sam did it his way." Phillip looked unhappy. "Sam talked to Del and to me right before...well, it was just a few weeks before the plane crash. He said that he'd been in touch with Landrum and warned him to stay out of politics or Sam would go public with the photos. He said he'd videotaped a deposition relating the events of that last day on the Swift Boat and swearing to the authenticity of the pictures. Then he said a weird thing: he said that he'd given *you* the key to where he'd hidden them. But that you didn't know what it was."

"A key? An actual key? Or...Because I don't think..." Her mind was busy, sorting through drawers, old jewelry boxes, all the places in her house where incongruous assortments of small objects gathered. *There're some old keys in one of the little drawers of the secretary...and that basket in the mudroom has old house keys and car keys and...*

"No idea if he meant a real key or not. Del said Sam was really pleased with himself—like he'd come up with the perfect hiding place. Del thought it was pretty risky, doing it that way, and he tried to convince Sam to let him have duplicates of the photos and the taped deposition. Finally Sam said he'd get some copies and send them to Del right after Christmas."

"And then there was the plane crash."

"Right. Del never got any copies. And Landrum laid low for a while. Now he must have figured that, after all this time and with Sam gone, it would be safe for him to resume his political career. But he has to be sure those photos don't turn up. And this is what you need to understand, Elizabeth: Del thinks that Landrum has sent some of his men to find those incriminating snapshots and destroy them."

"Maybe they *did* find them. Maybe—"

"Elizabeth, Del knows who these people are. He says Landrum's people are still nearby. If they think that you know where this stuff is, their next move will be to threaten you. That's why I'm asking you to take this gun class—until those photos and Sam's deposition are found, you could be in real danger: these people have a lot at stake and wouldn't think twice about..."

His voice trailed off. Elizabeth pondered, looking around the living room, as if hoping to see a faded manila envelope protruding from behind a picture frame or an ancient scrolled key lying casually on the floor. *Ridiculous. Whoever tore the place apart would have found that stuff... if it was hidden here. But what if...?*

"What if the key Sam said he gave me is something like a treasure map, something that tells where this evidence is hidden? After all, he had the whole farm—barns, drying sheds, tenant house, equipment shed. There're lots of places he could have hidden a small package, wrapped to make it weatherproof."

"Now you're talkin', Sherlock." Phillip draped an arm around her and pulled her closer. "He said he *gave* you the key. Think about that. Was Sam a big gift-giver? Let's see, what are gift-giving occasions—birthdays? Christmas? anniversary? Mother's Day? Valentine's—"

"No, not all of those. Christmas and my birthday for sure, but not..." She felt compelled to explain, to come to Sam's defense. "Early on we decided to go easy on exchanging gifts with each other—there were too many things the girls or the farm needed and never enough money. Mostly we gave each other stuff we'd made—for our anniversary sometimes we went out to dinner, but we were more likely just to splurge on champagne and something really good and easy to fix from the Fresh Market. The same for Valentine's—if we remembered. The girls made Mother's Day presents, not Sam....I think that about covers it."

"Okay, let's see. We didn't know that Landrum was alive till...I think it was '98. Sam wouldn't have had reason to make the deposition till then."

"And Sam died in '99. So, let me think...what did he give me for Christmas and for my birthday in those years." She closed her eyes, remembering. "The one thing I can remember is what he gave me that last Christmas. It was already wrapped and under the tree—he'd really been on top of things that year."

And all the presents sat there, unopened till New Year's Eve. Memories of that bleak December crowded into her mind, as if released from some subterranean dungeon and eager for the light.

The fatal plane crash, just a few days before Christmas... *freak accident...less-than-skillful amateur pilot...light planes inherently dangerous...pilot appeared to be attempting a stunt...* The explanations had inundated her and she had become almost paralytic with grief...and anger. Grief at the loss of her husband, friend, lover; grief at the sight of the girls' wounded faces; anger at the stupidity of the accident.

Only tradition, passed down from her grandmother,

tradition that said it was bad luck to have the Christmas tree still up on New Year's Day, had roused her from the sleepwalking state that had settled on her. The irony of attempting to avoid bad luck at this particular dark moment had been apparent, but she had forced herself to make this return to normalcy, for the girls' sake, if not her own.

On the morning of December 31, she and the girls had sat round the Christmas tree. Its piercing fragrance filled the room. No one, in the shock and tragedy of the past week, had thought to fill the tub in which the big Fraser fir stood, inexorably drying and dying. In spite of the fact that its needles were dropping fast, the tree was still a lordly presence in the living room. One by one Elizabeth and her daughters had opened presents. By unspoken consent, they'd saved the gifts from Sam for last.

Finally there were only five unopened packages left. "You first, Laurie," Rosemary had said, with the authority of her twenty-three years.

Unwilling to cut the red yarn with which the packages were tied, nineteen-year-old Laurel had picked at the knots patiently till at last she could remove the yarn. Then she gingerly undid the paper on both packages, pausing to smooth and fold it away, finally opening the first box.

It was a beautiful edition of the works of Georgia O'Keeffe—something of an icon to Laurel at the time. An expensive, coffee table–type book, used but in excellent condition, it was crammed with exquisite reproductions and thoughtful commentary. Laurel read the inscription aloud: "'Merry Christmas, 1999, to Laurie, with love from Pa. Someday there'll be a book like this of *your* paintings.'"

Her voice had broken as she read the few words. Quickly she turned to the second gift. Inside the white cardboard box was another box, made of rich cherry-wood. On the lid was a spray of bay leaves, carefully carved from black walnut.

Rosemary's gifts had been similar: her book was a gently used first edition of Zora Neale Hurston's *Their Eyes Were Watching God* with the inscription: "Someday people will be collecting *your* first editions." The box Sam had made for his older daughter was of black walnut. On the lid was a half-relief rosebud, daintily carved from cherry.

Finally just one small package was left among the fallen needles. Laurel had retrieved it and held it out. "Here, Mum." A small box and a card that read "For Liz, who has deserved better, with all my love, Sam."

She had understood then why the girls had been so slow, so deliberate in the unwrapping of their gifts. *Sam tied this bow . . . and now I'm untying it. He placed this tape, folded this paper . . . and now I'm undoing it. This is my last present from Sam . . . there will be no more.*

No, no, never, never no more. The mournful refrain of an old ballad had sounded in her head as she pulled open the cardboard box. Inside was a tiny oval wooden box, smaller than those he had made for the girls. She had run her fingertips over the complex knot of initials incised on the lid and fought back the tears that had risen to her eyes.

And within the little box, resting on a piece of folded silk, had been an antique wedding band, its warm pink-tinged gold decorated with fanciful vines and leaves.

23.

LOST BAGGAGE

Monday, October 17,
Tuesday, October 18,
and Thursday, October 20

"**A ring, Sam** gave me a wedding ring that last Christmas. I'd lost my original one and he found a beautiful old band of rose gold. I took it off when you and I ... I don't know ... it didn't seem right."

"No, I see what you mean." Phillip was clearly uncomfortable with the subject, but he persevered. "I remember noticing it ... before. Leaves and stuff on it. I thought it suited you ... with all your herbs and flowers. Could I take a look at it? If it's the last thing Sam gave you, it could be what we're looking for."

It was in the top drawer of her bureau, in the little box Sam had crafted for it. She took the ring out, resisting the impulse to slip it onto her finger, and carried it to Phillip.

"Nothing engraved inside." He shook his head in disappointment. "And the design—you say you think the ring was old? No chance that he had it made?"

"No chance at all. Sam told me that he found it in an antiques shop in Asheville. And it just *felt* old, if you know what I mean—all worn and smooth."

Phillip held the ring under the reading lamp, turning it

this way and that. Finally he shrugged. "No, I don't think this is what we're looking for." He gave it a last admiring glance. "It does suit you. Sam had a good eye."

"There was another part of the present—the ring was inside a little carved box he'd made." She took the ring from him and absently slid it back onto her finger.

"I didn't know Sam was such an artist. This is really nice—great carving, all around the sides and across the top."

As he'd done with the ring, Phillip took the little box to study under the reading light. "He had to have worked under a magnifying glass. Amazing detail for such a small amount of surface area, and all of it carved. And these must be your initials, here on top—what's your middle name?"

"It's my maiden name: Grey. Which means, unfortunately, that my monogram is—"

"E.G.G." Phillip returned the little box to her. He grinned. "So that explains the shape of the box and the letters. Sam did love a pun. But, damn, for a minute I thought we had a clue."

The popping sound, followed almost instantly by the ding, made Rosemary catch her breath. Her dark eyes flicked to the bottom of the laptop screen where a flashing icon proclaimed INCOMING MAIL. Abandoning the story she was working on in mid-sentence, she opened her in-box. A smile spread slowly across her face. *Yes!*

The e-mail began abruptly:

I wish it were Thursday night already. I can't believe what's happened: the skinny little kid who lived next door—all long legs and big eyes—has turned into a college professor ... and a beauty. She's back in my life and Thursday we'll be together again.

You can't know, Rosy, what it means for me to be with you. You've brought something back into my life that I'd almost forgotten. I hope that we can spend a good portion of your fall break getting to know each other again—and much better.

But I'll save all of this for Thursday night. I just couldn't resist e-mailing, to remind myself that you're out there.

BTW, I've been thinking over what you said about that retarded man (Cletus?). You're right: he was definitely spooky and he did seem somewhat fixated on you little girls. I remember once he tried to get Krystalle to go with him up into the woods. He told her he would show her a nest of flying squirrels, or something like that. Of course, Patricia the über-mom was on the case and yelled at Krysty to come inside before she got her clothes dirty.

All of which proves nothing. And you tell me the man in question is dead. It may be hard at this point to prove anything. But I trust your instincts here and I respect your desire to pursue the question to some sort of resolution. I, too, would like closure.

Till Thursday night,

Jared

She read the e-mail through a second time, then printed it out and deleted it. She was reading the hard copy for a third time when a knock at her office door demanded her attention.

"Come in." Rosemary slid the printout into her desk

drawer just as one of her colleagues, an anxious-looking gray mouse of a woman, skittered in. "Hi, Letitia, you look harassed. Is there a problem?"

"No, not a *problem,* as such." Letitia perched on the edge of one of the office chairs and looked around the room as if in search of something. Her slightly prominent front teeth and almost nonexistent chin intensified her resemblance to a small rodent. *She always looks around like that, like she's afraid a cat will pounce on her. Or maybe she's just looking for cheese.*

"Well, Rosemary, as you know, Katherine, Nancy, Marion, and I have been planning a little trip over fall break—Charleston, Savannah, and the low country. Such an *evocative* area and so much fine writing has come out of there. We have all our arrangements and reservations at some really *nice* bed-and-breakfasts. And now Katherine says she won't be able to go.

"We *think*...." The mouse leaned forward and lowered her voice. "We *think* she's gotten involved with a *man.* So we were wondering... I know it's dreadfully short notice—but then, you don't have any family responsibilities, so we thought... we wondered if you might like to take Katherine's place. With four of us to share expenses, it's really a quite affordable jaunt." Her nose quivered. "Would you be interested? We plan to leave early Thursday morning."

"Thanks, it sounds terrific. But I have an appointment in Asheville on Thursday that I can't miss." She suppressed a fleeting desire to add, *And I think I've gotten involved with a man.*

It wasn't as if she'd never been involved with a man before, Rosemary reflected, driving toward Asheville on Thursday morning. There had been a few unsatisfactory interludes, none of any significant duration. The first had been during her freshman year, when she'd convinced herself she was in love with a tall, slim Bangladeshi graduate assistant who spoke beautifully accented BBC English. Hasibul had quickly disillusioned her: first, by suggesting that she bleach her hair; and second, when she declined to become a blonde, by finding someone who was. With a slightly guilty feeling of relief, Rosemary had returned to a life of chastity and scholarship until grad school.

Connor, of the pale skin, black hair, and piercing blue eyes, had been a fellow student, enrolled in many of the same seminars. This had led to late night study sessions at his apartment, which had led to very early morning sessions on the lumpy futon in his bedroom. It might have continued indefinitely—or at least through grad school— had she not dropped by his apartment one day to retrieve an overdue library book. There had been no answer to her knock, so she had used her key to let herself in.

Connor and Cassandra, a fluffy little MA candidate, hadn't made it as far as the futon. They were a tangled, half-clothed beast with two backs on the sagging old sofa. Ignoring Cassandra's squeals as she scurried for the bedroom and Connor's half-indignant, half-abject attempts at explanation, Rosemary had stalked to the table where she'd left the book, retrieved it, and stalked out the door, tossing the apartment key over her shoulder.

"We're all in this alone" had become an unspoken motto. Men betrayed you or wanted to change you. Happy marriages might exist—Mum and Pa's had been happy, eventually, in spite of those two… *indiscretions, surely nothing more.* But then Pa had been killed, leaving Mum with a burden of grief that had oppressed her for years.

Baggage, that's what the pop psychologists call it, Rosemary thought. *It was all that baggage weighing me down, making me so cautious about getting involved with anyone. I guess I just decided that a life alone was better than disappointment, betrayal, and loss.*

She smiled as she caught sight of the foothills, rising in the distance. *It's odd, I seem to have lost that baggage somewhere along the line. And so has Mum. She and Phillip are so sweet, pretending that nothing's going on between them.*

Elizabeth checked the car clock for the third time. It was almost one and still no sign of Rosemary. She glanced up at the façade of the shopping mall and grimaced at the bold green letters proclaiming that this was the home of Trish Trantham Lifeworks. *I am* not *going in there to talk with Patricia Mullins unless Rosemary's here. And I don't want to talk to Trish Trantham either. Whatever she calls herself, I call her a—*

"Mum!" Rosemary was rapping on her car window. "There was a huge traffic jam just outside Asheville or I'd have been here sooner. Let's go!"

The emerald green door was opening as they approached it, and a plump young woman, her brown hair skewered atop her head in an unbecoming and uncompromising knot, emerged. Her arms cradled a towering stack of padded mailers and she called back over her shoulder, "All *right,* I said I would, didn't I? Give it a rest, Trish."

Catching sight of Elizabeth and Rosemary, she smiled sourly. "Oh, my! Old home week!" Protuberant blue eyes studied them briefly through thick glasses. "She's waiting for you." The young woman bared her teeth in an unpleasantly knowing smile. "In there. Let the games begin."

GRAMMER GREY

September 1986

MUM'S MOTHER, *GRAMMER* Grey, *had finally come to visit.
At least five times since they had moved to North Carolina,
Grammer had called and said that she was coming—just for
a few days, just to see her darling grandbabies. Each time, a
whirlwind of cleaning and mowing and finishing incomplete
bits of the house had made life unbearable for several weeks,
and each time there had been the last-minute phone call.
Mum's face would go all blank, and after a few words she
would hang up and say, Well, girls, Grammer says to tell you
how sorry she is, but she can't come up after all. She's . . . not
feeling well.*

Rosemary remembered her grandmother Grey . . . sort of.
She had pale blond hair, red-lipstick lips, and was very thin.
Grand-mère *was what she had taught Rosie to call her, back
when the Goodweathers lived in Florida.* Only "Grand-
mère" *was hard to say and it had turned into* "Grammer," *no
matter how much Grace Howell Grey protested.*

Grace Howell Grey, *that's what Mum said when she talked
about Grammer to Pa.* Grace Howell Grey says we should send
Laurie to Montessori school—there's one in Asheville, *Mum
would say in a prissy kind of voice; or* Grace Howell Grey says

*Rosemary needs to go to dancing class; or Grace Howell Grey
wants to know when we're getting indoor plumbing.*

Never, if it'll keep that old harpy from coming here, Pa had
said.

But finally Grammer had come—not to the farm, but to a big
hotel in Asheville. She had driven out to the farm for lunch and
been taken on a tour of the house. *Everything looked beautiful,* Rosemary thought. Mum and Pa had stayed up late the
night before, waxing the living room floor till the broad oak
boards shone. She and Laurie had skated on them in their sock
feet till it was time for Grammer to arrive.

There were big vases of flowers everywhere. Rosemary had
helped pick them first thing in the morning—lavender chrysan-
themums, black-eyed Susans, the dangling pink begonias
whose seeds looked like paper airplanes. Even Laurie had
picked a bunch of those inky-blue wildflowers that Mum
called Great Lobelia.

But Grammer hadn't seemed to notice the flowers. Her
sharp blue eyes had darted everywhere as she came into the
house and her high heels had tap-tap-tapped on the shiny
floor. *Well, Elizabeth,* she had said to Mum. *Here I am.*

Mum had hugged Grammer and said, *I'm glad you're here.
I'll show you the house and then we'll have some lunch. I've
made chicken salad by your recipe.*

Pa was holding two interesting shopping bags with crackly
pink tissue paper sticking out of them. *Thank you, Sam,*
Grammer had said, taking them from him. *These are for the girls.*

They had both been disappointed to see that the presents
were just clothes, but at least Rosemary knew enough to smile
and say *Thank you, Grammer; it's very pretty*—even though
she hated dresses and wasn't crazy about pink either.

Laurie, prompted by a nudge from her mother, had reeled

off a ThankyouveerymuchGrammer, then had completely ignored the smocked green velvet dress in favor of putting the
shopping bag over her head and clumping straight-legged
about the living room pretending to be a robot.

Well. Grammer had said after the tour of the house. It's
rather small and rustic for my taste. And why in god's name
you don't have a proper bathroom, I cannot understand.
When I was a child in Alabama we visited relatives once—
second or third cousins—who lived out in the country. They
had an outhouse. I didn't think it was cute then and I don't
think it's cute now.

Mum had put pretty place mats and napkins on the table
and the silver had been polished too. There was chicken salad
on a lettuce leaf and a hot cheesy bread Mum said had a
French name—something like goo-jeir. Grammer ate most of
her chicken salad but only took one bite of the cheesy bread.
Too rich for me, Elizabeth, she said, and put it to one side of her
plate. I have to be careful if I don't want to put on weight. And
speaking of weight, how much have you gained since you've
been here? I hate to see you letting yourself go this way.

Three bloody pounds! That's what I've gained! And not a single nice thing could she find to say about the house, the view, the
garden, even the girls. Rosie's too quiet and Laurie's too loud...
and why didn't we give them family names instead of naming
them after herbs? If we'd had a boy, would we have named him
Basil? I tell you, Sam, there's nothing I can do to please her.

Relax, Liz. She's leaving tomorrow. We'll go in, have a nice
dinner, and say good-bye. We'll all be polite and pleasant to
the old harpy and that'll be it for a year or so. Maybe longer if
we don't tell her we're having a septic tank put in next week.

Rosemary could hear Mum fussing as she and Pa got
dressed. They were all going in to Asheville tonight to have

dinner at Grammer's fancy hotel. Very much against her wishes, Laurel had been put into the new green dress—I want to wear my striped overalls, she had insisted. Rosemary hadn't argued; that was for babies.

Pa and Mum came into the living room. Rosemary was reading Where the Wild Things Are *out loud while Laurie stomped around pretending to be Max in his wolf suit. Mum looked at them with a funny smile. I have to say, Sam, Grace Howell Grey has an eye for clothes. Don't they both look beautiful?*

Pa smiled too. They do clean up right good, Liz. He made his voice sound like Miss Birdie's husband, Luther. Fact is, yore a right handsome woman yore ownself, Miz Goodweather.

Mum was wearing a soft-looking white blouse and a dark swirly skirt that had little purple and green squiggles in it. Pa had on a pale blue shirt and gray pants and a dark blue coat. There was even a tie around his neck. Rosemary didn't think that she'd ever seen Pa with a tie on. She hadn't even known he had one.

Come on, all you fine-lookin' women, Pa said. We're off for dinner with Grammer. Best behavior, Miss Laurie Lou!

Laurel's red curls bobbed as she nodded vigorously. I'll be very nice to the old harpy!

By the time the dessert came, Laurie's eyes were heavy. She spooned up her ice cream laboriously, her eyelids drifting shut between mouthfuls. Finally Mum took Laurel from her chair and held her in her lap, where Laurie immediately went fast asleep.

Rosemary had been sleepy, too, but the arrival of her crème brûlée and the intense joy of cracking her spoon against the brittle caramelized sugar had awakened her. She ate the delicious creamy dessert very slowly, taking tiny spoonfuls to make it last.

The waiter was at the table again. He had brought first one and then another bottle of wine. Now Grammer was saying Three Irish coffees.

No, thank you, Grace, I have to drive, said Pa. *Just black coffee will be great.*

Just coffee for me, too, Mum said.

The waiter nodded and went away. Grammer poured the last of the red wine into her glass and lifted it. *Well, here's to the Goodweathers and their oh-so-happy life. Pardon me if I don't get it. I guess I'm just not a nature girl like my older daughter.*

Mum's eye darted toward Pa and she started to say something, but Grammer kept on. *I only asked you to let the girls spend the night here with me. There's a lovely heated indoor pool they could swim in tomorrow and I could drive them out to the farm before I head back for Florida.*

Thank you, Mother, but I don't think . . . anyway, they don't have their bathing suits—

There's a nice little shop right here in the hotel—all sorts of swimwear . . . I'll buy them some—

—and Laurie's never spent the night away from home—

She's old enough to start now. Grammer's face was growing red and her voice was getting louder. *I want to spend some time with my granbabies! You dragged them away from civilization—their grandmother, their aunt . . .* Grammer grabbed Rosemary's hand and the spoon with the last bite of crème brûlée fell onto the pink velvet, leaving a white smear. Grammer's hand held Rosemary's wrist very tightly.

Mum? Rosie looked at her mother, who was clutching the sleeping Laurel. Grammer was standing now and trying to make Rosemary get up and come with her.

Mum? Rosemary whispered.

She slept most of the way back to the farm. She had the whole back seat to herself because Mum was still holding Laurie. She woke up once to hear her parents talking softly.

I got her back to her room, Pa was saying. *She was pretty well staggering by the time we got there. And into the maudlin, nobody-loves-me thing. But she collapsed on her bed and told me to leave her alone and take you and the girls home.*

Mum didn't say anything and Pa continued in the same low voice. Rosie looked kind of freaked. What did you tell her?

Mum's voice was cold and hard, like a stone in the shade. I told her Grammer had too much to drink. Again.

Pa's voice was very soft. Liz, as I was leaving her room, she said, Tell my daughter I apologize.

Mum didn't answer at first. When she did, the stone had turned to ice. She always does, Mum said.

24.

CHRISTIANS MAY FORGIVE BUT ONLY FOOLS FORGET

Thursday, October 20

"Elizabeth, how nice to see you! And Rosemary! Let's go back to my office; we'll be more comfortable there. You just missed Krystalle ... or did you see her on your way in?"

The voice was familiar; the smooth, unaccented, woman-in-charge radio voice that dominated much of right-wing talk radio, weekdays from nine till noon. But the impeccably and elegantly attired woman who stood before them ...

"Patricia?" Elizabeth studied her ex-neighbor doubtfully. The bouffant yellow hair of the past had become a carefully toned ash blond, worn in a classic cut that fell just along Trish Trantham's classic, sculptured jawline. The tight, bright clothes that had adorned Mrs. Barbie were gone; Trish Trantham wore an artful and expensive layering of cashmere, silk, and suede: a symphony of understated taupe, gunmetal, and pearl. *And what happened to the big bosom? I saw her in a bikini. I know it was real, or at least, real implants. Where'd those go?*

"Was that Krystalle going out the door?" Rosemary asked. "I didn't recognize her. I think Jared said she works with you?"

Trish Trantham motioned them into a large office without replying. Ignoring the imposing desk, she led them to a sitting area furnished with a luxurious mole gray velvet sofa and wingback chairs covered in heavy silk the deep purple of a thundercloud. The chairs were pulled close to the sofa to allow for intimate conversation.

"One of my assistants will bring us coffee." Trish Trantham composed herself gracefully in a wingback, bestowing a benevolent smile on Elizabeth and Rosemary. "Yes, Rosemary, that was Krystalle. I'm not surprised you didn't recognize her. She's working through a number of problems at present, and choosing to ignore her appearance is one of the passive-aggressive mechanisms she's employing."

Trish kicked off her improbably high heels and pulled her feet up under her. She resembled nothing so much, Elizabeth thought, as a blue-point Siamese, right down to the huge sapphire eyes that had just turned her way with an appraising stare.

"You know, Elizabeth, I'm glad that you came with Rosemary. I'm afraid that after we left Mullmore I tried my best to forget everything about Marshall County. I didn't even know about Sam's death until I spoke with Rosemary. Please, may I offer my condolences?" She extended a manicured hand and lightly brushed Elizabeth's arm. "He was such a lovely man. Such a devoted father...and husband."

Elizabeth felt her arm tighten in an involuntary response. "Thank you, Patri—excuse me, *Trish*. Yes, he was that." *And you certainly did your best to undevote him back then.*

Why the hell did I agree to come? What bloody good is it to stir up the past this way? Sam's interlude with this woman was over almost before it began and my brief moment with Mike was just that—a moment. Sam and I were a faithful, loving couple for years and years afterward. And now, that one bad time's the main thing I can remember. Oh, bloody hell!

The door opened and a dark-haired young woman came in, carrying a silver tray. She set it on the coffee table in front of them.

"Thank you, Melissa." Trish Trantham uncoiled herself and picked up the silver coffeepot. "Have them hold all my calls, please. Elizabeth, do you take it black?"

The interruption helped; the small ritual of cup and saucer (thin, creamy porcelain—*you couldn't hurl this across the room in anger, not like a mug*) and fragrant steaming coffee forced Elizabeth back into the present moment and its purpose. *We're here for Rosemary—to talk about* her *memories, not mine.*

"...and we have to recognize that after all this time, none of us is the same. Obviously, you've grown up, Rosemary, but I mean something more.... I like to think that we've all grown."

Trish Trantham was in radio mode now. She set her cup and saucer back on the tray and leaned forward, elbows on her knees, chin resting on her interlaced fingers. "Let me share with you something of my journey since we left Mullmore. I'd like you to know who I am now before we go back to the old Patricia Mullins." She smiled a self-deprecating smile. "I often share my story with groups—parents who've suffered traumatic loss; they seem to take strength from it. Forgive me if it sounds a bit...practiced."

The story *was* obviously a well-rehearsed, often told tale. Silly young woman...dysfunctional family background...poorly educated...bad choices...lack of values...false goals...achievement of false goals...

realization of emptiness of life...and then disaster. Trish Trantham was unsparing in her condemnation of Patricia Mullins.

"My behavior in those years before we lost Maythorn was terrible, I confess." Trish held Elizabeth with a limpid gaze. "I knew the moment you walked in that you were still carrying anger toward me; your body language shouted it out. And Patricia deserved that anger—sad to say, she had the morals of a cat in heat. Elizabeth, I'm truly sorry for any pain that she caused you..." the sapphire eyes swiveled to encompass Rosemary "...or you, Rosemary. Please forgive Patricia, and know that granting of forgiveness is a step toward your own healing as well."

Something a friend had said years ago ran through Elizabeth's mind: *Any Christian can forgive. But only a fool forgets.* Repressing a powerful desire to repeat this, she nodded at Trish, who was holding out her lovely hands in somewhat dramatic supplication. "You're right, Trish. I *was* remembering several occasions. But as you say, we're none of us the same people anymore; Patricia has my forgiveness." *For what it's worth. And I still wouldn't trust her* or *Trish in my meat house with a muzzle, as Miss Birdie says.*

Trish sighed and leaned back. "Thank you, Elizabeth. You know, one of the truly important lessons that I learned from the loss of Maythorn was the power of forgiveness. Yes, I had to learn to forgive myself, as well as others. And I had to face the fact that my firstborn child was gone forever—accept the reality and go on with my life. It was then, in the depths of despair, my child ripped from me, my husband lost in the bottle, it was then that I found my strength, my voice, my true calling."

The second half of the Trish Trantham story: enlight-

enment...self-realization and actualization...the perfect mentor...the lucky break... *All made possible by the
extremely munificent divorce settlement she hasn't mentioned.
Rosemary said that Jared told her it was around ten million dollars. I may throw up if she says much more about the struggle of a
single mom. I don't know—I think I liked her better as Mrs.
Barbie.*

But at last the saga was drawing to a close. "So you see,
I've moved on. As *you* should, Rosemary. But, of course, I
want to help you. Let's treat this as if you're a caller to my
show."

Trish leaned forward again and stared into Rosemary's eyes. "Good afternoon, Rosemary, what's your
question? Tell Trish."

"Well, I guess—"

"No guessing. If you have a question, ask it."

Elizabeth watched—fighting back a growing annoyance *or is it jealousy?*—as her daughter struggled to
arrange words in an acceptable form. Finally Rosemary
said, "Trish, I think that Maythorn wants me to find out
what happened...to find *her*. Do you think I'm crazy?"

Trish Trantham studied Rosemary intently. "When
you say 'Maythorn wants,' do you mean that you believe
she's *spoken* to you?"

"No, nothing like that...I'm not hearing voices or
seeing ghosts. But I have had...well, it sounds ridiculous, but at various times I've been almost overpowered
with the feeling that she's trying to contact me, trying to
tell me to find out the truth."

"And you feel you owe her this because...?"

Elizabeth watched in horror as her daughter, typi-
cally so self-contained and unemotional, struggled to
answer, then began to cry. Without a word, Trish pushed

a strategically poised tissue container across the coffee table to Rosemary.

"Take your time, Rosie," said Trish Trantham. "Pull yourself together and then tell me why you feel it was your fault."

"What? You can't—"

Elizabeth's outcry was halted by Rosemary's uplifted hand. "She's right, Mum. It *was* my fault—I should have warned her."

25.

HIDEY HOLES

Thursday, October 20

"Yeah, I've told her what we're looking for. She says Sam never mentioned any deposition or photos. We're making a systematic search....Remember, he said he *gave* her the key—so we're looking at all the gifts Sam gave Elizabeth from the time we found out Landrum was alive to the time Sam died."

Phillip looked at his watch with some irritation. The voice on the cell phone went on and on. "Trust me, Gabby, I'm checking out everything....I know, Red was big into puzzles and codes. There's a little box he made with some intricate carving—I've sent it to Del for his people to look at, along with a ring; she thinks it's an antique, but the designs on it are pretty odd...could be a cipher of some kind. And both of these are things he'd gotten her for Christmas the year he died."

He looked at his watch again. "No, nothing new on the plane crash. But it's pretty obvious, isn't it, what a lucky break it was for Landrum....No, I haven't."

From his perch on the front-porch railing, he could hear the sound of Elizabeth's jeep. "Listen, Gabby, I'll get back to you later. You keep an eye on Landrum's people;

let me know if it looks like they're going to make another move.... Okay, will do."

He returned the little phone to his pocket and watched the approach of the car, moving slowly up the road, Molly loping gracefully alongside and Ursa trotting behind. James, who had been keeping him company on the porch, bounded down the steps and pattered along the stone path to be ready to greet Elizabeth. With an inward chuckle, Phillip followed the little dog.

"Afternoon, Miz Goodweather." His strong arms encircled her as she stepped out of the car. "How'd it go with the radio lady? Find out anything useful?"

She leaned into him, savoring the embrace. "Useful, I don't know. But I did find out that when it comes to Rosemary, I haven't had a clue. Just like I didn't have a clue about Sam and that Vietnam horror story."

She tried to keep the bitterness and hurt out of her voice. It had not been easy to sit and watch Rosemary unburden herself of the guilt she had carried so many years—*to watch her bare her* soul *to Trish bloody Trantham, of all people! And then to hear her accuse* Cletus.

"*Cletus?*"

Sitting there in that luxurious office, watching a professionally sympathetic Trish Trantham extract the story bit by painful bit from a weeping Rosemary, Elizabeth had at last grasped the meaning of the rambling, tearful account her daughter was giving.

"Rosemary? You mean you thought that *Cletus* was responsible for whatever happened to Maythorn? And it was somehow your fault?"

Trish had ignored Elizabeth's outburst. "I always said that it was that half-wit—excuse me, developmentally disabled young man. I said so over and over, but the sheriff was sure it had to be that other local, the one who had threatened Moon. Of *course* it was Cletus!"

Elizabeth had looked on in disbelief as Rosemary, fighting to control her voice, stammered out, "I...I should have told someone. If I'd just warned Maythorn, told her that he scared me..."

"Or you might have told *me*!" Elizabeth reached for Rosemary's hand. "Rosie, what did Cletus *do* that scared you? And why didn't you—"

"Oh, Mum, you and Pa and Laurie all loved Cletus so much. I felt bad that he made me feel creepy just because he was the way he was. But there was this one time..."

"Phillip, I don't know what to think. I'm glad Rosemary had plans with Jared tonight so I could talk to you about all of this before she comes back."

The temperature had dropped during the day and the heat of the logs crackling in the fireplace was welcome. They sat after supper, side by side on the sofa facing the fire, their feet propped up on the old chest that served as a coffee table. Phillip's arm was around her and the warmth of his body was even more comforting than that of the fire.

"So the incident that actually scared Rosemary was when Cletus skinned a squirrel?"

"Yes, and that, in itself, doesn't mean anything. Lots of people used to hunt and eat squirrels. Still do. She knows that. But she got it in her mind that he was going to do the same thing to her dog, Dinah, the little hound we had back then. Rosemary said that one day Dinah had been missing since the night before and she found Cletus in the woods leading Dinah on a rope."

"Why didn't she tell you at the time?"

Elizabeth was quiet for a moment. At last she spoke. "That's what makes me feel so bad. First Rosemary said that she hadn't thought we'd take her seriously. Then, after some of Trish's trademark badgering, Rosemary said it was because when she came to the house right after this happened, Sam and I were in our room with the door shut. She said that I was crying."

Phillip's arm tightened around her. After a pause he said quietly, "Did that happen a lot? Sam always gave me the impression that you two had a really happy marriage."

She laid her head against his shoulder and shut her eyes. "Like the curate's egg, parts of it were excellent. No, that's not fair—*most* of it was excellent. It was his dreams that were the problem. I told you, they were bad when we first moved here, and though they got less frequent, there were still times…I'd given up trying to talk him into getting professional help, but I still tried to get him to talk about it with me."

Elizabeth stared at the dancing flames. "You know, Phillip, during those first three years we were here, between getting going with the farm, taking care of Laurie, who was something of a handful, and worrying about Sam's state of mind, I was just thankful that Rosie didn't seem to need much attention. It took the loss of Maythorn for me to see that she did. And then she shut me out."

When the meeting with Trish Trantham had finally ended, Elizabeth had felt an urgent necessity to talk to her daughter alone. They had stood by their cars in the parking lot, both still shaken with emotion, reluctant to pursue the revelations just uncovered but unable to ignore them. Rosemary's dark glasses hid her eyes, but Elizabeth suspected that they were still wet with tears.

"Rosie, when are you meeting Jared? Could we go somewhere for coffee first? Or maybe to the Botanical Garden and take a walk?"

Rosemary had stood there indecisively, jingling her car keys and looking away. At last she said, "A walk would be nice, Mum. I'm not meeting Jared till five."

The winding paths of the UNCA botanical gardens were almost deserted, and Rosemary, still hidden behind her dark glasses, had set off at a brisk pace as though attempting to outdistance her demons. Elizabeth lagged a little behind, hoping that the exertion would calm her daughter and leave her ready to talk. Almost twenty minutes went by with only the muffled sounds of their footsteps on the leaf-strewn paths, birdsong, the chatter of squirrels, and the murmur of water in a distant creek. Finally Rosemary halted by a bench and waited for her mother to catch up.

Elizabeth sank down gratefully and tried to catch her breath. "Could we rest a bit before going on?" she implored. "And I need to apologize to you, sweetie."

Rosemary took off the sunglasses and sat beside her mother. "Apologize? For what?"

"For not understanding how you felt about Cletus, for not knowing how afraid you were, for all the things I did that were wrong or didn't do that I should have done... *We have left undone those things which we ought to have done; And we have done those things which we ought not to have done*—words of confession, seared into her brain by attendance at morning prayer in the dim past rose unbidden. *And there is no health in us.*

"Rosemary and I went for a walk after seeing Trish Trantham and we talked about things. We talked about Rosemary's shutting me out back then, just as I had, in a way, shut her out. Of course, I felt, and still feel, that I was protecting her." Elizabeth made a small, rueful sound. "In a weird way, that was *her* reasoning: she couldn't tell me how she felt about Cletus because she knew I liked him."

"And now that she *has* told you, do you think there could be any truth in it? In your opinion, was Cletus capable of murder?" Phillip's arm was still around her and his voice remained carefully neutral.

Elizabeth sighed heavily. "I don't know. My gut feeling is that Cletus would never have hurt anyone. And back then when people pointed fingers at him, Sam and I just saw it as ignorant prejudice. But now I'm thinking that maybe we were just as prejudiced *for* him as others were against him. I never even considered it as a possibility, that he could have done something like that."

"Motive, means, and opportunity," Phillip mused. "He would have had the last two, easy—didn't you say he always roamed the woods and always carried a shotgun?"

"He did. And a lot of the time Maythorn roamed the same woods all alone. But motive... Now, that's where my mind stops working. I can't imagine Cletus—you never knew him, but he was so *gentle*—I just can't imagine him hurting anyone."

Phillip stood to put another log on the fire. The dogs, who had been basking by the hearth, roused and moved away, James to the pillow in the rocking chair and Ursa and Molly to Elizabeth's bedroom. At last, almost to himself, Phillip said, "But what if it was an accident—say he thought he was shooting at a deer or something. You said the girls were always slipping around, trying to be invisible. What if he shot Maythorn accidentally and then—"

Elizabeth sat bolt upright. "He would have been terrified. There was always a threat that he might be institutionalized if Miss Birdie couldn't look after him. He knew about that and he probably had enough sense to realize that this was big trouble."

A memory—Miss Birdie sitting on the porch and laughing about what she had found under Cletus's bed. *Law, you wouldn't believe the plunder that boy has hid from me under his bed. Things he's broke or spiled some way. Now, you know I ain't never raised a hand to him, and that's the truth, but he purely hates for me to know he's made a mistake of ary kind.*

Oncet hit was a baby groundhog he hid under the bed—dead as a hammer. I knowed they was something there by the smell. Well, I skirmished around with the broom till I got it out. I tell you what's the truth, tore-up books and broken clocks is one thing, but corpses is another.

So I called Cletus in and asked him right stern how come that groundhog to be there, and the pore boy just busted out cryin'. Said he found the baby wanderin' around and there was sign that dogs had killed its mama. You know Cletus is plumb foolish about young uns of ary kind. So he put the baby in his poke and brung it home. Only when he got here and come to take hit out, hit was dead. I don't know if it smothered or just died of fright like wild things kin do. Everwhat, Cletus got skeered hit was his doin' and he hid it.

Ay law, Lizzie Beth, he was all to pieces over that corpse. I didn't have the heart to scold him.

Elizabeth looked at Phillip. "I have to admit, it's a possible scenario. And if that, or something like that, is what happened, I can see Cletus hiding the body."

She found all my hidey holes, Cletus had said of Maythorn. *She's pretty, like a baby deer.*

26.

"LIKE AN ANGRY BUZZ SAW"

Saturday, October 22

Bambambambambambambam...*bam.* The rapid fire of the seven other class members was punctuated by Elizabeth's slower response as she struggled to line up the center of the target in her sights. If only there had been time for practice at home. Unfortunately, an emergency with the main greenhouse's watering system had occupied the afternoon she had set aside to reacquaint herself with the big .357 Magnum that had been Sam's. She realized now, as she tried to accomplish the required five rounds in fifteen seconds—*and get them in the chest area of the target, Elizabeth*—that the mere possession of the big handgun had given her what was very probably a false sense of security.

Phillip had announced on Thursday that he had (*provisionally,* he had emphasized) signed her up for the concealed carry permit class.

"You ought to have a gun with you when you're driving around, and you might as well be legal while you're at it."

He had fixed her with a look of such seriousness that she swallowed the flippant reply trembling on her lips and said, "Okay, then. Nine at the library."

"Thanks, Elizabeth." He had kissed her heartily. "There're some rough characters out there and I'd be a lot happier knowing you can defend yourself."

As she returned the kiss, a phrase from Robert Heinlein's *Glory Road* popped into her always vagabond mind. One of Sam's favorite books, it featured Star, the lusty, busty heroine, who was, coincidentally, the Empress of Twenty Universes. Because of her title, Star was in perpetual danger of assassination. It had, therefore, been determined that to increase her chances of survival, she should be trained in all the martial arts, should learn to "fight like an angry buzz saw."

Me too. But what's a buzz saw? Remembering the empress's penchant for fighting garb that was scanty or nonexistent, Elizabeth grinned.

"What's so funny, Miz Goodweather?" Phillip turned a suspicious eye on her.

"I just thought of a book you might enjoy—all about a woman and the handsome hero guarding her. Sam had a copy. I'll find it for you."

At five till nine on Saturday morning, Elizabeth and Phillip had pulled into a parking space at the Marshall County library. He had insisted on accompanying her and, as she looked at the group gathered in the parking lot, she was very glad he had.

About a dozen young men were milling in front of the library doors, apparently intent on one last cigarette before class. They seemed to be typical Marshall County good ol' boys: there were snuff can circles on the

pockets of more than one pair of jeans—there was spitting.

Elizabeth sat in the car, acutely aware of her outsider
status. Phillip seemed unconcerned as he got out and
pulled a little bag from the back seat. In it, she knew,
were Sam's .357 Magnum, a belt, a holster, hearing pro-
tectors, and several boxes of ammunition.

"Showtime," he said cheerfully as he opened her door.

The morning part of the class had been a piece of cake.
Phillip had introduced her to the instructor, whom he
seemed to know fairly well. Alex Sewell—"Call me Alex"—
was an imposing figure, with close-cropped blond hair
and blue eyes, who, at six-five, towered over Phillip but
treated him with the friendly deference due to a man
who was a close friend of the sheriff. Alex had assured
Elizabeth that she would be able to pass the shooting
range part of the test and had not seemed to find it
amusing that she was there in the midst of all the young
men.

And at the last minute, to Elizabeth's intense relief,
another woman had shown up. Elizabeth had heard her
tell Alex, "I already got my permit; I just come to help my
daddy. He's eighty-two, right deaf, and cain't read much
on account of he had to leave school early. I kin read the
test to him."

The morning had flown by in a blur of PowerPoint
presentations, very dull films, and repetitive drill, all de-
signed to hammer home the information needed to pass
the written test at the end.

"Once you have your permit," and it was encouraging
how Alex assured them that they would all be able to
pass the test, "if you're carrying and are stopped for a

traffic check or whatever, keep your hands on the steering wheel and *at once* inform the local great gray god that you are armed."

Elizabeth had frowned a question at Phillip, who was sprawled in the chair beside her, and he had leaned close to whisper, "Slang for 'trooper'—highway patrol wears gray uniforms."

Alex had enumerated the many, many places where, even with the magic permit, one could *not* carry a gun: public places where admission is charged; educational institutions and their campuses; places where alcohol is sold and/or consumed; courthouses; state property; Federal property; parades, demonstrations, picket lines, funerals; law enforcement facilities; Department of Corrections facilities; financial institutions; or anywhere the owner has posted a sign saying NO FIREARMS. *Well, hell, where* can *one carry a gun?* Elizabeth found herself thinking.

She had scribbled furiously, back in note-taking, high-achiever mode, aware of Phillip's amused eye on her. *I'll probably make an idiot of myself on the firing range, but at least I can do well on the written test.*

Alex had then moved into the very interesting and, in her opinion, somewhat contradictory part of the instruction covering the private citizen's right to use deadly force. After she copied the words in her notebook, she paused and reread them.

Deadly force. This is serious. And scary. And Phillip thinks I may need to do this to defend myself.

Could she kill in self-defense? She was pretty sure that she could. She had been startled once in the past at the wild vehemence of her response when Laurel had been threatened, and she knew that beneath her liberal, tree-hugging façade, a primal being lurked.

"...for self-defense against a real threat of death or

bodily harm. It should be a threat others would recognize as such. You may not have instigated the conflict. If you did instigate it and it threatens to escalate, you must attempt to withdraw and be rejected before resorting to deadly force. You may not use force beyond what is necessary to eliminate the threat."

Alex had continued slowly, stopping now and again to be sure that his listeners grasped the meaning of the law.

"There is the duty to retreat. You must retreat in face of a threat, *unless* there is a threat of death, serious bodily harm, or sexual assault. If you are in your home or your business premises, there is no duty to retreat."

At those words, Phillip had nudged her. "That's important."

Alex had scanned the class, his blue eyes commanding the attention of each participant. "Now listen up. You have the right to use deadly force in defense of a life. You do *not* have the right to use deadly force in defense of your TV set."

A ripple of laughter had run through the class. Alex held up a hand. "You may not use deadly force in defense of property. You may not use deadly force to stop a simple assault—say Charles there slaps me, I'm not allowed to shoot him. Or if Hawkins over there calls me an S.O.B., that's not a legitimate reason. You may not use deadly force because of threatening or violent language *or* because of past violence *or* possible future violence."

Unless you're the current administration. The bitter thought had formed instantly. *Or someone like Landrum.*

The list of prohibitions against deadly force had continued: no deadly force to eject a trespasser, to arrest a criminal, or to prevent a criminal's escape. "You have to remember that in every case where deadly force is used, a criminal investigation *will* follow. There must be an imminent threat of severe harm—and since there will be an investigation, it should be a threat that others would recognize as such."

Alex grinned. "Now, I bet Miz Goodweather there is wondering how she makes that decision before blowing away the crank head she finds in her house some night. Well, she ought to know, sometimes the ladies get a free ride here. Not many juries are going to argue that she wasn't in danger.

"But if you *find* yourself in a situation, there's a saying worth remembering: better to be judged by twelve than carried by six."

Bambambambambambambam...bam!

Once again, she was slower than the others. But her shots seemed to be hitting within the chest area of the gray torso outline hanging downrange an easy five yards away. The test required two rounds of five from three, five, and seven yards. "Mamaw could do this, if she was still alive," Alex had said.

Phillip had discreetly coached her into what Alex had called the isosceles stance: both arms fully extended at shoulder height, wrists and elbows locked, feet apart, knees slightly flexed. She knew how to line up the front and rear sights, but kept forgetting which eye to close.

Finally, however, after a few practice rounds, she seemed to have it. Some shots had actually hit dead center and Phillip had given her an enthusiastic thumbs-up.

The timed test passed quickly in a blur of sun, the acrid reek of gunpowder, the muffled sounds of volleyed shots, and a whirl of last-minute instructions. She had concentrated on lining up the sights after each shot, as the recoil of the big pistol seemed impossible for her to overcome. When the last round had been fired and all pistols emptied and holstered, they had inspected their targets. Passing score was 70, but all around her were scores of 97 and 100. At last Alex came to her, at the end of the line. He studied her target briefly and nodded.

"Ninety-one."

While the second half of the class shot their qualifying rounds, Elizabeth and the first group stood, as directed, behind the twenty-five yard line. The firing range was located within the county landfill, and as her car had wound through the grim wasteland, she had been able to catch a glimpse of her own roof in the distance, its dull aluminum shining in the sun, the familiar outline of Pinnacle Mountain rising behind. Now she looked around, marveling at the strange set of circumstances that had brought her to this place.

The eight qualifiers of the second group lined up, and Alex began to go over his instructions. At the end of the line, the deaf old man pulled out his gun and drew a bead on the target. At once, Alex was at his side, explaining loudly that he must wait. The deaf old man grinning happily at him, nodded with perfect incomprehension.

"Hawkins." Alex jerked his head, motioning Phillip to go to the old man's side. Elizabeth watched, fascinated, as Phillip, with great and tender care, stayed by the old man's side throughout the exercise. The old man was shooting a very large revolver of ancient and unknown manufacture, and now the sound on the range was *BOOM . . . bambambambambambambam.*

"Your man knows just how to talk to Daddy," the deaf man's daughter declared between rounds of gunfire.

"Daddy didn't want me helping him while he was shootin'—claims I aggravate him."

My man. Elizabeth smiled. The words sounded good. And suddenly it felt perfectly natural and even desirable to be at the landfill, at the firing range on a fine October day. The exciting smell of gunpowder drifted toward them and the sun glinted silver and gold off the brass of discarded cartridges littering the wiry brown grass. The deaf man's daughter pointed behind them to a gentle rolling ridge overlooking an acre or so of heaped garbage. "My mamaw and papaw used to have a big old house up there. Mamaw had ever flower you could name out front. It like to broke her heart when they had to leave."

The second group finished and Phillip stayed with his charge to make sure the old man's pistol was safely empty. Then he returned to Elizabeth's side.

"I thank you fer helpin' Daddy. How'd he do?" the daughter asked.

"Ninety-seven," Phillip answered. "He's a good shot. He said he'd have made one hundred, but I aggravated him, standing so close."

They gathered under a large shed at the rear of the range and Alex collected their checks, recorded their scores, filled out their certificates, and wrote down the registration number of each weapon. Many of the participants were examining and comparing handguns, each vocal in praise for his weapon of choice. Elizabeth was charmed to note that one young man, wearing a T-shirt blazoned with the name of a local Baptist church, had a large mother-of-pearl cross inlaid in the black grip of his pistol. Immediately the question formed in her mind: *What handgun would Jesus carry?*

THE REAPER GAME

Early October 1986

THE SMELL OF *freshly sawn lumber was enticing, as was the empty interior of the newly constructed chicken house. It sat there beneath the big black walnut tree, a perfect little building with one window, a door, and a smaller door just for the chickens. Pa had finished building it last week, but there would be no chickens till spring. Until then it was Rosie's own possession—a fort, a clubhouse, a hideout.*

She had furnished her lair with a few old cushions and a wooden box for a table. The row of nest boxes on the wall were her bookcase, and some of her books and notebooks filled the little cubicles, where, this time next year, fat hens would lay their brown eggs.

She stood and looked out the window, her *window. Maythorn was late. And there was no sign of her on the hillside. The butterscotch squares that she and Mum had made after lunch were getting cold and the milk she had brought in a jar was getting warm. No more waiting.*

She sat down on the largest of the cushions, opened her copy of The Hobbit, *and began to read. Her hand went to and fro from the tin of cookies, alternating now and again with the jar of milk. Like the hobbits, Rosemary was always ready for a little something to eat.*

Footsteps outside the chicken house startled her and she was no longer Bilbo Baggins, cozy in his hobbit hole in the Shire. She looked with dismay at the tin of cookies and saw that she had eaten almost all of them. A meager few inches of milk sloshed in the bottom of the canning jar.

The door opened on its squeaky hinges and Pa stepped into the chicken house. He was carrying his toolbox. Hey, Rosebud, he said. I didn't know you were here. He looked at the nest boxes and made a face. Uh-oh, I'm going to have to ask you to move your books out of the nest boxes; I'm not quite done fixing them.

They look done to me, she said, slowly removing the books. What's wrong with them?

Pa had a funny look on his face as he watched her stack the books neatly on the floor. The hammer in his hand tapped impatiently on the side of the nest box.

Just needs more nails to make sure it stays put, he answered, grinning at her. Once those big fat hens your mum's planning on raising start laying, we don't want the nest boxes to come crashing down, do we? Think of the scrambled eggs!

Oh, Pa. Rosie giggled and settled back with her book.

You better run on out of here—I think maybe I saw Maythorn up by the scuttle hole—reckon she's waiting for you.

The big goof, Rosie groused. She was supposed to come down here. But with a glance at the almost empty milk jar and cookie tin, she picked up her climbing stick and started off.

As she was crossing the branch to begin the hike up to the scuttle hole, she remembered the book Uncle Wade had sent her. It was all about the Cherokee Indians and she was eager to show it to Maythorn. There were even pictures in it of people named Blackfox—maybe Maythorn's kin.

She ran back to the little building. Bangbangbangbang—
*Pa was making sure the nest boxes didn't fall down. His back
was to the door and he didn't hear her as she stepped into the
chicken house. His hammer was tapping busily inside one of
the nests and he didn't even notice as she took the book from
the floor.*

Suddenly Pa whirled around. Rosemary! I thought... *He
glanced back at the row of nest boxes. His face looked funny,
almost angry, but then a big smile spread itself across his face
and he dropped the hammer into his toolbox.* Hey, girl, you
snuck up on me like an Indian. You nearly made me jump out
of my boots.

Forgot my book, *she explained, and was out the door and
on her way back up the hill.*

There was no sign of Maythorn at the scuttle hole. Rosie
checked under their secret message stone—a flat gray rock the
size of a turkey platter that they had wrestled, with much difficulty, from the pasture below. There was no message in the
plastic bag where a notepad and ballpoint awaited use.

Rosie hesitated, wondering if she should take the path
down to Mullmore. It wasn't fun anymore, going to
Mullmore. The big house had come to feel cold and unfriendly
and the people who lived there never seemed quite real. It was
like they were all telling secrets to one another behind her
back. Their voices said one thing but their eyes said something
else.

And the worst thing—now Tamra was around all the time.
Her mom worked for the Mullins most days, so Tamra rode
the bus home from school with Maythorn and Rosie. She was
there all afternoon till her mother went home at six, and having her around changed everything.

She always wants to play that dumb reaper game. I hate it.

*Rosie stared down toward Mullmore, where the glistening
water of the swimming pool winked at her through the trees.
I wish Jared had never started that dumb game.*

The huge basement, crowded with boxes and stored furniture was where they played it. With the lights off, the basement
was black dark—and, according to Jared, a perfect place for
the game. He would wait behind the door upstairs, counting
slowly while, with the lights on, the girls hid. Then all at once
the lights would go out and the door at the top of the stairs
would open. A shaft of yellow light would appear and, standing black against the light, Jared. The door would shut, and in
the darkness he would start down the stairs, intoning the
words: *Here comes the reaper to put you to bed. Here comes
the reaper to chop off your head.*

It's just hide-and-seek, Maythorn had said when Rosie
protested that the game was creepy. And it was.... But the
darkness and the words and the black thing that Jared covered
his head with made it all too scary. Once, jammed into a narrow space between a stack of boxes and the wall, Rosie had
crouched, heart pounding, as the Reaper paced nearer and
nearer, chanting the chilling words in a strange, deep voice.
His hand had brushed so close to her face that she could smell
the heavy scent of the clove cigarettes Jared and Mike liked to
smoke, and a sudden spurt of pee had soaked her underpants.
Hot with shame, she had escaped up the basement steps when
at last the game had come to its close and Jared had allowed the
light to be turned on.

Tears burned in Rosemary's eyes. *It's all changing. Why do
things have to change?*

27.

HIDDEN SECRETS . . .

Sunday, October 23

The morning air was crisp and clear. A light frost the night before had wilted some of the tenderest vegetation, but in sheltered spots, great mats of rich green chickweed still flourished, bearing a myriad of tiny white star flowers. More and more leaves were falling and they rustled underfoot as Rosemary led the way up the trail to the scuttle hole, followed by her mother and Phillip Hawkins, all wielding stout sticks to aid in the climb.

The three dogs accompanied them—Molly and Ursa ranging in an ever-widening circle, James staying very close. Rosemary set a brisk pace, anxious to visit Mullmore again, but she paused at the sight of the little dog, who had stopped to investigate a huge, dry puffball. Unable to resist, she reached out her stick to tap the globular mushroom. It burst on contact, releasing a small brown cloud of spores, and James retreated, sneezing reproachfully.

At the scuttle hole she paused again, waiting for her slower-moving elders to catch up. She had found her feet flying up the old trail, and could almost believe herself ten years old again, so effortless was the ascent. "I've got four-wheel drive" had been her standard response when her parents marveled at how easily she ran up and down the steep slopes.

Her mother reached the top of the ridge where the line fence divided Full Circle Farm's pasture from Mullmore's wooded slopes. She was breathing hard.

"I'm impressed, Rosemary. For a supposedly sedentary academic, your four-wheel drive is still pretty good."

Elizabeth turned to look at Phillip, still toiling up the path. When Rosemary announced at breakfast that she absolutely *had* to go to Mullmore, he'd insisted on accompanying them. "There's been no sign of Bib Maitland, but I'd like to tag along... if you ladies can put up with me."

The night before, Rosemary had read late, right through all fourteen of her spy notebooks. She had followed her younger self through the early, happy, innocent days to the last few notebooks, those which recorded her growing unease with Mullmore and its inhabitants.

Propped up in her narrow bed under the low eaves of her childhood room, she looked around at the familiar surroundings. Her favorite childhood books, the collection of plastic horses, temporarily restored to their own shelf, a small framed reproduction of Van Gogh's *Starry Night,* which she still loved, in spite of deeming it too much of a cliché to hang in her own house—all these old friends should have comforted her.

She shivered and pulled up the faded patchwork quilt Mum had made for her. The soft pastel squares—many salvaged from outgrown or worn-out family clothing— told stories of their own, and she let her fingers trace some of the most familiar.

The pale blue pieces are from work shirts, Mum's and Pa's; this lavender used to be really bright purple—scraps from those awful curtains in Laurie's room. The green was a dress Grammer Grey sent Mum.

Her hand stopped on a soft rose patch. *This was from the Cherokee dress Granny Thorn made for me. Maythorn had one just like it. I wore mine till it fell apart, and Mum was able to get only a few patches out of it.*

The last of the spy notebooks lay across her knees. Reluctantly she opened it and began to read.

> *We were in our special tree near the old ~~sem~~ cemetery when Jared and Mike came along. They'd been hunting with their bows and arrows and they had two dead rabbits. They pulled their skins off just like Cletus did that time, but I didn't get sick. We stayed very quiet and they never knew we were there. Jared messed up his rabbit, trying to cut it apart, but Mike did his very quick, just like Mum cuts up a chicken. Mum says you have to pay attention to where the joints are and then the knife will slide through. Mike is good at it. He laughed at Jared when Jared got mad, and Jared picked up his rabbit and threw it off into the bushes.*

The chime of her cell phone brought her back to the present and Rosemary reached for it eagerly. As she had expected, the caller ID told her it was Jared.

"Not too late to be calling, I hope." His soft voice in her ear was like a caress. "I had a dinner meeting that went on and on. Can I see you tomorrow?"

She tossed the notebook aside and curled up more comfortably. "Hey, Jared, I was just reading about you."

*   *   *

He hadn't much liked being reminded of his teenage self. "For god's sake, Rosemary, that was nineteen or twenty years ago! I know I went through a weird stage—horror movies and Stephen King and bad music. The therapist said I was getting back at Moon for bringing me to live out there in the boonies. Yes, I'm embarrassed to say I did get a kick out of scaring you little girls—Maythorn and Tamra particularly. They were always hanging around, and to be honest, I think they liked being scared."

He hadn't remembered the words to the Reaper Game that had terrified her so. Nor had he remembered the incident with the rabbit.

"I do remember playing hide-and-seek in the basement with you girls. Didn't I dress up in a Dracula costume or something? I think I used to have one, left over from a big Halloween party. Pretty childish behavior for a teenage boy—Rosemary, do you think we could talk about something else now? Like maybe dinner tomorrow night?"

I shouldn't have told him about the notebooks. It embarrassed him. Stupid of me. He's a totally different person now—what's that thing about how all our cells renew every seven years? I certainly wouldn't be spending time with him now if he still wanted to play the Reaper Game.

But they had plans for dinner the next night and more plans for the following weekend. With a contented sigh, Rosemary returned to the final notebook.

"I finished reading through all the spy notebooks last night. There were a bunch of odd things, actually.

Maythorn and I were pretty obnoxious, I see now, with all our sneaking around and spying."

Elizabeth, Phillip, and Rosemary were resting on a fallen tree before starting the climb down to Mullmore. Elizabeth watched her daughter attentively but said nothing, waiting to see where Rosemary's reading had taken her.

"Some of the stuff I wrote—I don't know if I was making it up or exaggerating or . . . or what." Rosemary stood and walked to the scuttle hole. "That's why I want so much to go back down there: I need to see it again. Then maybe I can sort out things."

She slipped through the narrow opening and started down the trail, James trotting behind her. Phillip sighed and stood, stretching out a helping hand to Elizabeth.

"Onward and downward," she said, and cautiously angled through the scuttle hole. "It's worth seeing, Phillip. Honest."

They followed Rosemary, who was moving with great determination along a secondary trail that slanted off to the left. "I wanted to go to our special tree first," she called back to them. "It was a big maple with wide branches and we had a rope to help us climb up."

Nothing was left of the rope, and the maple had undoubtedly grown even bigger. A little way down the slope was a small knoll; here and there a crooked tombstone protruded from the long grass. The knoll top was free of the brambles and saplings that were slowly choking the rest of the open land, and Elizabeth realized that family members must come once a year to mow and trim around the graves. Indeed, she could see a few wreaths of plastic flowers leaning drunkenly amid the grass.

Rosemary laid one hand on the trunk of the big

maple. "We spied on Maythorn's Uncle Mike and Tamra's mother from up there. She worked for the Mullins as a maid or something, and she'd sneak off when Mrs. Barbie was away. They used to meet in the old cemetery down there and…kiss…and paw at each other." She glanced at Elizabeth then quickly looked away, a blush rising on her cheeks.

"Was that in your notebook or are you just now remembering it?" Phillip asked.

"In the notebook. What little toads we were!"

They walked on, through the old family cemetery, where the rough gravestones bore dates from the 1800s to as recent as 1978. The family name on most of the stones was "Ridder."

Below the knoll lay the tennis court and, to the right, the swimming pool and gazebo. Rosemary stared at the empty pool with a faraway look and said, "Once, when I was spending the night with Maythorn, I woke up because the moon was bright and it was shining on my face. I went to the window and looked out."

She leaned on her stick, her gaze fixed on the pool. "Down there, on one of the chaise longues, there were two naked people. I knew what they were doing and I knew that one was Mrs. Barbie. And I was almost positive that the other one was Mike…or Jared."

Elizabeth started to speak but stopped herself. *Poor Rosie—what a terrible example all of the adults in her life seem to have set. No wonder she's been in no hurry for a relationship.*

"Sure it wasn't Moon?" Phillip asked. "From that picture I saw on the Christmas card, all three of them were similar in looks."

"Not Moon." Rosemary's voice was definite. "He was out of town; I remember that."

"What about Maythorn?" Elizabeth asked. "Did she see them too?"

"Maythorn was asleep. And I never told her. She wouldn't have believed me."

"Really?" Elizabeth raised her eyebrows. "That surprises me. I never had the impression that there was that much love between Maythorn and Patricia."

"Me either. I always thought Mrs. Barbie was more like Maythorn's wicked stepmother than a real mother. But Maythorn didn't see it that way." Rosemary stabbed her hiking stick into the hard-packed earth. The faraway look was in her eyes once more.

"There was one time...I remember it was really hot and Maythorn had called to see if I wanted to go swimming. I was coming down the path, and as I got near the gazebo, I could hear Mrs. Barbie in there. She was yelling at Maythorn and saying horrible, awful, mean things. And then I heard a sound like a slap and saw Mrs. Barbie hurrying away to the house. Her high heels went *click-click-click* and then the door slammed.

"When I got to the gazebo, I could tell Maythorn had been crying and there was the red imprint of a hand on her face. But when I said something to her about it..." Rosemary looked pained. "Something like 'I think your mother's mean,' Maythorn got all mad with me. For *spying* on her. She denied entirely that Patricia had slapped her."

They wandered about the deserted grounds, following Rosemary, who was moving like a sleepwalker. Elizabeth watched her daughter closely, suspecting that the rush of memory was beginning to take its toll. *She's just about overwhelmed with all of this. I need to get her out of here.*

"You know, sweetie, if we're going to have lunch, it's probably time to start back."

Phillip was quick to agree. "I'll be happy to ride shotgun with you another time, Rosemary. But I'm with Elizabeth—it's a long climb back up, and somehow all those pancakes I ate for breakfast have worn off."

Rosemary hesitated on the leaf-littered steps leading down to the sunken garden—then, with a last look all around her, nodded. "Okay, another time. I wish I could get into the house. And I wish I knew where Maythorn used to hide *her* spy notebooks. You know, Mum, I'd been thinking that I was right to suspect Cletus back then, but now...now I'm not so sure. What if the *spying* was the cause—something she saw that someone had to keep secret?"

When they reached the scuttle hole once again, rather than starting back down the trail, Rosemary made her way to the foot of a big locust tree and began to poke around in the grass with her hiking stick.

Elizabeth could hear her muttering, "It has to be here still—weeds have grown over it, but it couldn't have washed away or anything."

"What are you looking for, Rosie?" Elizabeth inched her way down the slope, with Phillip close behind.

"Our message stone was here. We used to leave messages for each other under it." Rosemary jabbed her stick into the weeds. "For a year or so after she disappeared, I would come up here and leave notes for her—in case she was still...out there."

At last the stick hit rock, and Rosemary dropped to her knees to sweep the debris from the flat surface of the stone. As she worked, she continued her explanation. "I had to sneak out when you and Pa weren't watching; after Maythorn, you all didn't like my roaming the woods. And mostly I didn't. But this was something I had to do. After a couple of years though, I quit coming up here. It was just too . . . sad."

She stood and thrust the end of her stick under the big rock. Using the stick as a lever, she slowly raised the message stone.

In the bare dirt that lay revealed were two fat red-and-black millipedes, coiled into tight circles, and a clouded plastic zipper bag. Rosemary knelt again. "I just wanted to see if my note was still here."

She opened the bag and took out a stained and mildewed notepad. A slim pencil was stuck through its metal spiral. As Rosemary leafed through the few remaining pages, Elizabeth could see that there was no writing on any of them.

"I thought sure I'd left a note that last time. I don't know, maybe I finally realized how futile it was." Rosemary's disappointment was evident. Again she paged through the little book.

"What else is in that bag, Rosie? It looks like there's something down in the bottom."

"Remember that green malachite heart you and Pa gave me? When Christmas came I brought it up here and left it for Maythorn. So she'd have a present."

Rosemary upended the bag and a small black stone fell into her outstretched hand. She looked at it in disbelief, then held it out to Elizabeth and Phillip. A carved figure, no bigger than a bantam's egg, nestled in the cup of her trembling palm—a sleeping fox, curled up, its sharp nose resting on its plumy tail. Great wings sprouted from its shoulders and lay folded along its flanks.

28.

. . . AND CONUNDRUMS

Sunday, October 23

Rosemary lifted her eyes to meet Elizabeth's gaze.

"No one knew about this hiding place—no one but Maythorn and me."

Phillip leaned closer to examine the beautiful little carving. "Fine work. Like those little Japanese whatsits—*netsukes*, I think they're called. But you said you left a green heart.... When was that?"

Rosemary took the carving and turned it to examine all sides. "I don't understand." The words were barely audible and she seemed not to have heard Phillip's question.

"Christmas of '86—is that when you put the heart up here, Rosie? They'd quit searching for Maythorn by then."

"Yes...That was when I left the first note...and the heart. And the heart was still here the last time I left a note. That was two years later. I was about to turn thirteen and I had decided that it was childish to keep coming back and leaving notes that were never answered."

She glanced around, her eyes vacant. "It had snowed hard the night before, but I was determined to make the last trip up here before my birthday...before I became a teenager. I remember that the stone was hard to lift because it was frozen to the ground. I broke my stick trying to pry it loose."

Rosemary brushed a stray lock of hair away from her cheek. "Nothing had changed. All the notes I'd written before were still there, along with the little green heart. I wrote one last note and told Maythorn good-bye. And I never came back."

She looked from the overturned stone to the little sleeping winged fox, nestled in her hand.

"Mum..." It was the voice of a young girl. "Mum... where did *this* come from? I don't understand."

"I don't understand, Phillip. Who could have switched the carvings? And why?"

The three of them had debated the question during lunch, without reaching any conclusion. The little carving sat on the dining table, its sleek black shape revealing nothing. Soon after the meal, Rosemary had left for Asheville. She and Jared planned to search newspapers on file at the library for references to Maythorn's disappearance, in hope of finding some overlooked item that might suggest new avenues to explore.

Phillip looked up from his textbook on criminal justice and the notes he was preparing for his class. Elizabeth had brought a stack of unpaid bills to the dining table and sat opposite him, quietly working her way through them. The sight of her across from him, brow furrowed in concentration, hair escaping from her long braid to curl around her face, was infinitely pleasing—a quiet domesticity that now seemed to him the way that life should be. *Elizabeth, my love.*

But quiet domesticity could not last in the face of so

many unanswered questions. Elizabeth had picked up the carved fox and was frowning at it. "Rosie was so definite that no one else knew about that secret stone. So how did *this* get there? And what happened to the notes Rosie left?"

He put down his pen. "I was thinking about that. Who else would have known about that rock? Who else spent a lot of time in the woods and might have seen the girls hiding things?"

He watched her face as she considered the implications. Several unwelcome ideas seemed to be suggesting themselves to her. "Jared might have seen them. Or Mike. Patricia and Moon weren't much on being in the woods. And anyway, by the time Rosie left the last note, they'd all moved away. This was put there after the Mullins were gone."

"And who was still around...and was out in the woods a lot?"

"Cletus. You think it was Cletus." Her eyes were deep pools of sadness. "Do you think that means Cletus was the one responsible for what happened to Maythorn?"

"No, not necessarily." He reached out for the little carving. "I don't know...in a way it seems to me that whoever left this might have been trying to make Rosemary feel better somehow—like all her notes to Maythorn had finally been answered." He studied the enigmatic black fox. "It's really fine work; where would Cletus have gotten something like this?"

"Cletus carved things...animals...I remember he gave Laurel a little wooden pig years ago. It was beautifully done."

"Maythorn's real name was Blackfox—right? And this black fox has wings—is it saying she's in heaven, maybe? I don't know—seems like a fairly sophisticated way to express something. Everyone keeps referring to Cletus as simple—could he have come up with this concept? This is more like something Sam might have thought of. Like those—"

"Like those boxes he made for us that last Christmas, all with carving that referred to our names. And Sam might have seen Rosie going up that way after Maythorn was gone...." Elizabeth's voice took on a defensive tone. "She wasn't supposed to roam around alone anymore; I didn't think she was. But obviously there were lots of things I didn't know."

She turned to stare out the window at the distant mountains. Her pen tapped absently on the tabletop and her lips were half-parted. Phillip waited.

"Maybe Sam made it and put it there for her to find... but she never went back." Elizabeth's words were slow and halting. "But I would have thought he'd have told me if he knew about the message place and that Rosie was leaving notes for Maythorn. I would have thought..." She seemed unable to go on.

The sorrow in her voice stabbed at him and he set the little carving down. "Elizabeth—" he began and, as he spoke, the cell phone Gabby had given him vibrated against his hip. "Oh, hell, it's a call I've got to take," he apologized, and stood and moved toward the kitchen.

Elizabeth's gaze wandered over the warm shades of the mountains' autumn foliage, vivid in the afternoon sun. From the kitchen she could hear the confidential murmur of Phillip's voice.

She reached for the carved stone fox. *Could Sam have made this? I don't think he ever worked in stone. It was always wood. This is more like some of the carvings we saw over in Cherokee—soapstone, I think. Is this something Driver made? All of his carvings were life-sized, but this... the scale is so different.*

The little figure slumbered on, its secret safe within the sheltering wings that wrapped it round.

Phillip emerged from the kitchen, returning the cell phone to his waistband. "That was one of Del's people—they've been looking at your ring and the box Sam made and they don't think there's any hidden message in either one. They're sending them back." The chair scraped noisily on the red-brown tile floor as he resumed his seat. "We're running out of time here—word is Landrum's appointment will be announced November 1—a week from tomorrow. If we find the deposition before then, Del is certain that Landrum will withdraw his name, just on the threat of it becoming public."

Elizabeth dragged her thoughts away from the enigma of the little fox. "But even if Landrum did get named Secretary of Defense—if we found the deposition eventually, couldn't your friend still use it to discredit Landrum, force him to resign?"

Phillip looked uncomfortable. "Thing is, it would get tricky for Del—possibly ruin his career if it all went public. Too many questions—why did we wait so long to bring this up?...what are Del's personal interests here? It could get very ugly. And once Landrum was in the Cabinet, there'd be the whole loyalty question. They'd be asking Del why he hated America." He pushed aside the textbook. "No, our best bet is to find the deposition and find it soon." His brown eyes were steady on her. "Let's go over this again, Elizabeth. Try to remember what gifts Sam gave you, beginning in '98."

Four gifts: a small table, an outdoor bench, an early copy of *Girl of the Limberlost*, and a simple box for stationery, free of any cryptic carving or false bottom, were all that Elizabeth could remember.

"That's it, Phillip. Sometimes he gave me a plant or flowers on our anniversary, but I just don't think there's anything else."

Phillip was riffling through the pages of the book, examining them closely. Finally he closed it with a disappointed sigh. "Not a mark. An old book like that, you might expect to see something. It's a not uncommon way of sending a message—low tech but—"

"An old—wait a second!" Elizabeth jumped up and darted away, returning almost immediately with a small book.

"I'd forgotten; he gave me this at some point during that last year, not for any special occasion but to replace one he'd lost—and there *are* some marks in it."

She held out the copy of *Walden* that he had seen on her bedside table. With a rising feeling of excitement, he took it from her. On the title page were the words "For Liz—Here are things that mustn't be forgotten. With love, from Sam."

The inscription was dated February 12, 1999. Phillip began slowly to turn the creamy pages. The table of contents caught his eye with the faint check mark by the words "What I Lived For."

Turning to the indicated chapter, he began to grin. "Miz Goodweather, this could be it!"

29

A VOICE FROM THE PAST

Sunday, October 23

"What do you think, Jared? Would your father be okay with our looking around the house at Mullmore? I'd really like to find Maythorn's spy notebooks. Do you think he'd let us have a key?"

Jared took a sip of his espresso before replying. They had spent several hours at the Pack Library, scanning the microfilmed pages of the *Asheville Citizen-Times* for November and December of 1986. At last, frustrated by the paucity of information, Rosemary had called a halt and the two had moved on to the coffee shop at a nearby bookstore.

Now Rosemary watched him, supremely aware of his nearness across the tiny table. In these surroundings, peopled mainly by the younger, more raffish of Asheville's denizens, with a sprinkling of aging hippies, Jared's impeccable and conservative clothing, as well as his sleek good looks, set him apart.

He smiled at her, perfect white teeth against the smooth tan of his face, gray-blue eyes regarding her with something like amusement, and suddenly she felt like the awkward little girl she had once been, seeing her friend's brother as a being from another plane: untouchable, unknowable, unattainable—yet eagerly vying for his attention.

"Would the notebooks still be there? The movers packed up most of the furniture and things—and even if you did find them, do you really think there'd be anything useful?"

"I'm sure she hid them well—not in her dresser drawers or under her bed or anything easy." Rosemary leaned toward Jared. "I think she said something about the basement—that they'd be safe there because we were the only ones who spent time down there. And yes, I think they could be important—Jared, what if she saw something she shouldn't have and that was the reason—"

He put his hand over hers but didn't answer for a moment. At last he nodded. "You could be on to something; it's certainly a possibility, anyway. God knows, everyone has secrets, including me. If we find those notebooks, I fully expect to see myself revealed as a drug fiend." The blue gaze held her. "I have to plead guilty to buying the occasional baggie of home-grown marijuana from our redneck neighbors on the backside of the mountain. And I know that Maythorn knew. But so did Moon and Patricia—I took care to let them see how very bad I could be."

He winked at her and murmured, "Promise you won't turn me in, Rosie, and we'll go talk to Moon about the key to Mullmore right now."

"Jared and I went to see his father, and Mr. Mullins said he would meet us at Mullmore on Friday and

let us in so Jared and I can look for Maythorn's notebooks."

Elizabeth and Phillip, decorously reading in the living
room, looked up to see a flushed and exuberant
Rosemary standing in the doorway, a paper bag in one
hand.

"Mum, we went to that mission place you told me
about. It was just like you said, all those people in the
front yard and everything. And Mr. Mullins was really
nice—almost as if he'd been expecting us. When I explained what I wanted to do, he just nodded and said
that he thought it was a good idea and that I should let
the Higher Power guide me. He said that he'd been
avoiding Mullmore all these years, but that perhaps it
was time for him to go back and face the past."

She waved the bag at them as she approached. "I
picked up some bagels for breakfast, and some lox and
cream cheese spread. Oh, and Mum—Mr. Mullins
wanted you to call him. I've got a card with his number
on it right here."

Rosemary thrust the little rectangle at Elizabeth, then
disappeared into the kitchen. They could hear her humming as she opened and closed the refrigerator.
Elizabeth looked at Phillip.

"Well," she said, reaching for the telephone, "I guess
I'll see what he wants."

Her one-time neighbor picked up on the first ring.
"Redemption House. This is Moon. How can I help?"

"Moon, this is Elizabeth Good—"

"Elizabeth! Thank you for calling. I have someone
here who wants to talk to you."

"Moon? Who—"

There was a rustle of sound as the phone changed

hands. Then a second voice murmured in her ear. "Elizabeth? This is Mike. I'm back."

How can the sound of a voice do that to me? Almost twenty years since I've spoken to him and I can still see him, the way he looked when I told him I'd made a mistake, that I couldn't hurt Sam. The way he just stared at me with that uncanny stillness. And then he said—what was it—No, I think you're making a mistake now. And he walked away and my heart nearly broke at the sight of his back, the way he held his shoulders as if supporting some invisible weight.

Elizabeth had sought the refuge of her bathroom, too unnerved by the call to explain to Phillip the significance of this unexpected voice from the past. Phillip, aware of her penchant for long, soaking, tub baths, had not seemed to notice her agitation, but had continued on with his preparations for tomorrow's class. Mercifully, Rosemary, too, had not asked about the call. Instead, she'd said good night, lost in her own thoughts, and explained that she would be leaving early in the morning to return yet again to Chapel Hill.

As she lay back in the tub, Elizabeth's mind was busy. Old dreams, long forgotten, and once well-buried regrets seemed to rise with the steam from the surface of the lavender-scented water.

It all came down to the simple fact that I was convinced Sam no longer loved me . . . and that Mike did. I felt like Sam was ignoring me and I was hungry for love. And so . . .

And so she had come close to tearing apart the life they had begun to build at Full Circle Farm.

Thank god for that blessed bell . . .

* * *

April 1985: their first spring on the farm. Sam, plagued by the nightmares of the past and the almost overwhelming job of learning to run a farm, had been unusually short-tempered as he struggled with the plowing and the planting. To his credit, she thought, he had always managed to remain easygoing and loving around the girls. *Thank goodness for that. But on that one day, when so many things seemed to be going wrong and all I wanted was for him to put his arms around me like he used to do . . . to tell me it would be okay . . .*

Tears were running down her face, already damp from the steam of the bath. *Instead, he was so cold, so hateful, that I felt like he was some stranger inhabiting Sam's body. And then he walked out of the house, saying he didn't know when—or if— he'd be back.*

She had watched the truck out of sight, then, when Laurel had asked where Pa was going, had concocted a quick story. She had gone through the rest of the day with mechanical cheerfulness when Laurel was around, but with a foreboding that knotted her stomach.

As soon as Rosie gets home from school, I'll go for a walk in the woods. If I can just get off by myself for a little while, I can figure out what to do.

Finally Rosemary had appeared, trudging slowly up the road, an open book held before her. As soon as she reached the house, Elizabeth had charged her with watching Laurie, "Just for a half an hour," had put on her old straw hat, and headed for the woods.

Thick-growing wild iris made a pool of lavender-blue on the slope at the edge of the wood and she sat down on a fallen tree, hoping that the flowers' cool beauty would calm her and soothe the pain she felt. She was staring unseeing at the flowers, numb and unable to think, when she felt a hand on her shoulder.

His hair was silver-gilt in the afternoon sun and his eyes mirrored the iris. He knelt beside her and brushed his fingers against her cheek.

"Rosie called Maythorn to say she had to stay home with Laurie." His breath was sweet and clove-scented. "I wondered if I might find you here again."

I forgot about the time; I forgot about the girls; I forgot about all the promises I'd made—for better or worse. He made me feel... treasured.

And then, like a savage intruder into a peaceful dream, had come the frantic clanging of the farmhouse bell on the front porch, the bell that was reserved for emergencies. She had been on her feet and racing toward the house almost at once, without a backward glance.

On the porch, a white-faced Rosemary ran to her, clutching at her hand and dragging her toward the door as she stammered out an explanation. Laurel, climbing the steep steps up to Rosemary's bedroom, had slipped and tumbled down the stairs. "She won't wake up, Mum! She's breathing but she won't wake up!"

Horror-struck, Elizabeth had burst into the house to find her younger daughter sprawled at the foot of the stairs. Far down the hill the welcome sound of Sam's returning truck grew louder.

They had bundled both girls into the truck and, pausing only to leave Rosie with Miss Birdie, had pushed the vehicle to its rattling, groaning limits for a nerve-wracking trip to the emergency room in Asheville. There had followed hours of anxious waiting, the exchanging of bitter self-recriminations, and then, finally with the dawn, the joyful news that Laurel was conscious and would make a full recovery. And somewhere in those awful, endless hours between night and morning, their marriage bonds, strained and worn almost to the breaking point, had been mended.

And now Sam's gone ... and now Mike's back. ... Did Moon tell him about Sam? Could that be why?

30.

MISS BIRDIE'S DAYBOOK

Monday, October 24

So the brother's back. And how does she feel about that? Surprised, for sure. But there's something more going on... there's a back story of some kind with her and this Mike Mullins.

The forty-minute drive from Marshall County to AB Tech for his 10 o'clock class had become so routine that Phillip Hawkins was free to give almost all of his attention to pondering the implications of the return of Mike Mullins. He had noted Elizabeth's agitation at hearing from this long-lost... *friend? neighbor? lover? What the hell was this guy to her? And why is he reappearing after so many years?*

The memory of the handsome figure in the old photo taunted him. *Tall, lots of blond hair, a friggin' Aryan poster boy. And then there's me—balding, something of a gut, just barely taller than her. Shit... what if...? It didn't sound like there were plans to see each other.... Of course, he could call again....*

The cell phone on his belt vibrated and he took advantage of a nearby exit to pull over.

"Hawkins... Yeah, I think I've got something.... No, it's at the house.... I couldn't make any sense of it but I think it could be the key. I'm going to spend some time studying it; if I can't make any sense out of it by Thursday, I'll express it to DC and let Del's boys take a look....No, don't bother...besides, she doesn't know you....Hell, Gabby, she might think you were one of Landrum's people and call the law on your ass."

"Lizzie Beth, you don't look so pert this evening. What's ailin' you? Git you a chair and come set a spell. You kin keep me company whilst I tie this quilt."

A wooden frame covered by a bright quilt stitched from large, irregular blocks of red and orange corduroy, highlighted by a few smaller bits of purple and black, hung from the ceiling of Miss Birdie's living room. The quilting frame was so large and the room so small that the few pieces of furniture had been pushed to the walls, and Elizabeth was forced to sidle around them to find a straight-backed chair.

"Let me help for a while, Miss Birdie." Elizabeth reached for the ball of black crochet thread and took a stout needle from the faded red pincushion resting in the middle of the half-tied quilt. "Who's this one for?"

She had finished her morning chores, and after lunch, realizing that she was unconsciously waiting for the phone to ring, hoping that it might be Mike, she had forced herself to leave the house. *What's wrong with you, Elizabeth? What about Phillip? And for all you know, Mike has a wife and children—grandchildren, maybe—back in California. Get over it, for god's sake....But he did say he'd see me soon.*

With a last glance at the silent telephone, she had fled

the house, remembering to lock the doors—a still unfamiliar task that aroused her anger each time she turned the latch. *Just do it, Elizabeth, Phillip had urged her. It won't be forever, but for now you need to keep things locked up . . . take precautions. Blaine's got people keeping an eye on the place, and I know Julio and Homero are on the alert. And you've got your gun.*

As she drove down her road, she could see Julio and Homero, bent over the beds of frost-nipped nasturtiums, harvesting the ripened seeds for next year's crop. She stopped the car and got out.

"I'm going down the road to see Miss Birdie, Julio." She had to shout to make herself heard above the noise of the boom-box that was Homero's constant companion. "You all keep an eye out, okay?"

"Sí, Elizabeta, no problema." Julio's tanned face split in a wide grin and he patted the scabbarded machete at his waist. "We take care of anyone who don't belong here."

God help the wandering Jehovah's Witness who makes the mistake of trying our holler. At least Julio knows the meter reader.

The needle made a satisfying *pop* as she poked it through the thick layers of the brilliant bedcovering and pulled the strong thread through the pieced top, the fluffy poly-fill batting center, and the sturdy flannel that was the back of the quilt. "Quilt" by courtesy only, as its fabric was far too heavy to allow for the intricate decorative running stitches that set off seams or traced fancy patterns while performing the mundane task of holding the three layers together. Miss Birdie's colorful creation, a far more utilitarian product, was tied at intervals with strong square knots, and would be completed in a few hours, rather than the months that a true quilt would require.

"Now, this is fer Calven, Dor'thy's nephew. He's a sweet child, Lizzie Beth, fer all that he's not had no proper raisin'." Birdie's gnarled fingers drove the needle relentlessly through the multiple layers.

She peered over the tops of her gold-rimmed spectacles at Elizabeth. "And looks like he's goin' to be on Dor'thy's hands fer good—that sorry mama of hisn, that Prin Ridder's run off, just like her sister done. There she was in the hospital, takin' on like one thing and givin' out that she ain't got long to live—why they took up a special collection for her at church, to help with the doctor's bill, and they was planning on holding a singin' too."

Miss Birdie jabbed her silver needle into a purple square with unnecessary force and continued. "Dor'thy told me that when her sister Mag went to the hospital yesterday, Prin was gone—had slipped out in the night, takin' all that money with her. Dor'thy believes that Prin was in trouble with the law and hadn't never been sick atall, just bidin' her time till she could leave out of here. She'd been took up, several years back of this, fer passin' bad checks, and Dor'thy believes that Prin was up to her old tricks again."

"What about Calven? Surely she'll come back for him?"

"Dor'thy don't think so. She says Prin ain't no kind of a mother to that poor boy. And Mag ain't able to look atter him." *Pop...pop...swish.* Another length of thread was set into the quilt, looped, and firmly knotted by those implacable old fingers.

"Dor'thy'll see he's raised right. Calven'll be better off with her, oncet he gets over thinkin' his mama cares a lick fer him."

Miss Birdie cut another length of black thread and brandished her worn scissors at Elizabeth, *Like a cheerful little Atropos,* Elizabeth thought, seeing her neighbor as a rather incongruous personification of one of the Fates.

"Lizzie Beth, when you was here before, talkin' about that Maythorn child, well, I got to thinkin' back on that time. You know how I keep my daybook. Well, I got to studyin'."

Miss Birdie pointed her scissors toward the silently flickering television set. "Just reach me that book that's settin' atop the TV, if you don't care, Lizzie Beth."

The little hardbacked composition book was faded and the label on the front cover was marked "1986" in Birdie's spidery handwriting. Elizabeth knew that her neighbor had kept a kind of journal all her married life— every day she recorded the weather, what she did, who she saw... anything unusual. With her prodigious memory and this additional written record, Miss Birdie Gentry was a veritable archive of life on Ridley Branch over the past sixty-odd years.

She took the book from Elizabeth and began to leaf through it. "April 12, old Pet brought two bull-calves... July 23, put up forty-four quarts of runner beans... August 9, that was that dreadful rain... Here it is: 'October 31, brown Ford truck passed by right before first dark. Believe it was Maythorn's uncle, the one that took her and Rosie off to Cherokee back on October 4. Still got them old long braids, looks like two big blacksnakes.'"

As Elizabeth turned up her driveway, she was startled to see Calven sitting patiently on the big flat rock at the foot of the road. He seemed unalarmed at the sight of her, waving cheerily and coming to the side of her car when she stopped and put down her window.

"Hey there, Miz Goodweather." He stood on tiptoe to peer into her car. "Where's ol' Yoursa and Molly?"

He already seemed to have put on weight and the unhealthy gray pallor was giving way to a sun-touched pinkness. A knapsack with schoolbooks spilling out of it lay on the ground nearby.

"Hey, Calven. I guess the dogs are up at the house." She eyed him curiously. "I've been at Miss Birdie's and she told me you were staying with Dorothy. What are you doing here? Won't she wonder where you are?"

"Naw, ol' Dor'thy said I could ride the bus home with the Robertses. Travis Roberts is in my room at school; him and me's friends. We been playin' in the woods up there, but I'm supposed to meet Dor'thy here at five." Calven held out a thin wrist adorned with a wide-banded watch. "She give me this here watch so's I'd be on time." He gazed at the timepiece with immense satisfaction. "I ain't never had me no watch till now."

Elizabeth glanced at the car's clock. "It's only four-thirty, Calven; you could have stayed up there a little longer."

The boy shifted uneasily from foot to foot. "I come away 'cause they was fixin' to sneak into that big ol' place up yon. Son, I tell you, I had me enough of that place when I was there with Bib. You know, the Robertses live just this side of that big ol' wall, and Travis has knocked footholes in it so's to climb it. They even take that little Asheley with 'em."

He stepped close. In a low tone, he confided, "That Asheley, she's just a girl, but she's the worst of 'em all. She's got her an invisible friend named Maydern, or some such, and her and Maydern makes play houses in the woods. Miz Goodweather, do you think there's such things as ghostes?"

BACK TO CHEROKEE

The Qualla Boundary, October 1986

At last October *had come, and with it the long-awaited trip back to Cherokee. When Maythorn and Rosie had gone to Cherokee last time, Mrs. Barbie had driven them, complaining in a whiny voice all the long way. The traffic was terrible; the stores were tacky; Maythorn's father's family were rude and backward—the trip had seemed to go on forever.*

But this time Mrs. Barbie and Krystalle were off at a pageant, so Driver came for them in his truck. They set off as before, down Ridley Branch, but instead of crossing the bridge that would take them to the road that led to the big highway and Asheville, Driver turned left onto Bear Tree Creek.

Rosemary nudged Maythorn, who seemed unconcerned. Maythorn, she whispered in her friend's ear, he's going the wrong way.

Driver must have heard her, because he reached over Maythorn and squeezed Rosemary's knee. Hey, Rosie, he said, I'm taking you by a secret Indian shortcut. This is the way the old Cherokees would have come, back when they traveled over here to hunt.

Rosemary's heart thudded with excitement. She knew that

Indians had hunted in Marshall County long, long years ago. Pa and Mum had found spearheads and flakes of flint in the big field near the barn. And she herself had once found a tiny bleached seashell with two holes drilled in it. Mum had said that it had probably been sewn to a shirt as a decoration. Just think, Rosie, this shell got here all the way from the ocean or the gulf. Maybe an Indian down on the Gulf Coast found it and traded it to someone who lived a little farther north, and she traded it, and so on till it ended up here—far, far away from the salt water.

Driver drove to the end of Bear Tree Creek, to the place where it turned into two narrow roads. He pointed the old truck up the road to the right and they began to climb, twisting and turning, higher and higher up to the top of the mountain.

The road was narrow and unpaved, with woods pressing close on either side, and Rosemary became Shining Deer, the only woman who, because of her superb skill with a spear, was allowed to accompany a band of hunters. She herself had slain three fat bucks.

We're at the top now, Driver announced. *This is what the white folks call Troublesome Gap. And down there's Spring Creek.*

As they descended, the woods changed to farms and pastures, and houses, more and more houses. They passed through a tiny cluster of buildings that Driver said was a place named Trust. *And on up here a little ways is Luck.*

Maythorn pointed to a store that bore a sign reading PINK J. PLEMMONS, GROCERIES AND FEEDS, and she and Rosemary both began to giggle at the idea of someone named Pink.

And then they were on a highway, and the lake called Junaluska was to their right. *That lake's named for a famous Cherokee chief,* Driver told them; *no one but rich white folks live there now.* He spat out his window and went on,

The white folks love us Indians when we've been dead long enough.

The roar of the waterfall was even louder than she had remembered, and once again the sight of the white foam tracery against the sheer rock cliff caused her to stand mesmerized. And Granny Thorn was waiting for them, like before. She hugged them both and hurried them into her cabin, where a fire was crackling in the hearth. From out of the ashes she pulled a black iron skillet, full of what looked like cornbread. She spoke to Maythorn in Cherokee and Maythorn nodded, a little dubiously.

She wants you girls to have some of her chestnut bread, Driver explained, cutting his eyes over to the hesitant Maythorn. Go on, Rosie, try some; it's good.

As they helped themselves to the crumbly, slightly sweet bread, Granny Thorn continued to talk in the whispering sounds that were the Cherokee language. Driver tried to keep pace with her, putting her words into English. Granny says that it's the Fall Festival this weekend and we'll all be going. She wants to show you about the dances—and to Rosemary's amazed delight, Granny Thorn began a slow shuffling step, accompanying herself with a repetitive chant in her high, thin, old voice. Her gnarled and calloused bare feet beat out a rhythm on the dusty planks of the floor.

It was the most wonderful day she had ever spent. Granny presented her and Maythorn with real Cherokee dresses of a deep rose-red to wear to the festival. And at the festival, she and Maythorn had been taken under the wing of a pretty young woman who seemed to know Driver very well. Sary Littlejohn had shown them how to do the Beaver Dance, and best of all, had asked Rosemary what clan she belonged to!

She thought I was a Cherokee! Rosemary hugged the thought to herself as they jolted back up the road to Big Cove and Granny's house by the waterfall. Maythorn's head was nodding and Granny and Driver were talking softly.

Some of us are going up to Swimmer's house later tonight for the Man Dance, she heard Driver tell Granny. If don't anyone do it, it'll be forgotten. And seems like to me, us Cherokee need it as much now as we ever did.

31.

THE BOOGER DANCE

Tuesday, October 25

The People were crowded into the house, hip to hip, knee to back, close-packed on the big, smooth-worn logs that circled the central hearth. A faint sheen of sweat covered their eager faces, for although First Frost had come and the night air outside was crisp, the smoky interior was warm with the heat of so many bodies. All eyes were fixed on the tanned deerskin that covered the doorway, and when it was drawn back briefly as one of the men stepped outside to relieve himself, the huge orange moon hanging impaled on twisted, leafless branches illuminated strange shapes flitting back and forth in the purple night, manlike but for their grotesque heads.

The children squirmed beside their mothers in an ecstasy of anticipation and terrified delight as the five Callers, with their seed-filled gourds, and the lead Caller, with his water drum, accompanied the dancers circling the hearth. The pebble-filled tortoise shells bound to the legs of the dancers provided an extra layer of percussion to the measured thump of feet tracing the age-old pattern of the stomp dance.

The sixth song ended. In the momentary hush, a pale shiny face, its long, obscenely drooping nose surrounded by black fur, insinuated itself into the sliver of space between the deerskin *and the doorframe. The hideous face surveyed the expectant crowd for a long moment then withdrew. There was a prolonged, inhumanly loud farting sound from beyond the door. And suddenly, in a jumble of flailing limbs and lewd gestures, the six masked boogers clumped into the lodge and the Booger Dance began.*

Rosemary hunched forward, lost in the words as they scrolled down the computer screen. A recently posted article on a Web site devoted to Cherokee lore had popped up in response to her search. Suddenly, vague, half-remembered images had coalesced into a firm conviction.

This is it; one of the things I've been trying to remember. Driver was going to a dance at a neighbor's house. But there were only grown-ups there. And it was in a regular house, with the furniture pushed back to leave room for the dancing. We weren't supposed to be there, but when Granny Thorn went to sleep, Maythorn whispered to me that she knew the way to where they were dancing. We snuck out and followed a path through the woods to another little cabin. We could hear the drum and the rattles and we watched through the window until someone saw us. Then Driver came out and took us back home.

He had been annoyed with them for interrupting his good time, but beneath the irritation was a surprised admiration. *You girls came through the woods in the dark? Pretty good Indian stuff. But this dance is just for grown-ups—parts of it, a little X-rated maybe.*

As he accompanied them along the dark path back to Granny's cabin, he had explained the significance of the Booger Dance. *See, the boogers are the bad guys, like the boogeyman—nothing to do with the stuff that comes out of your nose,* he had said as Rosemary stifled a rising giggle. *We call it the Man Dance, too, because . . .* He had hesitated, but both girls knew what he was talking about, having seen some of the dancers with penis-like gourds between their legs, making a great show of their artificial equipment. *Well, that's just another name for it. But the reason we do the Booger Dance is to make fun of our enemies. You see? You saw how the dancers were acting silly and falling down. The dance tells us to laugh at the bad guys and not be scared of them.*

Then they had heard the roar of the great waterfall and, as they had rounded a curve in the path, they had seen the little cabin's outline against the ghostly veil of falling water. The tiny windows had been dimly aglow with the light of the oil lamp Granny had left burning to guide Driver back home.

And Maythorn told Driver that she wanted to make a Booger mask so she wouldn't be scared of someone—and Driver said he would help her.

"Mum, I'm glad I caught you. I've remembered something really important." Rosemary's breathless enthusiasm bubbled in Elizabeth's ear. She listened apprehensively as her daughter detailed the elements of this new revelation, ending with a somewhat diffident note.

"But I called because I thought … Mum, do you think you could possibly go to Cherokee and try again to find Driver Blackfox? If he can remember the mask Maythorn made, it might tell us who she was afraid of. And if we knew that, it could get us closer to knowing what happened to her."

Elizabeth glanced at the clock. Eight-thirty in the morning and a day's worth of wreath-making ahead of her. Phillip had already left for school, and she had been on the way out the door when the phone rang.

"Today? Now? Why would I have any better luck at

finding him than we did before?" *And what makes you think that I'm sitting around like some unemployed private eye, just waiting for a call so I can spring into action? For god's sake—*

"Mum, I know you're busy, but listen. I did a little on-line research and ended up phoning a gallery in Cherokee where Driver's got a show right now. I talked to this woman and told her that I was doing an article on Cherokee artists and that I wanted to interview Driver Blackfox but had been having difficulty getting in touch with him. She was really nice and said that he was bad about returning calls or answering letters but that if I could get to Cherokee today, Driver would be at the gallery this afternoon."

32.

TRUST TO LUCK . . .
AND BEYOND

Tuesday, October 25

Reluctantly, Elizabeth had allowed herself to be convinced. Rosemary's excitement was compelling. "And, Mum, you really ought to try going by the back way—I wish I'd thought of it earlier; it's the way Driver took us the last time we went to visit Granny Thorn. You just go down Bear Tree and over Troublesome Gap to Spring Creek—really, Mum, I think you'll love it. And call me tonight and let me know if you talk to Driver."

The day was clear and cold as Elizabeth drove up Bear Tree Creek. Frost blanketed the fields still in shadow, and almost every little house was marked by a plume of white smoke. At the head of the creek she took the fork to follow the gravel road that wound high and steep toward Troublesome Gap. Rich brown leaves carpeted the woods, and the sun, winking through tree trunks and bare branches, highlighted the few trees whose red or yellow leaves had not yet bowed to the inevitable. Huge old rhododendrons, dark and wilted with the cold—leaves "querled" up, in the mountain dialect—clung to steep banks.

Higher and higher, surrounded by leafless trees she drove. Through a gap, she could see distant mountains, dark and hazy blue, stretching along the horizon. Above her, the sky was a perfect clear deep azure, and before her, newly fallen brown leaves lined the roadsides, leaving a narrow trail down the middle, making the gravel road seem no more than a footpath.

This is incredible—like going back centuries. I haven't seen another vehicle since that one pickup back near the bridge. She was very near the top now. Tilted vertical outcroppings of rock loomed above the road; in the pervasive shade, icicles and wilted ferns clung to the folds of the boulders.

At the top of the mountain she stopped the car to enjoy the view. In the distance a grid of roads was sketched on a cleared mountainside, and farther down the road she could see a single car. A small litter of beer cans in the ditch revealed that others had paused here.

Oh, well, back to the present. Down and down, dodging in and out of shadows and sunlight that lay across the twisting road. Far below her lay Spring Creek, its houses and fields in the mountain's shadow still heavy with frost. Two horses, little more than dark silhouettes against their silvered pasture, looked up as her car approached.

Close by the road rose an abandoned log cabin, the original edifice studded with additions from different periods—a frame addition to the front, a crude plywood enclosure scabbed on to the back. Sentinel pines stood in a line beside the old house, and across the road were a traditional corn crib and shed. Just beyond the house a log barn still stood, straight and true, though a plank addition sagged slightly. *There's a story there in that home place— probably spanning several generations. But now they're all gone.*

The somber thought was dispelled by the sight of a

sheaf of orange-coral leaves illuminated by the sun, be-hind the dark loom of a huge poplar trunk. And now the woods gave way to fields, and before her were more and more houses in a broad valley and beautiful mountain slopes warmed by the sun and punctuated by globular green pines. Soon she was through Spring Creek and into Trust, a little handful of buildings that seemed to have been recently renovated: a general store, a large house with a well-maintained lawn, a gazebo, a chapel, a covered bridge: an immaculate little fantasyland amid the quiet surroundings.

Luck was next, another minuscule community, and Elizabeth smiled at the sign on a defunct grocery and feed store. Mr. Pink J. Plemmons's store might be shut-tered, but his name still endured, proudly blazoned in faded lettering on a sign that hung askew across the building's façade. *Till some antiques picker gets hold of it and sells it to a transplant to put on their living room wall because it's "quaint."*

To her disappointment, she realized that the magical part of the journey was over, and she found herself on a busy highway, speeding through Junaluska, past Waynesville, and on to Cherokee. The odd feeling of having come in through a secret back door lingered—*almost like L'Engle's "tessering" through a wrinkle in time*—but now the scenery was familiar: the same that she and Rosemary had passed not quite two weeks prior—except that now there was a snowmaking machine on the roadside in Maggie Valley, turning out a pathetic little slope of white granules for tourists to slide down on inflated rubber doughnuts.

Mystic Grounds, the coffee shop and gallery where Driver Blackfox's work was on display, was an unexpectedly cosmopolitan little sanctuary in the midst of the tourist kitsch of Cherokee. Fancy coffees, quiche, and *pain au chocolat* were on the menu; Edith Piaf was followed by Tracy Chapman on the sound system. Elizabeth paused in the doorway, wondering if her quarry was on the premises.

A sign with an arrow directed her to the gallery—a spacious, windowless room. The first thing that met her eye was a carved mask, painted a lurid blue and surmounted with a stiff fringe of flame-colored hair. Beneath it, she was delighted to see, was an artist's statement and a picture of Driver Blackfox.

A handsome, chiseled face with a somber expression looked out from the color photograph. *He still has the long braids Birdie mentioned but, like mine, they're not as dark as they used to be.* The artist's statement was brief. It mentioned Blackfox's commitment to Cherokee themes, his fascination with animal totems and spirit guides, and his longtime interest in mask-making.

Elizabeth made her way around the room, studying each piece. Superbly carved animals rendered in wood or stone were displayed on log pedestals. A life-sized Great Horned Owl with outstretched wings dominated the display, flanked by smaller works of various birds and beasts. Masks lined the walls, some carved and painted, others constructed from gourds. Many depicted animal heads: a realistic bear with mouth opened in a red snarl; a demure raccoon; a comic possum, with pointed, grinning snout and tiny sharp teeth. Others were human, with exaggerated features. *These have got to be caricatures: doesn't that one look like Rush Limbaugh? And that's got to be—*

"Sometimes people from outside see these masks and think Blackfox is abandoning Cherokee themes.

Actually, they're just the latest expression of a very old tradition that he's keeping alive."

A dark-skinned young woman was standing in the doorway. Her paint-daubed jeans and shirt suggested that she, too, was an artist. She looked closely at Elizabeth.

"I thought maybe you were the one who called, the one who was doing an article on artists from the Boundary. But I had the impression she was younger...."

"You spoke with my daughter; we're working on the piece together." Elizabeth pulled her reading glasses from her pocket and put them on, in a feeble attempt to look like someone who would write an article. "My daughter wasn't able to get away, so I came. Do you expect Mr. Blackfox soon?"

The young woman looked abashed. "Well, that's the problem. Right after I talked to your daughter, Driver came in and took care of the stuff he was going to do this afternoon. He said he had an important client coming to talk to him about a big commission."

"Will he be back later?"

"Afraid not. He said he was having lunch with the client at the casino and that he had some other things to do after that." A frown wrinkled the young woman's smooth forehead. "Did you make a special trip? I'm sorry."

Her face brightened. "But if you went to the casino, maybe you could catch him there. I think he said he was meeting the client at one."

33.

AT THE MOUSE HOLE

Tuesday, October 25

The casino stretched out endlessly, row after row of slot machines and video poker games. Lights flashed and blinked, music blared, and the smoke of innumerable cigarettes spiraled like incense from myriad altars up to the massive exhaust fans. Elizabeth made her way down a row of machines, a stranger in a strange land. Disconcertingly, many of the gamblers seemed to be plugged in, a cord growing from chest to machine as if for intravenous feeding or some electronic life support.

At first the players seemed to her to be all alike: mindless automatons feeding money into mindless automatons. Soon, however, she began to pick out individuals and relish their particular idiosyncrasies. A tiny old woman, evidently toothless, judging from the set of her tight-lipped jaw, was nodding and bouncing to the driving rhythm of the relentlessly upbeat music as one hand punched the buttons before her in perfect time. Beyond her, a matron with tight-curled iron gray hair rode her tall chair with insouciant ease, one foot propped up on a steel tray, the receptacle into which the machine would, with luck, disgorge its bounty of nickels. At her side, a neglected cigarette smoldered in a black plastic ashtray.

Elizabeth picked her way through the rapt gamblers, heading for the offices at the back, where she had been told she would find Driver Blackfox. Suddenly a siren whooped. She looked back to see a thirty-something woman with dirty blond hair, tight white slacks, and a cigarette dangling from her lips executing a slow, hip-swiveling, triumphal dance in the aisle by her machine. The beacon light atop the machine was proclaiming a win that could not be satisfied by rattling coins, and a uniformed attendant was hurrying to make the payout.

Other players looked up briefly, then resumed their methodical feeding of the machines. A tall man came striding down the lane, looking for an unoccupied seat. He brushed past Elizabeth and made for a vacant, flashing monster.

Okay, he gets the prize. Elizabeth tried not to stare, but the man was already attached to his machine and oblivious to her. A little embarrassed, she yielded to curiosity and studied the newcomer carefully, absorbing every detail of his outfit—fur-lined boots, *very* short cutoff jeans with slits reaching precariously high, an open denim vest, and a large gold medallion, prominently displayed on his bare chest. His confidence in his fashion statement was clear, but with his long white hair and beard, the latter slightly yellowed about the mouth, he looked like nothing so much as a Santa gone very wrong indeed.

At last she came to the hallway at the back of the main gaming room. It was marked NO ADMITTANCE, but the helpful woman at Mystic Grounds had told her that if she waited there, she couldn't fail to intercept Driver Blackfox.

I hope she knew what she was talking about. Elizabeth took up her station, just to the right of the hallway. *Like a cat at a mouse hole.*

Or one of the damned in Dante's inferno. Twenty minutes of waiting: being bombarded by flashing lights, bells, buzzers, the rattle of coins in the metal trays, and the occasional siren for the large wins, as well as the pervasive cigarette smoke. Elizabeth had a growing suspicion that somewhere back at the coffeehouse, two Cherokee artists were having a good laugh at her expense.

She was watching a woman near her light her fifth cigarette, oblivious of the four still smoldering in an overflowing ashtray. The woman, eyes locked on the ever-changing display in front of her, exhaled jets of smoke from her nostrils.

"I can't promise it any sooner than June."

"We can live with that—I don't think we'll have the site ready much before June, anyway."

The voices were almost beside her, and Elizabeth hastily looked around to see the man she had been waiting for.

Driver Blackfox was even handsomer than his photograph—slim and athletic, he had avoided the paunchiness that was the curse of so many of his fellow tribesmen. He wore faded jeans and a neatly pressed white dress shirt. His braids were iron gray, and the aquiline severity of his copper-hued face was softened by the faint tracery of laugh lines around his dark eyes.

The two men stood, exchanging a few more words, while Elizabeth feigned interest in the smoking woman's play.

At last good-byes were said, and to her great relief, the

client—supremely uninteresting: smallish, pinkish, with what was either a bad toupee or a terrible haircut—returned to the inner sanctum and Driver started for the exit. He strode rapidly away, gliding down the rows of slot machines as if along a deserted woodland path. Elizabeth hurried after him, not wanting to accost him here, doubting that she could make herself understood in the heart of this buzzing, whirring, dinging, sparking bedlam, but determined to keep him in sight.

At last Driver was at the main entrance, flashing a brilliant smile and nodding to the two pretty Cherokee women stationed there to greet the patrons. He pushed through the doors and started for the parking lot.

"Mr. Blackfox!" Elizabeth dashed through the door. "Mr. Blackfox, can I speak to you for a minute?"

To her immense relief, Driver Blackfox turned to look at her. "Mr. Blackfox, I'm Elizabeth Goodweather... Rosie's mother. You knew Rosie—she was Maythorn's friend."

Explanations, apologies, more explanations. Driver Blackfox stood as still and inscrutable as one of his own carvings as Elizabeth told him about Rosemary's belief that she could solve the mystery of her friend's disappearance.

"I know it sounds ridiculous, but Rosie's convinced herself that Maythorn wants her to do this. It's become almost an obsession—maybe that's too strong—but I don't know what else to call it."

Maythorn's uncle said nothing. Instead, he began to walk toward a nearby section of the huge parking lot. Elizabeth kept up with him.

"Rosie had just one thing she wanted to ask you. It was about the booger mask you were helping Maythorn make. Rosie—"

He didn't slow his long-legged stride but he did break his silence. "What does Rosie know about booger masks?"

"She knows that Maythorn was making a mask to represent someone who scared her. Kind of like your Rush Limbaugh mask. Or the one of the President."

"Yeah, they scare me, all right." His eyes twinkled, but his mouth remained stern. He stopped at the side of a worn old pickup.

"So, do you remember what the mask Maythorn made looked like? It would be such a help. . . ."

Her heart sank. Driver Blackfox was climbing into his truck. He was turning the key in the ignition and the truck was roaring to coughing, sputtering life. Laboriously he cranked down the clouded window and began to back the truck out.

Elizabeth stood there, bitter disappointment sweeping over her. With a grinding and clashing of gears, Driver forced the old truck into low. Just before he released the clutch, he put his head to the window, leaning toward her. "Maythorn didn't make *a* booger mask. She made *two*."

HUNTERS' MOON

September 1986

AS THE FULL *moon's glowing disk slowly came into view behind the peaks and gables of Mullmore, its cold light bathed the watching face of the girl in the gazebo. Maythorn Mullins watched, motionless, as the great orange ball gradually struggled free of the mansion's silhouette to begin a stately ascent into the velvet sky. At last she nodded. Now, now was the time to finish it—now when the magic would be strongest.*

Below her, the big house pulsed with light and hummed with a crazy confusion of sound—talk, music, the rhythmic clatter of tap shoes, gunfire, and the squeal of tires in a car chase emanated from various rooms as Mullmore's other inhabitants pursued their chosen entertainments.

Silently, Maythorn counted them off on her fingers: Krystalle was perfecting her Tap 'n' Twirl routine under the critical eye of her mother; Moon was in his den watching Beverly Hills Cop; and Jared and Mike were in the great room, where the television was tuned to some scary movie. In the kitchen wing, where the cook and her husband—the houseman—were cleaning up, a radio added its voice to the others.

Standing alone in the gazebo, Maythorn stared down at the

house. A cold breeze herded a rustling flock of dry leaves across the wooden floor and around her running shoes. She pulled her jacket closer to her thin frame and shivered. The house looked so warm. Kids at school envied her for what they thought was a perfect life. When the class had come out for a picnic and a swim party at the end of school last year, she had seen how everyone had looked around. All at once, girls who had made fun of her long braids and dusky skin now wanted to be friends. And even Brian, who had whispered "Red nigger" whenever she passed by him . . . even Brian had been nicer to her since the picnic.

Brian's eyes almost jumped out of his head when he saw Mama in that tight T-shirt. And all those stupid girls, saying how darling Krystalle was. They didn't pay her much attention once Jared came out to play lifeguard—acting all grown up and showing off how he could do fancy dives.

Maythorn sniffed in disgust. Every last one of those dumb girls was giggling and trying to get Jared to notice them. They all had crushes on him for a long time—bad as Tamra. I knew that was why they all of a sudden wanted to be friends—so they'd get to come back here and see him. *And I bet it was Debbie or Tiffany who kept calling him all summer. Dumb idiots.*

As the moon soared higher above the great house, its angry orange-red softened to a creamy yellow. The girl watched its progress for a few more minutes, then, leaving the gazebo to the skittering leaves, she made for the little shed behind the pool house. Gardening supplies and tools were stored in the shed; at this time of year, no one ever came here. Her secret project would be safe from curious eyes.

Thrusting a hand into her jacket pocket, she felt for the precious envelope—still there. It hadn't been easy to get hold of what she needed, but at last the opportunity had come, just in time for the full moon—the Hunter's Moon, Driver called it, when trees and fields were bare and the light of the moon made it easy to spot the prey.

Her fingers curled around the soft package, and the ends of her mouth lifted in a triumphant smile. Anything the booger had worn next to their skin, Granny Thorn had said. But for the strongest magic, hair from the booger was best.

Rosie, what are you going to be for Halloween?

Mum looked up from her sewing machine set at one end of the dining table. She was stitching another strip of bright polka-dotted fabric onto the gypsy skirt that was going to be Laurie's costume.

Will you wear your Indian outfit again? If you want something different, you need to decide now—I'll be finished with this as soon as I add the rick-rack.

The machine buzzed back to life and Mum's head bent over her work. Rosemary considered the question while watching her little sister, who was painstakingly wrapping her arms, legs, torso, and head with strips of cloth from Mum's scrap bag. Orange, purple with pink flowers, green stripes, blue—with crows of delight, Laurie found a new place for each scrap. Her bright red curls were already adorned with a scattering of little bows.

Make my hair all fancy, the little girl had demanded. I want lots of bows. Odd ends of bias binding (lucky Mum never threw anything away) had served for ribbons, and now Laurie's head looked as if a flight of tropical butterflies had landed on it.

But her face . . . Rosemary looked at her sister with undisguised displeasure. The chubby face was garish with pink lipstick, blue eyeshadow, and two clown spots of rouge on her fat cheeks.

Mum, where did Laurie get that . . . that stuff? She looks like Mrs. Barbie.

The whir of the sewing machine stopped as Mum looked up. She made a funny face and whispered, I know, it's awful, isn't it? Don't you remember—the Mullinses gave it to her for her last birthday, almost a year ago. She wasn't at all interested in it and I put it away. Unfortunately, she came across it this morning when we were rummaging around for stuff to make her a costume. She decided that makeup would suit the look she's working on now.

They watched Laurie, who was standing on one foot and slowly raising the other behind her. Her arms, trailing bright strips of cloth, waved languidly up and down.

Now I'm a bally dancer. Aren't I beyootiful, Rosie? But for Halloween I'm going to be a gypsy princess. With big earrings!

The leg and arms came down and Laurel looked at her sister with an appraising eye. You can use some of my Little Princess makeup, Rosie. You can be an Indian princess.

Somewhat hobbled by the various bits and pieces of fabric dangling from her small person, Laurie moved carefully to a nearby chair, where a round purple plastic case lay open. She picked out a small pink tube and held it out. Here, try this. It'll make you pretty too.

Yuck! I wouldn't put that stuff on my face for a million dollars. You look dumb. Besides, who ever heard of an Indian with makeup on?

Laurie's lower lip began to stick out and her face got the look that said a loud outburst wasn't far away.

Indians did use war paint, Rosie. It would work with your costume. You don't have to use the colors like makeup—be creative! And don't call your sister dumb. She's just playing. Mum lowered her voice and winked. The sooner that stuff gets used up, the better. And it does wash off, sweetie—at least, that's what it says on the case.

Rosemary pondered. War paint. That might be fun. She and Maythorn had never done war paint. But she had seen pictures of Indians with bold patterns on their faces, right there in the museum in Cherokee, the time Driver took them. Yes, that settled it.

Okay, Mum. I'll be an Indian again. Sorry I called you dumb, Laurie. I didn't mean it.

The little girl grinned and tumbled in a brilliant heap on the floor. Now I'm a chicken hiding my eggs, she announced, as she crouched above the bag of scraps.

Rosie studied the contents of the purple case. She picked up a container labeled Pretty Princess Blusher. She opened it, frowned, snapped the lid shut, and selected a little pot of turquoise eyeshadow. Prying off the top, she put in a cautious finger.

Shining Deer, her face painted with the slashes of blue, green, and red that marked a Cherokee princess prepared for battle, made her stealthy way toward the Council House. The message had been clear: come quickly and quietly; come alone. The longed-for return to the old alliance, the sisterhood of blood, had come at last and Fox-That-Watches had sent for her—and her alone.

She looked back to her family lodge. A blue banner of smoke rose to the sky from the hearth fire. Already, on this fall afternoon, the sun had slipped behind the steep hump of the mountain that marked her people's western border and the chill breeze nipped like the wolf in winter. But as she reached the boundary ridge and looked down on the land held by the clan of Fox-That-Watches, she was warmed again by the waning rays of the sun, as yet unblocked by the lower hills at the western end of this neighboring hollow. With a brief pause for an openhanded salute to the setting disk, Shining Deer hurried on.

When the Council House was in sight, she halted again and

gave the secret signal. *Kee-o-wee! Kee-o-wee! She called twice, waited five beats, and called a third time.*

The door of the Council House opened halfway and Fox-That-Watches could be seen. Her impassive eyes scrutinized the markings on her friend's face for a long moment. At last she said, That looks cool, Rosie.

Then, recollecting herself, she reached into the pouch that dangled at her hip. Raising the dark circle of the Looker Stone to her eye, she intoned, Shining Deer of Over Hill, I see you. Enter.

34.

ARMED AND DANGEROUS

Wednesday night, October 26

Elizabeth shivered and peered through the dusty workshop window. The fading light outside warned her that it was growing late—probably after five. Sighing, she placed the wreath she had just finished in its box and added it to the stack of others waiting for the FedEx driver. *Two more to do, if they're all going out in the morning.*

She flipped on another light and took down a straw wreath form from a shelf. *Maybe I can get one more done before Phillip gets back. At least there's not much to do about supper—just heat up the soup and bread and make a salad.*

She shivered again and stalked over to the wood heater—a green enameled Jotul woodstove that usually kept the shop reasonably warm. Yanking open the door, she saw only a glowing bed of coals—all that remained of the oak logs that had been burning so vigorously.

Way to go, Elizabeth. No wonder it's so bloody cold in here. You have to keep adding wood if you want to stay warm, you dunce.

The coals raked forward, she added a few small sticks and scraps of wood, then shoved in two split locust logs.

That ought to do me through one more wreath. She shut the stove door and adjusted the damper to allow more air into the chamber, glanced out the window again, and returned to her worktable.

There, she began to gather stiff, dried lavender spikes into little bunches and affix them, one by one, to the straw form, using strong pins that were shaped like tiny croquet hoops. A slanting row of aromatic lavender clumps began to spiral around the wreath, short green stems overlapped by the purple blossoms of a second row. A third row of lavender was followed by a row of mixed yellow and white statice, then more lavender.

She held up the half-completed wreath and frowned at it, unsure about the design. *A bit stripe-y for my taste, but it's what the customer asked for.*

The shrill ring of the shop telephone interrupted her aesthetic assessment and she reached for the receiver.

"Hey there, Elizabeth. Just checking to see if you wanted me to pick up anything at the store. I tried the house and your cell and you didn't answer. I was starting to worry, then I finally remembered you might still be in the shop. What are you doing working so late, anyway?"

Elizabeth smiled. It was nice to have someone worry about her—*I could get used to this,* she decided.

"I've got a big order that needs to ship tomorrow. I'm just finishing up the next to last one now—there'll be time to do the other one in the morning. There's nothing I can think of that I really need at the store, but I appreciate your checking. Where are you now?"

"On the bypass—in the grocery store parking lot. On my way home as soon as I hang up."

Home. How good it was to hear him say that. Phillip's temporary stay at Full Circle Farm was still officially temporary, but his presence in her house—*and bed...and life*—was becoming more and more an accepted thing.

"Elizabeth, sweetheart..." His voice was hesitant. "Ah...do you have your cell phone with you? It would probably be a good idea."

She chuckled. "You forget, my phone isn't one of those snazzy satellite hookups like yours. You know how funky the reception is out here. My cell works fine at the house, but it's useless down here in the workshop—I might as well be in a deep, dark hole, as far as it's concerned."

Phillip made a discontented sound that hovered on the edge of tsk-tsking. "Well, I don't like nagging, but while I'm on the subject, how about your gun? Do you have *that* with you?"

Several days after the concealed carry class, Phillip had brought her a snub-nosed .357 Magnum. "It's just like Sam's gun, but with the shorter barrel it'll be easier for you to carry." He had offered her the deadly little weapon with an air of embarrassment. "I brought some different holsters, too, so you could see which one you liked best—dammit to hell, Elizabeth, don't laugh! This isn't the kind of present I want to give you, but for now it's what you need."

Subdued by the utter seriousness in his voice, Elizabeth had meekly submitted to trying out the various holsters. Both the shoulder harness and the ankle holster seemed uncomfortable in the extreme, and she finally convinced Phillip that the pocket holster that could clip to her waistband was her best choice.

"Yeah, I'm armed and dangerous," she assured him, looking at the revolver, lying in its holster on the nearby workbench. *For god's sake, Elizabeth, remember to put that on before you head back to the house.* "Listen, if I finish before you get back, I'll leave the jeep down here for you and walk on up. I need the exercise. See you soon."

Phillip switched off his cell phone. No sooner had he started the car than his second cell—the one Gabby had given him—buzzed.

"Shit!" he muttered, and turned off the ignition. He listened intently to the voice at the other end, asked a few terse questions, jotted a line in a pocket notebook, then nodded reluctantly. Ending the call, he pulled out his other phone. She was evidently no longer in the workshop—nor at the house. *Probably walking up.*

He left a quick message on the house phone, then, with a feeling of mounting excitement, started his car and headed out of the parking lot, back toward Asheville.

"Señora Elizabeta, why you work so late? *Y dónde está* Señor Felipe?" Julio's stocky frame appeared in the open doorway. Behind him, his slightly taller brother-in-law shifted from foot to foot.

"Have to, Julio—but I'm almost finished." Elizabeth jabbed the U-pin around another bundle of yellow and white statice and pushed the prongs deep into the straw of the wreath form. She paused to look at her two friends, both shining clean, hair carefully combed, crisp white shirts tucked into new Levi's. Homero was turning a new straw cowboy hat around and around in his hands and grinning expectantly at her.

"Wait a minute—this is the night you all were going into Asheville, right? I'd forgotten."

"*Sí,* we are meeting *amigos* at El Chapala. There is *lucha libre*—wrestling on the big television and—"

Homero nodded vigorously. "*Sí! Con El Alacrán Rojo y El Diablo del Muerte y también Los—*"

Elizabeth smiled and waved the two away. "Go on, you guys—I just talked to Phillip. He'll be here in a few minutes. You don't have to do guard duty anymore."

"*Seguro, Elizabeta?* We can wait...."

But Homero had already smiled his happy thanks and headed for Julio's truck, which, like the two men, was in a state of high polish. Julio hesitated.

"Really, Julio, go. I'm almost done here and I'm going to walk up to the house. Phillip knows to bring the jeep up. Truly, I'll be fine. Besides—" she picked up the holstered gun and clipped it to the back of her waistband "—I've got this, remember?"

The spiral wreath was in its box, the woodstove damped down, the shop lights turned off, and still no Phillip. *Maybe he had some shopping to do for himself; he said something this morning about getting some ice cream.*

She pulled on her barn coat and started up the dark road. The dogs had long since given up on her and taken themselves off on their own recognizance. There was no moon, but enough light remained to show the outline of the gravel road stretching out before her. Crisp, chill air suggested that there would probably be a frost by morning. Elizabeth sniffed appreciatively, sorting out the many smells: wood smoke drifting in the air, the lavender that lingered on her fingers, the not unpleasant odor of cows, busily cropping the grass in the pasture next to the road, the autumnal aroma of the fallen leaves in the woods just to her left. Higher up, the haunting call of a barn owl echoed through the hollow.

With a feeling of perfect happiness, Elizabeth breathed

wordless thanks for the fate that had brought her to this beautiful place. Then, remembering the meal to prepare and the dogs to feed, she quickened her step up the well-known way.

She had reached the chicken house when she heard the familiar sound of her jeep coming up the road. As the headlights' beam swung around the barn just below the chicken house, Elizabeth stepped to the side of the road, extending a thumb and cocking a hip in what, despite her heavy jacket and baggy jeans, she hoped Phillip would recognize as a sexy hitchhiker pose. As expected, the jeep pulled to a stop beside her and the figure at the wheel leaned over to open the passenger-side door.

"Hey, mister, goin' my way?" Elizabeth climbed into the welcome warmth of the car. "What's happened to the overhead light? Isn't it working?"

35.

STAKED OUT

Wednesday night, October 26

Where the hell *is Gabby?* Phillip glanced at his watch. *He didn't say where he was calling from, but it sure seems like he would've have been here by now.* From his parked car, Phillip could see the entire lot, dimly lit by three mercury vapor lights; the entrance and exit; as well as Room 222, where, according to Gabby, Landrum's henchmen had just checked in. Though the room was illuminated only by the fitful blue glow of a flickering television, at least one figure could be seen moving slowly just beyond the partially drawn curtain.

Phillip tried Gabby's number, but was immediately met with a gabble of static. *Strange, that shouldn't happen.* A second trial was equally unsuccessful.

Don't try anything without me, his former shipmate had warned. *And don't involve the local boys. Del wants this all to stay as quiet as possible till we have that deposition in our sweaty little hands. Don't worry, this isn't wet work; we're just going to take them into custody. There're only two—we'll have them in cuffs, in my car, and on their way to DC before they know what happened. Del's arranged a quiet little holding facility where these two can be kept out of the way till we have the deposition—or till we fail and Landrum gets the confirmation.*

Phillip groaned and ran his hand over his balding head. He and Elizabeth had gone through the copy of *Walden* the night before, page by careful page, noting every pencil mark, and there were many; every underlined word or passage; even every stain and flyspeck.

At one point they had both been sure that a pattern of some sort was emerging. "This is reminding me of... Oh, hell, Phillip, there's something familiar about this, but I can't quite..." Elizabeth had pored over the pages, until finally, unwilling to admit defeat, she declared, "I just need to step back for a while—it'll come to me. Let's try again tomorrow night. If we can't figure it out then, maybe your friend in DC can."

If something there makes sense to her and she can figure out where Sam might have put that stuff, maybe I'll be sending Del the photos and the deposition tomorrow. And that'll be the end of that sorry son-of-a-bitch Landrum's political career. Sweet Jesus, a hundred-something acres, three houses, barns, outbuildings—it could be anywhere. Come on, Sam, old buddy, give us a clue to your clue, for god's sake.

A sleek black Mercedes sports car pulled into a slot near the door of 222. Phillip slouched down in his seat but kept his gaze fixed on the new arrival. A silver-haired man in a suit got out, swept the parking lot with a furtive glance, and hurried to open his passenger's door. A young woman in a very short, very tight black skirt writhed her way out of the car. A pink camisole top ended just below her very improbable breasts, leaving exposed a long expanse of tanned flesh, while a wide belt of sparkling rhinestones rode low on her hips, well below the top of her skirt. As the woman and her nervous escort passed beneath one of the parking lot's tall lights,

Phillip could see the black triangle of her thong high above the back of her tiny skirt.

He groaned, remembering having seen his daughter, Janie, in a similar outfit, and watched as the pair exchanged a lingering kiss outside the door of 226. As the man's hand traveled down the curve of her skirt, the young woman turned her head and yawned.

A sudden movement to the left caught Phillip's eye. The door to Room 222 began to open and the silver-haired man abruptly ceased his explorations. In one eye-blurring movement, he pulled wide the door of 226, yanked his companion inside, and slammed the door firmly shut.

A hunched form stood in the doorway of 222, head turned back and evidently speaking to someone in the room. Phillip's hand went to his automatic but he forced himself to stillness. *Not unless they both come out and try to leave,* he told himself. *Wait for Gabby.*

The person in Room 222 wavered, hand on the door, deep in shadow. At last the conversation came to an end and the object of Phillip's scrutiny moved through the door and into the light.

Phillip stared at what seemed to be an old lady. Fluffy white hair formed a halo around her gently bobbing head. Her purple sweatpants were topped by a white sweatshirt on which, as the woman passed under the light beside her door, Phillip could plainly read the words "World's Greatest Grandma." As she slowly moved away from the open door, Phillip could see an elderly man sitting on the edge of the bed, a walker beside him. He appeared to be absorbed in a television program.

The old woman reached her destination—a nondescript light green car with a "We Still Pray" sticker on its rear window. She fumbled in first one pocket and then the other before locating her keys. At last she opened the back door and leaned in. After some moments of searching, she backed out, bringing with her a large shopping bag. Painfully, she began the trip back to her room, hesitated, returned to the car, locked it, and resumed her hobbling progress back to Room 222. Inside, the old man had not moved.

Phillip watched with mounting incredulity. *Sweet Jesus, did I get the room number wrong? Or the motel?* He scrabbled in his shirt pocket for the little notebook and wrenched it open.

This is where he said, all right. Phillip stared at the enigmatic door of 222. *Disguises? I suppose it's possible, but…*

He tried Gabby's cell number again. But the same frustrating static answered his call. Next Elizabeth—house, cell, workshop—no joy. A nameless trepidation began to swell within him.

"Goddammit to hell!" he whispered as he jumped out of his car and sprinted to the window of 222. Through the gap in the curtains he could see the old man and woman with the contents of the shopping bag laid out on the table just inside the window. A hasty glance before he returned to his car showed him a homemade picnic—sausage biscuits, a jar of applesauce, and two thick slices of layer cake.

"What's going on here?" he growled, grabbing his cell and keying the DC number.

Del answered almost immediately. "Do you have it, Phil? We're running out of time here."

"I think we're close, but first you need to tell me about Landrum's people—what do they look like?"

"Look like? I talked to Gabby this morning and he told me he was tailing a little dark Colombian guy and a big African-American who looked like he could've played some football. But I told him not to worry about them anymore, because you and the lady thought you were about to crack the code. I told Gabby all he needed to do was to keep an eye on Sam's Liz."

36.

MIND IF I CALL YOU LIZ?

Wednesday night, October 26

"Been keeping an eye on you, Liz," said the stranger behind the wheel. Elizabeth gasped and grabbed the door handle just as a loud click sounded.

"These childproof locks are a fine invention. Keep you from running off when all I want is to have a little talk. Don't mind if I call you Liz, do you? Red always called you that, and he talked about you so much, well, that's how I've always thought of you."

The man beside her reached out and twisted a knob on the instrument panel. It lighted and in the pale glow, she could see the glitter of little metal-rimmed spectacles and gray hair pulled back in a straggling ponytail. She could also see the small automatic pistol in the man's left hand. He held it easily, keeping it trained on her head.

"Now, I know you've been taking lessons, even got your permit. Wouldn't old Red be proud of his bride?" An unpleasant baring of crooked teeth was accompanied by a mirthless laugh. "But just so we don't have any mis-understandings, I need to know where that piece Hawkins gave you is. I already checked your glove compartment, and it wasn't there."

Like a striking snake, the stranger's right hand shot out and fumbled at her breast through her jacket. He leaned closer, bringing the cold gun muzzle to her head while his free hand crept, fingers digging and searching, over her torso, between her legs, and down to feel around her ankles.

"Nothing here ... or here. Let's see about ... here. We just may need to have a real good pat down when I get you to the house." The man's breath was strong with cigarettes and rotten teeth. "I don't suppose old Red would mind me getting up close and personal with his bride ... like his buddy Hawkins has."

She could hardly breathe, paralyzed by shock and fear. Somehow she remained aware of the lump of metal at her back—her pistol in the little holster clipped at the back of her jeans' waistband. She froze, motionless in her seat, hoping to buy a little time. *Phillip's on his way.*

Elizabeth turned her head away from the mocking smile of her captor to look down the dark road. She desperately wanted to see Phillip's burly form trudging up the road. *If he's coming, I'll need to warn him somehow—if he sees the car stopped here, he might think—*

"Looking for your boyfriend, Liz? Don't strain your eyes; he's off on an errand for old Gabby."

The hand had finished now and the man had moved back, but the automatic was still aimed at her left temple.

"Gabby?" The word was a croak, forced from a mouth dry with fear. "Who's Gabby? Who are *you*?"

"Now, Liz, that hurts my feelings. You mean Hawkins never mentioned his old shipmate, Gunner's Mate First Class Gabby Hayes? Gabby Hayes, sent specially from DC to help him find old Red's little bombshell deposition? Maybe you ought to wonder what else Hawkins hasn't told you."

"Mac, can you get a unit out to Ridley Branch right now? I'm on my way, but it's going to take almost thirty minutes. I've got a bad feeling...."

Phillip was speeding through the darkness toward Marshall County, cell phone pressed to his ear. The vague sense of uneasiness had blossomed into full-blown conviction. *What if Gabby sent me to that place on purpose? There's been something squirrelly about this whole setup ... the way he kept me out of the loop from the beginning ... and now his cell's not working ... and why the hell can't I raise Elizabeth?*

Mackenzie Blaine's reply didn't help. "What do you mean, 'on your way'?" the sheriff said. "You should have been there forty-five minutes ago, by the schedule you gave me. Listen, Hawk, I've got a small department and we're stretched thin as it is. I can't keep a man out there 24/7. What about those Mexican fellows? They're there, right?"

Phillip groaned. "This is their wrestling night. They're probably in Asheville, unless they waited—but Elizabeth would have told them I was on my way. Dammit all, Mac, this may be bad! Listen..."

He put his foot down, maintaining a steady, if illegal, seventy-five. A cold misgiving lay like a lump of lead in the pit of his stomach.

Elizabeth watched helplessly as her captor slid from the driver's seat and walked around the car to her door, all the while continuing to train the automatic pistol on her. *He's the one Phillip's been talking to ... but he's supposed to be working with Phillip ... why is he threatening me?* She could hear James's high-pitched barking. All three dogs were probably on the porch, waiting for their long over-due supper. *Three rottweilers, that's what I need. But he'd just shoot them.*

A terrible thought hit her. As the ponytailed man opened the door and motioned her out, she could see the three dogs trotting down the path toward him.

"They won't bite!"

Even as she said it, the dogs had stopped. Molly began to whine, but James whirled and dashed away, tail tight between his legs. Ursa and Molly held out an-other uneasy moment, but as the man called Gabby made an abrupt move in their direction, the pair whirled and ran, following James to the safety of under the porch.

"Well, what about that! *They* remember old Gabby." The steel-rimmed glasses glittered at her.

"Remember ... ?" Understanding dawned. "You were the one who tore up my house ... but, why? What was the point of that? And what do you want with me now?"

Keep him talking. The bulk of the snub-nosed revolver nestled against the small of her back was a distant com-fort. *If he doesn't think of looking there, I still might have a chance....*

No sooner had the words formed in her mind than they were overridden by a second voice. *Right. Forget it, Elizabeth. He's holding a gun on you.*

But say he puts the gun down ... for some reason.

Gabby jerked his head toward the house. "Ladies first, Liz. We'll talk about what I want once we get in-side."

All the strength seemed to have gone out of her legs, and the walk along the uneven stone path was unexpectedly difficult. The pistol riding at her back felt huge, and with each step she expected that the man following her would notice it.

But the heavy barn coat and the lack of light were her allies: she reached the porch with her secret still undiscovered. Gabby pushed by her to the front door.

"Why, Liz, you've *locked* it! Was it me ruint your faith in mankind?" His mocking words were accompanied by a brusque gesture with the gun toward the lock. "Open it."

She obeyed, reaching for the key in her pocket, and was stunned by an excruciating pain as Gabby knocked her hand back. An involuntary gasp escaped her.

"Ah, ah!" The hand dove into her jacket pocket and retrieved the door key on its metallic blue mini-carabiner. "Allow me." With a gesture of mock gallantry, Gabby opened the door and stood aside to let her enter. "Now let's go in and have our little talk, Liz."

Inside, he flipped on the lights and glanced around in amusement. "Can't even tell I was here. You three did a real good job cleaning up."

Elizabeth stood hunched and shivering, even in her heavy coat. Something didn't make sense, something... *How does he know who cleaned up? And where the hell is Phillip?*

Her breath was coming in shuddering gulps but she forced herself to ask, "What do you want? I don't understand what this is about."

"Why, Liz, I expected more of you. Red always told us how smart you were, and your boyfriend Phil seems to think highly of you too. He said you've just about figured out where old Red hid that deposition of his."

The cold eyes behind the little glasses studied her. "Well, I've got other plans for that deposition, and I'm tired of waiting. I want you to get that Waldo book you and Phil been puzzling over. You and me'll see if we can't untangle Red's message."

37.

WHERE'S WALDO?

Wednesday night, October 26

"Waldo?" She spoke the word, and instantly the germ of a desperate diversion formed in her mind. "How did you know—Oh, of course, Phillip must have told you."

"Let's just say I found out. Now I want to see that special book." Gabby emphasized his demand with a thrust of the automatic in her direction.

Elizabeth hesitated, weighing the chances of her idea. "It's...back there, in a bookcase by the guest room. Do you want me to—"

"I'll just go along with you. Don't want you doing anything stupid."

As she led him to the bookcase where an assortment of books were kept—light reading and children's books for the entertainment of various visitors—her mind was racing furiously. *I know it's there and I think I remember that it's pretty marked up. If I can just stall him for a while, till Phillip gets here, maybe there's a chance....*

Where's Waldo? that perennially favorite picture book, was buried under several *Doonesbury* collections, an album of Gary Larson cartoons, and a battered *Calvin and*

Hobbes. She disinterred the volume and held it out to Gabby, who looked skeptically at the brightly colored cover.

"*This* is the book Red gave you? Said it was so important or whatever the fuck it was?"

She hurried to provide a plausible explanation. "It didn't make any sense to me at the time, but now…" Her hands were shaking as she opened the book. *Please let this work.*

Where's Waldo? had been a favorite with her girls. They had spent hours poring over its pictures of densely packed crowd scenes in search of Waldo with his striped stocking hat and round glasses. And when that had ceased to be entertaining, they had embellished the already crowded pages with their own drawings and remarks.

"See," she said, opening to the first page where a dialogue balloon had been drawn over Waldo's head, saying, in Rosemary's careful, minuscule printing, " 'You found me but can you find six apples and a sponge?' And on the next page—"

"And this is supposed to tell you where he put the photos and the deposition?" Gabby took the book from her and glared at it. "Where's all the notes and shit you two were making about this so-called code?"

"I guess Phillip took them with him this morning.…I think he was going to try to—"

He stood there, squinting at the page in front of him, then, motioning with the pistol, followed her back to the living room and directed her to the end of one of the sofas. He took the seat to her left and, laying his weapon on the empty cushion beside him, began to study the pages with their teasing commentary.

"What's this? 'Look on page 22'…and on page 22

there's an arrow pointing to a truck...and the sign on the truck says..."

Jammed into the corner of the sofa, Elizabeth was breathlessly aware of her gun at her back, still hidden by the heavy coat—and Gabby's pistol, so near to his hand. *Not a prayer, not now. Oh, Phillip, where are you?*

She had to fight to keep her eyes from turning toward the dining room, where, around a corner and just out of sight from the living room, the marked copy of *Walden* and the sheaf of paper with her and Phillip's copious notes were stacked on a chair seat. *Stupid! Why did we leave them out in plain view?*

After only a few minutes of paging through the picture book, Gabby looked up from the bright illustrations. His eyes narrowed.

"I believe you've been messing with me, Liz. That's what I think. And that makes me mad."

The chilly fury in his voice forestalled any further explanation she might have tried.

"I thought it was Waldo or some name like that, but *this*—" He tossed the book away from him. "—this is shit. I'll just check on something here, refresh your memory like. Then maybe you'll be a little more helpful, Liz."

She watched as Gabby pulled a small electronic device of some sort from his pocket. Slightly larger than a television's remote control, it had a little display screen which lighted as he punched a button.

"Hours of stuff on here—mostly boring. I erased that. But I saved the parts where you two were talking about the key Red gave you and what this and that might mean." A grin creased his weather-beaten face. "I saved some other parts—for my listening pleasure, you could say. Long about oh-three-sixteen's a good one."

He pressed a tab and the little device hummed. A second press and she heard a tinny variation of her own voice. "...*can talk about it another time.*"

There was the creak of bedsprings, giggling, and more. Quite a bit more. Elizabeth looked away from Gabby, who was listening with rapt attention. Her face was blazing hot.

He has my bedroom bugged...the whole house maybe. Did he do that when he tore the place apart? Or—

"I really like the part where you start making those little squealing noises and old Phil starts huffing and puffing." He had turned off the recorder now and was looking at her appraisingly. "Pretty hot stuff for folks our age. But you might want to think about the strain on Phil's ticker. The way you two lovebirds been going at it, he's likely to drop dead right on top of you one of these nights."

His hand reached out and slid inside her jacket and under the layers of flannel and knit to run lasciviously over her breasts.

"Bet *I* could make you squeal, Liz." The rough fingers clamped around a nipple with a vicious twist.

She stifled an exclamation, biting down on her lip. Her eyes began to drip tears and her whole body stiffened in fear and revulsion. The hand withdrew.

"Liz, baby, that's nothing. You don't give me your full cooperation, I'll show you what real pain is."

Gabby cocked his head and studied her. "No offense, Liz, but you're a little old for my taste—I like 'em fresh." He continued to appraise her, seemingly toying with some interesting thought. "Still, it's been a time since I had me someone...expendable. And if you don't help me out, that's what you'll be—expendable."

And if I do, I'll be even more...expendable.

The recorder began again and she closed her eyes as she heard the unmistakable sounds once more.

"That's another good one, but we don't have time for fun just now, do we, Liz?" Gabby frowned and keyed the little device again. "Somewhere, right about ... here."

A canned and diminished version of Phillip's voice spoke: *"Miz Goodweather, this could be it! Walden. I remember he carried around a paperback copy of it till it got lost during some mission. He knew that book backward and forward ... and look, there are little marks here in the margin—"*

Her face must have betrayed her. Gabby cut short Phillip's recorded exclamations and slipped the recorder back into his pocket. He picked up the automatic.

"Not Waldo. *Walden.* Right, Liz? You were just having a little fun with old Gabby." The automatic's muzzle stroked her cheek. "No more games. You're going to get me the right book or I'm going to put a bullet through your foot. Then your other foot, then move up to your knees. You won't be able to get around your farm so good when I'm done with you, Liz."

38.

IF YOU FIND YOURSELF IN A
SITUATION . . .

Wednesday night, October 26

As he rounded the last curve and came in sight of the driveway to Full Circle Farm, Phillip saw a pair of taillights disappearing up the road toward the workshop. With squealing tires and a spray of gravel, he swung his car into the drive. The car ahead of him, a big black SUV, he recognized immediately as belonging to the sheriff's department. It made a semicircle in front of the workshop and came to a stop, its headlights trained on his vehicle.

Phillip braked, leaving his car where it would block the road; cut the engine; and jumped out, keeping his hands visible and away from his body. *I think all of Blaine's folks know me, but just in case this is some skittish new deputy . . .*

"It's Hawkins," he called out as he stepped forward. "Phillip Hawkins. I asked Sheriff—"

"Get in, Hawk." Mackenzie Blaine cut the headlights and called out from his open window, "I was the only body we could spare. Come on; we'll ease on up there nice and quiet and just see what's up."

* * *

With a feeling of hopeless defeat, Elizabeth choked back tears of frustration and rage. "Okay, I'll get the book. But would you tell me why? If you were part of the crew the day Landrum massacred all those people, don't you understand—"

"Lieutenant Landrum risked his life to save *me*, Liz. That's more important to my mind than a bunch of stinking gooks. Plus, he pays good. When the lieutenant first heard from Red, old Red with his bullshit ideas about honor and right and wrong, he got hold of me. I'd worked for the lieutenant before and he knew he could trust me. He's counting on me to make this problem go away, and that's exactly what I'm going to do. The book, Liz. I want the right book, and I want it now."

What choice do I have? Maybe one last chance... "It's in there, on the chair in the corner." She pointed toward the dining room and slowly began to get to her feet.

As she had hoped, Gabby left her where she was and with a few quick steps was by the chair where the precious copy of *Walden* lay, holding down the stack of papers with all the scribbled notes that she and Phillip had made.

"Well, hot-doh-cocky-damn! Look at this!" In his excitement, he laid his gun on the chair seat and began to leaf through the pages of notes. As he turned away, to bring the pages under the hanging light over the table, Elizabeth slid off her jacket and reached behind her. The gun's grip was in her hand.

Gabby was examining the pages, looking quickly from one to another. "I can't make heads or tails of this shit. You better not be messing with me again."

He moved a step closer to the light... and a step farther from his gun, lifting the pages to the lamp and peering through his little spectacles at the confusion of numbers, words, and letters before him.

The .357 Magnum was in both her hands now, carefully gripped as she had been taught. Her arms were extended, wrists and elbows locked in the isosceles stance. She lined up the sights on Gabby's torso and waited.

"Mac, leave the car just below the barn, where we're still out of sight of the house. It might be better not to announce ourselves. Maybe Elizabeth's up there by herself—and maybe not."

Leaving the big car in the road, the two men went quickly and quietly up the grassy track that led to Ben's cabin. Phillip could see that lights were on in Elizabeth's house, but there was no sound of music, nor any smell of cooking, none of the usual signs of a usual evening.

Both men had their weapons drawn now. Phillip led Blaine past the silent darkness of Ben's cabin and across the narrow stream that ran between house and cabin. Just ahead lay the French door that led into the guest room at the back of the house. Silently, Phillip stepped up on the little porch and tried the handle.

The door swung open with a tiny creaking sound. Phillip froze, but could hear nothing. The room's other door, the one leading to the hallway, was shut, a bar of yellow light shining beneath it. Motioning to Blaine to follow him, Phillip crept toward the closed door.

"What the fuck do you think you're doing?"

Holding the papers in both hands, Gabby looked at Elizabeth with a mixture of scorn and incredulity. "Where'd that come from?"

His eyes flicked to his own gun and back to Elizabeth. She stood, frozen in place, certain what was coming next. Disjointed facts and pronouncements, from the concealed carry class bombarded her.... *right to use deadly force in protection of your life... He said I was expendable... if you are in your home, there is no duty to retreat... He threatened to cripple me, at the very least... Oh, shit... what if he reaches for his gun?... Can I fire quickly enough?... Can I hit him?*

"If you try to reach for your gun, I'll shoot you."

Phillip's heart leapt as he heard Elizabeth's muffled voice. *She's in the living room, but what...?* She sounded a little shaky. He inched the bedroom door open and slid into the hallway, Blaine at his heels.

They moved noiselessly down the hall, guns at the ready.

"I believe you just might try it, you crazy bitch. But could you hit me, that's the question. How's your aim with that short barrel? I don't know, maybe I'll take my chances—"

"Sure about that? She can take you out, no problem, Gabby." Phillip stepped into the living room, his weapon trained on his one-time shipmate. "And so can I, and so can the sheriff here. It's over."

MULLMORE

October 1986

AT LAST THE *house was quiet. The shrill nagging and whining that had accompanied the preparations for Krystalle's trip to the Pumpkin Pageant had died away when mother and daughter climbed into the car packed with costumes, tap shoes, hair spray, cosmetics, as well as motivational tapes for Krystalle to listen to during the forty-minute drive to the auditorium in Asheville.*

From her bedroom window, Maythorn watched the green Range Rover pull away. Tears smarted in her eyes but she swiped them away with the back of her hand. On the pink-and-green coverlet of her bed lay the mutilated remains of her beloved Indian costume—the one Rosie's mum had made. Next to the worn brown shirt and trousers, now slashed and torn, lay the fluffy lavender ballerina costume with its matching shoes and tights. The scissors Mama had used lay open on the floor.

No more! I'm sick and tired of seeing you skulking around like some dirty reservation brat. There're going to be some changes with you, missy, Mama had said before dragging her off to the beauty parlor again.

It had been bad enough when her braids fell to the floor and the stylist had started cutting at what remained of the glossy black hair. Maythorn had shut her eyes tight, not wanting to see what was happening, but there was no escaping the words that came at her in minty, smoky puffs.

She may not like it right now, the stylist was saying. But when we get done and she sees how pretty she looks—ssst, ssst, ssst, the scissors kept up their merciless song—when she sees how much she looks like her gorgeous mama and little Miss Krysty, why she'll thank you and me both. Now, you run along and get Krysty to her class. Me and Maythorn'll do just fine. When you get back you'll see a different little girl.

And then her head was in the sink and there was the stink of chemicals and the endless washing and rinsing. Honey, did the shampoo get in your eyes? You're not crying, are you?

Maythorn sat, stoic and silent, as the stylist twisted her hair around the little rods. There was an awful, penetrating smell. Maythorn kept her eyes squeezed shut—a single glimpse in the mirror had been enough. Is this what Mama wants—a different little girl?

Maythorn pulled off the red hat and turned to her mirror. The face that looked back at her was unfamiliar. She leaned closer, but there was no sign of Fox-That-Watches, only a stranger with fluffy yellow curls framing a thin dark face that stared hopelessly back at her. She scooped up the red hat and pulled it down over her ears. Then, from under her mattress she pulled out the leather pouch that held the Looker Stone. Putting it to her eye, she looked again into the mirror. The stranger was gone and Fox-That-Watches smiled back at her.

I see you, she whispered.

* * *

Telephone for Rosie! Telephone for Rosie!

Laurel's bellow echoed through the house and Rosemary raced down the stairs to take the phone from her little sister.

It's me. Meet me at the scuttle hole.

I thought you were coming over to spend the night. Mum's making pizza and we've got a movie to watch. And why weren't you at school today?

I can't spend the night; I'm grounded. But I want you to take the Indian suit your mum made for me and see if she can fix it. It got cut up.

Maythorn tiptoed into the back room that her mother called Moon's "den." Yes, like a hibernating bear, he was sleeping in the dark, sprawled in the big green recliner and snoring noisily. Eleven empty beer cans ringed the nearby wastebasket and a twelfth lay in a puddle on the floor just under Moon's limply outstretched fingers. A trail of spittle led from the corner of his gaping mouth to the headrest, and as she watched, the dark stain on the green velour spread larger.

She felt in her pocket for the Looker Stone. It would be safe to look at him now—not like that other time. That had been her mistake, not waiting. But she had been so curious. *He just turns into an animal when he has too much to drink,* she had heard Mama telling Uncle Mike. And though she knew that was only something people said, still, she had thought, *if I look at him through the Looker Stone, maybe I'll see what kind of animal he really is.*

But she had no sooner raised the Stone to her eye than Moon had staggered toward her and pulled her off her feet. He was tickling her all over and his sour breath was in her face. *Stop,* she had said. *I don't like that.*

Later she had asked her mother not to let Moon tickle her anymore and her mother had said, What are you saying, missy? And she had answered, They said at school that we have to tell if someone is touching us in a way we don't like, and Mama had slapped her and called her a liar. Moon's your meal ticket, missy. If he wants a little sugar, you give it to him.

39.

THE CLOUD OF UNKNOWING

Thursday, October 27

A shaft of sunlight lay across her pillow. Elizabeth groaned, rolled over, and yanked the covers over her eyes. *It must be eight o'clock.*

The temptation to seek oblivion in her soft pillow was powerful. She felt bone-weary, as if she had just hoed an endless field of tobacco or trudged uphill for many tiring miles. *I think every muscle in my body was clenched tight from the minute I got in the car and realized it wasn't Phillip till Phillip actually showed up.*

She slid an exploratory leg to the other side of the bed—cool sheets and an empty space. The tempting smell of coffee, as well as bacon, suggested that Phillip had been awake for some time. Bowing to the inevitable, Elizabeth sat up and opened her eyes.

As always, the three eastern windows that faced the bed were a triptych worth enjoying. The sun, far to the south, peeped over the darkness of a mass of trees on the nearby ridgeline. A pearly mist, barely tinged with pink, was lifting from the river. Far in the distance, the dusky violet outline of the Blue Ridge Mountains met the morning sky.

Elizabeth stretched, threw back the covers, and stiffly—*damn, my muscles* are *sore ... it's not just my imagination*—got out of bed.

Standing by one of the north-facing windows, she pulled on her jeans and an old sweater, watching a flock of wild turkeys moving across the field just below Ben's cabin, busily feeding as they went. The early rays of the sun touched their bronze plumage and set alight the rich colors of the surrounding trees.

"Morning, Annie Oakley."

She turned to see Phillip leaning against the doorframe, a mug of steaming coffee in each hand.

"I thought I heard you stirring." He set the mugs down and came around the bed to fold her into his arms. "You were dead to the world when I got back last night—I figured you needed the sleep."

His arms tightened around her and he spoke in a low, husky tone. "Thank god you weren't hurt. I should have known there was something not right about Gabby. But you—you were amazing. I'm glad we got here when we did, but like I told Mac, I've got no doubt at all that you would have dropped that scumbag right where he stood."

He stepped back to look at her with fond affection. "You're some woman, Miz Goodweather."

"What's left of her." She smiled wearily at him. "I'm glad I didn't have to find out if I could shoot him. But you're right, I sure would've tried. After you and Sheriff Blaine took Gabby off last night, all I wanted to do was to take a bath and get in bed. I thought I'd hear you come back but ..."

Phillip retrieved the coffee mugs, setting one on her dressing table and taking the other with him as he sat on

the bench at the foot of the bed and watched her brush
and braid her hair.

"You were totally zonked, sweetheart. I came in and
said your name, but you were down for the count."

"So what have you done with Gabby?"

"Blaine's booked him on everything from attempted
kidnapping and assault with a deadly weapon to bad
breath and dog-scaring. I've been in touch with Del. He
thinks he can get the Feds involved—don't ask me how,
'cause Del wasn't saying. Anyway, Gabby will be safe in the
Marshall County jail for the foreseeable future. And I've
sent Del that copy of *Walden*, along with our notes—took
it with me last night and put it in the FedEx drop by the
bank. I think Gabby was working alone, but just in case he
wasn't, now there's nothing for anyone to come after."

"Except the deposition itself—and the photos."
Elizabeth twisted an elastic fastener around the end of
her braid and turned to Phillip. "Wherever they are."

She hesitated, her mind turning over a confusing assortment of possibilities. "You know, Phillip, the more I
think about it, the less sure I am that we're on the right
track with *Walden*. What if we've been fooling ourselves,
reading meaning where there was none? If I was able to
come up with some sort of explanation for the scribbling
the girls did in *Where's Waldo?*...I don't know, maybe
we're making it all too complicated."

She picked up her mug and joined Phillip on the
bench. Silently they watched through the eastern windows as the morning mist rose higher and higher, to become a fog blotting out everything.

"It all just seems so hopeless, Phillip—like we're spinning
our wheels and getting nowhere. Not only are we no

closer to finding the deposition, but this whole Maythorn thing is still completely unresolved. Rosemary may say she's remembering more and more important things about that time, but…"

They had finished the massive breakfast that Phillip had prepared in an attempt to make up for the meal missed the previous evening. He had announced that he would not be going in to AB Tech today and so, replete with eggs and bacon and English muffins and coffee, they were strolling along the pasture path toward the woods. "Let's just take it easy today, sweetheart. Or at least this morning."

She had agreed, welcoming the diversion and hoping to distance herself from the questions and puzzles swirling madly in her mind.

To no avail. As they neared the woods, the sight of the faint path leading up to Maythorn and Rosemary's scuttle hole brought all the questions surging back.

"…but maybe Rosemary's just spinning her wheels too. You know, Phillip, sometimes I think that all this so-called 'looking into what happened to Maythorn' has turned into a way for her to spend more time with Jared. I've never seen her so interested in a man, not since old what's-his-name—the one who looked like an Irish poet—back in college."

Elizabeth sank down on the little bench that was just at the edge of the woods and stared unhappily at the pasture where her cattle were cropping the last of the grass. It would soon be time to move them to the lower pasture, where the tractor could keep their feeding rings supplied with the great round bales of hay trucked in from Tennessee. The farm barely broke even on the small herd of cattle—beef prices were low and hay was not cheap—but without the cattle, the open fields and pastures would swiftly revert to woodland.

Phillip sat down beside her. She was aware that he was uneasy, could see his hand start for his head in the familiar gesture, then return to his side.

She turned to look at him. "What?"

The hand came up again but paused. He rubbed his chin vigorously. "Yesterday I had lunch with Hank—you remember, Elizabeth, Hank with the Asheville PD—he asked about you and I told him a little bit about what was going on with Rosemary. Well, he remembered the Mullins case, and, get this, *he* says at one time there was some thought that it was linked to what they called the Halloween Vanishings. I did a little research...."

The Halloween Vanishings: the headline tag the media had given to a baffling string of disappearances—all young girls who had gone missing on Halloween night. There had been one in nearby Barnardsville in 1984, and one in Asheville in 1985, and then, of course, Maythorn in 1986.

"I remember that phrase...." Elizabeth's face screwed up in an effort of recall. "But there was never anything really conclusive to link them, was there?"

"No, and there're runaway and missing children every night of the year, these days," Phillip added. "But I got Hank to do a little more checking. I found out that the Mullins family moved here from Greeneville, South Carolina—"

"I could have told you that."

"And..." He overrode her interjected comment. "...and there was a Halloween disappearance in Greeneville in 1983—*while* the Mullins were living there."

"Phillip." A sudden chill of apprehension touched her. "Are you saying that one of the Mullins family—"

"I'm not saying anything. Matter of fact, in the Greeneville case, a neighbor of the girl confessed in a suicide note. Said he'd put the body somewhere it would never be found."

Phillip rubbed his chin again and seemed to be studying a nearby cow with rapt attention. He added, in a noncommittal tone, "There *was* still some doubt as to whether the neighbor was really guilty, or just deranged. And since Maythorn's disappearance there've been several more, but like I said, runaway and missing children are all too common."

"So what's your point here?" Elizabeth reached for Phillip's hand, which was once again starting its upward journey, captured it, and held it close to her heart.

"Hank gave me the number of a retired cop he knew, one who was in Greeneville back in '83, then transferred to Asheville a few years later. Hank suggested that I call him."

"And . . . ?"

"This fellow, his name is Evans, must be lonely since he retired. He insisted that I come over to his house in Oakley. Said he'd buy me a beer and fill me in on what he knew about the Mullins."

Evans had had plenty to say. According to him, the Mullins family had been well connected and well known in Greeneville. "Families like that, any bad publicity and they attract a lot of attention; could be that's why they finally moved—make a new start maybe."

When Jared's name came up, Evans had let out a low whistle. "Now, there's a turnaround for you. You know,

I've kind of made a study of Jared Mullins. First knew about him when he was a juvenile in Greeneville. Boy was one nasty piece of work back then. His mother couldn't control him and only the fact that his father's family was so important kept him out of the detention center. There was an incident with a neighbor's cat...he'd killed it with his hunting bow, then skinned it and disjointed it. He brought in the pieces and was starting to cook them, and his mother got suspicious."

Evans popped open another beer and thrust it toward Phillip. "A few years later, I'm with the department in Asheville and I hear that name again in connection with a drug bust—Jared Mullins. Well, I find out it's the same kid and I figure he's probably gotten into some deep shit now. But turns out, once he moved in with his dad way out there in Marshall County, there was evidently quite a change. It was *Jared* who called the sheriff on a gang of marijuana growers near the Mullins place."

Evans had laughed at the odd twist the one-time delinquent's career had taken. "Hell, after that, young Jared started talking about going into law enforcement. He hung around the department and took a few criminal justice courses. He had a lot of friends in the department; still has, as a matter of fact. But in the end, he decided he wanted to be a lawyer instead."

Evans studied his beer bottle. "I *guess* that puts him with the good guys."

40.

FOR THE SAKE OF ARGUMENT

Thursday, October 27

"I was hoping I'd catch you in your office. Can you spare me a few minutes, Rosemary? I just want to hear your voice again."

Rosemary, receiver to her ear, glanced across her desk at the singularly unattractive young man whose self-righteous monologue had just been interrupted by the buzz of her telephone. Slouching low in his chair, he was surreptitiously picking at a blackhead on his unwashed neck, hand half hidden by a veil of lank dark hair.

She smiled, seeing in her mind's eye the clean good looks, the silver-blond, short-cut hair, gray-blue eyes, and smooth tanned skin of her caller.

"Hold just a moment, will you, Jared?"

She laid the phone on her desk. "I'm afraid there's nothing I can do about your grade, Mr. Horton. You've cut class time and again; your work is shallow and uninformed; and the fact that you can't be bothered to proofread is an insult. Creative genius, if that's what you think you have, can't overcome shoddy presentation. The grade stands."

The young man struggled to his feet, shooting her a look of pure venom as he replaced the iPod in his ear.

"Whatever," he mumbled, shambling toward the door.

As the door slammed, a little harder than necessary, Rosemary picked up the phone again. "Sorry about the wait, Jared. I was hoping you might call. Are we still on for tomorrow?"

There was a chuckle at the other end. "You were pretty rough on poor Mr. Horton, don't you think? Good thing I like dominating women."

Rosemary winced. "Jared, if you knew what I've put up with from that...that...*lout*. He fancies himself the next great misunderstood voice of his generation, but in truth, he's just a lazy little plagiarist with a big library of rap music. I sat through a ten-minute rant before your call gave me an excuse to shut him up."

She glanced at her watch and her voice softened. "Just eight more hours and I'll be back in Marshall County... and tomorrow we'll be together...."

"Phillip! You know, that's more than a little unsettling for a mother to hear. Rosemary's been spending a lot of time with Jared—I'd say she's pretty well smitten with him. But this...what you've just told me about him—that's a little scary."

"I thought you *knew* he was a lawyer—ouch! Sorry, couldn't resist—"

Phillip broke off, laughing as Elizabeth pinched his arm viciously.

"This is bloody serious, Phillip. It's my *daughter* we're talking about."

"Elizabeth, according to this guy Evans, Jared has been

straight-arrow Dudley Do-Right ever since he was responsible for the breakup of that ring of dope growers. And, by the way, our Bib Maitland was part of that gang back then. Anyway, it was Evans's theory that Jared realized it could be pretty exciting to be one of the good guys."

Elizabeth frowned. "Well, why did you tell me that awful story about the cat? I've read that children who torture animals are far more likely to grow up psychotic or criminal or something like that."

"I'm sorry; I should have kept quiet about that. I guess the point I was trying to make was how much he's changed. Besides, Jared was pretty young to be a serial killer, wasn't he?"

Elizabeth leaned into his warm bulk. "I'd think so. Though god knows, from the things you read, nothing's impossible. But when the Mullinses moved out here, they had Mike with them and Jared was almost always under Mike's eye."

See, you can say his name without it meaning anything. "Mike once said that, at first, being Jared's quote 'mentor' was a bit like having a rattlesnake strapped to his leg. But as time went on, he and Jared developed a real friendship—and Jared stopped being a problem."

"That fits in with Evans's story." Phillip stood and put out a hand. "Come on; let's walk some more."

As they continued along the path into the woods, they went over the list of potential suspects. "What about Moon? Was he ever suspected? He's another turnaround—from a drunk to a saint."

Phillip nodded. "I asked about that, but aside from the usual questioning, there was never any real suspicion attached to Moon. They investigated the whole family—father, mother, uncle, stepbrother: the whole shooting match."

"As far as I ever knew, Moon was never what they call a *mean* drunk. But, for the sake of argument, say he maybe hit Maythorn when he'd been drinking. She could be a little unsettling at times, with her creeping around and her spying. Say he hit her harder than he meant to and killed her. So he hid the body somewhere. But then guilt overwhelmed him, and his giving up all his money and running a homeless shelter is a kind of…atonement."

"Or a way of getting easy access to the most helpless children of all?" Phillip added. "Just for the sake of argument."

They walked on in silence, but for the dry rustle of the leaves underfoot. In the distance Elizabeth's rooster crowed and a hen announced, with a frenzied cackle, the arrival of an *egg*, a miraculous *egg!*

"Phillip, what about Bib? He resented the Mullinses, and if Jared called the cops on him about the marijuana, he'd have even more reason to hate them. And, according to Rosie, Maythorn was all over the place with her spy games; what if she was the one who told Jared about the marijuana. Maybe—"

"Remember, Bib was the main suspect at the time. They investigated him up and down but never could pin anything on him—he did *his* time for almost killing a trooper who tried to arrest him for DUI. The story was that Bib's wife ran off and took their little girl with her. Bib was pretty well liquored up and going to look for them when he was stopped. He was just wanted for questioning, but then it was obvious he was drunk. He was arrested just shortly after the Mullins child was last seen. They did their best to make a case against him for kidnapping Maythorn, but there wasn't any hard evidence."

"And lots of people suspected Cletus," Elizabeth said slowly. "Rosie did for a long time. Here again, I suppose it's possible—but he definitely couldn't have been responsible for any of the other ones—the Vanishings. Cletus couldn't drive."

Deeper and deeper into the little woods. The path curved around a small, still pool at the base of a huge beech tree and emerged at the top of a cleared hogback ridge. The last of the several benches—"Stations of the Walk" Sam had dubbed them—was here, and once again they sat, enjoying the sun's warmth after the cool shade of the woods.

As Elizabeth looked out across the fields and down to the valley below where the Ridley Branch road wound its way from the bridge across the French Broad to the foot of the road to Mullmore, another idea presented itself.

"Phillip, Miss Birdie told me she saw Driver Blackfox's car on the day Maythorn disappeared. What about *him*? Was he questioned?"

"Her real father's brother? Oh, yeah. But he swore that he'd had a call from Maythorn to come get her. He said that he waited at the foot of the road for almost an hour—and when she didn't show, he left. Said he figured her mother had changed her mind about letting Maythorn go to the res for the weekend. He was questioned, all right—I think they even searched his truck and his house, but it didn't come to anything. He'd been the subject of another investigation a few years before— when he shot his brother in a hunting accident."

"Was it really an accident?"

"There seems to have been no doubt that it was."

Elizabeth was silent, remembering the stone wall of silence she and Rosemary had encountered on their first trip to Cherokee. *If someone there wanted to keep a secret,* she thought, *it wouldn't be hard.*

41.

A Feather on the Winds of Time

Thursday, October 27

The steady hum of traffic on the highway was so familiar now, after her weekly trips home, that Rosemary could allow her mind to wander. Scenes of times long past sprang unbidden—clear and complete—into her memory. She made no effort to direct her thoughts, far less to analyze the memories that drifted into her consciousness like feathers caught in a fickle air. But she listened to their whispered tales...and remembered.

A potluck party, the standard weekend gathering for the young, recent arrivals to the community, one of the few the Mullins family had attended. A big bonfire...people sitting around it in little clusters. Mum holding the sleeping Laurie in her lap. Herself—eight? nine?—leaning against her father and sleepily rubbing her face on his shirt. And Mrs. Barbie, who pointed and said to Mum in a harsh voice, They can be such little sluts with men—especially their daddies, can't they?

Greensboro, and though the traffic slowed, there was not the usual congestion that brought all lanes to a nerve-testing crawl. Her thoughts floated effortlessly through layers of time.

Maythorn and the booger mask she's making from one of Mum's big gourds. When it's finished, she says, I'll do the Booger Dance like Granny Thorn showed me. Then I won't have to be afraid of boogers anymore. But you have to promise never ever to tell. Blood promise of a blood sister.

Strip malls and outlet stores, used-car lots and fast-food restaurants: the unlovely legacy of an automobile-based society spooled by in an unseen blur. Rosemary rubbed her little finger against the rough fabric of the car seat. The finger—*the one we cut so I could be Maythorn's blood sister*—was tingling. *Never tell, no matter what.*

At last the first mountains appeared and Rosemary's foot bore down on the accelerator. Jared was waiting.

Rosie in the pool house, waiting for Maythorn. Just out of sight she could hear the angry voice of Mrs. Barbie: He's your daddy and you can give him a little sugar if that's what he wants.

And Maythorn's reply: He's not my daddy! My daddy is dead. The angry crack of an open hand on soft flesh.

Her own hasty retreat for home and her shocked report to her mother: Mum, I don't think Maythorn's mother loves her!

And the offhand answer: Of course she does; mothers always love their children.

Past Asheville now, its lights already twinkling in the twilight, and on to the final stretch of interstate.

Maythorn at the scuttle hole, a bright red hat pulled down to hide her hair. She looks like she's been crying, but Indians never cry. When she talks Rosemary sees that Maythorn has lost one of her upper teeth, the pointy one that had been threatening to fall out for a week or more. Maythorn moves through the scuttle hole to hand over the bundle she's carrying, but the red hat snags on a low-hanging branch. The hat pulls off, revealing Maythorn's hair: the shining, silky mass of dark hair has been cut and bleached to golden blond, tortured into a semblance of Krystalle's fluffy curls. With a growl of despair, Maythorn re-

trieves her hat, tugging it over her ears. She runs back down the path to Mullmore. It is the last time Rosie will ever see her.

Marshall County. In the distance, lights were blinking on in the houses on the hills. The lights danced and blurred through the tears in Rosemary's eyes.

42.

DREAM QUEST

Friday, October 28

"She's determined to go over there this afternoon with Jared and his father." Elizabeth's near-whisper was charged with urgency. "She says she wants to look for Maythorn's spy notebooks. I'm really worried, Phillip. She's acting so weird, almost like she's in a trance. I can't let her go off like that with Moon and Jared, not when there's a possibility... Please, we have to go too. Can you be back by one-thirty?"

"No problem; I'm almost done here. Is Rosemary still at the house?" Phillip shifted the cell phone to his other ear and glanced at Mackenzie Blaine, who was ostentatiously absorbed in a lengthy printout. On the desk in front of Blaine was a small digital tape recorder.

"Yes, she is—which is why I'm whispering. She wanted to go in and have lunch with Jared, but I convinced her to invite him out here. Phillip, after what you told me... the thing about the cat and then about the missing girl in Greeneville... Maybe I'm overreacting, but I know I don't want Rosemary to be alone with Jared till we're sure—"

"Have you told her what I told you?"

"Kind of...some of it. I started to issue a sort of disclaimer and a motherly warning—she just looked at me with those big soft eyes and said that Jared had *told* her about his wicked ways as a teenager and that *I* should know that everyone makes a mistake now and then. That people *can* change."

Phillip frowned. Elizabeth sounded near tears—a rare thing. "Listen, sweetheart, I'll be there at one-thirty. Blaine and I are just wrapping up a few details. There's a U.S. marshal on his way to take Gabby off the county's hands. Don't worry, you and I'll tag along on this trip to Mullmore."

The call ended, Phillip shot a look at Blaine. Aware that Phillip's eyes were on him, he looked up from the printout with an innocent smile. "Sweetheart in trouble again, Hawk?"

Sighing heavily, Phillip spread his hands wide. "What can I tell you, Mac? The lady and I are...involved."

"I'd say you are." The innocent smile blossomed into a knowledgeable grin and Mackenzie Blaine nudged the digital recorder in front of him. "This was on Gabby when I did the pat-down. Evidently he had bugs in her house and in your cell phone so he could keep track of your progress looking for that deposition." Blaine assumed an unnaturally somber expression. "There was some...extraneous material on the recording—nothing relevant to the case; I've erased it, out of respect for the lady." The grin returned. "You *dawg*, you!"

Just as he had promised, Phillip was back before lunch was over. Declining anything to eat—"Took the sheriff to lunch. I owed him a favor."—he poured himself a cup of coffee and settled at the table with the others.

There was an odd tension at work between these three—Elizabeth, Rosemary, and Jared. Elizabeth, though trying hard to act normally, seemed nervous and talked more than was usual for her. Rosemary was very quiet, lost in her own thoughts. And Jared...

It was difficult to imagine this charming, soft-spoken man as the juvenile terror the old cop had described. He'd jumped to his feet when Phillip entered and was introduced, and although he'd bowed to Phillip's request not to be addressed as "Mr. Hawkins," every "Phillip" was followed by a deferential "sir."

"My father and Uncle Mike are going to meet us at the gate at two," Jared was saying. "That should give Rosemary plenty of time to look for Maythorn's notebooks before it gets dark. Of course, the power's been off at the house for years."

Elizabeth pushed her chair back and began to clear the table. Phillip stood to help her.

"Just put the dishes by the sink," Elizabeth insisted, a strange chord of excitement in her voice. "I'll deal with them later. It's after one-thirty now and we don't want to keep them waiting."

Only the solid warmth of Jared's body next to her on the back seat of the jeep anchored her to the moment, thought Rosemary. Without him, she would rise and float away, insubstantial as the dreams and memories that had been her constant companions since leaving Chapel Hill for this tormenting quest. *Dream quest, like Maythorn said, back when we tried to get high.*

In the front seats, her mother and Phillip were talking but the roaring, a constant hurring sound as if she were holding a seashell to her ear, made their voices seem thin and far away. Rosemary closed her eyes to concentrate on the memories endlessly dancing and teasing just beneath the surface of her understanding.

The car pulled to a stop and Mum and Phillip were getting out. Jared tugged at her sweater sleeve.

"We'll have to walk up from here, Rosie. Dad says there's been some erosion just ahead and the pavement's fallen in."

Opening her eyes, Rosemary looked out her window to see Moon, and beside him, slightly taller, and slightly younger, the Uncle Mike of her memory. She looked from Moon and Mike to Jared and back again. *I've fallen into a house of mirrors—they're still so alike.*

And now Mike was opening her door and helping her out. The little party set off, up the long curling driveway to Mullmore. With every step, the years seemed to fall away. Rosemary felt blind to the overgrown roadside, the once beautiful landscaping inexorably absorbed by native growth, the gaping cracks and potholes in the drive. It seemed that at any minute she might round a curve and the depredations of time would be undone: Mullmore would stand shining in the midst of its perfectly manicured lawns and gardens and Maythorn would come running to greet them, black braids flying behind her.

Elizabeth hurried after her daughter, whose pace seemed to increase the nearer they drew to the big house. They were all half jogging now, trailing in the wake of the young woman who moved as if drawn by some irresistible influence.

I've seen him again...he's as handsome as I remembered...

but thank god, he no longer has the same effect on me. Back then I was unhappy and needed someone who cared ... but now ...

She looked at Phillip, keeping pace at her side. Had it been her imagination or had he been watching with particular interest when she first spoke to Mike, watching her reaction to this man from her past? *It doesn't matter what fantasies I might have had at one time about Mike—I'm happy with the reality of Phillip.*

She smiled at that solid reality beside her. Phillip winked at her and grabbed for her hand, gave it a brief squeeze, and released it.

No one spoke as the great house came into view. All eyes were on Rosemary, who ignored the broad entryway and led them through the brown and dying weeds to the basement door at the side of the house. Wordlessly, Moon searched through a heavy ring of keys till he found the correct one and put it to the lock.

"Rosemary," Elizabeth stepped to her daughter's side and took her hand, "Rosie, are you sure you want to do this? You don't—"

Blank, brown eyes met hers and Rosemary answered in an unfamiliar voice, high and breathless. "Maythorn told me to meet her here."

Moon pushed open the door and stood aside. Without a moment's hesitation, Rosemary went down the steps and into the vast room. Pale throngs of sheeted furniture and stacks of dusty, cobwebbed boxes filled one end of the space, but she ignored them all and walked deliberately toward the furnace that sat in the middle of the basement.

"She looks like she's sleepwalking, Phillip," Elizabeth whispered. "I don't like this; I think we should—"

Phillip raised a hand. "Wait," he cautioned.

Suddenly, Rosemary dropped to her knees. With her

bare hands, she began frantically sweeping the dirt from the concrete apron around the big furnace, cold for so many years. With a cry, Elizabeth started for her daughter, but Phillip held her back.

Rosemary ignored them, scraping at the dirt with filthy hands, pushing it away to clear a small rectangle. At last the frenzied activity ceased and Rosemary sat back.

Elizabeth leaned closer to read, in straggling letters, the words: "ROSIE GOODWEATHER," a date, and a handprint. As they watched, Rosemary laid her hand atop the smaller impression and her slim body jerked as if she had received an electric shock.

When at last she spoke, it was as if she were a ten-year-old again. Her voice, usually low and musical, was high and shrill, like that of a frightened child.

"I was looking for Maythorn. She was supposed to meet me at the scuttle hole. We were going trick-or-treating and she wasn't there. I looked in the garden shed and she wasn't there either. And I did our special call but she didn't answer. Then I saw the basement door was open so I went down the stairs. Mr. Mullins was there, scraping the top of some wet cement, and he was crying. He said it was allergies but I knew he was crying. I asked him where Maythorn was and he said she was in her room, being punished for talking back. He told me he was fixing a place to set a new furnace on. He was pulling a piece of wood over the top of the wet cement and he stopped and said, 'Hey, come here, Rosie, you want to write your name?' "

Elizabeth turned to look at Moon. Tears were streaming down his face, but he made no effort to move. "She's there," he rasped. "God help me! She's under there!"

HALLOWEEN

1986

THE MENDED INDIAN *outfit had been under the message stone, just where Rosie had said she would leave it. A note was in the plastic bag with it.*

> *Dear F-T-W,*
>
> *Mum said this was the best she could do for now. She'll make us both new ones for Christmas. Pa will take us trick-or-treating at 5. He put hay in the back of his truck so we can have a hayride. I'm glad your not grounded anymore. Meet me here at 4:30.*
>
> *See you then!*
> *S.D. of O.H.*

Maythorn carefully unfolded the precious garments and, dropping her jeans and sweatshirt on the floor of her bedroom, she pulled on the mended trousers and shirt. There were odd, slanting lines where Rosie's mum had sewn the pieces back together, and both top and bottom fit more tightly than they had before. But the fringe down the trouser legs still jiggled when she walked and the bone beads on the shirt still traced their intricate zigzag patterns.

She slid her hand under the mattress and pulled out the big scissors that Mama had thrown down on the floor. Opening and closing them a few experimental times, Maythorn watched the long vicious blades slash the air. Satisfied, she turned to her closet where the ballerina costume was hanging, and began her work.

When the closet floor was littered with shreds of lavender satin and little wads of netting, she shut the door on the destruction. In her head she could hear the echoing chant—the chant she had heard that night in the woods when she and Shining Deer had watched the men do the Booger Dance.

Like a ghost, Maythorn slipped down the hall to the stairs. It had worked; Mama and Krystalle had left for the pageant without her, thinking she was with the Goodweathers. The house was still and empty, except for Moon, who was fast asleep in his den. Down the stairs and into the back hallway, moving on silent moccasined feet, Fox-That-Watches crept through the deserted house. In the hallway by the kitchen she froze, listening with all her might, but no sound came to her. Even the cook and houseman were gone.

The stealthy Cherokee edged out the door, into the cool afternoon air, bound for the secret hiding place of the masks. They were waiting. She would put on the face of the enemy and, so doing, would dance them into nothingness. She would become fearless. The wail of the chant echoed in her head as she padded past the deserted pool house, her lips moving silently.

The crack of a black walnut falling on a metal roof made her jump and she spun around. *Who is it?* she whispered, but there was no answer, nothing but the rattle of bare branches overhead, restless in the small breeze.

Be brave, like Driver said, she told herself. *Be strong like all the ancestors. Put on the face of your enemy and dance the Booger Dance.*

At the little shed, she looked around once more before reaching for the latch. Her breath was coming fast and the chant was loud in her head.

She put out her hand, and at her touch, the door swung open. In the shadows, the booger stood before her.

43.

SHE WANTS TO BE FOUND

Friday, October 28

"She's under there, just where Rosie wrote her name."

Moon sank to his knees, his face a study in anguish. "I put her there, and not an hour passes that I don't beg her to forgive me." Sobs racked his thin body.

They watched, speechless and helpless. Jared moved to Moon's side and leaned close to whisper a few words in his father's ear. Moon shook his head and the horrible, broken sounds continued while the rest of them stood frozen, dreading further revelations.

At last the fit of weeping subsided and Moon looked up. His eyes went at once to Rosemary, and when he began to speak it was as if his words were for her and her alone.

"I was drunk; I didn't know what I was doing. I swear it. When I came to and saw her lying there, I thought it was a hallucination...I had no memory of what had happened...what I must have done. I still don't. But God help me, there must have been a devil in me to have hit her like that—again and again. Her face was so swollen and battered that I wouldn't have known it was Maythorn, little

Maythorn...except for that Cherokee Pride sweatshirt she always wore."

They listened in horror as he described waking up on the basement floor, the child's body at his side, a bloody shovel by his hand.

"My head was spinning. Nothing made any sense. But there she was, and her blood was on me. And there were bags of Qwikcrete piled to one side and the workmen's tools and the place where the new furnace was going to go. The dirt was soft—"

"Dad, stop, you don't know what you're saying...you couldn't have..." Jared gripped his father's shoulder to stop the dreadful flow. "He used to have terrible hallucinations back then...that's what he's remembering. He couldn't have done a thing like that."

"Jared's right." Mike Mullins moved forward. "Moon, it was a nightmare, not something that really happened. Between your drinking back then and the loss of Maythorn, it's not surprising—"

"Will somebody listen to me?" Moon struggled to his feet. His eyes were still wild but his voice had become calm, almost peaceful. "I knew when Elizabeth first came to Redemption House how this was going to end. I'm tired of pretending, of trying to live with the horror of who I was...of what I did."

He turned and walked to a sheet-covered table, leaned down, and brought out a pickaxe. "I came out here a few days ago, thinking I'd get it over with. I was going to uncover her, to ask her forgiveness again," The pickaxe dragged behind him as he slowly approached the concrete pad.

"I thought I could do it, but I kept hearing sounds...

sounds that frightened me and wouldn't let me think. God help me, I ran away...again."

"Dad, please...please don't say these things." Jared stopped his father as the pickaxe began its upward swing. Gently he took the heavy tool from the older man.

"Son, please, she's tired of being hidden; she wants to come out!" The frenzy had returned to Moon's voice. Phillip took a step forward, but Mike intervened.

"No. Let him see the truth—let him see that this is all a fantasy, just a product of his illness. Give me the pickaxe, Jared."

Without a word, Jared handed the implement to Mike, who lifted it high over his head, bringing it down with a resounding crack in the loop of the *R* in the inscription. To Elizabeth's surprise, the concrete broke at once, revealing that it was just a few inches thick.

Only the repeated thuds broke the strained silence as the pickaxe swung again and again. Moon fell to his knees, watching the tool bite eagerly into the thin concrete. As the material shattered, Mike paused, allowing Jared to reach in and lay the pieces to one side.

At last an area was cleared. In a voice raw with emotion, Moon called out, "Stop, you'll hit her! I can't bear it if you hit her."

Like a medieval penitent, Moon Mullins, still on his knees, approached the newly revealed patch of soil. Just as Rosemary had done, he began to sweep aside the dirt with his bare hands, muttering as he worked.

Elizabeth pulled at Phillip's sleeve. "He's insane! Shouldn't we try to—"

Mike, who had been watching his brother with an inscrutable expression, turned to her. "We might as well let him work through this, Elizabeth. Let him see for himself that there's nothing—"

"No!" A cry of despair rang out and Jared was on his knees beside his father. "No!"

Even as he cried out, Jared's hands were working frantically to uncover the smooth brownish-white object that was emerging from the soil—the elegant fanlike shape of a small bone protruding from a gray piece of cloth and the horrible shattered teeth of a partially hidden skull. Clumps of matted blond hair still clung to the bone.

"Mike, Jared, get him away from there. This is a crime scene. I'll call the sheriff—we can't do anything till he gets here." Phillip had his phone in his hand. Suddenly he looked puzzled and took a careful step nearer to the half-revealed bones. "But this... this was a blonde—I thought Maythorn..."

"It's dyed. Patricia thought it would make Maythorn look more like one of us." Jared helped his father to his feet and slowly pulled him back from the excavation. Phillip had his cell phone to his ear as he shepherded them all up the steps and outside. They obeyed him without protest, happy to be away from the darkening basement and the subtle stench of dirt and decay.

"I never went back down there, I never could.... When the men came to set up that furnace, I was dead drunk...."

While they waited on the steps of the mansion for the arrival of the sheriff, Moon talked incessantly. Words tumbled out of him as he looked from one to another of them, his eyes begging for understanding, for compassion, for forgiveness.

"I've tried to pay... to make my life count for something... to help others. It didn't seem right, that I should have to go to jail, maybe even die for something I couldn't remember doing."

His filthy hands reached out to his son. "Jared, forgive me, but for a while I was able to convince myself that *you* had accidentally killed her—you had such a temper back then—and I told myself I was protecting *you.*"

The haggard face turned to Rosemary. "And Rosie, when you came looking for her, I lied, I said Maythorn was in her room. And I let you write your name and make your handprint...and all the time, she was there... under there."

It was a long, sad wait. Jared's arm was around Rosemary and he was whispering to her. Moon, babbling and weeping, was hunched over, his face buried in his hands, as his brother tried to calm him.

When Sheriff Blaine arrived at last, he quickly took charge. A deputy read Moon his rights and led him, stumbling and dazed, to a waiting car. Jared and Mike followed.

"Hawk, you take the ladies home. No need to keep them out here. We'll get statements later, after we see what's down there."

"Moon's made a full confession, Elizabeth." Phillip came to sit beside her in front of the fire.

On returning home, Rosemary had refused dinner, saying only that she wanted to go to sleep, that she might wake later and fix a sandwich. Elizabeth had watched without comment as Rosemary climbed the stairs to her old room. *This has been terrible for her—but at least it's at an end. Sleep is probably the best thing for her right now.*

"Evidently Jared's taking it pretty hard." Phillip put

his arm around her. "He doesn't believe his dad knows what he's saying."

"And Mike?"

"Mike . . . Well, Blaine said he got the impression that Mike might have had some suspicions about his brother all along. Something he said implied that was one reason he moved so far away.

"Blaine said Mike's talking about staying around a while, maybe even moving back here." Phillip was looking directly into her eyes now. "Would it make a difference to you if he did?"

She was silent, thinking of all the might-have-beens. Finally, she answered. "Years ago, when Sam and I were having . . . difficulties, I was attracted to Mike. He was a sympathetic ear and a shoulder to cry on. But in the end, Sam, my marriage, and my family were more important. Now . . ."

It was with a joyful burst of revelation that she found the words. "Now it's *you* who's more important." She grinned happily. "As Laurel would put it, I am *so over* Mike Mullins."

44.

UNSETTLED

Saturday, October 29

Rosemary lay still, listening to the morning sounds below: the gurgle of the coffeepot; James's excited bark as he danced, toenails clicking; her mother's cheerful "Go play, you dogs;" and the opening and closing of the front door. There was the chunking sound of logs being added to the fire and Phillip's deep gravelly tones asking some question.

Phillip. He seems to be a part of life here now. Mum is finally having to acknowledge what's going on between them. Once the guy who did the break-in was in jail, she didn't really need a bodyguard anymore. But he's still here.

Rosemary rolled out of her bed and reached for her jeans. Her quest was over: Maythorn had been found; her murderer had confessed.

It's what I thought she wanted. Why do I feel so...unsettled?

"I talked to Jared, Mum. I won't be here for supper; we're eating at his place."

Elizabeth looked up from the computer, where she

was wrestling with the end-of-month billing. Rosemary, her face pale and drawn, stood fidgeting in the doorway of the little office.

"How is Jared doing with all this, sweetie?" *And how are you doing, my dearest baby?*

"He's trying to line up a legal team for his dad. I don't think he can accept what happened. He keeps saying that his father couldn't have...Oh, Mum, I saw the skull. Maythorn's teeth had been knocked out...and the bones around the eyes all shattered. How could someone do that to a child?"

How could someone do that to a child? She and Phillip had talked late into the night, asking that same question. Eventually the subject had turned to Calven.

"Miss Birdie says he's having trouble settling down. 'That pore little young un keeps thinkin' his no-good mama's gonna come back fer him. Won't hear nary a word agin her even though she's treated him like a sorry cur' is how Birdie put it."

Phillip's eyes were distant. "I worked a few child abuse cases and that's one of the saddest things—seeing the kids defend their worthless mothers and fathers—fathers who abuse them, mothers who'd sell their kids for a bag of crack. But the kids fight to believe that their parents love them, particularly their mothers. They'll beg to stay with her even when she's mistreating them."

Phillip left for Weaverville to pick up his mail, and mother and daughter ate lunch in almost complete silence. *We should at least be relieved that it's all over,* Elizabeth thought, watching Rosemary pick at the carrot sticks beside her half-eaten sandwich. *But she's still so . . . bemused, almost like that strange, fey state she was in yesterday. Of course, seeing what was left of her friend, imagining what she'd suffered . . .*

Rosemary pushed her chair back. "Sorry, Mum, I'm just not very hungry. If you don't mind, I'm going to change and go on to Asheville early. Laurel wants me to come by where she's working on that mural. I'll hang out with her for a while. Maybe poke around some bookstores. Phillip's coming back, isn't he? I hate to leave you here alone. . . ."

Elizabeth smiled at her. "Hey, I'll be fine, sweetie. All the bad guys are where they belong. But, yes, he is coming back."

And at some point I'm going to have to stop blushing about it.

Elizabeth drove Rosemary down to her car and watched the little vehicle depart. She was filled with an irrational feeling of unease. *It was Moon, not Jared. Rosie's perfectly safe with Jared, you fool.*

She crossed the little branch and began a leisurely inspection of the beds of perennial herbs and flowers, now nestled under thick blankets of mulch in preparation for the coming winter. She was leaning down to break off a few branches of variegated sage when she heard the now familiar sound of Phillip's car.

He spotted her across the field and waved. Pulling up beside the drying shed, he flung open the car door, sprang out, and started jogging toward her. Agreeably surprised at his impatience to see her again, she hurried to meet him.

"I missed you, too, Phillip." Smiling, she took his hand. "You took a long time picking up your mail."

He leaned forward to kiss her briefly. There was no returning grin.

"I had a call from Mac—Sheriff Blaine—so I went into Ransom on the way back." Phillip's expression was solemn. "Mac said that he'd had Doc Adams come take a look at the skull—at the teeth—before the remains went off to the ME."

"Doc Adams? The dentist? *My* dentist?"

"The one in Ransom, yeah. Anyway, Mac said he figured since Doc Adams is the only dentist on this side of the county, it was likely he'd had the Mullins family as patients. Mac gave the doc a call first thing this morning and asked him about it. Sure enough, the doc remembered the whole family—said he still had their dental records. He came right in, with a quick stop by his office to get Maythorn's file.

"Mac said it didn't take thirty seconds—Doc Adams took a look at the teeth in the skull and said that he'd bet his license to practice that those remains weren't Maythorn."

Maythorn Speaks

Halloween 1986

I WATCHED AS *the booger untied her from the chair and laid her on the floor. He had made her put on my clothes before he started—not the fancy ones she always liked but just my old jeans and my Cherokee Pride sweatshirt I'd left on the floor in my room. Now they were all soaked with blood, and where she had wet herself when she finally understood it wasn't a game anymore.*

I knew that she was dead now, and that the booger couldn't hurt her anymore. There at the end, those last things the booger had done, she hadn't made any noise. And before that, the duck tape he put across her mouth, like he had done to me, kept her from screaming. All she could do was make low, awful, gurgling sounds.

There was a hole there in the basement floor and a shovel where the furnace men had been working. The booger looked at the shovel and then picked it up and whacked the dead girl in the face. Her body was all cut up and limp, but it jumped when he hit it, and even though I knew she was dead, I started to vomit. The booger heard me and came right over. He ripped off the duck tape fast. I don't want you choking on your own puke, he said. Oh, no. I have plans for you, little Indian.

When I'd finished and there was nothing left to come up but thin yellow stuff, I tried to call out for Moon to come save me. But he was asleep upstairs and I couldn't make more than a sad little sound. The booger just laughed and slapped the tape back over my mouth. You want Moon? Just wait here; I'll go get him for you.

He looked at me close and ran his knife along my leg. The cloth of my Indian pants fell apart like there was a zipper there, and the booger smiled his booger smile as he watched the blood come out and spread. Why, you're going to be a real red-skin, Mary Thorn Blackfox. Just what you always wanted. But first I'll go get Moon for you.

He left me alone and went quiet and careful up the basement stairs. I started working against the ropes at my wrists. I folded my hand as small as I could, and soon I pulled it free. My heart was beating fast and the tape on my mouth made it hard to breathe.

Both hands were loose now, and I was scratching at the knot that held my ankles when I heard bumping on the floor over my head. The basement door opened and the booger started down the stairs, left foot, right foot, feeling for each step. He had Moon across his shoulder, like he was some fireman saving him from a burning building. At first I thought that the booger had killed Moon, too, and I felt sorry. Moon had never been mean to me except when he was drunk.

But when the booger laid him on the floor, there by what was left of the blond girl, I could hear that Moon was saying something. He never opened his eyes though, not even when the booger marked him all over with the dead girl's blood and wrapped his hands around the handle of the bloody shovel. The booger was so busy that he didn't notice when I pulled off the last of the ropes and ran for the stairs. Then he yelled out and started after me.

I slammed the door and turned the lock. In a second the booger was there and he rattled the knob and beat on the door and yelled terrible things as I took off out the kitchen door into the night.

I ran up the dark trail as fast as I could, feeling my way among the trees and rocks I knew so well. When I got to the top I stopped to listen.

Everything was quiet, but back down below, I could see the strong beam of a big flashlight searching all over, looking in the pool house and then in the garden shed, where my masks were hidden. I knew that when the booger didn't find me there, he would come after me.

My mouth was sour from the vomit and my leg burned like fire where his knife blade had run. The pieces of my Indian pants flapped around my leg and caught on the bushes as I ran toward the Goodweathers' house.

Their porch light was on but I could see that the truck was gone. Then I remembered about trick-or-treating and knew that Rosie's house would be empty. But that's where the booger'll expect me to go, I thought, and kept climbing, up the hill to the Cave of the Two Sisters.

45.

BONE AND STONE

Saturday, October 29

Elizabeth stared at Phillip. "Not Maythorn? How could Doc Adams be sure of that? The teeth were all battered in."

As they walked back to his car, Phillip explained. "Not all of them. The canines were untouched. According to Mac, Doc Adams showed him on Maythorn's chart where she'd been in his office on the twenty-third, just a week before she disappeared. There was a note on the chart to the effect that Maythorn's upper left canine was loose. And, as Doc Adams saw immediately, both canines in that skull were fully mature teeth—there wouldn't have been time for the loose tooth to come out and be replaced. And what's more, he pointed out that the teeth showed signs of untreated decay. Maythorn's records indicated healthy teeth and no decay. Doc said these were the kind of teeth he sees in low-income kids—the ones who drink a lot of Mountain Dew and eat a lot of sugary junk food."

Phillip pulled a small duffel bag from the back seat of his car and transferred it to the jeep. Elizabeth watched him, her mind busy with the ramifications of this new revelation.

"Then if it wasn't Maythorn—"

"Who was it? Blaine's asking that same question. Moon swears it was Maythorn he buried, but he's not the most rational of witnesses. Mac's checking through the records of runaways and missing—"

"Missing…" They climbed into the jeep, and as Elizabeth reached for the ignition, a name flashed into her head. "Wait a minute. Tamra! The other little girl."

"Phillip, it was in Rosie's notebook. Rosie wrote about a Tamra who lived near here and played with her and Maythorn some of the time. And Tamra was blond…." *The prettiest little yaller-haired girl called Tamra, Miss Birdie had said.* The words were coming more slowly now as she sorted through her memories. "Miss Birdie told me about her… Tamra was Bib Maitland's daughter."

"Oh, yeah, the one he was supposedly looking for when he got drunk and assaulted an officer. But I thought her mother took her away?"

"Let me think." Elizabeth tugged on her braid and twisted it impatiently. "Okay, Birdie said that first Tamra's mother ran off and then… then she must have come back because the child left a note saying she was going to be with her mother. And Bib came home and found the note—"

"Or said he did." Phillip was reaching for his cell phone. "We need to see if Mac's thought about Tamra… and Bib."

Phillip watched as Elizabeth skimmed through the notebooks she had brought downstairs from Rosemary's room. She was paging intently through the second one, the remaining dozen on the sofa cushion beside her.

"Rosie mentions Tamra several times in here. She

didn't like her much—jealous, I guess. I haven't read all through these…I'm just looking for any mention of Tamra and…and of Moon…maybe there'll be some hint of how he reacted to the girls…or what Rosie thought about him." She looked up at him, her blue eyes troubled. "It's just so unbelievable to think of *Moon*…" And she was lost again in the pages of the slim book in her lap.

Phillip watched her for a few more moments, then, realizing that this search could takes hours, picked up the worn paperback copy of *Glory Road* that Elizabeth had found for him. *This Heinlein fella's a hoot. I think I remember reading some of his science fiction when I was a kid.*

He read on, falling deeper and deeper into the story of Star, the Empress of Twenty Universes, and Oscar, the Hero she had recruited to find the Egg of the Phoenix—the repository of the memories of all her predecessors.

Maybe we should hire a Hero to look for Sam's stuff. Or for the little Mullins girl.

The clock in the office had just struck three when Elizabeth slammed shut the notebook she had been reading. "Phillip, we need to go find Rosie and Maythorn's cave."

She had been adamant—no, she didn't want to wait till tomorrow so Rosie could show them the way; she felt almost positive she knew where it was. She was on her feet and pulling on her hiking boots and jacket, in such a fever of excitement that he simply laid aside his book and got ready too.

As they climbed the hill behind the house, she explained. "In her spy notebooks, Rosie keeps mentioning a place she calls the Cave of the Two Sisters. Evidently,

she and Maythorn used it as a kind of secret clubhouse.
She talks about how it was hard to find the way in, that
you had to get down and crawl. She says it's a perfect hiding place."

Elizabeth's face was flushed with excitement and she
was setting a rapid pace, slanting across the semi-
wooded hill. Ahead, a clump of buckeyes marked the beginning of the woods that extended to the top of
Pinnacle Mountain.

"Okay, but why is this so important?" He paused to
catch his breath. Though they were only slightly above
the house's roofline, already there was the feeling of
looking down on things from a great height.

Her eyes glittered. "It's important—or it *may* be
important—because I think this is the same cave that
Miss Birdie told me about a couple of years ago—a cave
that Cletus found when his dog followed a rabbit into it.
She told me he had to crawl under a big ledge of rock to
get in, and that's exactly how Rosie describes it." She
pointed up the hill. "See where it looks like two huge
boulders are leaning against each other? I bet you anything that's where the cave is—it fits the description."

"Elizabeth, sweetheart, I still don't see what the
point—"

"I'm sorry. I haven't told you the important part." She
was quivering with eagerness to be climbing again. "I
think the cave may be where Maythorn is. Cletus told
Miss Birdie there were bones in there."

He had followed as Elizabeth went straight to the tall leaning stones, as if walking a familiar path. She had explored
around their base, prodding at various rocks with her hiking stick until she found the opening under the ledge.

Crawling under the ledge had been the hard part. Though Elizabeth had assured him that the cool weather meant that any snakes would be, if not actually dormant, at least sluggish; still, it had been an unpleasant, claustrophobic thirty seconds, writhing on their bellies through dry leaves and sandy soil to pass under the rocky ledge.

"It's not really a cave, more of a rock lean-to." Elizabeth was on her hands and knees, investigating the farther recesses of the little hidden room.

Phillip looked down at the sandy floor—a scattering of dry leaves, a small pile of fist-sized stones, a few lengths of rotting branches. With an inward sigh, he dropped to his knees to help Elizabeth in her search.

She was working her way methodically around the perimeter. Looking up, she saw that he was doing the same. "No bones, huh?"

"Not over here." His answer was more brusque than he had intended and he added, "But it was certainly worth a look. Interesting place."

"Oh, Phillip, I'm sorry I dragged you up here. It was just…It was just that I had this sudden vision of Maythorn…coming here to hide, and then maybe something happened and she couldn't get out. But I guess that if Cletus saw bones, they were probably animal bones, and other animals have taken them away by now."

Phillip was only half listening. There, before him, wedged in a crevice, lay a round, flat stone with a dime-sized hole in its center. A bleached sliver of bone was jammed through the opening.

46.

THE EGG OF THE PHOENIX

Sunday, October 30

For the third time in a half hour, Elizabeth went to look at the kitchen clock. She glanced at Phillip, comfortably ensconced on the sofa, a second cup of coffee in one hand, *Glory Road* in the other, serenely oblivious to her unease.

Only ten after eight—too early to be calling. Laurel, whose bartending job kept her up till the very wee hours on Saturday nights, generally slept quite late on Sunday mornings, and presumably, so would Rosemary. If Rosemary had stayed with Laurel. On the other hand...

When she and Phillip had returned yesterday from their search of the so-called cave, the blinking light on the answering machine had announced a message.

"Mum," Rosemary's quiet voice had said, "I'll be staying in Asheville tonight. See you tomorrow, probably after lunch."

Stop fretting. Either she's with Laurel or she's with Jared. She's a big girl, Elizabeth.

"Worried about your daughter?" Phillip was looking at her over the pages of his book.

"No...well, a little. I wish I knew if she was at Laurel's or..."

With a sigh she dropped onto the sofa beside him. "Really, I just wanted to tell her about the bone we found and ask her if she ever went to the cave after Maythorn disappeared."

He put the book down. "She'll be back after lunch and we'll ask her then. We'll show her the stone with the hole and see if it means anything to her. And then I'll take the bone to Mac. It looks like a human finger bone to me, but I could be wrong. Mac'll send it off to the ME, and if it is human, they'll do DNA testing. It'll all take a while, but eventually they ought to be able to establish if the bone is Maythorn's."

Phillip read on, thoroughly enjoying the swash-buckling fantasy. Now Oscar the Hero was trading rhymes and swordplay with Cyrano de Bergerac, guardian of the Egg of the Phoenix. Now he was crawling through endless tunnels in search of the egg. *Pretty corny, but fun to read. I remember Sam telling me about this book. He kind of identified with the hero—Oscar was a "military advisor" in Southeast Asia, which turned into the Vietnam War.*

The egg that holds the knowledge. In search of the egg. Where would you look for an egg? Phillip blinked, put the book down, and went into the kitchen, where Elizabeth was filling a jug with water to take down to the chickens.

"I wonder..." He saw her amused look as his hand moved toward his head, and he stopped himself from making the habitual gesture. "This is probably pretty wild, but I was thinking..."

* * *

"You can see there's not much of anywhere to hide things in *here*."

They were both crowded into the little building. A rectangular box, of about nine feet by five feet, the chicken house's bare, uninsulated board walls and hay-strewn floor were unpromising. One red hen eyed them warily from a nest box, while the others milled about the metal garbage can where the laying pellets were kept.

"I clean it out every spring and I've certainly never seen anything hidden down here." Elizabeth reached into the can and tossed several handfuls of feed out onto the bare ground of the chicken yard. With a flurry of feathers, the chickens raced to gobble up the pellets. The red hen, with an agitated squawk, abandoned the nest box and half jumped, half flew between them and out the door.

"Idiot biddy! In such a hurry she broke a couple of eggs." Elizabeth reached into the nest box and retrieved the eggs, throwing the broken ones out the door. Quickly abandoning the laying pellets, the hens hurried to suck up the bright yellow yolks, pecking and jostling one another aside.

"Cannibals," Elizabeth muttered. "You should see them with chicken bones. It's a regular feeding frenzy."

Phillip was making a careful examination of the interior of the little structure. "Sam built this, right?"

"Yep, pretty soon after we got the house done. Rosie used it for a clubhouse for a while—till I got chickens. It was really cute—she kept books in the nest boxes and had cushions on the floor—oh, yuck, the hay in this nest's all covered with egg. If you'd move outside a minute, I'll clean it out."

Elizabeth fetched the old hoe that hung outside the chicken house and used it to scrape out the slimy hay.

"There's a loose bale of hay just under the barn shed over there. Would you bring me about a quarter of it? I'll go on and clean out all four nest boxes and put in clean hay."

She was pulling the old litter out of the last nest box when Phillip returned with an armful of fresh hay. He stepped into the house and began to pile the sweet-smelling dried grass into the first box. "There we go, ladies, clean sheets for your boudoirs—"

He stopped and dropped the rest of the hay to the floor. "Look at this, Elizabeth. Why is this third nest shallower than the others?"

Without waiting for an answer, he felt for the bottom of the nest box. "Outside, the bottom's the same as the others, but inside..." He reached for his pocketknife. Moving with a contained impatience, he inserted the blade at the edge of the false bottom and lifted.

The small flat aluminum box was filthy with dust and powdery dried chicken droppings that had sifted through the cracks around the edge of the false bottom. Phillip gave her a grin of wild glee and reached for the little tin.

"I believe we've got it—Sam's Egg of the Phoenix!"

It was all there—the fading snapshots documenting the horror of that long-ago afternoon and the videotaped deposition. Phillip had played just enough of it to make sure that it was still functional. She had watched as Sam's face, nervous and unhappy, filled the screen, but after the first few sentences, she had left the room.

Soon Phillip had come looking for her. She was sitting on the bench at the foot of her bed, staring out the big windows. He sat beside her and took her hand.

"I've talked to Del. He's flying in tonight to pick up the tape and the photos. I'll meet him at the airport and hand them over personally." He lifted her hand to his lips and kissed the palm. "Sweetheart, are you okay?"

She turned toward him. "I am. It was sad seeing Sam on that tape. But I was just thinking that, with your help, he's finished what he meant to do. The end of his chapter. I'm ready to turn the page now and find the end of Rosie's too."

47.

ONE MORE DAY

Sunday, October 30

Two masks.

One proudly displayed, smooth and painted, fashioned from a large gourd. The other, half hidden under an old towel, crudely formed from an abandoned hornet's nest—an amorphous mass of gray, papery material; ragged holes forming two empty, staring eyes and a small mouth, perpetually open in a soundless scream.

Rosemary awakened with a jolt, still seeing the images that had dominated that last incoherent dream. *She showed me the gourd one, but she didn't tell me who it was supposed to be. And I only saw the other one by accident, before she covered it back up and pretended it wasn't anything.*

She got out of bed quietly and began to dress.

"Rosie, where are you going?"

Jared rolled over and favored her with a lazy smile.

Phillip and Elizabeth were eating lunch and listening to the rebroadcast of *Prairie Home Companion* when the ring of the telephone chimed in with the Powdermilk Biscuit theme.

"That's probably her now." Elizabeth pushed back her chair and darted to the study. She emerged almost immediately and handed the telephone to Phillip. "For you. The sheriff."

"Mac?...Sorry, I must have turned my cell off....I was going to call you....There's an interesting development...."

Elizabeth listened as she finished her soup, but her mind was preoccupied. *As soon as he gets off the phone, I'm calling Laurel. She and Rosemary are probably up by now and just sitting around yacking.*

Phillip was telling the sheriff about their discovery, explaining the location of the hiding place and their speculations about the single bone. "It could be human—but I'm no expert....After all this time, uncovered bones could certainly have been dispersed by animals...but we may be jumping to conclusions....I'll bring it in this afternoon. And I've got some other good news—but I'm forgetting, you called me. What's up?"

Uh, oh, it looks like there's something wrong. Elizabeth felt a sudden uneasiness as she saw Phillip stand and begin to pace, phone to his ear.

"You're kidding me!...Mac, what the—what's going on here?...Okay...right...right. Okay, I'll be there in..." He looked at his watch. "Twenty minutes."

He set the telephone on the table and looked at her with an inscrutable expression.

"What? Phillip, what is it?"

He shook his head. "They've been excavating more of the basement over there at Mullmore, looking for Maythorn. This morning they found more remains."

She stood and picked up her empty bowl. A dull ache established itself in her heart. "So Moon killed them both—Tamra, if it was Tamra, and Maythorn. So the bone we found must be from an animal."

He shook his head again. "No, maybe not. Mac says the second skeleton's an adult—probably a woman. He's thinking if the first skeleton is Tamra, this might be her mother—Bib's wife. They're bringing Bib in for questioning."

Elizabeth slammed down the phone in frustration. Laurel wasn't answering her cell, nor Rosemary hers. *She said she'd be back after lunch. What time is it, anyway?*

James's shrill bark caught her attention and she hurried to the front porch. Rosemary was hiking up the road, accompanied by Ursa and Molly.

Instant relief flooded her and she went inside to do the dishes with as nonchalant an air as she could assume.

"Mum? I'm back. I passed Phillip on the bridge—I thought he was staying here."

"Hey, sweetie." Elizabeth hugged her daughter, a little harder and longer than usual. "He had to go into Ransom. I'll tell you.about it."

Rosemary held the flat stone in one hand, then brought it to her eye and peered through the little hole at her mother. *Just Mum, thank goodness. Yesterday, today, and always.*

"This was definitely Maythorn's. She called it the Looker Stone. It was something Granny Thorn gave her and it was very precious to her. She kept it with her most of the time. There was a leather pouch for it, but sometimes she stuck her finger through the hole and carried it that way."

Mother and daughter were both silent, staring at the little stone as if willing it to divulge its story. At last Rosemary spoke.

"I'm staying over one more day. I've called my department head and made arrangements about tomorrow's class. Jared and I are going back to Mullmore tomorrow afternoon to look for Maythorn's notebooks."

She met her mother's surprised stare. "He couldn't do it today; he needed to go see his dad and talk over the plans for his defense."

Her mother didn't speak but reached out and took the Looker Stone. She turned it around and around, studying it with apparent fascination.

Rosemary watched her mother. *She's worried about something, but I know her, she'll bite her tongue rather than interfere if she thinks it's not her business.*

"Mum, Jared's sure that Moon didn't kill anyone. I want to help him. We're hoping there'll be at least a hint in the notebooks about who Maythorn was afraid of—who the booger she talked about was."

When her mother remained silent, Rosemary reached for her hand. "What's the big deal, Mum? It's just one more day."

HALLOWEEN

1986

IT WAS WARMER *in the cave and I curled up in the dead leaves way back under the lean of one of the sisters. My heart was still beating so hard that it was like a drum, filling the room with thunder. I lay still, feeling the burn of the cut down my leg but knowing that when daylight came I could get away. She would hide me from him; I knew that she would. I called her again with my mind and asked her to help me. My eyes got heavier and heavier and I knew that I was falling asleep, like a rabbit, snug in its hole.*

The sharp crack of a dead branch snapping woke me and I opened my eyes to see a beam of light coming from the entrance tunnel. The light swooped and danced on the walls and I choked back the scream that wanted to come out.

Then I heard the booger call me. Little Indian, little Indian, I know where you hide. I stayed still, hoping the way in would be too small for him but the sounds kept getting closer.

Your Cherokee blood gave you away, little Indian. There were scraping, pulling sounds as he inched through the tunnel, talking all the while.

Oh, little Indian, it was a slow game, but a good game for a

Halloween night, tracking you through the dark woods, one red drop at a time, right to your hiding place. The best Reaper Game of your life—and we're not done yet.

He laughed and began to sing. *Here comes the reaper to take you apart; here comes the reaper to cut out your heart—* and then he was filling the narrow entrance and I remembered how wild things always had a bolt hole—another way out. But there wasn't a bolt hole in the Cave of the Two Sisters, not unless I could turn myself into a bird and fly up through the open place high above my head.

I shoved the Looker Stone onto my little finger to keep it near and made myself small against the rock face. I was shivering all over but still I tried not to cry. The booger pulled himself all the way in and his eyes were as cold and silver and sharp as the blade he held. His hair looked white in the dimness and he said *Little Indian, little Indian, say your prayers and go to bed.*

I pushed up against the wall, wishing I could melt into it. He came at me with the knife and grabbed my hand. At first I thought that he only wanted to pull the Looker Stone off, but then I felt the cold blade slicing through the knuckle of my little finger. I screamed with pain and with the fear of what was coming. The sound filled the cave and I watched my finger and the Looker Stone fall to the sandy floor. They were still stuck together and he kicked them both away from him. Then he turned to me and I could see the booger looking out of his silver eyes. He caught my bleeding hand and pulled my arm out straight.

We're just beginning, little Indian, he said, and ran the knife from my shoulder to my wrist-bone. The sharp blade sliced through the shirt sleeve and left a bloody track down my arm. He watched the blood soaking into the cloth, then he smiled, as if he was remembering something, and reached for my pointer finger. All of a sudden there was a terrible sound that filled the cave, like some giant bird was in there. The booger jumped back and turned around to see what it was.

And I picked up one of the branches me and Rosie had drug in for a pretend fire. It was thick and long, like a baseball bat, and I swung it with all my might. I got him on the side of the head, right at the temple where I knew the bone was thin, and he fell over. He didn't move and I hit him again and he still didn't move and I knew that I'd killed him.

Good, I thought, and crawled over his legs and out into the chill night air. With the bleeding stump of my finger pressed against my shirt, and the blood running from the cuts he'd made on me, I ran through the woods of that black Halloween night. The giant bird was screeching in my ears and I felt sick and dizzy, but I ran, on and on down the long gravel driveway, past the dark buildings. I was almost to the hard road and my legs were heavy. My head felt light, as if I was flying, and then I fell. Just ahead I could see the dim outline of a truck and I began to crawl to where I knew she would be waiting for me.

48.

ANOTHER HALLOWEEN

Monday, October 31

"**Do you ever** get any trick-or-treaters, these days? I remember once Laurel and her friends got too sophisticated for trick-or-treating, there were years no one ever made it all the way up here." Rosemary sat on the cushioned bench, lacing up her hiking boots.

Elizabeth pointed to the oven. "I've got a pan of brownies baking. Morris Roberts brought his stepkids up in his truck last year. Took me by surprise. I didn't have anything remotely treatlike in the house so I ended up giving them money. This time I'll be ready. And Dorothy called to let me know that Calven was coming too."

She came to sit beside Rosemary. "Are you still planning on bringing Jared back to dinner?"

Rosemary's head was bent over her boot and her fingers were busy pulling the laces tight. "Mum, would you mind very much if I canceled? When I asked him to come here, Jared said he'd already made reservations at that new place in Biltmore. We thought we'd look for the notebooks and then just go straight on in to Asheville. I've already put my stuff in my car. If I stay in

Asheville tonight, I can get an earlier start in the morning."

At last she raised her eyes. "I'm sorry, Mum, I should have told you sooner."

Somehow, Mum can make me feel ten times worse by what she doesn't say. I should have told her right off what my plans were. Just putting it off to avoid that look, I guess.

Rosemary found herself humming as she strode down the hill to meet Jared. . . . *Rode till he came to Miss Mousie's hall; Gave a knock and he gave a call—a hum, a hum, a hum, a hum. . . .*

Jared's car, an elegantly simple Saab, was parked by the barn and he was standing beside it, checking his watch. Looking up, he caught sight of her. "Four o'clock on the dot. Our reservation is for seven-thirty, plenty of time to find those notebooks, if they're where you think they are."

He looked at her little car. "All packed? Why don't you follow me over to Mullmore? That'll save us a few minutes, not having to come back for your vehicle."

They were turning up the gravel road of the next holler—the road that led to Mullmore's iron gates—when a utilitarian pickup truck came rattling down the road, its bed full of costumed children. As the truck inched by them, its strange cargo began to howl and gesture in their direction.

Rosemary smiled, recognizing her mother's neighbor Morris Roberts and his brood. There was a small boy in a Superman outfit and another with the black, pointy-eared mask and cape of Batman. An older boy had no mask but was wrapped in gauze from head to toe. She raised her hand to wave and then caught sight of the two other children—both in ordinary clothes, each wearing a mask from her dream. *One, smooth and painted, made from a large gourd. The other crudely fashioned from an abandoned hornet's nest—ragged holes forming two empty, staring eyes and a small mouth, perpetually open in a soundless scream.*

But there was a difference. As the child with the hornet's nest mask turned to face her, she saw that the mouth had been ringed with bright red lipstick and iridescent blue paint decorated the staring eyes.

She sat there in her car, watching the truck and its nightmare passengers crawling along Ridley Branch toward Miss Birdie's house. *Am I hallucinating or something? Those were the booger masks from my dream.*

Blinking her eyes, she shook her head to clear it of the rags and tatters of old memories. Jared's car was moving forward now and, with a quick tap of his horn, he recalled her to the task at hand.

The iron gates were open and another car was parked just inside. She pulled in beside Jared's car, ready for the walk up the drive with its cracking and fallen-in pavement.

"Whose car?" she asked, as Jared came to open her door.

"Uncle Mike's." Jared's face betrayed an odd annoyance. "The foundation's going to put the house on the market and Mike came out earlier to make an inventory. I thought he'd be gone by now."

The great front doors of Mullmore were open, but Jared led her quietly around to the basement entrance on the side of the house. "You thought they were down here, right? Let's get started."

Rosemary hesitated, looking at the yellow crime scene tape across the door. Jared brushed it aside with an impatient gesture. "The sheriff's people finished this morning. I talked to Blaine and he said it was okay for us to go in."

"Jared, I was just thinking—now that they've found the second body...set of remains...whatever it was, Phillip said the sheriff is looking for Tamra's father. That makes things look better for your dad, doesn't it? Maybe we should just forget about the notebooks."

A strange reluctance to go down those stairs, back into that basement, was creeping over her. Memories of the Reaper Game, played in the claustrophobic darkness...

Jared fumbled through a set of keys, at last selecting one and fitting it into the lock. "Rosie, nothing's certain. They're only guessing that those remains belong to Tamra and her mother. At this point, after the confession he made, Dad's going to need all the help I can give him. If you think you know where Maythorn's notebooks are, let's go find them."

He turned the key and pushed at the door, but it stayed firmly shut.

"Damn! Mike must have bolted it from the inside. He was worried that those kids down the road would get to wanting to see the scene of the crime and come poking around."

As Jared gave the door a final, futile shove, there was a soft flurry of wings just above their heads. In the deepening shadow of the afternoon, an early owl was hunting. It swooped low, almost grazing Jared's head.

"Jesus Christ!" he exclaimed and, grabbing her hand, pulled Rosemary after him back to the front of the house and through the open doors.

49.

THE LAST NOTEBOOK

Monday, October 31

Rosemary shook off her reluctance and followed Jared deeper into Mullmore. As they moved through the house, footsteps echoing hollowly on the marble floor of the hall, she could hear someone walking about in an upstairs room.

"That's Mike up there. He must be almost done." Jared didn't pause but made straight for the open door at the back of the hall.

The smell of fresh dirt filled her nostrils as she descended the stairs. Over there, where she had knelt to discover her handprint, the furnace had been dismantled and more concrete removed. A great hole gaped black in the center and a heap of fresh dirt lay to one side.

The room was dimly lit by the fading light that trickled through the few dust-smeared windows. Rosemary motioned to the sheeted furniture and stacked boxes standing undisturbed: mute spectators to unimaginable horrors.

"Back there, behind those boxes. There used to be a plastic storage bin where Maythorn kept some stuff."

A sudden picture of her lost friend filled her memory: Maythorn, in jeans and flannel shirt, gazing disconsolately at the frilled and fluffy canopied bed, the fussy throw pillows, the yellow-haired dolls ranged on her window seat. *I came back from visiting Granny Thorn and it was like this—a surprise, she said. They put all my old stuff down in the basement.*

The storage bin was still there, pushed under a table that was covered with a stack of dusty, cobwebbed boxes. Together they dragged it out and carried it to an open area under a window. Rosemary lifted the lid.

A faint smell of mold rose from the interior. Folded on top was the rose-red dress Granny Thorn had made. A lump formed in Rosemary's throat and tears prickled at her eyes as she lifted the soft garment out of the box and laid it to one side.

A jumble of objects was next: a threadbare handmade stuffed fox that Rosemary recognized as her mother's handiwork; a cheap plastic doll, dark-skinned, with black braids and a beaded faux-buckskin dress; a Cherokee blow gun and a clutch of down-feathered darts; another fox, a beginner's attempt, carved in pale soft wood. And beneath the rejected treasures—a stack of notebooks.

"Here they are!" She pulled out one at random and held it to the light. The dates were on the cover—June 1985–September 1985. Flipping it open, she glanced at the small, precise printing. *SD and me worked on the fort.*

"It's a little hard to read in this light." She reached for another book. "I guess the thing to do would be to take them back with us, but . . ." She looked at the cover of the notebook in her hand.

August 1986–There was no terminal date. *This is the last one she wrote in.* Rosemary began to page through the notebook, struggling to read in the fading light.

Jared picked up one of the little journals, glanced briefly at its first page, then dropped it back into the box. "I'll go open the door to the outside—give us a little more air and light."

Rosemary nodded, turning pages rapidly. A phrase leapt out at her: *He cut off the rattail today and I got it out of the wastepaper basket to put on the mask.*

She read it a second time, struggling to understand. *The rattail. Then one of the masks was supposed to be Jared. It was Jared she was afraid of—oh, dear god, it was Jared....*

Her breath was coming fast and her knees felt as if they'd give way at any moment. Jared was at the top of the stairs to the outside, struggling with the bolt, muttering angrily as he rattled the door.

Very quietly, very afraid, she moved to the foot of the stairs that led up to the hall. Just as she mounted the first step, Jared turned.

"Rosie, where are you going?"

"I've got to get something from my car." Bounding up the steps, two at a time, she could hear him hurrying after her. In her haste, she stumbled, almost fell, regained her footing, and ran on—through the door and into the hallway. She just had time to slam the door in Jared's startled face and turn the latch.

"Rosie, this isn't funny; what the hell do you think you're doing?" The door rattled alarmingly.

She whirled and dashed for the entranceway. The tall front doors that had stood so invitingly open were closed now. The rattling of the basement door increased as she snatched at the pair of tarnished brass knobs and wrenched them with all her might.

Locked! *Oh, god, no! Mike must have left, not realizing we were here. . . . Jared didn't want him to know.*

She looked down the darkening hallway at the basement door. The rattling had stopped and Jared was silent. She thought of the kitchen door, or the French doors to the terrace—*or a window . . . anything; I just have to get out before—*

The harsh sound of splintering wood made her catch her breath. The tip of the pickaxe Moon had left in the basement appeared in the midst of the thin wooden door, wiggled, and was withdrawn.

Without waiting for the second blow, she wheeled and ran for the nearest window. She threw back the heavy drapes, only to be met with a blank wall—the plywood that blocked all the windows on the ground floor.

Stifling a sob, she ran through the library and down a little hall, past the housekeeper's rooms, past the butler's pantry, and toward the kitchen. Behind her, the shattering, rending sound continued—the sound of thin, brittle wood yielding to merciless steel.

The huge kitchen with its blinded windows echoed with the frantic thud of her boots. Just ahead lay the little mudroom and the door to the service drive. If only—

As she scrabbled in the near-darkness at the bolt, the sound of her own rapidly beating heart thrummed in her ears. Panting, she bent to look at the stubborn bolt.

She had just succeeded in tugging it loose when strong hands gripped her throat, fingers digging into the soft flesh. She tried to turn, to face her attacker, but the relentless fingers squeezed tighter . . . tighter. Her vision blurred as she clawed at the hands that held her.

50.

The Masks

Monday, October 31

"Trick or treat! Trick or treat! Give us something good to eat!"

Elizabeth had heard them coming up the road but stayed discreetly out of sight in the living room, waiting for the knock and the traditional chorus. She picked up the basket, heaped high with little black and orange beribboned bags, each containing several dark brownies decorated with candy corn. She opened the door to the accompaniment of delighted squeals and giggles.

"Trick or treat! Trick or treat!" The two small superheroes jumped wildly up and down, eager for a look at the contents of the basket. Behind them, a somewhat larger mummy lifted his bandaged arms and let out a slightly embarrassed "Ooooooh." She offered the basket and the children grabbed at the bags of brownies, then, with hasty thanks thrown over their shoulders, were tearing off, down the steps and back to the waiting truck.

Elizabeth was turning to go inside and finish dinner preparations when she heard a whispering and shuffling coming up the steps. Two strangely masked small figures appeared, one leading the other by the hand.

"Treat or treat, Miz Goodweather!" The taller figure, the one in the painted mask that seemed to be made from a big gourd, came forward. "It's me, Calven. Asheley here got kindly shy about coming to the door but I told her you was a nice sort of somebody."

Asheley advanced slowly, holding her strange mask in front of her face. "Trick or treat," she whispered.

Elizabeth bent down to look at Asheley. *A hornet's nest. Cut in half and hollowed out. And holes for eyes and mouth. But she's put lipstick and eyeshadow and, heaven help us, false eyelashes on it.*

The effect was bizarre beyond belief, but, offering the basket of treats to the children, Elizabeth mustered a smile. "Well, those are some masks, Calven. Did you all make them yourselves?"

The gourd face turned toward her and Calven said, "Naw, these is some maskes Asheley and her brothers found up at that big place over yon." He waved one hand toward Mullmore and reached into the basket with the other.

Asheley tugged at Calven's arm and whispered, "Maydern told me where they was."

Pocketing two treat bags, Calvin leaned toward Elizabeth and confided, "Maydern's her nimaginary friend she plays with all the time. Travis said they found these here maskes in an empty garbage can what was in a little toolshed over there. He was gonna wear this one but then he decided to be a mummy instead." The boy's hand slipped carelessly into the treat basket again, withdrawing two more bags.

From the driveway could be heard the rattle of a diesel engine as Morris Roberts cranked up his truck.

"We got to go now. Thank you, Miz Goodweather. Come on, Asheley."

"Thank you, Miz Goodweather," Asheley whispered.

Elizabeth watched as Calven turned to help the little girl negotiate the steps. The long thin braid of blond hair affixed to the back of the gourd mask caught her eye, stirring an uneasy memory.

51.

THE REAPER

Monday, October 31

Her throat was sore and it was hard to breathe with the tape over her mouth. She was cold. Rosemary swam back through the murk into painful consciousness. She was sitting on a chair, chin slumped to her chest, hands tied behind her, and ankles firmly bound to the chair legs. Her heavy jacket was gone. Without moving her head she opened her eyes just a slit.

Dark, deep darkness to one side and flickering lights to the other. And just beyond, a huddled body, limply sprawled at the edge of the pool of light. The face was turned from her but she saw the pale hair.... She could feel the beginning of a scream building and knew that her body was trembling beyond her control.

A flash of silver. Something cold lay against her cheek, slid along her face in a lingering caress.

"Wake up, Rosie," said the Reaper.

The knife moved under her chin and the flat of the blade began to lift. Through her half-closed eyes she saw him, haloed by the light of dozens of little candles set in a semicircle on the floor behind him. It was the same nightmare figure, in the same long black robe, the same black hood covering his face. It was the teasing, taunting shape that had led the Reaper Game of long ago, while she and Tamra and Maythorn shivered and hid from his grasp.

"Hold up your head and open your eyes, Rosie. It's time." The knife slid away from her chin. She forced her eyes open and the Reaper nodded.

"Good girl, Rosie. That's better." The black hood turned toward the body on the floor. "It couldn't have worked out more perfectly: Halloween night again and the perfect scapegoat on hand. A quick blow to the head, the fireman's lift, down the stairs with him, and there we are—just like Moon, nineteen years ago."

The Reaper held the silver blade before him, angling it this way and that to watch the play of candlelight on its polished surface. When he spoke, his voice was soft and dreaming.

"Nineteen years ago . . . You should have been part of it that time. You and your—what did she say you two were? . . . blood twins, was it? I'd never done it with two at one time, but the way you and Maythorn were always together gave me the idea. I wanted her to watch—she always liked to watch, didn't she . . . to spy.

"I wanted her to see exactly what was going to happen. So many times they're still alive, but they aren't really fully *participating* anymore. I wanted Mary Thorn to experience it all vicariously first. And it would have been so perfect if she could have watched it happening to you, her blood twin, knowing that every cut to your body would be repeated on hers."

The Reaper brought the blade back to her and ran the point of it lightly along her arm. He talked on, almost crooning, like someone reliving a bittersweet memory.

"Your . . . substitute was weak and fainted too soon. A

disappointment. Oh, Rosie, it would have been so perfect. But you're different now. It's best with those lovely, prepubescent, androgynous beings, creatures of fire and air—but you, you've become a woman, tied to the earth and the rhythms of the moon."

He trailed the knife thoughtfully along her arm, the lightest pressure on the razor edge. The thin flannel of her shirtsleeve split open and a narrow thread of scarlet followed the blade as Rosemary watched, frozen with terror. He shook his head thoughtfully. "I'm sorry, Rosie—I don't think you and your twin will have much in common anymore when you meet in the afterlife.

"Oh, but wait!" His sudden laugh was harsh and ugly. "I was forgetting, Maythorn was an *Indian,* a proud Cherokee! She'll be in the Happy Hunting Grounds, won't she? No, you won't be finding your twin, I'm afraid. You'll be stuck in the white-bread, hymn-singing, Christian side of heaven, if you've been good."

She whimpered as the blade touched her other arm and began its slow descent. A second trail of blood appeared. "You *have* been a good girl, haven't you, Rosie?"

52.

THE REAPER REVEALED

Monday, October 31

"Phillip, where are you?" Her voice was frantic in his ear.

"Just crossing the bridge; Elizabeth, is something wrong?"

"Everything! It *was* Jared that Maythorn was afraid of. I just realized, and Rosie's at Mullmore alone with him right now. I've called the sheriff and I'm heading out the door this minute. I'll meet you at the mailbox. Hurry, Phillip!"

The blood had soaked her shirt and her jeans. At first it was warm and fluid but it quickly grew cold and sticky in the chilly air. Rosemary watched, feeling a strange detachment, as the Reaper tested the blade of his knife against his thumb. He frowned and looked over at her. "Oh, good, you're back with me now. I hate it when the subject passes out too soon. Of course, it's inevitable: you will *eventually* lose consciousness before we're done, but if I do say so, I'm getting better and better at this. The last one was with me for fifty-seven minutes."

The black-hooded countenance seemed to study her judiciously. "But you're a grown woman and probably have more endurance." He shook back the dark flowing sleeve of his robe and glanced at his watch. "Twenty-three minutes so far." Behind the slits in the hood, his eyes glittered. "Yes, I think if I don't let myself get carried away, we can set a new record tonight, Rosie."

He leaned closer and she could smell the musty fabric of his robe. "You won't mind waiting while I touch up the edge, now, will you, Rosie? Nothing worse than a dull knife, I always say. You don't get that exquisite fine line."

He moved to a workbench against the far wall and Rosemary could hear the steady grind of the steel edge on a sharpening stone. Her eyes drifted shut. She was so tired and sleepy. It was almost too much effort to breathe. Sleep was tiptoeing closer, a familiar, welcome friend, beckoning to her, calling her to the comfort of oblivion. But someone was yelling and breaking things.

"Mac's got a car on the way."

"We can't wait." Elizabeth jogged steadily along the winding driveway. Just ahead lay the brooding mass of Mullmore, a dark shape against the moonless sky.

"Listen, Elizabeth, let me go in there. You wait outside. I don't want—"

"You can go first. But I'm coming too." She was pulling her revolver from its holster as she cast him a look of such deadly seriousness that any further objections died unsaid.

As they drew closer to the house, Phillip could see a shadow figure slipping around the corner, moving toward the basement entrance. Silently he motioned to Elizabeth to follow.

Bang! Bang! Bang! The noise echoed through the basement, louder at every crash. With a great effort, Rosemary opened her eyes again. The Reaper was backing away from her, looking up the stairs that led outside. Lazily, for nothing seemed to matter anymore, Rosemary followed his gaze. The door at the top of the short stairway was bulging inward with each blow.

In a whirl of black draperies, the Reaper threw off his robe and hood and fell on the limp body that lay, still unmoving, at the edge of the pool of light. The knife flashed in Mike Mullins's hand, and the unconscious Jared jerked convulsively.

Loud footsteps descending the stairs, a roar of anger, and Bib Maitland hurled himself across the room onto the killer, knocking the bloody knife from his hand.

"You goddammed piece of outlander shit! It was you, you she run off to be with. And it was you killed her and my baby girl too. Sheriff brought me into the jail and showed me their bones, thinking to frighten me into saying I done it. And when I seen that little gap between the front teeth, I knowed it was Precious. And I knowed the other had to be my baby girl, my little Tamra."

The basement door lay in splintered pieces; from below could be heard the sounds of two men fighting to the death. Cautiously, Phillip eased down the steps, gun at the ready. Elizabeth, close on his heels, saw two men locked in a close struggle. One—heavy, unshaven, greasy dark hair obscuring his face—she recognized as Bib Maitland. The other—slim, athletic, and silver-blond—was Mike Mullins. Then, surrounded by a bevy of flickering votive candles, she saw Rosemary, bloody cuts on her arms and legs, sagging against the ropes that held her.

Elizabeth tried to push her way past Phillip but he put out one hand to block her. He raised his automatic to point at the ceiling; there was the deafening sound of a gunshot, and ringing echoes reverberated through the dark room.

"Stand away from each other," Phillip cautioned as he descended the steps, gun trained on the two combatants. "That was just to get your attention. The next one—"

The two broke apart and Mike turned to face them, his silver-blue eyes seeking Elizabeth. "Thank God you're here. I was upstairs and heard noises. When I got down here, Jared was dead and this monster had Rosie tied and was using his knife on her. I tried to get him off her, but she's bleeding so bad—"

As he spoke, he hurried to Rosemary, swooping to pick up something from the floor as he went. Elizabeth thrust her way past Phillip just in time to see the blade in Mike's hand moving toward Rosemary's throat.

"NO!" But even as she cried out, Bib flung himself on Mike. His hand moved swiftly to knock the blade spinning to the floor. Holding Mike by the throat, he scooped up the knife, pulling the choking, flailing Mike after him.

Bib's hand moved again, like a striking rattler. It buried the blade between the other man's ribs, and Mike fell to the floor, gurgling and twitching in a final spasm.

Ignoring the life and death struggle, Elizabeth pushed past Phillip to get to Rosemary.

Bib dropped the knife and stood by the dying man, hands casually in the air. He looked at Elizabeth with a sly grin.

"Your girl's okay, Miz Goodweather. I got here before he done any real damage. But this piece of shit," he said, kicking the body, which had finally fallen still, "this piece of shit is dead as a hammer, I guaran-damn-tee. One thing you learn inside is how to kill—slip in between the ribs and give a pretty little twist."

DREAMTIME

Halloween 1986

MY FATHER'S STRONG *arms were picking me up and carrying me. I knew then that I had died and was with him, like I wanted to be. A-do-do, I said in Cherokee, Father, I've killed the booger. Please, take me with you and keep me safe.*

And then I was in Granny's arms and I knew she must be dead, too, and I whispered to her that I never wanted to go back to the other place but would stay here with my father and her.

I heard someone say, We have to take her to the hospital, and I wanted to laugh because they didn't know I was dead. The hospital and the police, the voice kept saying, but Granny hugged me close.

There's no need for the hospital now, said Granny, and she whispered to me in Cherokee, telling me that I would be safe on the Boundary, among my own people forever and ever.

You'll have a new name and Mary Thorn will disappear. No one will ever tell your secret.

I whispered back, in Cherokee because now that I was dead I could talk it as good as she could. Ever, ever, Granny Thorn?

* * *

The child's blue lips scarcely moved and her words rode lightly on the faintest of exhalations. The old woman considered, consulting some inner knowledge. At last she leaned down to whisper to the child, who was smiling peacefully even as she slipped toward oblivion. I'll keep you safe on the Boundary, my little daughter.

The child's eyes drifted shut, her thin, torn body sagging in her great-grandmother's arms. The old woman talked on, crooning to the unhearing child. And one day, and it may be many years off, could be your blood twin will come and call your true name. Only then will you be safe in both worlds. Sleep now, child; sleep safe in Granny's arms.

At the wheel of the truck, jolting along the dark road to Cherokee, Driver Blackfox let out a great howl of despair.

53.

ALL SOULS DAY

Tuesday, November 1

The guard stopped them at the gate of the Oconaluftee Village, the living history museum of the Cherokee on the Qualla Boundary. "Sorry, closed for the season." He pointed to the sign by the entrance.

"Driver Blackfox left a message that—" Elizabeth stepped forward.

There was a slight softening of the dark features, then the guard nodded and opened the gate to let Elizabeth, Phillip, and Rosemary pass. "Follow the arrows that point to the Council House," he said, waving them down a path.

"I wish I knew what this was about." Phillip took Elizabeth's hand as they followed Rosemary through the village. In the summer, the re-created village was packed with tourists: families on vacation and busloads of kids from the nearby summer camps. Now it was eerily silent and deserted—a fitting home for ghosts.

"I don't really know; there was a message from Driver Blackfox that we should bring Rosemary to the Indian Village today and take this special tour they're doing at eleven for some school group. He said something else, that Granny Thorn had told him it was time. I have no idea what he meant—I thought Granny Thorn was dead years ago."

They sat in the empty Council House, waiting for the eleven o'clock presentation. Outside, a muted din announced the arrival of more visitors.

A beautiful dark woman with long braids was shepherding a flock of schoolchildren and their teachers into the Council House. Wriggling and shoving, the boys and girls took their places on the rows of log benches that ringed the central hearth. The woman lifted her hand for silence and Rosemary stifled a gasp when she saw that the little finger was missing. Once the children fell silent, the woman began her story.

"Many years ago, when the Cherokee were troubled with enemies from other tribes and other countries, they struggled to find a way of not letting fear overcome their spirits. Some wise elder invented the Booger Dance and the People began to make masks and dress up like the very enemies who threatened them. They called the enemy the boogers and they did a dance that showed just how stupid and clumsy these enemies were. The People would watch the boogers falling down and making fools of themselves and they would stop being afraid."

A girl on the front row raised her hand. "Did you ever do the Booger Dance?" Two boys beside her elbowed each other and whispered.

The guide was unperturbed. "Only once. But it worked...eventually."

"Did a booger bite off your finger?"

The guide raised her left hand, palm out. A broad gold band circled the ring finger. She regarded her hand quizzically, as if noticing for the first time the missing digit. "As a matter of fact, he did. But I got away and that booger never bothered me again." Her smile was serenely untroubled.

On the bench beside Elizabeth and Phillip, Rosemary was trembling with excitement as the guide continued her story. At last the talk ended, questions were answered, and the children began to follow their teachers out the door. The guide looked at the three of them.

"Did *you* have any questions?" Smiling, she took a step toward them. "That was the kiddie version of the tour—if you've read any of the material you probably know there's a bawdy side to the Booger Dance ritual that I didn't get into."

"Maythorn." Rosemary's voice was choked and low.

The other's brow wrinkled. "I'm sorry, what did you say?" Her smile wavered, then vanished.

"Mary Thorn." Rosemary's voice was stronger now and she stood.

The young woman's hands clenched. "No, you've made a mistake. My name is Mary Owl."

Without shifting her gaze from the guide, Rosemary put her hand in her pocket and drew out the Looker Stone. Lifting it to her eye, she stared through it at her childhood friend. "Mary Thorn Blackfox: I *see* you."

54.

KNOWING

Tuesday, November 1

"Mary Thorn Blackfox, I see you."

This time the words were tinged with scorn. Years of sorrow, years of guilt, and now recognition of an old betrayal trembled in those words. The eyes of the two women were locked—brown to darker brown. They stared at each other silently till Mary Thorn, with a single strangled sound, turned her head.

"You ran away, Maythorn. You ran away and left him free to hurt more little girls." Rosemary was shaking with anger and she grabbed the other woman's arm. "How many more did he kill? We found bones in the basement and I cried and cried because I thought they were yours."

Maythorn twisted away. "It was Tamra. He wanted me to call you, Rosie, but I called her instead. I told her that her mother was waiting for her in the basement....When Tamara came, he put my sweatshirt on her and made me watch...."

"Maythorn, I always thought you were so brave—why didn't you tell someone about him?"

"She couldn't....We couldn't."

They all turned at the sound of the new voice.

Driver Blackfox stood in the doorway of the Council House.

"Maythorn got away from him but she was near about gone when we found her that night. She couldn't hardly talk but she swore that she'd killed the booger who hurt her. That was all she said, then her eyes rolled back and I figgered she was dead. I put her in the truck, into Granny's arms, and we headed out for the Boundary, like Granny said. I told Granny we ought to take Maythorn to a hospital, but Granny shook her head, said that if Maythorn lived, she'd be blamed for the death—Granny never trusted that the white law was the same for us Indians. Besides, she said, most likely Maythorn wouldn't last out the night. Granny was bound and determined to get Maythorn back to the Boundary, where she belonged."

Driver entered the Council House and went to his niece's side. Gently, he led her to one of the benches. She dropped down, arms wrapped around her chest, making herself as small as possible.

"Well, like you can see, she didn't die," Driver told them. "But she was a long time coming back. And when her body was healed, her spirit was still broke. She didn't talk for almost a year, and when she did begin to speak again, it was only in Cherokee, like Granny Thorn had talked to her all those months she was in bed, sick with fever and fear and Granny tending her with the old medicine ways. Granny said it was like a baby learning to talk and that the old half-blood Mary Thorn had died and come back a true Cherokee. That's when Granny gave her a new name—Mary Owl. And that's when Granny made me promise never to tell anyone about that night."

"Driver, I don't understand! How did you just happen to be there when Maythorn got away? How could you know? Did she call you? I don't see how...." Elizabeth looked from Driver to Maythorn and back again. Neither met her eye.

Driver Blackfox drew a line in the dirt of the floor with his boot, then scuffed it out. "Maythorn called someone, all right. But it wasn't me she called and she didn't use no telephone."

He lowered himself to the bench next to his niece. "The way it happened was this: my phone rang—it would have been early afternoon of that day—and it was Granny Thorn. She said we had to go get Maythorn, said she had a 'feelin'.' Well, we weren't supposed to go after her till the next day, but I told Granny I'd be over to pick her up after a while and we'd go get Maythorn. I'd known since I was little that Granny wouldn't take no for an answer when she had one of her 'feelings,' but I was in the middle of a carving—two foxes out of black walnut that I was going to use as the centerpiece for a show."

Driver was deep in the memory, not looking at his rapt audience, but gazing instead into the distance as if seeing the picture his words painted. "The wood was doing right; my knife was sliding through it like it was butter and the foxes were coming clearer every minute—like just one or two shakes and they'd be free from the wood. Anyway, I kept at the carving, thinking a few more minutes wouldn't make any difference to Maythorn."

He paused and looked at each of them in turn. "All of a sudden I hear this high-pitched screech that makes me jump and the knife slips on the wood and buries itself in my forearm. I think I'm in real trouble, but I pull it out careful and there's no bleeding to speak of. I get my first-aid kit and clean and bandage the wound. Just as I finish wrapping the gauze around it, the phone rings. I know right off who it is. She doesn't even say hello, just, 'Boy, you get over here now. I ain't tellin' you again.'"

Driver shook his head. "Well, I did like she said. Granny Thorn had powers and I figgered I was lucky she hadn't hurt me worse than what she had for not minding her right off. We drove to Marshall County as fast as I could in that old truck of mine. Granny said we'd wait at the foot of the road, by the mailboxes. We waited there till it was dark and I thought Granny had dropped off to sleep. But then I hear her say, 'Maythorn's coming.' And I get out and there's a little whimpering noise and there she was, pulling herself along, coming down not the road from Mullmore, but the next one over, your road, Miz Goodweather."

"Rosie, I was so afraid...." Maythorn looked at Rosemary with pleading eyes. "I almost died and Granny Thorn kept me away from everyone for such a long time. When I was better, there were things I couldn't remember...things I thought might have happened and things I thought I must have dreamed. It finally seemed like it might all have been a dream, except for the scars and this...." She extended her mutilated hand, then tucked it back under her elbow and looked away.

Tears were rolling down Rosemary's face, but she made no move toward Maythorn.

"Driver," Elizabeth said, "why didn't *you* do something? When you found out that she hadn't killed him, that Mike was still alive—a monster who could hurt a little girl like that—how could you just walk away?"

Blackfox shrugged. "I didn't know what to do. For a long time Mary Owl wasn't talking, and when she did start, she wouldn't say who it was cut her. And she didn't want to go back to that mother of hers, that was for sure. The police had been out here—took me in and asked me questions, even got into the old thing with my brother's death. They roughed me up till I damn sure wasn't going to give *them* any help. Finally when they had to let me go, I came back here and stayed put. Later I heard the whole Mullins family had moved away from the place in Marshall County. Didn't know where they went. And didn't try very hard to find out."

"But your mother, Maythorn? How could you let *her* go on all these years, wondering what had happened to you?" Elizabeth persisted, trying to understand, in spite of a growing feeling of apprehension.

"My mother!" The young woman's words were black and bitter, stones dropping into an icy, bottomless pool. "Do you know what my mother used to tell me, back when I was Mary Thorn Mullins? Time after time, she told me that I was a curse to her with my dark skin and Indian looks; she said I should never have been born—"

"She couldn't have meant that. She—"

Quietly and deliberately, Mary Owl began to unbutton her blouse. She walked over to Elizabeth and pulled open the garment.

A neat procession of puckered scars—some small and faint, others indicative of deeper wounds—marred the smooth brown skin of Mary Owl's back and shoulder, a cruel chronicle of years past.

The young woman reached back to lay slender fingers on the ugly marks. "Mama had an old-fashioned curling iron she used on Krystalle's hair. She heated it on the stove, said it worked better than the new kind."

Mary Owl traced the length of the scars, one after another. "That last year she used it on me too, when she'd had too much to drink."

Nausea swept over Elizabeth and she stumbled

blindly toward the door. "The other mask was for *her*. Oh, god! I should have known....Me, of all people. I should have tried to do something...."

Outside, Phillip caught up with her at the bench where she was sitting, head in her hands. "Elizabeth, sweetheart, how could you have known anything? She never told you...."

Just as Mary Owl had done, Elizabeth began to unbutton her shirt. She pulled one arm free and held it out for him to see the ragged procession of barely visible burn scars that marked the surface of her inner arm.

"*These* are why I should have known—I should have recognized a child who was living through the same sort of misery I'd known years before. *My* mother didn't have a curling iron, just a cigarette. She was always so sorry afterward. And I covered up for her, told her it was okay." Elizabeth's voice faltered but she continued. "I never told anyone the whole truth about her—not even Sam. Even when I had my bad dreams and he would wake me and make me feel safe again. I could have told him, but that would have made it...made it real. If it was just a dream..."

She looked at Phillip with a bleak gaze. "If it was just a dream, I could still believe she was just sick, that she really loved me."

Hot, angry words rose to Phillip's lips, but as he met Elizabeth's eyes and saw not the woman but a still-vulnerable child looking out, the anger gave way to another feeling. With infinite tenderness, he bent his head to lay his lips on the old wounds.

ABOUT THE AUTHOR

Vicki Lane has lived with her family on a mountain farm in North Carolina since 1975. She is at work on an addition to the saga of Elizabeth's Marshall County.

If you enjoyed

Vicki Lane's

OLD WOUNDS

you won't want to miss any of her novels of
suspense featuring Elizabeth Goodweather and
Full Circle Farm. Look for them at your
favorite bookseller.

And read on for an exciting early look at
Vicki Lane's next novel

IN A DARK SEASON

Coming soon from Dell

In a Dark Season

Coming soon from Dell

1.

The Madwoman and the House

Friday, December 1

The madwoman whispered into the blue shadows of a wintry afternoon. Icy wind caught at her hair, loosing it to whip her cheeks and sting her half-closed eyes. She brushed back the long black strands and peered through the fragile railing of the upper porch. Below, the broad fieldstone walkway was dusted with white and the ancient boxwoods were capped with snow. Beyond the house, the terrain sloped to the railroad tracks and on down to the gray river where icy foam spattered on dark rocks and a perpetual roar filled the air.

Her thin hand clutched at the flimsy balustrade as, eyes fixed on the stony path far below, the madwoman began to pull herself to her feet. Behind her, a door rattled on its rusty hinges and slammed, only to creak open again.

She paused, feeling the house around her—feeling it waiting, crouching on its ledge above the swift-flowing river. The brown skeletons of the kudzu that draped the walls and chimneys rustled in a dry undertone, the once-lush vines diminished to a fine netting that meshed the peeling clapboards and spider-webbed the cracked and cloudy windowpanes. From every side, in its small mutterings and rustlings, the old house spoke.

None escape. None.

As the verdict throbbed in her ears, marking time with the pulse of blood, the madwoman began to feel her cautious way along the uneven planks of the second story porch. A loose board caught at her shoe and she staggered, putting out a thin hand to the wall where missing clapboards revealed a layer of brick-printed asphalt siding. The rough material curled back at the exposed seam, and she caught at the torn edge, tugging, peeling it away from the wood beneath. The siding ripped away to show the heart of the house—the original structure beneath the accretions of later years.

She stilled her trembling hands, splaying them against the massive chestnut logs. *A palimpsest, layer upon layer. If I could tear you down, board by board, log by log, would I then discover where the evil lies . . . or where it began?* Resting her forehead against the wood's immovable curve, she allowed the memories to fill her: the history of the house, the subtext of her life.

The logs have seen it all. Their story flowed into her, through her head and fingertips, as she leaned against them, breathing the dust-dry hint of fragrance. *The men who felled the trees and built this house, the drovers who passed this way, the farmers, the travelers, the men who took their money, the women who lured them . . . and Belle, so much of Belle remains. Her dark spirit pervades these logs, this house, this land. Why did I think that I and mine could escape it?*

No answer came, only the mocking parade of memories. The thrum of blood in her ears grew louder and the madwoman turned her back on the exposed house wall and moved to the railing. Leaning out, oblivious to the cutting wind, she fixed her eyes on the stony path thirty feet below. *Far enough?* She hesitated, looking up and down the porch. A stack of plastic milk crates filled with black-mottled shapes caught her eye.

Of course, there would be a way. The house is seeing to it. Belle is making sure.

Snatching up the topmost crate, she lifted it to the porch railing. Mildew-speckled dried gourds tumbled down to shatter on the stones, scattering seeds over the path and frozen ground. The madwoman set the empty crate beside the balusters and slowly, painfully, pulled herself up to stand on its red grating-like surface. Then, holding to the nearest upright, she placed a tentative foot on the wide railing.

The words came to her, dredged from memory's storehouse. When her own thoughts faltered, one of the poets spoke for her as they always did, one of the many whose works she had loved and learned and taught.

Balanced on the railing, the madwoman hurled the words into the wind's face.

"'After great pain a formal feeling comes—'"

She closed her eyes, willing herself to go on.

"'The snow—
First chill, then stupor, then
The letting go.'"

The house waited.

2.

THREE DOLLS

Friday, December 1

As the car negotiated the twisting road down to the river, Elizabeth Goodweather saw them once more: three naked baby dolls, their pudgy bodies stained with age and weather, twisting and dancing in the winter wind like a grisly chorus line. They had hung there for as long as she could remember, dangling by their almost non-existent necks from the clothesline that sagged along the back porch of the old house called Gudger's Stand.

The house lay below a curve so hairpin-sharp and a road so narrow that many travelers, intent on avoiding the deep ditch to one side and the sheer drop to the other, never noticed the house at all. It was easy to miss, lying as it did in a tangle of weedy brush and household garbage, perched well below the level of the pavement on a narrow bank that sloped away down to the river rapids.

I wish I'd never noticed it. It wasn't until the power company cleared some of those big trees that you could even see the house.

Her first sight of the house and the grisly row of hanged dolls had been on a fall day some years ago. *Sam was still alive. He was driving and the girls were in the back seat....*

The memory was sharp: the abrupt shock of the missing trees on the slope below the road; the sudden appearance of the hitherto-unseen house with its long porches front and back; the row of hanging dolls and the hunched old man sitting in a chair beneath them, belaboring their rubber bodies with his lifted cane. *And a woman just disappearing into the house; I only saw the tail of her skirt as she went through the door. The whole scene was bizarre—and unlike anything else I'd seen in Marshall County. I started to say something but then I couldn't; it just seemed too awful—those helpless little dolls—I didn't want the girls to see that old man hitting the dolls.*

Ridiculous. Of course, the next time the girls had ridden the school bus some ghoulishly eager schoolmate had pointed out the newly visible house and the trio of dangling dolls. Rosemary and Laurel had come home cheerfully discussing the meaning behind the display.

"Shawn says it's where old man Randall Revis lives—and that he's had three wives and they've all run off. So old man Revis pretends the dolls are his ex-wives and he whacks them with his walking-stick."

Rosemary's matter-of-fact explanation, punctuated by slurps of ramen noodles, had been followed by her younger sister's assertion that a girl on *her* bus had said the old man was a cannibal who lured children into his house and cut them up and put them in his big freezer.

"Like the witch in Hansel and Gretel! And every time he eats one, he hangs up another doll!" Laurel's eyes had been wide but then she had smiled knowingly.

"That's not true, is it, Mum? That girl was just trying to scare the little kids, wasn't she?"

"That's what it sounds like to me, Laurie." Elizabeth had been quick to agree, adding a tentative explanation about a sick old man, not right in the head.

But really, the girls just took it in stride as one of those inexplicable things grownups do. I think they quit even seeing the house and the dolls. I wish I could have. For some reason I always have to look, and I'm always hoping that maybe the dolls or the cords holding them will have rotted and fallen away. Or that the kudzu will have finally taken the whole place. The old man's been dead for years now; you'd think some one would have taken them down.

Elizabeth shuddered and forced her thoughts back to the here and now. Sam was dead; the girls were grown; it was Phillip Hawkins at the wheel of her car on this particular winter afternoon. But still the hanging dolls seemed to hold some implicit warning.

"What's the matter, Lizabeth?" Without taking his eyes from the road, Phillip reached out to tug at her long braid. One-handed, he steered the jeep down the corkscrew road and toward the bridge that crossed the river at Gudger's Stand. Snow plows had been out early and tarnished ridges of frozen white from the unseasonable storm of the previous night lined the road ahead.

She caught at his free hand, happy to be pulled from her uneasy reverie. "It's just that old house—it always gives me the creeps."

Phillip pulled into the deserted parking lot to the left of the road. For much of the year the flat area at the base of the bridge swarmed with kayakers, paddlers, and busloads of customers for the various whitewater rafting companies, but on this frigid day, it was deserted except for a pair of Canada Geese, fluffed out against the cold.

"That one up there?" Phillip wheeled the jeep in a tight circle, bringing it to a stop facing away from the river and toward the house.

She nodded. "That one. It's as near to being a haunted house as anything we have around here—folks tell all kinds of creepy stories about things that happened there in the past—and ten years ago the old man who lived there was murdered in his bed. They've never found out who did it."

They sat in the still-running car, gazing up the snow-covered slope at the dilapidated and abandoned house. Low-lying clouds washed the scene in grim tones of pale gray and faded brown.

"What's that?" Elizabeth leaned closer to the windshield, pointing to a dark shape that seemed to quiver behind the railings at the end of the upper porch. "Do you see it ... something moving up there?"

"Probably just something blowing in the wind." Phillip followed her gaze. "One of those big black trash bags, maybe—"

"No, look!" Elizabeth frowned in an attempt to make sense of the dark form that had moved now to lean against the wall of the old house. "It's a person! But what would anyone...I wish I could see—"

Phillip was already pulling out of the parking lot and toward the overgrown driveway that led up to the old house. And even as he said "Something's not right here" the angular shape moved toward the porch railing. There was a flash of red and a tangle of rounded objects fell to the ground.

"I think it's a woman." Elizabeth craned her head to get a better look at the figure high above them. "What's she doing...climbing up on something or...?" The question in her voice turned to horror. "Phillip! I think she's going to jump!"

The car was halfway up the driveway when they were halted by a downed tree lying across the overgrown ruts. High above them they could see the woman balanced on the railing. Clinging to a porch pillar, she swayed in the wind.

Elizabeth shoved her door open and leaped from the car. Pulling on her jacket as she ran, she pounded up the steep drive, the climb made even slower by frozen mud and ice-covered puddles. Behind her she could hear the steady thud of Phillip's boots. Ahead she could see the scarecrow form of the woman, still teetering on her precarious perch. The woman's black hair writhed around her head, obscuring her face. A long black coat lofted out in the wind, making her look like some great bird preparing for flight.

"Stop!" Elizabeth's voice was little more than a thin quaver against the wind and she took breath and tried again. "Please!...Wait!...Talk to us!"

This time her cry reached the woman on the railing, who turned at the sound. Her pale face stared at Elizabeth and her lips moved but the words, if there were words, were carried away by the pitiless wind.

Elizabeth gasped. "Nola!"

She tried to run faster, even as she shouted to the figure high above her. "It's me, Nola—Elizabeth Goodweather. Please, get down from there before—"

The woman on the railing hesitated, wavered. Then she lifted her head as if listening to a far away sound.

"Just wait where you are, please! We'll help you..." Elizabeth's side was aching and her voice was a rasping croak, but she forced herself up the road and toward the old house. In the distance a siren began its urgent howl.

Phillip was at her side now, pointing to the stairs that led to the upper porch. "Keep talking to her; I'll try to get up there."

The siren was louder now, very near. Elizabeth kept moving toward the porch, breathless with fatigue.

"Nola, were you looking for the will you told me about? Let us help you." She labored to be heard, to be understood, to get closer, to make eye contact with this woman she met only a short few weeks before. "Please, be careful; that railing looks—"

Above her the black-haired woman slowly shook her head. Elizabeth heard the emergency vehicle turn into the drive behind her. The siren shrieked once more and died away.

She turned to see a Marshall County sheriff's car stopped just behind her jeep. Its light was still pulsing in blue rhythmic bursts as two men in uniform, followed by a smaller figure in jeans and a purple fleece jacket, emerged from its interior and began to race up the drive.

Whirling to see what effect this new arrival would have, Elizabeth was just in time to see the black-clad figure release her hold on the post, spread her arms wide, and plunge—a great raven tumbling from the sky.

"How the hell she survived that fall . . . just missed the stone walkway and landed on one of those old boxwoods."

The EMTs had responded quickly, strapping the crumpled, unconscious body of Miss Nola Barrett to a backboard and loading her into the ambulance for the trip into an Asheville emergency room. The young woman in the purple jacket had gone with Miss Barrett.

"She's the one who called us," Sheriff Mackenzie Blaine had explained. "Miss Barrett's niece or something—been visiting her aunt. She said Miss Barrett started acting kind of squirrelly—obsessing about this house. Evidently the house belongs to Miss Barrett—or she thinks it does. Anyway, the niece—what's her name, Jan, Janice?—said she went to the store after lunch and when she came back, her aunt was gone."

As soon as the ambulance had been loaded, Phillip had led Elizabeth to her car, started the motor, and turned the heat to high. In a few moments the car filled with warmth but Elizabeth, her face pale and drawn, continued to shiver. Phillip put an arm around her as Mackenzie Blaine slipped into the back seat. Behind the jeep, his deputy waited in the patrol car. Clouds of white exhaust billowed from both vehicles.

Blaine stared out the car window at the old house. "It's a sad thing, seeing a woman like Miss Barrett come to this. Folks always thought a lot of her around here—hell, there's a couple of old boys I know, they think she hung the moon. Funny thing—"

"Mac," Phillip interrupted, "Why'd the niece call you? How'd she know her aunt wasn't over at a neighbor's house or—"

"Oh, there was a note—and it worried the niece enough that she called us right away—well, you saw what happened— Miss Barrett was trying to kill herself."

Blaine opened the back door and stepped back out into the cold air. " 'Fraid she may get her wish—the EMTs weren't sure if she'd make it."

He leaned back into the car and cast a sympathetic brown gaze at Elizabeth whose face was wet with tears. "You knew her, you said?"

Elizabeth gulped and nodded. "I met her for the first time a few months ago. But, Mackenzie, Nola Barrett was not *squirrelly*...or suicidal...at least not when I saw her a week ago. My god, the woman has a memory like...like..."

She faltered, unable to find a strong enough comparison. "Well, her memory's amazing. Just a few weeks ago I was telling her about how Sam and I left suburbia to learn to farm...how we wanted a garden and cows and bees...and all of a sudden she launched into 'Nine bean rows will I have there, a hive for the honey-bee...'"

She broke off, seeing puzzlement spread over the sheriff's face. "It's from a poem by William Butler Yeats. Nola knew it all by heart. She told me that she had memorized page after page of poetry and still could go on for hours without repeating herself. She was...she was the most..."

The memory of that nightmare figure on the upper porch, the pathetic crumpled form, and the still, white face that disappeared into the ambulance was too much. Betrayed by a rising tide of tears, Elizabeth turned away, unable to go on.

Blaine's eyes met Phillip's and he said gently, "You all go on home. I'll be in touch."

When the sheriff's car had gone, leaving the way clear, Phillip backed slowly and carefully down the rutted drive. Elizabeth stared up at the old house. The blank windows stared back, watching and waiting under the lowering sky.

In spite of the car's heater and her attempts at control, her body continued to shiver. As they pulled farther away from the house, once again she could see the dolls on the back porch, stirred into a writhing, endless dance by the chilly wind sweeping down the river gorge.

LYDY GOFORTH AND THE DROVERS' ROAD

1860

I

When first I seen Belle Caulwell she was standin in the midst of a great drive of hogs, her dark green skirts not swayed a lick as the flood of swine, all a-slaver at the smell of the corn wagons, parted and passed by to either side of her, like as a rushin creek will divide at a tall rock. She stood there not payin the brutes no mind a-tall and just a-starin at me, them dark eyes of hern like fire-coals burnin their way right into my breast.

The lanky youth fell silent. He laid one bony hand over his heart and stared up at the tiny patch of sky just visible through the high barred window, his gaze as intent as if he could see the burning eyes watching him still.

The Professor shifted on the planks of his bunk, picked a bug from the ragged gray blanket that was the whole of his bedding, and cracked it against the wall where a scattering of red dots told the tally of his kills.

Circe, he pronounced, shaking his head. *Circe and John Keats' merciless* dame, *the two subsumed into one.* He scratched at an odiferous armpit. *Boy, I begin to see why it is you find yourself in such a dire predicament. But, like the blind singer Homer, you have initiated your narrative* in media res. *Perhaps you would indulge my curiosity and begin at the beginning. I take it that these mountains are your native heath?*

The young man frowned and shook his head as if reluctantly

returning from a happier world to the chilly reality of the Marshall County jail. He shot a suspicious glance at his cellmate.

The Professor, a man in his mid-thirties, wore a black frock coat. His once-white shirt was adorned by the tattered remnants of a dark blue cravat—the garments of a man with some pretensions to gentility. With a soft exhalation, he settled himself more comfortably on the narrow bunk, his head cocked expectantly, awaiting an answer to his question.

The young man, whose homespun shirt and threadbare jeans trousers were faded to a muddy gray-brown, lowered himself to the uneven bricks of the floor, casting a last, longing glance at the little window before replying.

Well, I see why it is they call you the Professor—all them fine words just a-spewin out yore mouth. Now I don't know nare singer called Homer, nor do I understand the half of yore fancy talk. But I reckon you kin tell me first who it is you are and how come you to be here afore I unburden myself to you. Hit'll do to while away the time. And my name hain't Boy, hit's Lydy Goforth.

The Professor rose and made a little bow in the direction of his companion. My most humble apologies, Mr. Goforth. Allow me to introduce myself—Thomas Walter Blake, the second of that name, native of Charleston, South Carolina, late of Harvard University, and completely at your service. In view of our enforced intimacy, may I suggest that we dispense with formalities hereafter. If it meets with your approval, I shall call you Lydy and I beg that you will make use of my own praenomen, my familiar appellation, my given name . . . in short, please call me Tom.

Lydy's eyes narrowed. Reckon I'll stick with Professor, iffen you don't keer. Hit don't seem fitten fer a body with so many big words in his craw to be called by a name any common he-cat might carry.

The Professor shrugged and sank back to his bunk. As you will, my young friend, as you will. He leaned back and crossed one black-trousered leg over the other, assuming the air of a gentleman at his club, about to embark on a leisurely narrative.

You may ask how it is that I, scion of a distinguished Charlestonian family and graduate of Harvard University, how it is that I find myself in this verminous cell, in this backwater of civilization—

Shitfire, Professor! Lydy broke into the flow of words. I be *damned iffen I know what it is you're talking about. What I asked is how come you to be in jail?*

Aah. You prefer a concise account. Very well. It appears that I am being held for carnal knowledge of a minor. The professor straightened his cravat. Or breach of promise. The father of the damsel in question has not yet made up his applejack-befuddled mind.

Lydy dragged the rough homespun of his shirtsleeve across his eyes. *Law, Professor, looks like hit's the love of woman that's over-throwed the both of us. Hit's a fearsome, powerful thing, that kind of love is. I've studied on hit but be damned iffen I can make it out.*

He looked down at his big, rough hands and slowly turned them, palms up and then down. His face wore a puzzled frown, as if the hands were strangers to him. After a moment's study he wrapped his arms around himself to hide the hands in his armpits. His voice trailed into a dreaming whisper.

You know, some of the time hit seems like a hundred years ago and other times I'd swear hit was only yesterday that I was back at my uncle's place, way up there on Bear Tree Creek.

Lydy leaned his head against the wall, once again fixing his eyes on the little window.

What brung me here ... I'd have to say it started back there, back on this one day when I was huntin a little spotted heifer what had come in season and had took a notion to travel. Well sir, I followed her trace clear to the top of Old Baldy. When at last the heifer come into view, I seen that she had found what she was atter. Hit was a red and white bull what I hadn't never seed before and he was a-ridin her like one thing. I seen there weren't no way of turnin her back down the mountain till they was done so I set down there in the grass to wait.

Hit was late spring of last year—eighteen and fifty nine—and the day was one of them bright clear ones with all the world looking like hit had been washed clean. Old Baldy's the highest peak on Bear Tree and with the sky so close hit seemed like hit wouldn't be no trouble atall to reach out and maybe grab God's shirttail.

The bull got done at last but I just set there, thinking how I had spent all of my life down in the holler, a-clearin my uncle's ground, bustin his wood and choppin his corn, with my eyes looking at the dirt till it grew too dark to see. Then hit would be back to my pallet in the loft and up before first light to begin all over again.

Off in the far distance I could see the mountain humps a-stretchin out in blue rows till they kindly melted into the sky. And then it come to me as how I'd like to travel beyond them mountains some day, maybe see the great ocean that my kin had crossed, back when they first come to this land. I stared off into that blue far-away and, like I had heard the preacher say one time, my spirit took wing.

The young man was on his feet now, still gazing up at the little window and the darkening sky beyond.

And then, all to once, there's my uncle, a-standin over me afore ever I heared his step. He had come a-lookin fer the heifer too; and when he saw her and the bull croppin grass and me just a-settin there not doin nothing, why he commenced to whup on me with his ole walkin stick. Called me a worthless, loaferin woods-colt and said though he'd kept me on like his sister had begged on her death bed, now I had plagued him a time too many. I thought to fight him but he was a stout, full-growed man and I feared I'd be beaten bad.

I left him there, a-shoutin vile curses at me whilst I lit out down the mountain. Weren't none of the others to the house so I took the blanket offen my pallet and rolled my good shirt in hit, along with my few other bits of plunder. I took cornbread from the safe and put hit in my pocket and then I took my papaw's long rifle and set out down the creek.

Hit was late evening when I come to the river and the old man with the ferry had just set down Silas Gentry and his wagon. I didn't have no money but bein as the ferry had to go back fer a man and a mule what was waitin on the far bank, the old man agreed to put me across iffen I did the haulin.

I'll ride like a gentleman for once, says he, and set hisself upon an empty nail keg. That ole man grinned like a fool whilst I hauled his flat bottom raft across the fast runnin waters of the French Broad. Hit was a stout rope he had strung over the water and hard though my hands were with the use of the axe and hoe, by the time the far shore was nigh, I had raised me a blister or two.

But I paid no mind to the burning of my hands for there on the slope above the turnpike was the place I'd been making for—the inn on the drovers' road. I looked up at that fine big place with its porches and galleries and its two stone chimbleys reaching up so tall and hit seemed to me that Gudger's Stand had been a-waitin fer me all the years of my life.